Blue Helmets

Blue Helmets

THE STRATEGY OF UN MILITARY OPERATIONS

Second Edition

John Hillen

BRASSEY'S

Washington, D.C.

Second edition 2000

Brassey's Editorial Offices: Brassey's Order Department:
22841 Quicksilver Drive   P.O. Box 605
Dulles, Virginia 20166   Herndon, Virginia 20172

Library of Congress Cataloging-in-Publication Data

Hillen, John.
    Blue Helmets : the strategy of UN military
operations / John Hillen—2nd ed.
      p.   cm.
    Includes bibliographical references (p.   ) and index.

    ISBN 1-57488-236-8 (2nd edition pbk.)
    1. United Nations--Armed Forces. 2. PeaceKeeping Forces. 3. International Police.
I. Title.
JZ6374.H55   2000
327.1'6--dc21   00-062150
                      CIP

Typeset by Benchmark Productions, Boston, MA

10 9 8 7 6 5 4 3 2 1

Printed in the United States of America

For My Father

fellow warrior,
fellow scholar,
best friend

Contents

List of Illustrations, Tables, and Maps

Foreword

Starting in 1989, there was an exponential increase in the number, size, complexity, and forcefulness of what was commonly labeled "peacekeeping," i.e., operations involving international military forces under the direction of the United Nations. From only sparing use, with almost no military participation by major powers, the term suddenly became commonplace in the lexicon of the United States and other major military establishments, while the practice became the choice of statesmen and strategic thinkers for resolving problems of the post–Cold War world. Military commands and schools around the world, including those of the United States, produced multiple manuals and introduced many courses of instruction and practical training on the new doctrine. It was studied, refined, broken into components, and variously called such things as peacemaking, peacekeeping, peace enforcement, and operations other than war.

The first surge in 1989 sprang from the resolve of the Soviet Union and the United States to put the Cold War behind them and end several long-burning regional conflicts in which they had been supporting, directly or indirectly, rival parties engaged in large-scale, violent struggles for power, particularly in Namibia, Angola, Mozambique, Nicaragua, El Salvador, Afghanistan, and Cambodia. In each instance (except Afghanistan), the United Nations Security Council mandated and deployed peacekeeping forces numbering upwards of five thousand soldiers for the purpose of helping implement prior agreements to end the combat and secure the peace. As John Hillen points out, these operations, although somewhat larger and more complex, were not too dissimilar from earlier, traditional UN peacekeeping missions such as the United Nations Emergency Force of 1956. They were also largely successful, despite numerous difficulties.

The second surge started in 1991-92 and was inspired by the recent cooperation of the five permanent members in using the UN Security Council not only to help resolve smaller regional conflicts, but also to help defeat Iraq in the Persian Gulf. The United States, the Soviet Union, France, and Britain, with Chinese acquiescence, agreed on a still more active, broader UN role in attempting to resolve large-scale internal crises in a number of terribly troubled states. An unprecedented meeting of the Security Council at the chief of state level was held on 31 January, 1992 and endorsed the concept of "strengthening the capacity of the United Nations for preventive diplomacy, for peacemaking and for peacekeeping." The New World Order was at hand.

Several of the new operations were larger in size and more complex than previous actions and were authorized to employ military force actively rather than passively; they were undertaken either without agreement or with only fragile, limited agreement of the warring parties. Hillen calls them "second generation peacekeeping." By 1995, 80,000 personnel from scores of countries were deployed in some 20 peacekeeping operations, and UN expenditures for that year reached $3.6 billion. (In 1987, only 10,000 personnel were deployed in seven operations.)

However, even by 1994, enthusiasm for this military-diplomatic instrument had begun to wane in many countries. This was especially true in the United States, which was shocked by the death of 18 of its young men and the wounding of 78 more on 3–4 October, 1993 in Mogadishu, Somalia, in conjunction with a UN operation (UNOSOM) and discouraged by the failure of the UN operation in Bosnia (UNPROFOR) to protect civilians and end the combat. UN peacekeeping became an object of opprobrium and ridicule, as well as a source of fierce political attacks on the Clinton administration. The "Somalia syndrome" caused the United States to retreat politically from "assertive multilateralism" toward troubled states and to place such a high priority on the avoidance of casualties that it interfered with the conduct of operations.

Had those responsible for UN Security Council resolutions and national decisions establishing the mandates and approving the dispatch of military forces for peacekeeping understood what John Hillen has so clearly explained, they would have been able to avoid the excessive enthusiasm and irrealism at the outset and the excessive negativism later. They would have known about the inherent limitations of the UN in managing military forces and been available to avoid tasking both the UN organization and the forces in the field with missions that were so obviously unachievable. They would also have known that the success of peacekeeping operations — and there have been many successes — comes from the contribution that the military elements of an operation make to the achievement of overall political objectives, not from conventional achievement of military objectives.

Particularly in peacekeeping, one should always keep in mind Clauscwitz's axiom that "war is nothing but the continuation of policy with other means." Time after time, we see in this comprehensively researched yet easily readable book that UN military operations of various types and sizes have been undertaken for political rather than military purposes. The planning, preparation, and other prerequisites for successful military operations were often almost totally overshadowed, as witnessed by the overnight establishment of UNIFIL in south Lebanon in 1982 in order to save the peace talks at Camp David and by the sudden creation of UNEF in 1956 to preserve the cease-fire between Egypt and Israel. Yet, in these and numerous other operations, the political objectives were achieved even if the military elements of the operation left much to be desired. (The Camp David talks were successfully concluded rather than being disrupted by Palestinian guerrilla attacks out of Lebanon on Israeli civilians, although UNIFIL completely failed to protect the border from infiltration.)

It is probably the excessive focus upon the political aspect of UN peacekeeping operations that explains why no one before John Hillen has undertaken such a systematic, thorough examination of their military aspects and of the capability of the UN as an institution to manage military operations. He examines how the national policy makers, time after time, either failed to see or deliberately ignored the extreme difficulties that the military forces to be deployed would have in fulfilling their military objectives. He points out how the UN became the scapegoat for failures by the members of the Security Council, particularly the United States, to mandate objectives clearly beyond the capabilities of the organization. Somalia and Bosnia are two clear examples. (The U.S. combat forces in Somalia that suffered casualties were never under UN command, although the administration allowed this myth to spread unchallenged for two years. UN forces in Bosnia never had the strength to protect safe areas established by the Security Council, although it was held responsible, rather than the governments most directly involved in approving the mandate and providing the forces to carry it out.)

Hillen's military experience and keen analytical eye have enabled him to identify the strengths and weaknesses of the UN in deciding on and managing critical components of military activities such as force structure, objectives, and command and control, including major problems such as "force turbulence" (i.e., difficulty in recruiting and maintaining properly trained forces and in ensuring that they adhere to UN rather than national command structures). He makes practical recommendations on how to alleviate the problems, including contracting out to more powerful, better organized military entities for large, conflict-prone operations. He also recognizes that with the right civilian and military leadership on the ground, many peacekeeping missions have been able to innovate and adapt, compensating for UN military weaknesses and successfully carrying out the overall mission.

This book will contribute significantly to the understanding of how the UN actually functions in strategically managing of military activities, what its true capabilities are, what military tasks and resources it should and should not be given by its member states, and how these factors relate to the political objectives. Hillen's conclusions are particularly relevant for members of Congress, the administration, and policy makers from the other permanent members of the Security Council, who often seem all too willing to give the UN a military mission well beyond its inherent capabilities. Such understanding will be most helpful in deciding how best to deal with the inevitable future problems of troubled states and regional conflict that the United States, the United Nations, and the international community must continue to confront. Peacekeeping should and can be improved, because the situations requiring its use will not disappear.

AMBASSADOR ROBERT B. OAKLEY

Acronyms

Current Peacekeeping Operations

MINURSO: United Nations Mission for the Referendum in Western Sahara; Laayoune; April 1991 to present.

UNAMIR: United Nations Assistance Mission for Rwanda; Kigali; October 1993 to present.

UNAVEM III: United Nations Angola Verification Mission III; Angola; February 1995 to present.

UNDOF: United Nations Disengagement Observer Force; Syrian Golan Heights; June 1974 to present.

UNFICYP: United Nations Peacekeeping Force in Cyprus; Nicosia; March 1964 to present.

UNIFIL: United Nations Interim Force in Lebanon; Southern Lebanon; March 1978 to present.

UNIKOM: United Nations Iraq–Kuwait Observation Mission; Umm Qasr, Iraq, in demilitarized zone between Iraq and Kuwait; April 1991 to present.

UNMIBH: United Nations Mission in Bosnia and Herzegovina; Sarajevo; December 1995 to present.

UNMIH: United Nations Mission in Haiti; Port-au-Prince; September 1993 to present.

UNMOGIP: United Nations Military Observer Group in India and Pakistan; India–Pakistan border, in state of Jammu and Kashmir; January 1949 to present.

UNMOP: United Nations Mission of Observers in Prevlaka; Prevlaka peninsula Croatia; January 1996 to present.

UNMOT: United Nations Mission of Observers in Tajikistan; Dushanbe; December 1994 to present.

UNOMIG: United Nations Observer Mission in Georgia; Sukhumi; August 1993 to present.

UNOMIL: United Nations Observer Mission in Liberia; Monrovia; September 1993 to present.

UNPREDEP: United Nations Preventive Deployment Force; Skopje, the former Yugoslav Republic of Macedonia; March 1995 to present.

UNTAES: United Nations Transitional Administration for Eastern Slavonia, Baranja, and Western Sirmium; Vukovar, Croatia; January 1996 to present.

UNTSO: United Nations Truce Supervision Organization; Jerusalem, Israel; June 1948 to present.

Past Peacekeeping Operations

DOMREP: Mission of the Representative of the Secretary-General in the Dominican Republic; Santo Domingo; May 1965 to October 1966.

ONUC: United Nations Operation in the Congo (now Zaire); Leopoldville (now Kinshasa); July 1960 to June 1964.

ONUCA: United Nations Observer Group in Central America; Costa Rica; El Salvador, Guatemala, Honduras, and Nicaragua; November 1989 to January 1992.

ONUMOZ: United Nations Operation in Mozambique; Maputo; December 1992 to December 1994.

ONUSAL: United Nations Observer Mission in El Salvador; San Salvador; July 1991 to April 1995.

UNAMIC: United Nations Advance Mission in Cambodia; Phnom Penh; October 1991 to March 1992.

UNASOG: United Nations Aouzou Strip Observer Group; Aouzou Strip, Republic of Chad; May 1994 to June 1994.

UNAVEM I: United Nations Angola Verification Mission I; Luanda; January 1989 to June 1991.

UNAVEM II: United Nations Angola Verification Mission II; Luanda; June 1991 to February 1995.

UNCRO: United Nations Confidence Restoration Operation in Croatia; Zagreb; March 1995 to January 1996.

UNEF I: First United Nations Emergency Force; Suez Canal, Sinai peninsula, and Gaza; November 1956 to June 1967.

UNEF II: Second United Nations Emergency; Suez Canal and Sinai peninsula; October 1973 to July 1979.

UNGOMAP: United Nations Good Offices Mission in Afghanistan and Pakistan; Kabul and Islamabad; April 1988 to March 1990.

UNIIMOG: United Nations Iran–Iraq Military Observer Group; Tehran and Baghdad; August 1988 to February 1991.

UNIPOM: United Nations India–Pakistan Observation Mission; border between Kashmir and the Arabian Sea; September 1965 to March 1966.

UNOGIL: United Nations Observation Group in Lebanon; Lebanese-Syrian border; June 1958 to December 1958.

UNOMUR: United Nations Observer Mission Uganda-Rwanda; Kabale, Uganda, on Uganda-Rwanda border; June 1993 to September 1994.

UNOSOM I: United Nations Operation in Somalia I; Mogadishu; April 1992 to April 1993.

UNOSOM II: United Nations Operation in Somalia II; Mogadishu; May 1993 to March 1995.

UNPROFOR: United Nations Protection Force; Bosnia and Herzegovina, Croatia, the Federal Republic of Yugoslavia (Serbia and Montenegro), and the former Yugoslav Republic of Macedonia; March 1992 to December 1995.

UNSF: United Nations Security Force in West New Guinea (now West Irian); Hollandia (now Jayaphra); October 1962 to April 1963.

UNTAC: United Nations Transitional Authority in Cambodia; Phnom Penh; March 1992 to September 1993.

UNTAG: United Nations Transition Assistance Group; Namibia and Angola; April 1989 to March 1990.

UNYOM: United Nations Yemen Observation Mission; Sana'a; July 1963 to September 1964.

Preface to the Second Edition

UN peacekeeping's hopes for the future and the tribulations of its past were all on display in Sierra Leone in May 2000. There, in that unhappy country torn by brutal civil war, the UN inserted international military forces into the conflict in an effort to force a peace. After a few years of relative quiet at the UN—much spent pondering past mistakes in places such as Somalia, Bosnia, and Angola—the organization in 1999–2000 geared up again in an attempt to push the boundaries of traditional UN military missions. In the new missions to Sierra Leone, East Timor, the Democratic Republic of the Congo, and elsewhere, the UN would not be simply an inert symbol of international presence and goodwill. Instead, the "Blue Helmets" would be a legitimate and authoritative referee able, by force of arms if necessary, to stem the most egregious violations of the frequent and ephemeral peace accords.

In Sierra Leone, the UN operations quickly turned into a fiasco. Several peacekeepers were killed, and over 500 were taken hostage by rebel forces. The British government sent in combat troops to openly support the local government and the UN mission, but those troops were under strictly British control and operating under rules of engagement far more robust than used by the Blue Helmets. The 8,000-odd UN peacekeepers thus became an expensive and somewhat aimless sideshow to the long-running conflict. Nonetheless, at UN headquarters in New York, the talk (especially from the United States) was of carrying through with a similar mission to the Congo—one that would also require an ad hoc peacekeeping force to try and impose peace when there was none to keep.

The lessons of this book, which examines almost fifty UN military operations undertaken since 1948, fly in the face of this new agenda for peacekeeping at the UN. In particular, the dramatic and costly lessons of the early–mid 1990s, when the UN failed in a series of expensive, large, dangerous, and ambitious military missions that bore little resemblance to the successful UN peacekeeping of the past. Nonetheless, memories are short and ambitions are large when it comes to using the UN to manage military operations. The new missions of 1999–2000 brought to mind the old soldier's marching song: "Here we go again . . . Same old stuff again . . . ."

This updated second edition tells again the story of the UN's fifty-two year involvement with managing international military forces: the ups, the downs, the successes, the failures. Well received when it was first published in 1998, I thought that it would scarcely need updating in light of how widely accepted the thesis was at the time, that the UN is inherently and immutably incapable of being the strategic manager of complex military operations. Conversely, the very traits that make it a somewhat bumbling leader of serious military missions make it a trusted and reliable manager of quasi-military peacekeeping missions. As author Peter Maass has written, "it is far easier to be the world's conscience than to be the world's policeman."[1] The book lays out in detail the political and military dynamics underlying this seeming paradox. It also attempts to answer the question of why the international community, and the United States in particular, cannot seem to the learn the lessons herein no matter how many times they applied.

Preface

In the years immediately following the end of the Cold War, observers of international relations theorized ad nauseam about the dynamics of the brave new world into which we were all entering. In a hasty world seeking bumper-sticker solutions to complex problems, "The New World Order," "The End of History," "The Coming Anarchy," "The Clash of Civilizations," "Assertive Multilateralism," "Neo-Isolationism," and other catchphrases and bywords crowded the pages of learned journals and the editorial sections of the major newspapers. This jumble of opinion sought to make sense of a new world in which the traditional roles of nation-states were seemingly being transferred to, undermined by, or devolved to substate ethnic or tribal groups, pan-state religious or cultural groups, transnational corporations, and international organizations. What roles were going where, who would be able to do what, and how would it all affect the human condition were the questions that provided much grist for the mill.

In the military field, one of the principal questions of the time concerned the role of the United Nations in the maintenance of international peace and security. The United Nations proper had always been a peripheral player in military affairs during its existence, sort of like a well-intentioned, but emasculated, uncle whose impartiality and distance from the family crises of the day made it useful as an honest broker in certain conflicts. On occasion, the United Nations even mobilized small military forces under its direction to aid in the resolution of military disputes between states. However, with the end of the era of superpower confrontation, many thought that a new security order might be in the offing and the United Nations would play a more central role in international military operations.

On the surface, the Persian Gulf War of 1991 appeared to presage these very notions. In that conflict, thirty-one member states fought united under the operational direction of a U.S.-led coalition, but in pursuit of political goals specified by the United Nations. In 1992 and 1993, the United Nations became further involved in the actual management of international military forces when it launched large, complex, and ambitious UN-managed military operations to the war-torn regions of Cambodia, the former Yugoslavia, and Somalia. By 1993, the United Nations was a significant player in international security affairs, forming and commanding almost 80,000 combat troops in some eighteen different military missions, some of which involved sophisticated and complex combat operations.

Having served in NATO and fought in the Persian Gulf War and now pursuing studies in international security affairs full-time, I was drawn in 1993 to the question of exactly what role the United Nations could competently play in military affairs in the post–Cold War world. Many political philosophers of the time were of the opinion that, once freed from the suffocating dynamic of Cold War tensions, the international community could now mobilize much of its political or military will through the United Nations instead of regional alliances, such as NATO, coalitions of the willing like the Persian Gulf, or even the age-old convention of unilateral action on the part of the nation-state. However, the soldier in me asked whether this newfound political consensus in the world would make any functional difference in the complex and emotive strategic tasks of putting together and managing complex and dangerous military operations. Would international political cooperation in the Security Council necessarily translate into military efficacy on the part of the United Nations? When the going got tough in the field, would the United Nations prove to have the legitimacy and authority to convince member states that it was the forum through which they should manage ambitious multinational military operations?

Although I had little doubt that the United Nations would play a more active role in international security affairs, I was curious about the way in which that would happen. Would the United Nations stay purely in the realm of political direction, as it had in the Gulf War? Or would the organization continue aggressively in the direction it was taking in 1992–1993, developing the institutions and procedures it would need to mobilize, organize, and deploy large and complex military forces under the command and control of the United Nations proper. At what level of military operations could a 185-member international organization get intimately involved to the benefit of those efforts, and at what level would the organization cease to be a useful forum for accomplishing certain strategic and operational military tasks?

Hence, between 1993 and 1996, I undertook a study of the ability of the United Nations to manage different types of military operations. This book is the result of that study. The data gathered in the course of this study were developed through an empirical review of thirty-eight UN-managed military operations and two multinational enforcement operations conducted under the political sanction of the United Nations. Given the tremendous increase in the number and type of UN military operations between 1988 and 1996, a significant body of evidence now exists for several different types of UN military operations. A study of those operations exposes the different challenges presented to the United Nations in managing those missions and the way in which the organization was able to succeed, fail, or merely muddle through. The evidence suggests that the ability of the United Nations (or any political entity for that matter) to act as a strategic manager is limited and that success is therefore clearly tied to the type of mission being undertaken and the extent to which the demands of that mission challenge the limits of legitimacy and authority inherent to the United Nations. In presenting these findings, this book considers different categories of UN military operations (observation missions, traditional peacekeeping, and second-generation peacekeeping).[1] It also looks at the UN role in large multinational enforcement actions in Korea and the Persian Gulf to examine why the United Nations was a political player but not the functional manager of those efforts.

This book examines the experience of the United Nations as a strategic manager through three analytical prisms that bring focus to the ability of the United Nations to manage military forces. These prisms are force structure, command and control, and military objectives. Questions of force structure revolve around the experience of the United Nations in recruiting and organizing a multinational military force. In each category of military operation, this book examines how UN military forces were created and what considerations and constraints, both political and military, influenced the size and composition of the force. Command and control "denotes the process that commanders use to plan, direct, coordinate, and control forces to ensure mission accomplishment."[2] Questions of command and control are centered on the military effectiveness of the United Nations' chain of command and the control procedures of UN operations. Last, an examination of military objectives is undertaken to explore the strategy of UN military operations (or lack thereof in some cases).[3] Strategy is defined here as the link between the political goals of a UN mission and the military objectives and modus operandi employed to help realize those goals. Ultimately, the questions considered through these three prisms give focus to the ability of the United Nations to form, direct, and employ military forces as well as the ability of those forces to achieve their mandate.

Using the conclusions from that empirical examination to support the thesis presupposes a measurable criterion for determining operational success or failure in UN military operations. The overall success and failure of UN military operations are difficult to judge for several reasons. First, all UN military operations were just one part of comprehensive, diplomatic, economic, and humanitarian efforts to achieve political mandates. As British Army doctrine notes in regard to UN operations, "military action cannot be viewed as an end in itself, but will rather complement diplomatic, economic, and humanitarian endeavors which together will pursue political objectives."[4] Thus, an operation perceived as a "failure" could in fact be a military "success" or vice versa. As James H. Allan, a former UN peacekeeper noted, "In the Congo, Cyprus, Egypt, the Golan, and elsewhere, violence was more or less controlled and superpower confrontation avoided: ergo success, even though the underlying political disagreements remained unresolved.

You could have successful peacekeeping and at the same time unsuccessful peace-making."[5] The second major difficulty is the tendency of judgments to change over time, especially in missions that have gone on for a number of years.[6]

Although these problems cannot be totally solved, a sharp analytical focus helps reduce those difficulties. Unlike the great majority of works concerning the United Nations and international security, this book is not a broad examination of the successes and failures of the United Nations' diplomatic, economic, humanitarian, and political attempts at conflict resolution. It therefore becomes important to focus on a strategic "end state" by which to measure the effectiveness of the United Nations as a political entity managing military forces and operations. This end state cannot be "victory" as traditionally defined by military studies. U.S. Army doctrine notes that "the concept of traditional victory or defeat is inappropriate in peace operations."[7] Instead, the two principal goals of the UN military operations over this period were to (1) limit armed conflict and (2) facilitate conflict resolution. The military objective in these goals is quite obviously "to limit armed conflict."

This objective will be used as the standard for determining the effectiveness of UN military operations and the UN itself as the strategic manager of these enterprises. As Paul Diehl noted in regard to peacekeeping missions, "one may judge the success of peacekeeping troops by their ability to prevent the onset or renewal of warfare, as well as to limit the death and destruction of violent incidents short of war in their area of deployment."[8] The United Nations has even further simplified this goal, noting that the basic function of UN military operations was to "maintain quiet," which gave UN military forces great value as a mechanism for aiding the resolution of political problems.[9] By helping to dampen military aggression and unlawful disorder, UN forces sometimes made an oblique contribution to the greater political goals of conflict resolution. The focus here is on that military contribution.

Many scholars have noted the difficulty of evaluating the United Nations, which, like other multinational organizations, "cannot be evaluated in quite the same terms as governments."[10] Moreover, many critical studies comparing the political legitimacy and authority of the United Nations to those of states fail to appreciate that "the UN cannot be adequately understood as simply the sum of its parts."[11] However, this book does not judge the United Nations writ large. It focuses on a particular set of functional tasks that the United Nations has attempted to manage. Although there is no standard model for a political entity managing these military tasks, other political entities, such as states, regional security alliances, or ad hoc multinational organizations have attempted similar tasks. In some cases, the experiences of these other entities are used for a broad basis of comparison, albeit a comparison that highlights the complex historical, institutional, political, and psychological factors that must inform such a method. While every organization is unique and every mission has its own genesis, missions initiated by other organizations, along with the thirty-eight UN missions under consideration, provide a considerable amount of evidence from which to draw conclusions.[12] The experiences of these other political entities are referred to in the book, with a special emphasis on their strategic capabilities and the extent to which these capabilities (military institutions, organizations, structures, and procedures) were drawn from the political legitimacy and military authority of the strategic manager.

The analytical method used in this study is therefore that of a historian in the empirical tradition. An examination of the ability of an institution to manage certain tasks could also be performed through sociological method or organizational theory.[13] Such an examination also would focus on institutions, structures, procedures, methods, and tasks. However, it was my intention to use the empirical method to identify the military tasks the United Nations has attempted to undertake, analyze the way in which it undertook these tasks, and, while accounting for the unique circumstances affecting each mission, draw conclusions about the competency of the institution to mount, direct, and employ military forces to pursue the tasks identified. Although some statistical methods are used to support analysis, the object of the book is to sustain the arguments through clear and understandable prose and without intricate systems analysis.

The existing body of literature about UN military operations describes and analyzes most clearly the international political or legal issues surrounding the use of military force by the United Nations. As might be expected, most of the literature focuses on the Cold War period and traditional peacekeeping missions. During the 1980s and in the immediate aftermath of the end of the Cold War, further studies were published that touched on the possibilities of second-generation missions, but still based most of their analysis on UN military operations carried out between 1948 and 1988. These included a comprehensive second edition of the United Nations' *The Blue Helmets* (1990), Alan James's *Peacekeeping in International Politics* (1990), Indar Rikhye's *The United Nations and Peacekeeping* (1991), Paul Diehl's *International Peacekeeping* (1993), and William Durch's *The Evolution of UN Peacekeeping* (1993).

Several deficiencies do exist in this body of literature about UN operations. Most of the comprehensive studies are dated, in light of the great expansion of UN military missions that took place in the early 1990s. As Mats Berdal noted in 1993, the "quantitative and qualitative expansion of UN peacekeeping in recent years has not been accompanied by any rigorous reassessment of the UN's capacity to engage effectively in its new range of activities."[14] Only monographs, journal articles, and edited volumes have gone some way to examining the recent "dramatic changes in both the volume and nature of UN activities in the field of peace and security."[15] Some of these notable recent efforts include monographs by Mats Berdal (*Whither UN Peacekeeping?* [1993]), Adam Roberts (*The Crisis in Peacekeeping* [1994]), and Charles Dobbie (*A Concept for Post-Cold War Peacekeeping* [1994]). There also have been edited volumes such as those from Don Daniel and Bradd Hayes (*Beyond Traditional Peacekeeping* [1995]) and Ramesh Thakur and Carlyle Thayer (*A Crisis of Expectations: UN Peacekeeping in the 1990s* [1995]).

In addition to the focus on traditional peacekeeping, most political studies do not specifically address the strategic aspects of UN missions; that is, the nexus between political goals and military means. This book necessarily recognizes the international political setting, but it focuses on the strategic and operational issues that arise after the decision to deploy military forces has been made. Moreover, it seeks to concentrate its conclusions on the ability of the United Nations to manage those strategic and operational issues. This book recognizes that many issues surrounding UN military operations are clearly a problem of international politics. However, a study of the United Nations' ability to manage certain types of military operations should take into account the nature of the task in the field and the military requirements of multinational forces as well as the limitations placed on the United Nations by politics in the region, on the Security Council, or in the international system as a whole. As former peacekeeper John Mackinlay noted about most UN military operations, "Peacekeeping is often discussed as a political problem in international seminars attended by politicians, UN officials and academics, but there is no effective military forum attended by the military cognoscenti to evaluate and anticipate the technical and procedural problems of deploying an international peace force."[16]

In this book I recognize some of those "technical and procedural problems," but I will attempt to use those findings to assess the capacity of the institution for managing the strategic tasks of managing military forces. By focusing on practical matters of strategy, I try to correct "much of the writings about the UN after the Cold War [which had an] excessive focus, both in academic and policy-making circles, on what is theoretically desirable rather than what is politically and practically feasible."[17] This book "drops" the level of analysis down to the strategic level. For instance, a former UN assistant secretary-general recently wrote that the secretary-general's involvement in the use of military force undermined the political credibility of the office itself.[18] This study takes such a political proposition and analyzes the actual organizations, mechanisms, procedures, and military operations conducted under the direction of the secretary-general and the United Nations to examine such a thesis even further. In the end, this study asks whether the secretary-general, the Secretariat, the Security Council, or the United Nations proper have had enough political legitimacy and military authority strategically to manage different types of military operations.

Studies that address strategy and operations do exist, notably James Boyd's *United Nations Peacekeeping Operations* (1971), John Mackinlay's *The Peacekeepers* (1989), and James Allan's recent *Peacekeeping: Outspoken Observations by a Field Officer* (1996). However, these works tend to address UN strategy only in the narrow context of observation missions and traditional peacekeeping. They also focus on details of issues at operational and tactical levels.[19] In contrast, this book focuses on the strategic level. It should be noted that in less complex military missions, such as observation missions, the levels of military operations combine; tactics become strategy in some of these missions. Kenneth Allard, a former U.S. Army strategist, has written that "because they are often a central focus of international attention, peace operations have a unique ability to combine the tactical, the operational, and the strategic levels of war."[20] However, as operations become more complicated militarily, the level of examination in this book remains focused on strategy.

Because the intellectual approach is strategic, this book can be more extensive than the fine works by Boyd, Mackinlay, and others. An examination of strategy allowed me to look at all UN military operations, not just traditional peacekeeping. I examined the United Nations and the use of military force in both passive missions, such as observation and traditional peacekeeping, and active force missions, such as second-generation peacekeeping, in addition to a brief discussion of large-scale multinational enforcement missions. In particular, case studies of certain missions will illuminate the practical difficulties that arose during these complicated military enterprises. It is hoped that this approach will satisfy both the need for a broad perspective on the issues and the desire for detail in the analysis.

The reader seeking technical minutiae of UN military missions may be disappointed. This study addresses many operational issues to determine firmly the military requirements of the missions in question. In this way the book is more meant to answer the strategic question concerning the ability of the United Nations to manage military operations. However, the study does not delve deeply into issues such as tactics, intelligence, logistics, finances, and military administration. For the military professional that may appear a drawback. These are indeed management functions, but of an operational, rather than strategic, character. To treat all these areas in depth could produce an administrator's manual for forces rather than an attempt to link the forces involved to the fundamental strategic capabilities of the political entity managing their operations. Thus, every aspect of military operations is analyzed for its utility in meeting the strategic questions at hand. Operational issues are not evaluated as ends to themselves. Ultimately, the questions of this book rest on the ability of the institution to carry out a set of military tasks and why it was or was not able to succeed.

This perspective is sorely needed to balance the current literature surrounding the recent travails of the United Nations. For instance, in a 1996 book review of Linda Melvern's *The Ultimate Crime: Who Betrayed the UN and Why* (1995), Francis Fukuyama writes that the author "ducks the questions of whether an institution such as the United Nations is really capable of moving beyond peacekeeping to peace enforcement, for which other international mechanisms may be better suited."[21] This book answers precisely that question. Ironically, although both this book and Melvern's work lay much of the blame on the permanent members of the Security Council, Melvern blames the big five for failing to support UN peace enforcement efforts, whereas I blame them for giving the United Nations such missions in the first place, missions for which it is uniquely unsuited. For Melvern and many other writers, it is a case of not supporting UN–organized collective security enough. For me it clearly is a case of permanent members using the false hope of collective security as a policy "cop-out" instead of more effective policies and military strategy worked through unilateral action, proven military alliances, or more focused coalitions of the willing. Either way, the United Nations got the blame and the member states were able to avoid difficult sacrifices in places such as Somalia and the former Yugoslavia. Ineffective half-measures taken through the United Nations gave everybody an excuse for inaction and set up a whipping-boy to boot.

I alone assume responsibility for the content of this book, although many others were involved in its creation. I am indebted to Professor Lawrence Freedman and Dr. Christopher Dandeker of the Department of War Studies at King's College, London, for their guidance as I first approached this subject. Dr. Martin Ceadel of New College, Oxford, was an early advisor, and Professor Adam Roberts of Balliol College, Oxford, provided useful direction at several stages. Professor Robert O'Neill of All Souls College, Oxford, deserves more credit than can be given in these pages for his patience and wise counsel. Others in Britain, where the majority of this book was written, merit special mention. Dr. Geoffrey Sloan, Professor Reiner Pommerin, and Dr. Jay Jakub provided useful points on geopolitics and British ales. Dr. Mats Berdal, Dr. John Mackinlay, and Colonel Charles Dobbie were friendly and helpful experts on the subject. Charles King, Lawrence Tal, Michael Dean, the Jesus College RFC, and especially Rachel Pearson need to be thanked for their friendship and support during my years in Oxford.

In the United States I am particularly grateful to my father, who edited many drafts at his kitchen table, and my wife Maria, who assisted in the most tedious tasks associated with the preparation of the manuscript. My grandmother, Aida Grassi, graciously hosted me during my research visits to UN headquarters in New York. Tom Timmons created the maps, figures, and other illustrations. Dan Patrick, Keith Olbermann, Rece Davis, Brett Haber, Stuart Scott, and Rich Eisen provided daily doses of inspiration. Renaissance man Mark Rader brought the book to the attention of Carol Mann of the Carol Mann Agency, where she, Gail Feinberg, and the tireless Christy Fletcher saw the book through to Brassey's. At Brassey's I am indebted to Don McKeon, who has been patient, supportive, and helpful. The manuscript itself would have never made it to his desk without the unflagging support of my mother, Lisa Hillen, to whom I owe so very much.

Introduction

On 1 January 1997, Kofi Annan of Ghana became the seventh secretary-general of the United Nations. He succeeded Boutros Boutros-Ghali, whose reelection to a second term was blocked by the United States because of many issues concerning the reform and direction of the United Nations. Events between 1992 and 1996 had, fairly or unfairly, caused the reputation of the United Nations to suffer in the United States, and President Clinton joined many critics on Capitol Hill and elsewhere in questioning the ability of Boutros-Ghali to lead the United Nations into the twenty-first century. Chief among these damaging events was the experience of the United Nations in managing ambitious military operations it deployed to ongoing civil wars in Somalia, the former Yugoslavia, and elsewhere. The failure of these expensive and costly missions reflected poorly on the United Nations and the secretary-general in particular. Critics in the United States demanded accountability and Boutros Boutros-Ghali's head was the first to roll. This bitter exchange between the United States, other members of the Security Council (who supported Boutros Boutros-Ghali), and the United Nations proper stood in stark contrast to the euphoria surrounding the United Nations and its military ambitions just a few years prior.

For many observers, the end of Cold War tensions in the UN Security Council and the subsequent display of unprecedented international cooperation during the Persian Gulf conflict of 1990–1991 heralded a new era for the United Nations and its role in international security. The role of the United Nations in the Persian Gulf conflict in particular seemed to presage a new dawn for an active United Nations. John Mearsheimer wrote that "the success of the American-led coalition that pushed Iraq out of Kuwait led some experts to conclude that the UN might finally be ready to operate as a collective security institution."[1] In addition, much of the thinking of this time maintained that because the United Nations was freed from the oppressive Cold War dynamic that dominated the Security Council, the organization could assume

1

a much more proactive military role in maintaining international peace and security. Adam Roberts and Benedict Kingsbury called these viewpoints "an attractively teleological view of the UN's place in the international order."[2] Conventional wisdom maintained that UN peacekeepers had been kept unduly constrained in their operations during the Cold War to avoid superpower confrontation over their deployment. Given the post–Cold War consensus on the Security Council, the United Nations could now free its military operations from their traditional restrictions.

In January 1992, the heads of state of the major powers met in the first-ever Security Council summit and declared, "the world now has the best chance of achieving international peace and security since the foundation of the UN."[3] The summit also asked the UN secretary-general to prepare a report on steps the United Nations could take to fulfill the expectations of a more active security role. The result, published some six months after the summit, was a report entitled *An Agenda for Peace*. In this document, the secretary-general proposed a greater military role for the United Nations in addition to its traditional peacekeeping missions. This more robust approach to military operations conducted under the aegis of the United Nations included a call for combat units constituted under the long-moribund Article 43 of the UN Charter. More controversially, this report called for "peace-enforcement" units "warranted as a provisional measure under Article 40 of the Charter":

> *I recommend that the Council consider the utilization of peace-enforcement units in clearly defined circumstances and with their terms of reference specified in advance. Such units from member states would be available on call and would consist of troops that have volunteered for such service. They would have to be more heavily armed than peacekeeping forces and would need to undergo extensive preparatory training within their national forces. Deployment and operations of such forces would be under the authorization of the Security Council and would, as in the case of peacekeeping forces, be under the command of the Secretary-General.[4]*

Some observers were skeptical about the efficacy of these proposals and echoed the sentiments of UN scholar Alan James, who faulted the secretary-general for having "muddied the conceptual waters" of the UN's military role with *An Agenda for Peace*.[5] Others had doubts about the ability of UN military forces to assume greater roles.[6] However, the optimism and enthusiasm over the prospects for an enhanced UN military role were reflected in numerous post–Cold War studies of the United Nations, peacekeeping, and collective security.[7] Much of this thinking maintained that the United Nations could now finally fulfill the vision of its founders and take its place at the center of the world's security structures.[8] A report by a distinguished group of international diplomats assembled at the U.S. Institute of Peace wrote that, once improved, the United Nations could "serve effectively as the primary vehicle for collective security originally envisaged in the UN Charter."[9] The secretary-general himself wrote that, "The machinery of the United Nations, which had often been rendered inoperative by the dynamics of the Cold War, is suddenly at the center of international efforts to deal with unresolved problems of the past decades as well as an emerging array of present and future issues."[10]

As if to test this thesis, in the two years following the Security Council summit, the United Nations initiated a large number of new military missions, including three very large and ambitious operations that the secretary-general and other observers referred to as the "second generation" of peacekeeping.[11] Two of these missions, in Somalia and the former Yugoslavia, had very significant combat capabilities and had mandates from the Security Council that included provisions for limited enforcement actions. These missions were infinitely more complex in their military structure and operations than traditional peacekeeping missions, and the mandate for limited enforcement provisions was a clear departure from the philosophy of traditional peacekeeping. As the missions evolved, they became expensive, intractable, and dangerous and were perceived by most as abject failures. Boutros Boutros-Ghali credited many of the problems in these operations to an attempt to mix the traditional precepts of UN peacekeeping with coercive enforcement:

> The UN operations in Somalia and Bosnia-Herzegovina . . . [were] given additional mandates which required the use of force. These were incompatible with existing mandates requiring consent of the parties, impartiality, and the non-use of force. The resultant combination was inherently contradictory. It jeopardized the safety and success of the peacekeeping mission. We have seen and felt the dangers of giving enforcement tasks to peace-keeping operations. In the future this must be avoided.[12]

In light of the problems experienced by UN forces in these missions and the recognition that the United Nations was being discredited by its attempts to manage large, active, and ambitious military operations, the secretary-general amended An Agenda for Peace. In January 1995, he retreated from his previous ambitions and released a supplement to An Agenda for Peace that called for the United Nations to rethink the concepts for these missions, especially their enforcement provisions. This new report highlighted the difficulties experienced by the United Nations in managing these new missions and called for scaled-down expectations and more limited missions. The secretary-general backed away from earlier proposals that would have the United Nations take an active role in managing large and complex military forces mandated for peace enforcement or large-scale enforcement missions.

> *Neither the Security Council nor the Secretary-General at present has the capacity to deploy, direct, command and control operations for this purpose, except perhaps on a very limited scale. I believe that it is desirable in the long term that the United Nations develop such a capacity, but it would be folly to attempt to do so at the present time when the Organization is resource-starved and hard pressed to handle the less demanding peacemaking and peacekeeping responsibilities entrusted to it.[13]*

By 1996, the United Nations had abandoned its most controversial missions and settled back into a more familiar and innocuous existence as passive peacekeeper. In late 1995, a senior UN peacekeeping official told the author that the United Nations was happy to be back in a "bear market" insofar as military operations were concerned.

The United Nations was forced to scale back its military ambitions because by 1995 the political legitimacy of large and complex second-generation operations was threatened by their failure to deliver results. This predicament was further exacerbated by the high cost of these missions in both men and materiel. All in all, the recent experience of the United Nations in managing large, complex, dangerous, and ambitious operations soured it and its member states on missions like those in the former Yugoslavia or Somalia. Ironically, the UN was most discredited among those very states (members of the Security Council) that charted the organization's foray into these new operations and, in some cases, actually pushed the organization into missions it did not want. Nonetheless, the series of recent UN adventures that took place after the end of the Cold War raised anew questions about the efficacy of managing military operations through an organization such as the United Nations.

Despite a consensus on the post–Cold War Security Council about mandating these new missions and methods, the United Nations proved it was not capable of managing large, ambitious, complex, and dangerous military operations. The United Nations' unique multinational character and institutional constraints made it inherently dysfunctional for managing such complex military operations in dangerous environments. The very nature of the institution did not allow it the sovereign legitimacy and political or military authority needed to develop the resources, structures, and procedures that were needed to manage dynamic military operations. Exactly what types of military operations suited the United Nations and why? The organization was capable of managing some military operations, but, despite post–Cold War "advances" in structure and methods, it remained definitively unsuited for managing other military missions. Therefore, what were the criteria and parameters that would spell out where the United Nations could constructively be involved? Moreover, if the United Nations was not the candidate for some sticky jobs in the post–Cold War world, who was? These are the questions that this book seeks to answer.

CHAPTER 1

The United Nations and Military Operations

Since its inception, the United Nations has had or developed institutions, organizations, structures, procedures, and methods that allow it to organize and manage military operations. The suitability of those components to the various military tasks at hand is examined throughout this book. However, it is helpful here to introduce the UN structure, the key organizations that deal with military operations, and the general UN procedures for managing those missions. A further explanation of the analytical structure of the spectrum of UN military operations is provided as well. This brief survey will show that in regard to military operations the United Nations has never used military force in the manner for which it was intended or designed. The relevant provisions of the UN Charter were never realized, and the Security Council, secretary-general, and the Secretariat were forced to use "creative interpretation and ingenious improvisation"[1] in managing military operations. This improvisation permeated all aspects of UN military operations and came to define its approach to managing their formation, direction, and employment. Before moving to an empirical analysis of that improvisation in this study, this chapter briefly illustrates the military provisions contained in the UN Charter; the political and strategic authority of the Security Council and of the office of the secretary-general; the organization of those parts of the UN Secretariat that deal with managing military operations; and the general military missions that UN forces have undertaken.

The Charter of the United Nations

The UN Charter alludes to the United Nations' possible military role in the first paragraph of Chapter I, Article 1: "To maintain international peace and security, and to that end: to take effective collective measures for the prevention and removal of threats to the peace, and for the suppression of acts of aggression or other breaches of the peace."[2] However, although this fundamental purpose is clearly stated throughout the Charter, the specifics about the organization, structure, and method of this military role are ambiguously spelled out in the document. It was undoubtedly the intention of the United Nations' founders to set up a framework in the Charter for collective military action, all the while recognizing that such a framework would depend almost entirely on the continued cooperation of the great powers, both with the United Nations and each other.[3] Some observers present at the United Nations' inception, such as Sir Brian Urquhart, have maintained that this was a supremely unrealistic expectation, given the divergence of interests among the allies that began to show at Yalta.[4] Urquhart wrote:

> The Charter had been based on the concept of an extension of the wartime alliance into peacetime. The "United" in United Nations came from the Atlantic Charter of 1941 and referred to nations united in war, not in peace. The permanent members of the Security Council with the power of veto were the leaders of the victorious wartime alliance, and the Charter assumed, with a stunning lack of political realism, that they would stay united in supervising, and if necessary, enforcing, world peace.[5]

Others present at the United Nations' creation thought the founders were less sanguine, and the statesmen creating the Charter knew full well that, if the document's provisions for collective military action were not realized, at least the United Nations gave the great powers a "constant forum, where nations must face each other and debate their differences and strive for common ground."[6] These guarded optimists thought that, although the Charter would put forth some guidance for a functional UN role in managing collective military operations, the organization might still play an important role in security affairs regardless of these provisions being fulfilled. Adlai Stevenson had such a view and noted that "The Charter . . . is only paper and no better and no worse than the will and intentions of the five [permanent Security Council] members."[7] Dean Acheson, the American statesman who had to represent President Roosevelt's desire for the ratification of the UN Charter before the U.S. Senate, "did his duty faithfully and successfully, but always believed that the Charter was impracticable."[8] President Roosevelt, despite the need to appear publicly optimistic, privately had no utopian expectations and conceded that no one could predict "how long [the Charter] or any other blueprint for world peace could last."[9] Thus, although international legal scholar Rosalyn Higgins writes that "the integrity of the Charter's collective security system was not intended to be dependent upon states' perception of where their national interests lay,"[10] most statesmen involved in the founding knew that the national interests of member states would very much affect the integrity of the Charter.

Nonetheless, if the United Nations was to become a political entity capable of managing multinational military forces, it needed the legitimacy of the Charter and the structure specified within to authorize the formation of security institutions and organizations. The Charter also broadly outlined the policy process, structures, and procedures by which the organization would recruit, organize, and command military forces. Chapters VI and VII are the parts of the Charter most relevant to the United Nations' practice of managing military forces. Those chapters explain the mechanisms and procedures by which the United Nations could hope to execute the enormous task of maintaining international peace and security, through both the "pacific settlement of disputes" and "action with respect to threats to the peace, breaches of the peace, and acts of aggression." However, the military role of the United Nations and UN military forces as outlined in the Charter never fully materialized. Instead, all thirty-eight military operations managed by the United Nations between 1948 and 1996 were improvised endeavors, ad hoc enterprises whose legal and political legitimacy were based on a loose interpretation of Charter provisions. In short, the UN Charter never provided an effective political, strategic, or military foundation for UN military operations in the way the framers of the Charter might have hoped.

Chapter VI of the Charter is entitled "The Pacific Settlement of Disputes." In six articles, it outlines the United Nations' role in negotiation, inquiry and investigation, mediation, conciliation, arbitration, judicial settlement, or other peaceful means of settling international disputes that endanger international peace and security. Chapter VI makes no reference at all to military operations of any kind, and yet, in the patois of most observers, the vast majority of UN military operations are referred to as "Chapter VI Operations." This approach relies on a broad interpretation of Charter provisions, such as Article 36, which states, "The Security Council may recommend appropriate procedures." This broad interpretation of Charter provisions is accepted by most UN legal scholars, many of whom note that political and functional considerations have constrained UN military operations much more than questions of legality and legitimacy.[11] Finn Seyersted writes that, "if the UN has not performed all types of sovereign or international acts which States perform, this is not because it lacks the legal capacity, but because it has not yet been in a practical position to do so."[12]

Some advocates of active collective security, such as former Australian Foreign Minister Gareth Evans, believe that under this broad approach, Chapter VI provides an acceptable legal and political foundation for observation and peacekeeping operations:

> The Security Council's principal activity under Chapter VI has
> been to establish, through recommendations under Articles
> 36–38, military observer missions and peacekeeping forces
> mandated to determine whether agreed cease-fires are being

> *maintained, and to act as a disincentive or provide a buffer to reduce the possibility of renewed conflict.[13]*

However, this is not by any means a unanimous interpretation of the Charter. There are those, such as Philippe Kirsch, who object on legal grounds. Kirsch offers a narrower interpretation of the Charter and maintains that "there has been no legal framework for the past fifty years of peacekeeping."[14] However, many of those who do not believe that military observation and peacekeeping missions fall clearly under Chapter VI base their argument not on legal interpretation, but on a functional argument. Chapter VI simply does not provide any clear and effective political or strategic guidance to conduct even low-level military operations such as observation or peacekeeping.

For instance, former UN Secretary-General Dag Hammarskjold called UN peacekeeping Chapter "Six and a Half," because the United Nations itself noted that observation and peacekeeping missions "fall short of the provisions of Chapter VII [but] at the same time they go beyond purely diplomatic means or those described in Chapter VI of the Charter."[15] This is a more pragmatic point of view, one that recognizes the gap between legal justification and political/military practicality. A consensus may have developed that Chapter VI provides legal justification for military operations, but those seeking to form, direct, and employ those operations do not derive much constructive guidance from Chapter VI of the Charter. Shashi Tharoor, former special assistant to the under secretary-general for peacekeeping operations, noted that, "in the unfolding confusion about whether UN peacekeeping was conducted under Chapter VI or Chapter VII, we were all at sixes and sevens."[16]

On the other hand, Chapter VII of the Charter was specifically intended to provide a policy framework for UN military operations. Chapter VII is entitled "Action with Respect to Threats to the Peace, Breaches of the Peace, and Acts of Aggression." This chapter lays out, in thirteen articles, a clear and logical progression of policy options and procedures—a progression that Adam Roberts and Benedict Kingsbury called "an ambitious scheme for collective security."[17] The incremental progression through all articles is not explicitly required, but the logic of Chapter VII's approach is implicit. Article 39 gives the Security Council the power to identify threats to the peace or acts of aggression. Article 40 empowers the Security Council to "call upon the parties concerned to comply with such provisional measures as it deems necessary or desirable." Article 40 does not specify the form or content of such "provisional measures," but it does emphasize the cooperation of the concerned parties. This emphasis on voluntary cooperation makes Article 40 the most explicit justification for observation and peacekeeping missions, which are "provisional measures" deployed with the compliance of the concerned parties.

Should those provisional measures fail, Article 41 gives the Security Council the power to impose economic, political, technical, and diplomatic sanctions on transgressors of the peace.[18] Although coercive, this article is the last nonmilitary method referred to in Chapter VII.[19] Should the methods referred to in Article 41 fail to address the problem, the Security Council can invoke powers under Article 42, which allow the Council to "take such action by air, sea or land forces as may be necessary to maintain or restore international peace and security." Article 42 does not specify exactly what those actions should be, referring only to "demonstrations, blockade, and other operations." Depending on interpretation, there is great latitude for a whole range of UN military activities to be conducted under Article 42. The emphasis, however, is clearly on the fact that these will be actively coercive operations.

The Charter brings the specifics of conducting these military operations into a somewhat sharper focus in Articles 43 to 49. Article 43 asks the member states to make some of their armed forces and facilities "available to the Security Council, on its call and in accordance with a special agreement or agreements." It is implied through the progression of articles in Chapter VII that Article 43 forces would be used for Article 42 actions. Rosalyn Higgins notes, immediately after outlining the actions of Article 42, that "it was envisaged that through Article 43 all members would enter into agreements with the Security Council to make armed forces and facilities available for *this purpose* [my emphasis]."[20] However, there is no explicit connection between the two articles, and Higgins goes on to note that "agreements under Article 43 are not a necessary prerequisite to military sanctions under Article 42."[21] Regardless, it is at this step that the entire policy structure envisaged by Chapter VII has broken down in practice.[22] Although much else has been done by the United Nations under Chapter VII, none of the "special agreement or agreements" called for in Article 43 have ever been concluded between the member states and the United Nations. Such agreements would conceivably give the United Nations a greater authority to mobilize, form, direct, and employ military forces in its military operations—including those alluded to in Article 42.[23]

Between 1945 and 1948, the member states of the Security Council negotiated for such agreements, but the rising tensions of the Cold War and the inherent infringement on national sovereignty prevented any useful result.[24] Adam Roberts has noted that

> the most obvious reason for the failure to implement the Charter provisions in the early years of the UN was the inability of the permanent members of the Security Council to reach agreement across the Cold War divide. However, there also appears to have been an underlying reluctance on the part of all states to see their forces committed in advance to participate in what might prove to be distant, controversial,

> *and risky military operations without their express consent*
> *and command.*[25]

Abba Eban, the former Israeli ambassador to the United Nations, recalled that the negotiations over Article 43 were effectively dead by 1947 and that, with the demise of that article, "the United Nations had renounced the special quality that was intended to distinguish it from its predecessor."[26]

Because the special agreements of Article 43 were never concluded, some of the subsequent articles in Chapter VII, which relied in some measure on the successful conclusion of Article 43 agreements, were effectively negated and their provisions have lain moribund since 1945—a "dead letter" in the words of Adam Roberts.[27] Articles 44 to 49 in fact provide the most useful policy guidance for the political and strategic direction of UN military operations, although these articles do not address what sorts of operations the UN forces would actually undertake. Article 44 invites force contributors to participate in Security Council decisions. Article 45 asks member states to "hold immediately available national air-force contingents for combined international enforcement action" in accordance with "limits laid down in the special agreement or agreements referred to in Article 43."

Articles 46 and 47 establish a Military Staff Committee (MSC) that would provide strategic guidance for UN military operations. Brian Urquhart writes that these articles "clearly imply that enforcement measures under Chapter VII will be under the control of the Security Council and its MSC."[28] As the Charter envisaged, the purpose of the Military Staff Committee would be "to advise and assist the Security Council on all questions relating to the military requirements for the maintenance of international peace and security, the employment and command of forces placed at its disposal, the regulation of armaments, and possible disarmament."[29] However, because of the disagreements among the great powers that started at Yalta and continued through the Charter negotiations and beyond,[30] Article 47 was left purposely ambiguous and stated that "questions relating to the command of such forces shall be worked out subsequently." As no Article 43-type UN forces were ever subsequently formed, no such questions were ever comprehensively addressed by the Security Council. Proposals were indeed made by the Military Staff Committee for forces, command and control structures, and other procedures,[31] but the failure of Article 43 negotiations and the reluctance of the great powers genuinely to consider working through the MSC doomed these proposals to irrelevancy.[32] Moreover, as Sir Michael Howard writes, "The Military Staff Committee . . . rapidly became a non-entity."[33]

In essence, the entire policy structure set up by the UN Charter for the conduct of military operations has never fully been realized. As Roberts notes, "The Security Council has never, in fact, had armed forces at its disposal in the manner apparently envisaged in Chapter VII of the UN Charter."[34] Consequently, all UN military operations had a political characteristic that permeated all aspects of operations: improvisation. Regardless of their expectations, the framers of the UN Charter set up a system for collective military action that envisaged some perpetuation of the successful wartime alliance. However, the UN Charter itself could not replace the sense of urgency, in the face of extraordinary threats, that drove the victorious allies to work together in unprecedented political and military cooperation. Thus the Charter, although not irrelevant for UN military operations, nonetheless failed to provide a legitimate, authoritative, and functional framework for managing UN military forces.

The Security Council

The UN Security Council is the UN body that has, according to Article 24 of the Charter, the "primary responsibility for the maintenance of international peace and security." Naturally, the failure of Article 43 agreements deprived the Security Council of reliable and rehearsed procedures for using military force. The dynamics at work in that failure, principally Cold War tensions between the Soviet Union and the West, also constrained the work of the Security Council. These tensions were manifested in vetoes cast by one of the permanent members of the Security Council. Between 1945 and 1991, over two hundred vetoes were cast.[35] In spite of these vetoes, some decisions were made during the Cold War, including the initiation of eleven of the thirteen UN observation and peacekeeping missions.[36] In contrast, the end of Cold War tensions saw a remarkable consensus on the Security Council, and there was only one veto cast in 1991–1993. As a consequence, that three-year period alone saw the creation of thirteen UN military operations.

Consensus on the Security Council allows for UN military missions to be authorized and created. In addition, the Security Council can revise the mandate of a UN military operation or terminate its mission. However, the functional authority of the Security Council is restricted to the political level. The actual direction of the military operation is the responsibility of the secretary-general, whose staff in the Secretariat forms and organizes the forces as well as sees to their administration and provision. The field commander conducts operations and answers to the secretary-general, who then reports to the Security Council.

The sharing of political and military responsibilities between the Security Council, the secretary-general/Secretariat, and the UN military commander in the field ensures that strategy—the matching of military means to political ends—is in the hands of several different bodies. The execution of this critical task, originally entrusted by the Charter to the moribund MSC, has had to be improvised as well. A 1993 report commissioned by the U.S. Institute of Peace noted that this "important link between clear political objectives and specific military objectives may be missing, especially in view of the weak UN Secretariat planning structure."[37]

In contrast, a state or military alliance also shares strategic responsibilities between several political and military bodies, but usually within a well-defined, well-staffed, and well-rehearsed system. These systems are based in law and treaty arrangements and are usually changed only by legislation or new international agreements. For instance, in 1986, as a supplement and update of sorts to the Constitution and the acts of Congress establishing a Department of Defense, the United States enacted the Goldwater-Nichols defense reorganization act. This legislation laid down clear legal guidelines about the strategic roles and responsibilities of the president, the secretary of defense, the chairman of the joint chiefs of staff, and the regional military commanders in the field.

The Secretary-General and the Secretariat

The secretary-general is described in Chapter XV, Article 97, of the Charter as "the chief administrative officer of the organization." It is indeed extraordinary that this important figure does not appear in the Charter until a discussion of the UN Secretariat, and even then is cast in a rather mundane role. This is a reflection of the fact that the critical role of the secretary-general in UN military operations was not intended, but rather evolved as a result of the failure of the collective security system envisaged by the Charter. In the absence of UN military forces foreseen under Article 43 and in the further absence of a functioning MSC to direct them, the secretary-general emerged as the virtual defense minister of the United Nations.

The secretary-general is empowered by Article 99 of the Charter to "bring to the attention of the Security Council any matter which in his opinion may threaten the maintenance of international peace and security." Thereafter, the secretary-general's role in these matters is not defined in the Charter. As noted, the Security Council can direct that a UN military operation be formed and issue its political mandate. However, because of the absence of workable charter provisions, what was supposed to happen next in this policy progression was unclear, a situation where "the gaps and inadequacies of the Charter system have been filled by creative interpretation and ingenious improvisation" referred to by Adam Roberts.[38] This improvisation meant that the functional challenges of managing military forces fell to the secretary-general and his staff on the Secretariat.

Article 29 in Chapter V of the UN Charter gives the Security Council the power to establish "such subsidiary organs as it deems necessary for the performance of its functions." These could conceivably be outside the Secretariat and directly under the Security Council, as was intended for the MSC. In practice, however, the relevant subsidiary organs of the United Nations that manage military operations are in the UN Secretariat. For the great majority of the United Nations' existence, these organs were fairly small. Between 1945 and February 1993, the secretary-general was assisted in strategic planning and force management by a small handful of staff in the office of the under secretary-general for special political affairs. Even in May 1993, when the United Nations was in the middle of the "explosion in peacekeeping," this office had only some twenty-three political and military planners.[39] A slightly larger, but separate, office, the Field Operations Division, handled the administrative and logistics support.

In February 1993, the UN Secretariat reorganized and created a separate office dedicated to strategic and military planning for the many new, large, and ambitious second-generation peacekeeping operations getting under way.[40] It split the responsibility for the other principal aspects of multifunctional peacekeeping between the Department of Political Affairs and the Department of Humanitarian Affairs. In September of 1993, the United Nations subsumed the Field Operations Division under the Department of Peacekeeping Operations (DPKO). The DPKO itself, beset by the planning challenges of the tremendous increase in the volume and scope of UN military operations, continued to increase in size throughout 1993–1994, the staff eventually growing to almost four hundred.[41] Several other initiatives also were undertaken in 1993, including the creation of a round-the-clock "Situation Center" to track field operations, plans to use a U.S.–donated management information system, and a general reorganization that included the creation of planning cells, training units, and analysis sections.[42]

Another initiative was the creation of a database to track "stand-by" forces that would be committed by member states to be oncall to the United Nations for future operations. By maintaining such a database, UN planners could identify units earlier in the planning stage, quickly obtain their commitment to the mission, and greatly reduce the habitual delays caused by having to recruit from scratch through time-consuming bilateral negotiations with member states. It was hoped that the concept of stand-by forces would circumvent the problems caused by the Secretariat's not having any sort of reliable access to forces. There also was an expectation that forces committed "conditionally" through the stand-by arrangements would mature into a semipermanent mechanism for recruiting UN forces.

However, because this system was ultimately predicated on voluntary contributions as well, it was subject to the same constraints as other methods of force recruitment. It did speed the negotiation process that had always been conducted between the Secretariat staff and member states, but it did not, in and of itself, increase the willingness of member states to participate in some of the new second-generation peacekeeping missions. The clearest and most tragic manifestation of this occurred in May 1994, where, despite the pleading of the secretary-general and the commitments of nineteen member states to the stand-by roster, not a single unit from those nineteen governments was offered for service in Rwanda.[43] It was an object lesson in the potential futility of enacting structural mechanisms that ran against the grain of an organizational culture that depends solely on voluntary contributions.

This vignette concerning the stand-by forces arrangement illustrates an important point about the relationship between new institutional structures and institutional efficiency. One does not necessarily give rise to the other. Throughout the period that witnessed the "explosion in peacekeeping," the United Nations took many steps to strengthen and "professionalize" its inherent capability to manage military operations. Between 1992 and 1996, through a more liberal interpretation of the Charter, a more aggressive and united Security Council, and a reinforced Secretariat, the United Nations greatly added to its legal and functional structure for creating and managing military operations. These changes were intended to fill what one report called a "fundamental institutional gap that must be filled if the use of collectively sanctioned military measures [by the UN] is to be effective."[44]

However, as will be seen, the nature of the much greater military challenges in the new missions the United Nations was now overseeing still threatened to overwhelm the organization. The large and complex military forces of the new generation of peacekeeping were a far greater management challenge than observation missions or traditional peacekeeping. Despite the political and functional steps taken to strengthen the inherent capacity for strategic management in the United Nations, traditional problems remained. In 1994, Mats Berdal noted that, despite the many studies and reports completed on strengthening the United Nations' management capability, "none have significantly enhanced the management of peacekeeping functions in the Secretariat."[45] Another observer dismissed the United Nations' recent structural changes as "mere window dressing."[46] The challenges posed by the new generation of UN military missions largely offset the reinforced United Nations and exacerbated the ability of the institution effectively to manage military forces in these complex and hazardous operations.

The Spectrum of UN Military Operations

Here UN military operations are defined as those missions conducted to pursue political objectives specified by the decision-making bodies of the United Nations, using military forces constituted from member states but managed by the United Nations in an effort to attain such objectives. These operations span a broad operational spectrum and differ considerably from one end of that spectrum to the other. This spectrum ranges from unarmed peace observation missions to large and dangerous multifunctional missions with mandates for limited offensive combat operations. In addition to these military operations, the United Nations has sanctioned, and even been symbolically involved in, the military management of some large-scale enforcement operations that were in essence tantamount to conducting a war against an intransigent state—in these cases, North Korea and Iraq. In this spectrum of operations, the operational nature of a UN military mission is determined first, by the environment in which the force operates and, second, by the level of military effort or force used.

The environment in which UN operations took place ranged from completely benign to very hostile and belligerent. This important factor largely determined the size, nature, and composition of the UN force and its tasks. The environment can be measured by several factors: (1) the sustainability of the peace settlement agreed on by all belligerents; (2) the official arrangements by belligerents and the United Nations that document the extent of their cooperation with the UN forces; (3) the *actual* level of cooperation by all parties, from national officials to local parties on the ground; and (4) the immediate environment in which the UN forces operated. The hostility of that environment can be measured by such variables as hostile violations of accords, shooting incidents, and UN casualties. Measuring these factors in a mission allows one to plot the relative belligerency of the operational environment.

The level of military effort and the force employed reflect the environment and opposing forces as well as the nature of the tasks to be performed. The force structure and the way in which that force operates differ markedly throughout the range of UN military operations. The type of force and how it was structured largely determined the military effort involved (or vice versa). Most missions were staffed by small groups of unarmed observers or lightly armed infantry troops. Other missions had large numbers of combat troops, organized in heavy mechanized and armored units, with organic artillery, air, and naval support. Generally, the larger and heavier the UN force, the more ambitious the military tasks. In some cases, limited enforcement measures were taken by heavy UN military forces to coerce belligerents into a pattern of peaceful behavior. Military force structure, operations, and objectives determine the level of military effort involved.

By measuring the operational environment and the level of military effort involved in all UN military operations from 1948 to 1996, one can actually plot the spectrum of operations as seen in Figure 1. Even though this spectrum is continuous, there are discernible subsets of missions that are subject to different political and military parameters. The resultant analytical framework places UN military operations into three general categories: (1) observation missions, (2) traditional peacekeeping, and (3) second-generation peacekeeping. A separate category, enforcement actions, also is considered as an addendum, although the two actions under consideration here were merely sanctioned by the United Nations and not managed by the organization. The spectrum may at times develop what appears to be chronological or regional patterns, but it is predicated solely on the military characteristics of the operation. Some missions (such as the Congo, Namibia, or Somalia) could be placed in one of several subsets because their military character was broadly defined or changed considerably over time. To illustrate that point, the Congo mission is shown in Figure 1 as an example of a mission that can be considered to span subsets. It should be noted again that the spectrum is merely a starting point for a comparative analysis and is not an attempt to rigidly categorize any one mission. For this reason the missions in Figure 1 are plotted to give a general idea of relative operational characteristics, but not labeled specifically. Map 1 shows the geographic distribution of all the UN operations from 1948 to 1996.

Observation Missions

Observation missions have presented the smallest management challenge to the United Nations, which explains why they make up the majority of UN military operations. There were twenty observation missions initiated between 1948 and 1996 (Table 1). Militarily, they represent the low end of the operational spectrum because of both the negligible military effort employed and the generally benign environment in which they operated. These missions consisted of no more than a few hundred military observers who were unarmed or were equipped with side arms only. The observers were generally composite groups of officers recruited from member states, chosen from "neutral" countries to make up an equitable geographic balance and to reinforce the appearance of impartiality. The force of observers was an ad hoc composition, usually determining its organizational structure and modus operandi once deployed to the area of operations.

The belligerent parties under UN observation had the power of veto over force composition and methods of operation. Thus, the key to success in observation missions was the goodwill and cooperation of the belligerents. Naturally, this left UN military observers beholden to the vagaries of their political environment. Needless to say, because of this, decisions about force structure, command and control, and military objectives were far more subject to political sensitivities than purely military requirements.

Because observation missions were completely reliant on the consent and cooperation of the belligerents for their success, there was no need for an overwhelming military presence on the part of the United Nations, one that it

Figure 1

The Spectrum of UN Military Operations

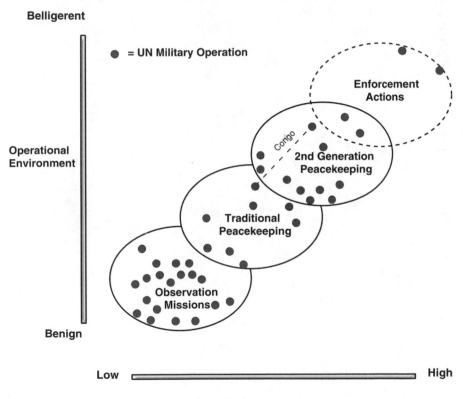

Belligerent

● = UN Military Operation

Operational Environment

Benign

Enforcement Actions

Congo

2nd Generation Peacekeeping

Traditional Peacekeeping

Observation Missions

Low   High

Level of Military Effort/Use of Force

Map 1

United Nations Military Operations, 1948-1996

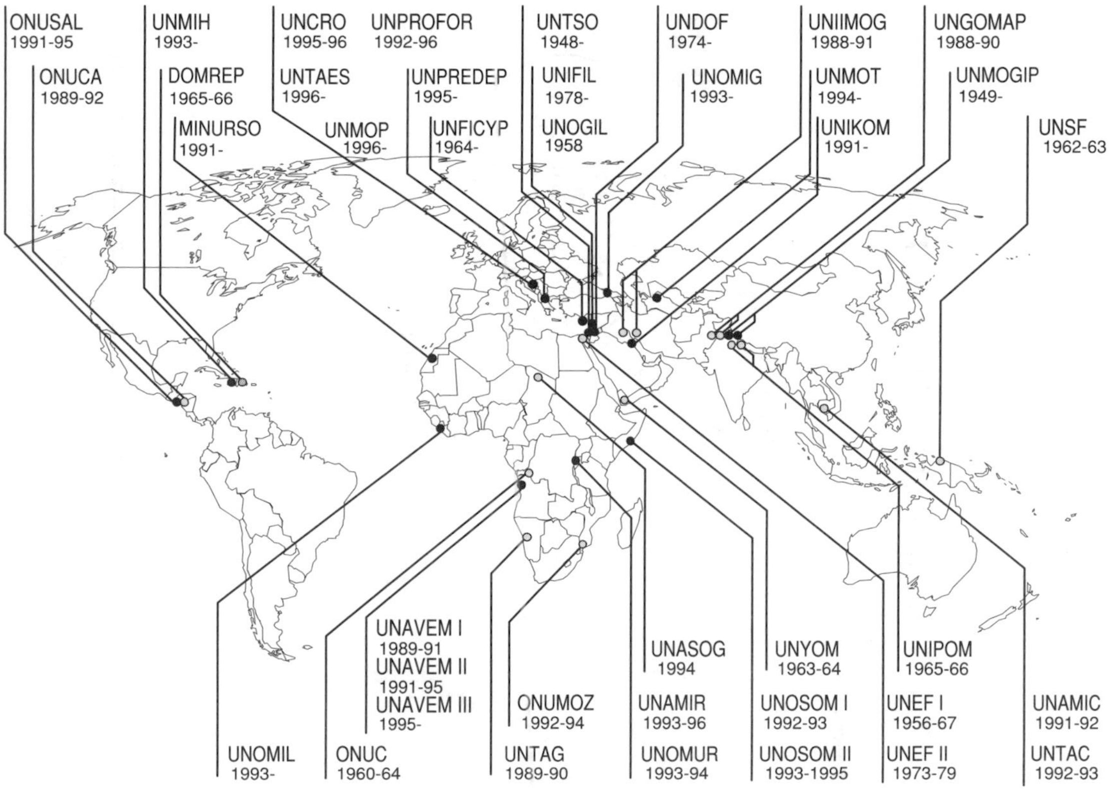

UNSF
1962-63

UNAMIC
1991-92

UNTAC
1992-93

UNGOMAP
1988-90

UNMOGIP
1949-

UNIPOM
1965-66

UNEF I
1956-67

UNEF II
1973-79

UNIIMOG
1988-91

UNMOT
1994-

UNIKOM
1991-

UNYOM
1963-64

UNOSOM I
1992-93

UNOSOM II
1993-1995

UNDOF
1974-

UNOMIG
1993-

UNASOG
1994

UNAMIR
1993-96

UNOMUR
1993-94

UNTSO
1948-

UNIFIL
1978-

UNOGIL
1958

ONUMOZ
1992-94

UNTAG
1989-90

UNPROFOR
1992-96

UNPREDEP
1995-

UNFICYP
1964-

UNAVEM I
1989-91
UNAVEM II
1991-95
UNAVEM III
1995-

UNCRO
1995-96

UNTAES
1996-

UNMOP
1996-

ONUC
1960-64

UNMIH
1993-

DOMREP
1965-66

MINURSO
1991-

UNOMIL
1993-

ONUSAL
1991-95

ONUCA
1989-92

Source: U.N. Peacekeeping Information Notes, 1996.

Table 1

UN Military Observation Missions

Name	Dates/Size*	General Mission
UN Truce Supervision Organization (**UNTSO**)	**1948 - Present** 572 (Max) 178 (1996)	Monitor Cease-Fire
UN Military Observer Group in India & Pakistan (**UNMOGIP**)	**1949 - Present** 102 (Max) 44 (1996)	Monitor Cease-Fire
UN Observer Group in Lebanon (**UNOGIL**)	**1958** 591 (Max)	Monitor Border Violations
UN Yemen Observation Mission (**UNYOM**)	**1963 - 1964** 189 (Max)	Monitor Disengagement
UN India-Pakistan Observation Mission (**UNIPOM**)	**1965 - 1966** 96 (Max)	Monitor Cease-Fire
Mission of the Representative of the Secretary-General in the Dominican Republic (**DOMREP**)	**1965-1966** 2	Monitor Cease-Fire
UN Good Offices Mission in Afghanistan and Pakistan (**UNGOMAP**)	**1988 - 1990** 50 (Max)	Monitor Troop Withdrawal & Disengagement
UN Iran-Iraq Military Observer Group (**UNIIMOG**)	**1988 - 1991** 350 (Max)	Monitor Cease-Fire/Withdrawal
UN Angola Verification Mission (**UNAVEM I**)	**1988 - 1991** 70 (Max)	Monitor Troop Withdrawal
UN Observer Group in Central America (**ONUCA**)	**1989 - 1992** 132 (Max)	Monitor Withdrawal & Demobilization
UN Iraq-Kuwait Observation Mission (**UNIKOM**)	**1991 - Present** 243 (1994)	Monitor Cease-Fire
UN Angola Verification Mission (**UNAVEM II**)	**1991 - 1995** 350 (Max)	Monitor Cease-Fire and Administer Elections
UN Observer Mission in El Salvador (**ONUSAL**)	**1991 - 1995** 30 (Max) 380 (Authorized)	Monitor Human Rights, Elections, and Government Restructure
UN Mission for the Referendum in Western Sahara (**MINURSO**)	**1991 - Present** 241 (1996)	Monitor Cease-Fire & Administer Referendum
UN Observer Mission Uganda-Rwanda (**UNOMUR**)	**1993 - 1994** 81 (Authorized) Subsumed into UNAMIR, 1994	Monitor Border Violations
UN Observer Mission in Georgia (**UNOMIG**)	**1993 - Present** 134 (1996)	Monitor Cease-Fire
UN Observer Mission in Liberia (**UNOMIL**)	**1993 - Present** 160 (Authorized) 26 (1996)	Monitor Cease-Fire/Embargo/ Demobilization
UN Aouzou Strip Observer Group (**UNASOG**)	**May 1994 - June 1994** 9 (Max)	Monitor Withdrawal
UN Mission of Observers in Tajikistan (**UNMOT**)	**Dec. 1994 - Present** 45 (1996)	Monitor Cease-Fire
UN Mission of Observers in Prevlaka (**UNMOP**)	**Jan 1996 - Present** 28 (1996)	Monitor Demilitarization Agreement

Note: * Number of military observers only.
Source: UN Department of Public Information.

no doubt would have had some trouble mobilizing. Observation missions were a self-help technique, and the belligerents provided the great bulk of the "help." As such, the authority of the UN forces was largely moral and political, not military. UN military observers rarely had the military manpower to carry out their mandate effectively without the active cooperation of belligerents and certainly had no power actively to coerce belligerents into cooperation. If in fact UN military observers were in danger from a bellicose environment and noncooperative belligerents, they were usually withdrawn or reduced significantly, as happened in Angola in 1993.

Traditional Peacekeeping Missions

Traditional peacekeeping missions also relied on the consent and cooperation of the belligerents, but were deployed with slightly more complex military tasks than just observation. Traditional peacekeeping missions consisted of no more than a few thousand lightly armed troops typically deployed in an interpositional buffer zone to separate warring belligerents. Like observation missions, these forces were constructed not on purely military requirements, but on factors such as equitable geographic representation, the neutrality of contingents, the approval of the belligerents, and the passive nature of the military operations themselves. As a result, traditional peacekeeping forces were small and light, usually composed of a few infantry battalions from neutral member states such as Fiji and Ghana or, more often, from the so-called "middle powers" of Canada, Sweden, Austria, Ireland, Norway, Denmark, Chile, and others. The distinction "middle" referred to the fact that these nations were, as a rule, neither great powers nor very poor developing states.

Although very different in their size, force structure, and employment from observation missions, these missions operated under the same basic political constraints. They were in many ways merely reinforced observation missions and yet less than coercive actions. As Professor Paul Diehl has noted, they were an improvised response to "the failure of collective security and the success of early UN peace observation missions."[47] There were eight operations of this kind, all but two initiated during the Cold War (Table 2). Traditional peacekeeping missions did not have ambitious military tasks. The missions of these forces were derived from their limited political objective. That objective was most often restricted to containing the armed conflict to provide a stable atmosphere for the further political resolution of the conflict.

The primary military objective of most traditional peacekeeping missions was therefore to occupy a clearly recognized and usually linear interpositional buffer zone. The buffer zone gave the small peacekeeping contingents a mechanism that could "stretch" and multiply its humble military capabilities. Much like observation missions, traditional peacekeepers were authorized to

Table 2

Traditional Peacekeeping Missions

Name	Dates/Size*	General Mission
UN Emergency Force **(UNEF I)**	**1956 - 1967** 6,073 (Max)	Occupy Buffer Zone & Supervise Disengagement
UN Security Force in West New Guinea **(UNSF)**	**1962 - 1963** 1,576 (Max)	Maintain Civil Order
UN Peacekeeping Force in Cyprus **(UNFICYP)**	**1964 - Present** 6,411 (Max) 1,165 (1996)	Occupy Buffer Zone (From 1974)
UN Emergency Force II **(UNEF II)**	**1973 - 1979** 6,973 (Max)	Occupy Buffer Zone & Supervise Disengagement
UN Disengagement Observer Force **(UNDOF)**	**1974 - Present** 1,052 (1996)	Supervise Disengagement
UN Interim Force in Lebanon **(UNIFIL)**	**1978 - Present** 4,614 (1964)	Occupy Buffer Zone
UN Preventive Deployment Force **(UNPREDEP)**	**1995 - Present** 1,085 (1996)	Monitor Border Area
†UN Operation in Somalia **(UNOSOM I)**	**1992 - 1993** 555 (Max)	Protect Humanitarian Supplies

Notes: * Size of the military component only.

On long-term missions if the peak strength differs markedly from the 1996 strength, both numbers are shown. Missions still active in 1996 show strength as of November 1996.

†UNOSOM I can be considered in several categories. However, in this book, it is treated as an overall part of the entire Somalia Mission and is therefore examined in Chapter Seven as part of the entire UN operation in Somalia.

Source: UN Department of Public Information.

use force only in a passive sense: in self-defense or in defense of the mandate when under armed attack. The light military capacity of traditional peace-keepers mitigated against always invoking the latter directive, as evidenced by the general lack of resistance from UN troops in Lebanon during the periodic Israeli excursions across its border with Lebanon.

The passive use of force was intended to preserve the impartial standing of the peacekeeping force and reinforce the concept of voluntary cooperation from the belligerents. Traditional peacekeepers were never intended to use active force to coerce belligerents and were of course never structured for this or mandated to do so. Despite this passive approach, operations were still often dangerous. As noted, many contemporary studies refer to UN observation missions and traditional peacekeeping as "Chapter VI Operations." However, as Chapter VI addresses the "Pacific Settlement of Disputes," it should be noted that not all operations have been so very pacific. In fact, almost 600 Blue Helmets have died in traditional peacekeeping missions and over fifty in observation missions.[48]

From its early experiences in managing observation and traditional peace-keeping missions, the United Nations developed a doctrine of sorts commonly known as "the principles of peacekeeping." This "body of principles, procedures and practices came to constitute a corpus of case law or customary practice" and was described by the then-under secretary-general for peacekeeping operations in 1993:[49]

1. They are United Nations operations. Formed by the United Nations from the outset, commanded in the field by a UN–appointed general, under the ultimate authority of the UN secretary-general, and financed by member states collectively.
2. They are deployed with the consent of all the parties involved and only after a political settlement had been reached between warring factions.
3. The forces are committed to strict impartiality. Military observers and peacekeepers can in no way take sides with or against a party to the conflict.
4. Troops are provided by member states on a voluntary basis. During the Cold War era, there was rarely superpower or even "big five" participation in these missions, and the majority of troops were supplied by the so-called "middle powers" to reinforce the concept of neutrality.
5. These units operate under rules of engagement that stress the absolute minimum use of force in accomplishing their objectives. This is usually limited to the use of force in self-defense only, but some missions have used force in situations in which peacekeepers were being prevented by armed persons from fulfilling their mandate.

These principles reinforced the political characteristics of a cooperative multinational organization that had no forces, structure, or mandates with which to manage a coercive military force. As will be seen, from a purely military standpoint the application of the principles of peacekeeping made observation and traditional peacekeeping missions somewhat militarily ineffective. The missions were improvised endeavors, thrown together from the disparate military elements of many different member states. They operated under a loose system of command that allowed for competition between the UN chain and national decision structures. There were few common control measures and little interoperability because of a lack of common doctrine, training, and equipment. And most frustrating of all, the missions were so buffeted by the tides of fickle belligerent cooperation that the Blue Helmets could not create the military conditions that would guarantee their own success.

However, because the military component of these missions was just one factor in a comprehensive diplomatic and political technique of conflict resolution, military inefficiency in and of itself would not necessarily wreck the entire mission. As peacekeeping veteran John Mackinlay recalled, "the importance of the military factor in the equation of success is considerably less than the political factor."[50] Ramesh Thakur noted that "the goal of peacekeeping units is not the creation of peace, but the containment of war so that others can search for peace in stable conditions."[51] Thus, expectations for what these UN military units could accomplish through force were kept low, and traditional peacekeepers merely held the line while other nonmilitary forces worked to resolve the conflict. Consequently, the military aspects of traditional peacekeeping missions were characterized by somewhat passive, innocuous, and unthreatening operations on the part of the UN force.

Second-Generation Peacekeeping Missions

Much of this traditional passive and cooperative peacekeeping doctrine changed in the early 1990s largely because of Security Council cooperation after the end of the Cold War and in the aftermath of the Gulf War. As UN diplomat Shashi Tharoor noted, "at the end of the Cold War, an unprecedented degree of agreement within the UN Security Council in responding to international crises had plunged the organization into a dizzying series of peacekeeping operations that bore little or no resemblance in size, complexity and function to those that had borne the peacekeeping label in the past."[52]

The new missions also reflected changes in operational environments and the complex and multifunctional nature of this new generation of peacekeeping. During this immediate post–Cold War period, the Security Council created operations that had to operate in less supportive political environments, often in the middle of intrastate wars. The old political prerequisite of a previously concluded peace settlement was no longer always taken into account. In addition, the missions were considerably more complex than inert buffer zone peacekeeping. More ambitious missions in unstable environments required larger and more robust UN forces that were equipped more aggressively.

Boutros Boutros-Ghali forecast the environments in which these large and complex missions would operate when, in 1992, he redefined peacekeeping as "the deployment of a United Nations presence in the field, *hitherto* [my emphasis] with the consent of all the parties concerned."[53] The secretary-general also wrote that his new concept "goes beyond peacekeeping to the extent that the operation would be deployed without the express consent of the two parties."[54] This foreboding observation, that the UN was free to launch peacekeeping missions without the full consent of the belligerents, was the conceptual seed for second-generation peacekeeping operations, some of which were being planned as *An Agenda for Peace* was being drafted.

Second-generation peacekeeping missions were qualitatively and quantitatively different from traditional missions, which the UN had characterized as mere "holding actions." These new missions were much more comprehensive, with the UN attempting a near-simultaneous management of political, societal, economic, humanitarian, electoral, diplomatic, and military initiatives. One magazine characterized the change by noting that

> *though still [sometimes] called peacekeeping, the concept of a true peacekeeping unit interposed neatly between two dormant belligerents has evolved into an untidy and intrusive host of soldiers and civilians who are supposed to demobilize guerrilla armies, run or monitor elections, train police forces and rebuild shattered infrastructures.*[55]

Moreover, the UN attempted to manage several of these large and complex operations at the same time, further stretching its management resources.

The newer operations were more hazardous, and the Blue Helmets were no longer "alert, but inert" in buffer zones. The UN forces now were spread among concentrated and mixed pockets of still-warring belligerents. In this environment they attempted at times *actively* to protect the delivery of humanitarian aid, disarm and demobilize belligerents, maintain and protect safe areas, enforce weapons-exclusion zones, monitor borders, monitor violations of human rights, repatriate refugees, assume temporary control of many government functions, and provide secure environments for elections and other "nation-building activities." The UN initiated ten of these operations after the relaxation of the superpower confrontation in 1987–1989 (Table 3). They took place in Namibia, Cambodia, the former Yugoslavia, Somalia, Mozambique, Rwanda, Haiti, and Angola. The larger and more active of these operations had a convincing historical antecedent in the UN operation in the Congo (1960–1964).

Table 3

Second-Generation Peacekeeping Missions

Name	Dates/Size*	General Mission
UN Operation in the Congo **(ONUC)**	**1960 - 1964** 19,828 (Max)	Supervise Troop Withdrawal & Restore Order
UN Transition Assistance Group **(UNTAG)**	**1989 - 1990** 4,493 (Max)	Supervise Cease-Fire & Government Transition
UN Transitional Authority in Cambodia **(UNTAC)**	**1992 - 1993** 15,511 (Max)	Disarm Factions, Maintain Order, Supervise Elections
UN Protection Force in Yugoslavia **(UNPROFOR)**	**1992 - 1996** 38,810 (Max)	Protect Delivery of Aid, Supervise Cease-Fires
UN Operation in Somalia **(UNOSOM II)**	**1992 - 1995** 29,545 (Max)	Protect Delivery of Aid, Restore Order, Disarm
UN Operation in Mozambique **(UNOMOZ)**	**1992 - 1994** 6,552 (Max)	Supervise Implementation of Peace Accord & Cease-Fire
UN Assistance Mission for Rwanda **(UNAMIR)**	**1993 - 1996** 5,442 (Max)	Supervise Cease-Fire & Provide Secure Environment
UN Mission in Haiti **(UNMIH)**	**1993 - Present** 1,200 (1996)	Assist Democratic Transition
UN Angola Verification Mission **(UNAVEM III)**	**1995 - Present** 7,350 (Authorized)	Supervise Cease-Fire, Provide Secure Environment
UN Transitional Administration for Eastern Slavonia, Baranja, and Western Sirmium **(UNTAES)**	**1996 - Present** 4,580 (1996)	Maintain Peace and Security

Notes: *Size of the military component only. On 31 March 1995, UNPROFOR was replaced by three separate but interlinking peacekeeping operations: UNPF, UNCRO, and UNPROFOR.

Source: UN Department of Public Information.

Attempting to manage these complex endeavors in dangerous environments was a tremendous challenge and required a significant increase in peacekeepers and supporting staff. In 1990, the United Nations was managing fewer than 10,000 personnel in eight observation and traditional peacekeeping missions. By 1993, it had control over some 80,000 troops in eighteen different missions.[56] Some missions, such as Namibia and Mozambique, were not unusually large or complicated in their military structure, but had complex and multifunctional tasks (including provisions for election security, humanitarian missions, and other nation-building measures).[57] Others, like missions in Somalia and the former Yugoslavia, were extremely large, dangerous,[58] militarily complex, and multifunctional as well. These missions not only sought to help end ongoing civil wars, but also to create an environment for political reconciliation and help rebuild "failed states."

The strategic and operational characteristics of many second-generation peacekeeping missions bore little resemblance to the classic "principles of peacekeeping." For instance, to manage the strategic challenges of these many complex and dangerous missions, the United Nations broke with its traditional recruiting formula and relied heavily on the sophisticated military forces of the great powers. In several missions, the United Nations even "contracted out" some military enforcement missions to member states, ad hoc coalitions, or regional military alliances. These limited enforcement operations were mandated under Chapter VII of the Charter and challenged the traditional UN peacekeeping requirement for strict neutrality and the passive use of military force.

The United Nations undertook these breaks with principle in some second-generation missions because it recognized that traditional peacekeeping, considering the innocuous forces and methods it employed, could only succeed in very favorable political conditions. These propitious political circumstances were not present or obtainable in several second-generation peacekeeping environments. As a result, some of these missions went ahead with a more "robust" and aggressive peacekeeping mandate. However, most second-generation missions, even those that were enormous military enterprises by UN standards, never had the resources, command and control structure, or modus operandi for effective enforcement. In addition, coercive force was used in conjunction with traditional peacekeeping precepts. As Berdal has noted, these attempts tended to obfuscate "the basic distinction between peacekeeping and enforcement action . . . [and] highlighted the particular risks of attempting to combine the coercive use of force with peacekeeping objectives."[59]

In some ways, many of these missions were only one step short of enforcement operations. However, that step to active and coercive enforcement is an important Rubicon that is not fully conveyed by the diagram in Figure 1. Second-generation peacekeeping missions, despite being labeled by many observers as Chapter VII or peace enforcement missions, were still based on the strategic consent of the belligerents.[60] Despite limited enforcement measures in some second-generation peacekeeping missions, the operations still relied on the belligerents for success and did not have the resources to coerce warring factions into peaceful coexistence. British Army doctrine concerning these missions articulated this point well: "Wider peacekeeping conflicts will [still] require resolution by conciliation rather than termination by force. Thus, as in [traditional] peacekeeping, military operations will be designed principally to create or support the conditions in which political and diplomatic activities may proceed."[61]

Thus it must be emphasized that it is an extraordinary leap in doctrine, attitude, effort, and capability from "consent-based" operations such as observation, traditional peacekeeping, and second-generation peacekeeping to large-scale enforcement missions. However, in the context of this study, there is a clear line of continuity between the management challenges of military operations as the United Nations progresses from observation to enforcement missions. The limited enforcement measures, complex tasks, and belligerent environments of some large second-generation peacekeeping missions accurately presage some of the challenges of managing large-scale enforcement missions. They also illuminated the limitations of the United Nations as an institution in managing active military operations.

Enforcement Actions

As will be shown, the United Nations suffered serious problems in trying functionally to manage militarily complex and ambitious second-generation peacekeeping operations. This phenomenon was, in a sense, foreshadowed by UN involvement in the Korean War (1950–1953) and the Gulf War (1990–1991). In both those large-scale enforcement missions, the United Nations sanctioned the active use of force by a coalition of member states and had to cede the functional management of operations to a major power. In Korea it even mandated a UN Command and made some provision for exercising limited oversight in its operations. However, in both cases the United Nations had little or no role in the strategic direction or functional military management of these extremely large and complex military operations. That role was left to the United States, which, as a major military power, could provide a legitimate and authoritative framework through which these enormous multinational military efforts could be mobilized, organized, and executed.

These missions represent the high end of the operational spectrum, taking place in a bellicose and adversarial environment that necessitates the use of large-scale military force. The operational characteristics of these campaigns are those of war. The roles and objectives of military forces in these enterprises are clearer than the somewhat ambiguous parameters of action in peacekeeping missions. No cooperation was expected from a defined enemy and there was no need for impartiality. Force requirements and operations were determined in large measure by military requirements that were tempered, but not overwhelmed, by political sensibilities. From a military point of view, these were the only types of military operations where the multinational forces could actually *create* the environment they needed to guarantee success.

Although these operations were not managed by the United Nations, and are not considered in this study to be UN military operations per se, each of these two crises presented a unique set of circumstances for large-scale military intervention conducted under the political sanction and, in the case of Korea, with the military forces under the symbolic auspices of the United Nations. Because in each case the command and control of the operation and the majority of forces were provided by the United States, many observers dismiss these operations as American wars. However, both were multinational operations authorized to use force by the Security Council. The fact that the United Nations was essentially following the U.S. lead in both cases illustrates an important characteristic of large-scale enforcement actions. They must have the wholesale participation of a great power to bring to bear the huge resources, sacrifices, and political will required to wage modern war against an intransigent state. Only a few states or groups of states can provide the complex infrastructure and large forces necessary to undertake complicated military enterprises such as Operation Desert Storm. A brief examination of these missions in the spectrum of operations makes for a more complete understanding of the strategic constraints inherent to the United Nations.

The spectrum of operations reflects an empirical and factual analysis of the military characteristics of UN military operations between 1948 and 1996. The spectrum is not a doctrinal guide for conducting military actions in UN operations.[62] A cursory look at the spectrum may imply that there is an operational continuum in UN military operations, and to some extent there is— between observation, first-generation peacekeeping, and second-generation peacekeeping missions. However, even within these three subsets, which often are elastically referred to as "peacekeeping," the differences in managing force structure, command and control, and military objectives are readily identifiable. The most dramatic changes for the strategic "manager" come when making the jump to large-scale enforcement missions, the only operations where belligerent consent for a UN presence is not the principal strategic imperative.

In the following analysis of the wide spectrum of military operations that the United Nations has undertaken since 1948, it will become clear that the organization is more suited for managing some missions than others. Operations that were small and unambitious, with simple and passive military operations, could be managed by a large and disparate multinational organization that had an impartial moral authority, but limited military credibility, few organic resources, and improvised structures and procedures. Larger, complex, active, and dangerous military operations needed to be managed by an alliance or coalition that had a framework state or group of states with real political legitimacy and military authority. This legitimacy and authority stem from the ability of a political organization to mobilize competent military resources, direct them through unambiguous and authoritative chains of command, and employ them in timely, rehearsed, and efficient operations.

CHAPTER 2

Observation Missions

The majority of UN military operations undertaken between 1948 and 1996 were observation missions. Twenty of the thirty-eight UN military operations addressed in this study were observation missions. In addition, two early missions in the Balkans (1946–1951) and Indonesia (1947–1950) had the fundamental characteristics of UN observation missions but are not treated as such by the United Nations and will be cited only briefly here. These two missions are not considered UN observation missions because the observers worked as members of national delegations and were not under the authority of the secretary-general.[1]

There are several pragmatic and rather simple reasons for the greater number of observation missions. First, they had unambitious and limited political mandates. It was simply less politically contentious to create an observation mission than a larger peacekeeping or enforcement mission. Second, because of that restricted mandate, the missions were small, relatively inexpensive, and had a modest operational profile that generally did not excite controversy. The UN could manage several observation missions at once and for long periods without undue financial, political, or managerial concerns.

In this regard, it is instructive to note that the two longest running UN military operations, the observation groups in the Middle East (UNTSO) and India/Pakistan (UNMOGIP), have been in continuous existence since 1948 and 1949, respectively. The mandate of these missions was renewed every year because their limited operations do not arouse much controversy about a UN military presence. Conversely, that same innocuous mandate and the very limited presence of unarmed UN observers has not compelled the belligerents in either of those long-running conflicts to come to a lasting political settlement. This is the fundamental political characteristic of observation missions: limited enough to form, fund, and deploy without undue controversy, but certainly not powerful enough to force belligerents to come to terms. Hence, the missions can continue for generations.

The operational military characteristics of observation missions are briefly sketched here before being examined in greater detail. First, they were military missions in that they were staffed predominantly by professional military officers whose technical expertise and professional standing were vital to the missions. Unlike peacekeeping, these missions did not include whole military units that were armed and capable of independent military operations. A few observation missions had whole military units involved for short periods (UNYOM, ONUCA, and UNIKOM), but their operational nature was overwhelmingly that of independently operating and unarmed observers. Second, the missions were small; the largest number of observers and supporting personnel was 591 deployed to Lebanon in 1958 as part of UNOGIL.[2]

Third, the small numbers of observers deployed did not always reflect the military requirements of their mission or area of operations, which were often large and difficult to inspect. The ratio of force to space in UN observer missions would be considered completely impractical by any military standards. As a rule, UN observers themselves could not fulfill their observation mandate because of their small force and the large amount of space under their "control." This reinforced the UN role as an impartial and limited force—an honest broker and secondary player in the conflict. The Blue Helmets were not an omnipotent or omnipresent military force. Fourth, as a result of these very features, the chief operational imperative of these missions was that they relied entirely on the cooperation and goodwill of the belligerents. UN military observers were a form of "self-help" for belligerents already committed to the conditions of a previously concluded peace settlement. The consent and cooperation of the belligerents toward the UN force were reinforced by the unquestioned neutrality and impartiality shown by the UN military observers during the mission.

Naturally enough, the reliance on belligerent cooperation, the innocuous political mandate of the UN mission, and the modest military capabilities of UN observers meant that they did not have the ability to plan or operate independently of those they were sent to observe. Acting only with the consent and cooperation of the belligerents, acting with strict impartiality, and adopting only a passive military posture were the pillars of UN military observers' modus operandi.[3] As noted, these operational characteristics were reflected in the "principles of peacekeeping," the de facto UN military doctrine that evolved from the United Nations' early experiences in observation and traditional peacekeeping missions. These principles and these methods of operation reflected the political characteristics of the United Nations itself, a multinational organization that was improvising quasi-military operations because it lacked legitimate, authoritative, and practiced mechanisms for recruiting, forming, and commanding larger and more active military forces.

This phenomenon is best understood in the explanations of force structure, command and control, and military objectives in the UN observation missions to be discussed. The primary analysis of observation missions is contained in the case study of UNIIMOG in Chapter Three. The purpose of the present chapter is briefly to examine general trends in observation missions and delineate the conclusions that can be drawn from them. The chapter first introduces the political atmosphere in which observation missions were formed and then examines how the military means functioned. This examination reinforces the point that the unique political characteristics and constraints of the United Nations helped form a distinctive doctrine for UN military observation missions. This doctrine made these ad hoc and improvised operations somewhat inefficient and impotent from a purely military standpoint, but they suited the nature of the mission itself and the nature of the organization managing the operations.

Creating Observation Missions

To understand more fully the strategy of these operations, the linking of military means to political ends, this brief section examines the political genesis of UN military observation missions. As noted in Chapter One, UN observation missions were not specifically addressed in the UN Charter. Therefore, there was no formal political mechanism for creating and deploying a group of UN military observers. Improvisation in the political arena therefore became a prominent feature of the management of UN observation missions, a characteristic that would permeate all levels of strategy and operations. As such, UN observation missions have sprung from many different political processes. According to William Durch,[4] these fall into three categories: Security Council initiatives, local initiatives, and brokered requests for assistance.

Before 1993, only three of fifteen observation missions were created through Security Council initiatives: the 1948 mission to Palestine (UNTSO), the 1988 Iran–Iraq mission (UNIIMOG), and the 1991 Iraq–Kuwait mission (UNIKOM). In all these cases, UN Security Council resolutions had demanded a cessation to the fighting and the Security Council's cease-fire proposal was eventually accepted by the warring factions. A Security Council proposal of impartial UN observers was considered a key inducement for belligerents to heed the warning to cease fighting and reach some form of settlement. This was the case in the war between Iran and Iraq, in which the deployment of UN observers to monitor the cease-fire was crucial to inducing those nations to end their war. In contrast, the deployment of observers to the demilitarized zone between Iraq and Kuwait in 1991 was unique in that it followed on the heels of an overwhelmingly successful enforcement action and left the Iraqis little choice in the matter of acceptance.

UNTSO, first established in 1948, also was the direct result of Security Council efforts to establish a truce in the Middle East. To adjust to the changes in local political conditions, it had its political mandate shifted almost every time there was a new armistice in the wars between Israel and her Arab neighbors.[5] In 1949, its mandate was restructured to reflect the four separate General Armistice Agreements between Israel and the Arab states at war with her. This new mandate was closer to a brokered request for assistance than a Security Council initiative. In fact, in 1972 the Security Council strengthened the mandate of UNTSO on a local request from the government of Lebanon that, "because of repeated Israeli aggression . . . wishes the Security Council to take necessary action to strengthen the United Nations machinery in the Lebanese-Israeli sector by increasing the number of observers."[6]

Similarly, two UN observation missions have been created as a response to local initiatives: UNMOGIP in Kashmir, and UNOGIL, which operated for six months in Lebanon in 1958. UNMOGIP was the result of India accusing Pakistan of sponsoring Muslim separatists in the Kashmir region.[7] UNOGIL is unique in that it remains the only recognized UN observation mission not created in part by some sort of political agreement between two belligerents, such as a cease-fire settlement. UNOGIL was authorized in response to charges by the Lebanese government that Syria (then linked to Egypt as the United Arab Republic) was smuggling arms and terrorists into Lebanon in an attempt to destabilize the regime.

After several efforts, a compromise Swedish resolution was accepted by the Security Council with the Soviet Union abstaining. Its language was brief, and it authorized action directly only to confirm or deny Lebanon's charges:

> *Having heard the charges of the representative of Lebanon concerning interference by the United Arab Republic in the internal affairs of Lebanon and the reply of the representative of the United Arab Republic, decides to dispatch urgently an observation group to proceed to Lebanon so as to ensure that there is no illegal infiltration of personnel or supply of arms or other materiel across the Lebanese borders.*[8]

On the other hand, the majority of UN observation missions come from political agreements that were brokered by one or more third parties. In most of these cases, the requirement for the United Nations to send an observation mission was a provision in a mediated cease-fire agreement. The mediator often was the United Nations itself or some combination of Security Council members, regional organizations, or just interested parties. For instance, the 1987 Central American leaders' summit, Esquipulas II, produced the political settlement that eventually spawned the United Nations' first military operation in Central America (ONUCA).[9]

The UN military observers sent to monitor the Soviet withdrawal from Afghanistan (UNGOMAP) were provided for in a "Memorandum of Understanding" attached to the UN–brokered peace talks in Geneva. As in most mediated settlements, the deployment of impartial UN observers was considered crucial to initial agreement and then implementation of the peace plan. After the accords were signed, the UN secretary-general officially asked the Security Council to authorize the mission that was agreed to in the peace accords. In some cases, the formal Security Council resolution authorizing the mission lagged far behind the actual deployment of UN observers.[10]

Most UN missions were created in this fashion, although the political impetus for their formation was as different as the settlements from which they originated. The UN observation mission in Yemen (UNYOM) was a result of a U.S.–brokered agreement between Saudi Arabia and Egypt. The initial UN observer mission in Angola (UNAVEM I) was the result of internationally mediated agreements between Cuba, Angola, and South Africa in 1988.[11] UNAVEM II was based on a later agreement among Angolan belligerents that was mediated by Portugal and the USSR, among others.

The common thread among almost all these missions (UNOGIL being the exception) was that they all resulted from a political agreement among belligerents. This most basic of political conditions had to be in place before the UN military observers were deployed. Unlike enforcement missions, where the military forces themselves could greatly influence and even create the environment needed for their success, observation missions had to accept the environment to which they were deployed. As such, a principal determinant in how the mission was structured, directed, and employed was the strength of the peace agreement itself and the consent and cooperation of the belligerents. When the consent was present and the environment was cooperative, the mission succeeded (UNAVEM I and UNGOMAP, for example). Conversely, when the belligerents were uncooperative, the mission failed (as in UNYOM and UNAVEM II). The inescapable fact is that the UN military observers themselves had little direct influence in the matter.

Thus, there was no regularly practiced and accepted political formula for creating and deploying UN observation missions. Political and functional improvisation was one common feature in the creation of these missions. The other common characteristic was that the missions resulted from a political agreement among belligerents. Naturally, some agreements were extremely tenuous and others were more reliable. Because of these political vagaries, over which the United Nations or its observers had little control, the UN force had to set low expectations for what their observers could achieve on their own. UN military forces in observation missions were important, but secondary, participants. As such, in these twenty missions, UN observers muddled through their operations, often buffeted by the fickle tide of belligerent cooperation, sometimes succeeding, sometimes not. It must therefore always be remembered that in operations at this end of the spectrum of UN military operations, the principles of consent, impartiality, and the passive use of military forces placed the prime determinant of mission success squarely in the hands of the belligerents, not the UN military observers.

Forming Observation Missions

The modus operandi reflected in the principles of peacekeeping greatly affected force structure decisions in UN military observation missions. The tenets of that doctrine that influenced the forming of a force of UN military observers were that (1) because the United Nations needed the consent and cooperation of the belligerents, the force was constructed with final approval reserved for the belligerents; (2) the force was structured on equitable geographic representation from member states; (3) the force was composed of national forces from neutral states and did not include great power participation; and (4) the force was structured on the assumption that military observers only had the moral authority of their UN status and could not resort to force of arms. These force structure guidelines were derived from the principles of peacekeeping and affected the size, composition, and nature of the observation force directly.

Because there were no rehearsed and reliable mechanisms for determining the composition of a UN observation mission, the UN secretary-general usually formed missions on the recommendation of his representative to the area or the head of the advance party. This official often suggested the number of observers and the types of support and equipment needed for their operations, and raised any host nation concerns. The initial UN observers were sometimes classified as military assistants to the secretary-general's representative and were not necessarily, at this early stage, part of an official UN military observation mission per se.

The secretary-general would then request that member states contribute the troops and equipment to satisfy his preliminary planning requirement. To expedite the process of staffing the missions, on many occasions the initial deployment of observers was taken from an existing mission. For instance, UNTSO deployed some of its observers to start UNOGIL and UNGOMAP. Observers in UNYOM were deployed straight from a peacekeeping mission (UNEF I) in the Sinai. Even after several UN missions had been undertaken, there still was no practiced and rehearsed pattern developed for forming and deploying UN observation forces. Naturally, this somewhat haphazard way of recruiting and building a force meant that the body of troops was not always a militarily effective force. As UN scholar D. W. Bowett noted, "in general, observer groups have been understaffed and under-equipped; they have also suffered from all the drawbacks of ad hoc constitution."[12] The planning stages of these missions were especially affected by the constraints and restrictions unique to the United Nations as it attempted to undertake (and improvise) military operations.

Composition and Size

The composition and size of UN observation missions clearly demonstrated the dominance of the political imperative over purely military requirements. Naturally, the principal assumption in force structure planning was that the military observers would be deployed in a supportive political environment. Within this consistent planning guidance, UN observation forces differed from mission to mission. Because the founders of the United Nations did not envisage military observation missions and the great powers had not concluded Article 43 agreements for UN military forces, the United Nations was forced to recruit individual military observers from member states on a case-by-case basis. Except in rare cases, the UN observer force did not comprise whole military units that had trained together for specific military tasks.

The United Nations could not circumvent its lack of regular and reliable military resources by using its civil servants (who *are* authorized in the Charter). UN observation forces needed to be organized around a core of seasoned, individual military professionals, usually middle-ranking officers. Because some observation mission tasks could conceivably be done by UN civilian officials, there was some early debate in the United Nations over the necessity of requesting and deploying the military officers of member states. However, there were several very important reasons why observation missions were predominantly staffed by experienced military professionals.

First, their technical expertise about military operations, gained through years of professional study and experience, was invaluable to observation mission tasks. Whether the observers were monitoring a cease-fire zone in Kashmir or the Middle East, patrolling a demilitarized area in Yemen or Central America, or monitoring a troop withdrawal in Afghanistan or Angola, military expertise was a prerequisite for success. Many newer observation missions had civilian and police components to monitor elections and other civil affairs, but the ability to observe and accurately report on military movements and actions was always the core function of UN observation missions.

Second, professional military officers staffing UN observation missions commanded the respect of their counterparts among the belligerents. Traditionally, military members of warring factions often were far more hostile to a civil servant or bureaucrat than a fellow in the profession of arms. In most UN observation missions, the UN observers accompanied the local commanders to verify cease-fire positions, investigate breaches of a truce, or gather information on troop withdrawals. The trust and cooperation of the local commanders, key components to UN success, often were more easily earned by UN military observers. As Bowett wrote,

> *The very nature of the observers' function, which consists of far more than simple observation, demands that the observer have an authority (and indeed personality) which will ensure respect; they have no armed forces on which to rely for authority. Hence the observers have been almost entirely commissioned officers.*[13]

Third, as discussed below, observation missions entailed limited military operations. Observation forces operated in difficult and inhospitable terrain, often in dangerous situations, and endured arduous living and working conditions. Between 1948 and 1996, over fifty UN observers lost their lives in observation operations.[14] One of the most horrific episodes included the 1988 kidnapping, torture, and hanging of a U.S. officer serving as an unarmed observer in UNTSO. Performing observation tasks under these conditions was something military professionals were trained for—the risks involved were part and parcel of the profession.

The composition of UN observation missions was based on individual officer observers, but there also were noncommissioned officers, enlisted observers, and support personnel under UN command. Early missions were made up almost solely of officers.[15] However, the commanders in the field soon came to realize that their operations were best supported by technical specialists in trained support units. In one early instance, the commander of UNOGIL requested noncommissioned officers and enlisted personnel to provide logistic and technical support for his mission, thereby freeing officers for observation duties only.[16]

Only in three instances have whole military units been deployed with UN observation missions. In the mission to Yemen, a Yugoslav reconnaissance company operated with the observers for a short time.[17] This Yugoslav contingent was drawn from a traditional peacekeeping operation in the Sinai, UNEF I. The company was withdrawn from Yemen and replaced by individual observers within months. The United Nations felt that, "in view of the cooperation shown by the parties and the peaceful and friendly attitude of the people in the area covered by the mission, it was no longer necessary to maintain a military unit in the demilitarized zone."[18] In ONUCA, once the mandate had been strengthened to include supervising the demobilization of the Nicaraguan resistance, a Venezuelan infantry battalion was briefly deployed to assist observers in that process. In UNIKOM, five infantry companies drawn from peacekeeping missions were briefly deployed to provide

security while the mission was in its early stages.[19] These units were somewhat symbolic and redundant, however, as the United States still had almost
two divisions worth of heavy combat troops occupying southern Iraq at the
time.

Although UN observation missions consisted mainly of ground observers,
many had small air and even naval elements as well. The air units were crucial to many operations because aerial observation could compensate for the
low-force to high-space ratio faced by most observation missions. For
instance, UNOGIL in 1958 was responsible for patrolling over 500 square
kilometers of Lebanese border in difficult terrain. Its ground force of 501
manned forty-nine observation posts and patrolled in over 200 vehicles, the
ninety air observers patrolled in eighteen aircraft and six helicopters and
were able to provide broad coverage of the border and direct ground forces
to areas of particular interest.[20] The missions to Palestine, Yemen, Central
America, and Western Sahara also included military air components.
ONUCA even included a naval component and operated with four
Argentinian patrol boats to help monitor the Gulf of Fonseca. Like all UN
observation forces, these additional military assets had to be recruited by the
United Nations on an individual and ad hoc basis as the need arose.

Neutrality and Equitable Geographic Representation

To reinforce the concept of force neutrality and impartiality, another principle of peacekeeping maintained that UN military observers would come
from neutral member states and would be chosen with equitable geographic
representation in mind. This tenet was made especially necessary by the
heightening of Cold War tensions in the 1950s, when it was decided that UN
military observers should be supplied almost exclusively by the so-called
middle powers. For instance, after the 1967 war between Israel and Egypt,
neither side would accept UNTSO observers from the nations who were
perceived to have armed and supported its opponent. Naturally, this ruled
out the superpowers or active NATO and Warsaw Pact members.
Consequently, the belligerents agreed on observers from Austria, Burma,
Chile, Finland, France, and Sweden.[21] The 1965 hostilities between Pakistan
and India also had Cold War implications, and the observers assigned to
UNIPOM reflected this.[22]

Conversely, UNMOGIP, founded in 1949 in the same area of India and
Pakistan as UNIPOM, but not as subject to Cold War ramifications, operated
with American and other Western observers. However, in the main, observa-
tion forces tended to come from nonaligned countries throughout the Cold
War. In contrast, operations initiated since the Cold War, such as those in
Western Sahara or Iraq/Kuwait, included observers from all five permanent

members of the Security Council. However, even these post–Cold War missions still operated on the principle of equitable geographic distribution, so no one member state or region dominated the force structure. For instance, the permanent five members of the Security Council contributed exactly twenty observers each to UNIKOM. The twenty-seven other member states contributed either seven, eight, or nine observers. As the mission evolved and numbers changed, the force structure priority was always to maintain that geographic and geopolitical balance.[23]

As will be reinforced in the case study, these types of political requirements most often superseded operational requirements. UN observation missions were never structured based on operational logic alone. Operational logic may have dictated that one country dominate the force structure to provide a rehearsed and authoritative command and control structure, dependable logistic support, and a consistent operational method. However, in an observation mission in which political sensitivity was far more important to mission success than genuine military efficiency, considerations of neutrality and equitable geographic representation were of greater importance.

To further explain how UN force structure planning was based on political requirements at the expense of military necessities, it is helpful to examine briefly some military planning considerations used in building a military force. In UN military operations, it was noted that factors such as belligerent approval, impartiality, and equitable geographic representation greatly influenced the force structure. In contrast, in more common military operations, many different planning factors are used when deciding on the force structure for an operation. The *mission* is considered first of all—what the force wishes to accomplish and what sort of force structure will ensure that the objective is reached. The *enemy* also is considered, both known belligerents, potential belligerents, and the general environment in which the force will be operating. *Terrain* is analyzed in great detail, as restricted terrain will require a much greater ratio of force to space to observe and control certain areas. *Time* is considered, as most missions have a set period in which it is advantageous to complete the operation. Finally, *troop availability* for the operation is considered and weighed against the ideal force structure arrived at from consideration of the other factors. This planning mechanism, known as *METT-T*, is just one standard process for analyzing force structure before initiating an operation.

In stark contrast, the United Nations did not have the luxury of planning its force structure based on the factors of METT-T. Because of its political constraints and lack of dedicated military forces, the United Nations had to approach the matter very differently. For instance, the "enemy" in UN missions were the belligerents themselves (who also were the allies!). Because the UN presence was merely intended to reinforce the goodwill and cooperation of the "enemy," these parties actually determined the parameters under which the UN force operated. In most cases, the previously warring factions decided the size of the UN force they were willing to tolerate and where that force could operate. Because the belligerents "sponsored" the mission and their political cooperation was vital for success, a purely military analysis of "enemy" was somewhat skewed and could not be used as a UN planning measure in the traditional military fashion.

In addition, troop availability was constrained by the fact that all UN forces had to be volunteered by member states. In many instances, especially in larger and more complex missions, the forces volunteered for service were less suited for their mission than forces that the commander would have chosen. However, the United Nations was limited in its power only to request forces. There have even been cases where member states simply refused to respond to the secretary-general's request and the mission was temporarily stymied. This happened most recently with peacekeeping forces in Somalia in 1992 (see the UNOSOM II case study in Chapter Seven) and Rwanda in 1994, as well as in the observation mission in Georgia in 1993. In addition, as noted, troops available during the Cold War were most often restricted to the middle powers because of the superpower polarization of so many local conflicts.

As a military manager, the United Nations had to deal with the political constraints inherent to a 185-member international organization that had to base force recruitment on voluntary military participation. Because of this, UN force structure planning for observation missions could never be conducted in an atmosphere where military practicability was the sole requirement. The additional constraints of local party cooperation and strict impartiality in the mission itself further restricted and limited force structure planning. Finally, because the United Nations had no standard and reliable practice for forming these missions, the composition of those groups was very much an improvised endeavor.[24] These features would also greatly influence the direction and employment of these forces once they were formed and deployed. All in all, the United Nations faced many more restrictions in recruiting and organizing simple military missions than other political entities, such as a nation-state or a credible military alliance.

Command and Control

Command and control, the processes and methods by which an organization plans, directs, coordinates, and controls its military forces, can be considered in two parts: the chain of command and control procedures. The problems of command and control in these two areas increase in complexity and consequence as military operations involve more units, more complicated operations, and more ambitious objectives. Consequently, the issues in both of these elements are brought into much sharper focus when considering peacekeeping and enforcement operations. Therefore, the principal discussion of command and control is undertaken in Chapters Four through Nine. However, they can be introduced here. Definitions also are explained in later chapters, but it is helpful here to use the paraphrasing of one peacekeeping report that noted "command is 'who is in charge of the military,' while control is 'how the military know what their own people are doing and how they tell them what to do.'"[25]

The first feature of command and control this book examines is "who is in charge." This is determined through a chain of command. The structure of the chain of command is critical to the success of a military mission because it establishes legitimacy, authority, responsibilities, and accountability at all levels in the organization. A clearly defined, authoritative, easily understood, and responsive chain of command is a key ingredient in successful military operations. The principal characteristic of UN chains of command is a loose interpretation of the concept of command. Because the United Nations temporarily had to borrow military observers from member states, it could never legally command these observers, but rather had temporary operational control. The nuances of these relationships are examined in detail in Chapter Four, but it can be appreciated here that the United Nations never had the same degree of sovereignty over its military observers as did the individual member states that contributed the personnel.

The second facet of command and control, control procedures, is used by the chain of command to ensure that decisions and actions taken at all levels are in close coordination with each other and calculated to achieve a common goal. In other words, "how the military know what they are doing." Military units spend a good deal of time rehearsing standardized and common control procedures to make sure all the efforts of the many units in military operations are planned for, integrated, and executed within a common operational framework and toward collective objectives. Because the United Nations had no standing military forces, it had no common control procedures, or even a standard modus operandi. Improvisation was therefore the key characteristic of the UN approach to control procedures and operational methods. This phenomenon is examined in greater detail in the observation mission case study and in following chapters. The more complicated operations undertaken in peacekeeping and enforcement missions clearly highlight these issues, although these two features of UN command and control did have great effect on UN observation missions.

Chain of Command

On the surface, the chain of command structure of UN observation missions seems to resemble that of orthodox military units. As seen in Figure 2, the observation mission operates with an overall political commander (the UN secretary-general), a field commander with a military staff, and groups of observers arrayed as "line" units (as in a standard military organization). The responsibility for strategy, linking military means to political objectives, was shared by the Security Council, the UN secretary-general, and the field commander. The somewhat ambiguous command provisions for ONUCA, written in 1989, were typical of most UN observation missions and illustrate this division of labor. These provisions stated, "Command of ONUCA in the field would be exercised by a Chief Military Observer, who would be under the command of the United Nations, vested in the Secretary-General, under the authority of the Security Council."[26]

Although setting the mandates and missions was the legal and functional purview of the Security Council, it was recognized early on that a sometimes fractious committee could not exercise effective and decisive day-to-day oversight of field operations. However, the exact role of the Security Council varied by mission. Indeed, in some missions the Security Council had almost no oversight responsibility at all, whereas in others it played a more active role. For instance, although regular UNTSO reports were scrupulously laid before the Security Council, periodic UNMOGIP reports stayed with the secretary-general and were not usually brought to the attention of the Council.[27] The disparity in the political processes that gave birth to these missions was clearly reflected in the great variation of their command and control requirements. For instance, UNGOMAP observers in Afghanistan were initially not the direct responsibility of the secretary-general because the treaty language described them as military assistants to a UN Good Offices mediator. Almost a year after its creation, UNGOMAP was accepted into the usual UN chain of command for observation and peacekeeping missions and its personnel were labeled military observers.[28]

The secretary-general was assisted in his role as the political commander of UN observation missions by an under secretary-general. For most of the United Nations' existence, this was the under secretary-general for special political affairs. The legal status, authority, and responsibilities of this official were somewhat ambiguous and were never formally codified by the United Nations. With most UN operations, the under secretary-general was the principal manager at UN headquarters and the senior advisor to the secretary-general on peacekeeping operations.

However, the influence and role of the under secretary-general varied according to the personality and prerogatives of that individual or his superiors.[29] In

Figure 2

Chain of Command in UN Observer Operations

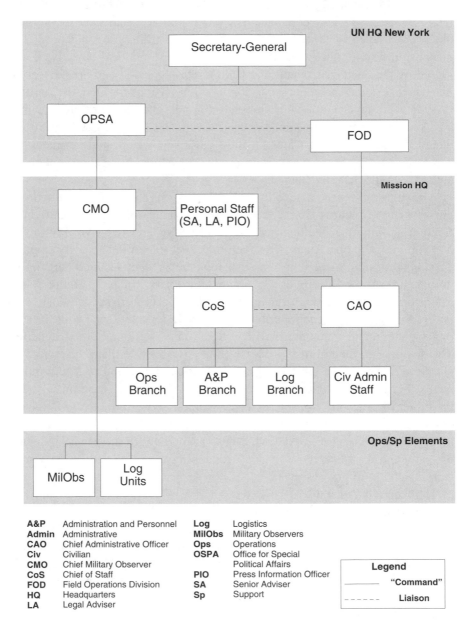

A&P	Administration and Personnel
Admin	Administrative
CAO	Chief Administrative Officer
Civ	Civilian
CMO	Chief Military Observer
CoS	Chief of Staff
FOD	Field Operations Division
HQ	Headquarters
LA	Legal Adviser

Log	Logistics
MilObs	Military Observers
Ops	Operations
OSPA	Office for Special Political Affairs
PIO	Press Information Officer
SA	Senior Adviser
Sp	Support

Legend

——————— "Command"

- - - - - - Liaison

Source: Based on UNDPI, *The Blue Helmets*, p. 409.

many ways, his position was similar to that of the chairman of the joint chiefs of staff in the American military establishment. The chairman is not in the warfighting chain of command, which runs directly from the president to the secretary of defense to the commander in the field. However, he is the senior military advisor to the president and, depending on the personal relationships between these officials, can exercise great or more limited command authority.

In February 1993, the UN Secretariat created an under secretary-general for peacekeeping and moved the responsibility for UN observation and peacekeeping missions to his new department. The role of this under secretary-general was somewhat ambiguous in that he appeared in the UN chain of command but in reality operated in much more of an advisory role, like a chief of staff in a military organization. In addition to this vaguely defined relationship, other key responsibilities in the chain of command for UN military operations were divided and diffused throughout UN headquarters. For instance, the Field Operations Division (FOD), which controlled all the logistic, financial, technical, and administrative support for observation and peacekeeping missions, did not become part of the Department of Peacekeeping Operations (DPKO) until September 1993.

The lack of coordination between the planning staff of the under-secretary responsible for the mission and the FOD was a considerable problem prior to 1993. The functional problems caused by this split were legion and are noted throughout this study. In only one of many examples, the senior military staff of ONUCA were brought to UN headquarters for two days of "mission familiarization." William Durch describes the incoherent process:

> The Field Operations Division, which does logistics and communication support, did not participate in the briefings . . .
> military and civilian staffers, and operational and support
> planning, followed separate, parallel tracks that did not meet
> until all parties deployed to Central America, where ONUCA's
> military chief of staff met his civilian administrative counterparts on December 2. At that point, the military side of the
> operation also had its first exposure to the FOD "standard
> operations document" that detailed basic UN field procedures
> and determined that much of the initial operational planning
> had to be scrapped.[30]

As in many military organizations, friction in the chain of command took place between frontline units (observers in this case), supporting military personnel, and civilian elements of the mission. This friction was exacerbated by the ad hoc nature of a cobbled-together and unrehearsed UN military formation. In one example, the former military commander of UNTSO bitterly complained that he did not always receive efficient and responsive support from his civilian staff in the Middle East.[31] This complaint, common to all military bureaucracies, was aggravated by the parallel lines of command coming from the UN headquarters in New York. With civilian administrative staff in the field effectively working for the FOD in New York, minor problems on the ground that could not be worked out would theoretically have to go to the secretary-general for resolution. This made the UN chain of command unwieldy, compartmentalized, and unresponsive to changes and the need for quick decisions.

The lack of a regular, authoritative, and legitimate chain of command had other effects, especially in field operations. The secretary-general's commander in the field was the chief military observer (CMO). On only one occasion did the CMO report to and was questioned by the Security Council directly.[32] Depending on the mission, the CMO reported either directly to the secretary-general or through the secretary-general's special representative in that country. In later missions it became more common for a civilian representative of the secretary-general to have overall command of the mission abroad.

The CMO exercised command over the UN observers in his mission. Sometimes the UN has confusingly labeled the field commander as the chief of staff. This is somewhat confounding because the function of a military chief of staff is to organize and coordinate the functions of the commander's staff. The chief of staff is not officially in the chain of command. The UN use of "chief of staff" to describe the mission commander (as in UNOGIL) means that the UN chief of staff himself needed a chief of staff to perform chief of staff functions. For clarity's sake, I always refer to the field commander as the commander. Regardless, the type of command authority invested in the UN commander was closer to a temporary variant of operational control. Even so, with the organization of the first UN mission in 1948 (UNTSO), it was decided to reinforce the United Nations' authority by stating that "during their assignments with the Organization, the observers were to take orders only from the United Nations authorities."[33] As noted, this was not the case in earlier missions in Greece and Indonesia.

The system of having volunteers temporarily working under a UN chain of command introduced a latent element of competition between member states and the United Nations. Indeed, in just one example, this friction was manifested when the Yugoslav reconnaissance element in the mission to Yemen occasionally received independent operational instructions from Belgrade.[34] This phenomenon was not typically a major problem in observation missions, but was exacerbated as missions became larger and more complex. As shown in later chapters, as the stakes rose in more ambitious and dangerous UN military operations, the legitimacy and authority of the UN chain of command were often called into question by the national chains of command of member states.

Further improvisation in the UN chain of command hurt the legitimacy of this UN system. Authority, reliability, and responsiveness in a chain of command stem largely from formal, recognized, and practiced structures. In contrast, the UN chains were forever shifting and changing. In the Middle East, where UNTSO worked in close concert with four large peacekeeping missions and UNOGIL as well, groups of observers were sometimes seconded to other missions and remained under their operational control for some time. As a military measure, this was not unusual in itself. In practice, however, these temporary relationships were ill-defined and ambiguous. One member of a UNTSO group operating with UNIFIL stated this vagueness when noting that his detachment was "formerly under the operational control of the UNIFIL's Force Commander, but it was more accurate to say that [his group] cooperates with UNIFIL by sharing relevant information than to say that it takes direct orders."[35]

In addition to this sort of improvisation in the chain of command, political circumstances further confused some command and control relationships (much as they skewed force structure planning). For instance, by agreement with the belligerents, UN observers in the Golan Heights cannot be from the permanent members (P-5) of the Security Council. Therefore, the UNTSO observers temporarily detailed to the Golan Heights peacekeeping mission (UNDOF) had to split into two groups. One in Damascus supported UNDOF but was not officially under its control, and one in the Golan Heights, which has no P-5 observers, was therefore under the official operational control of UNDOF.

In yet another instance of confusing and poorly defined command and control relationships, the secretary-general once assigned an officer to "informally exercise" command over both UN missions in India and Pakistan during 1965–1966 (UNMOGIP and UNIPOM).[36] This sort of informal command and control ambiguity could never be tolerated in traditional military operations. In those, organizational terms, such as *attached*, *operational control*, *tactical control*, and *administrative control*, are scrupulously defined to lay down specific and binding legal guidelines for such relationships. Improvisation in the chain of command is considered an immense liability in military operations.

The cause of this improvisation in command and control stemmed from the ad hoc political genesis and force structure planning of most UN observation missions. In UNOGIL, the command and control structure evolved with the mission instead of being in place from the very beginning. The UN commander described the command and control organization of his mission, built on the fly in Lebanon, thus:

> *In the initial stages of the mission, it was essential to send*
> *the maximum number of military observers into the field*

> *immediately after they arrived. Neither the time nor the per-*
> *sonnel were available for a complete headquarters organi-*
> *zation. . . . Finally, as the scale of operations steadily*
> *developed, the time came when it was necessary to divest the*
> *overburdened operations branch of responsibility for per-*
> *sonnel and for supply, separate staff sections being provid-*
> *ed for these matters. The headquarters is now organized on*
> *full military lines.[37]*

As highlighted later, improvisation also was the key feature of operational control procedures. This ad hoc approach to command and control made the operations less efficient in the performance of their military duties. However, because UN observation missions had very limited mandates and low expectations for the ability to exert direct influence, these military drawbacks did not doom many missions to failure. It must be remembered in a strategic critique of UN observation missions that military inadequacy was not necessarily a grave hindrance in missions that sought to work as supporting players to attain only modest objectives.

Military Objectives

With the exception of large-scale enforcement actions, the military objectives of all UN military operations were relatively limited. The objectives of observation missions were the most circumscribed of all UN operations and were generally limited simply to reporting conditions vis-à-vis the political agreement the observers had come to monitor. Within this general objective, one can distinguish three specific military tasks commonly given to UN observation missions: (1) border or demilitarized zone monitoring; (2) cease-fire, truce, or general armistice agreement monitoring; and (3) the supervision of the withdrawal of forces. Naturally, UN military observers also performed various "quasi-judicial" functions.[38] The first three missions were explicit tasks that involved military observation and reporting. The last category, which I treat only briefly, was a tacit mission that evolves from the role of the UN military observer as an impartial authority.

The guiding tenets of consent and cooperation, strict impartiality, and the passive use of military force discussed throughout this chapter also greatly influenced military objectives and operations. Because of their small size and innocuous role, UN military observers had only an oblique influence on realizing the military objectives of the observation mission. UN observers were very much cast in a supporting role. The exact amount of what leverage they could bring to bear depended principally on the cooperation of the belligerents and other events in the political and diplomatic arena. The case study in

Chapter Three of the UN Iran–Iraq Military Observer Group highlights this phenomenon. Before moving to that case study, it is helpful briefly to highlight the principal military objectives of observation missions and the operational imperatives that affected their success.

Monitoring a Border or Demilitarized Zone

Monitoring a border or demilitarized zone was the most common task for UN military observers, who were most frequently deployed to an area immediately following a political agreement between two or more belligerents to cease fighting. The immediate device for implementing that cessation of hostilities was the cease-fire line, demilitarized zone, or reaffirmation of the integrity of national borders. UN military observers monitored these lines or areas from static observation posts, traffic checkpoints, mobile ground and air patrols, and even sea patrols. The UN observers did not have the authority or capability to physically control these areas, that is, to regulate the movement of local forces and coerce any violators into compliance with the settlement. Reporting on the violations or lack thereof was the United Nations' only mandate. It was hoped that this moral authority and responsibility would give all the belligerents the confidence that the other side was not flagrantly violating the accords of the peace settlement. This would strengthen the trust needed to implement a cease-fire or peace settlement and help make a temporary peace into a permanent solution.

The principal difficulty faced by the UN observers in practically achieving this mandate was the ratio of observer force to space. Without exception, UN observation missions did not have the forces available to monitor effectively the territories under their mandate. This was another recognition of the fact that the doctrinal principles that guided the formation and employment of UN observers dictated that the belligerents, and not the UN military observers, would be primarily responsible for ensuring that the terms of the peace accord were upheld. Thus, force-to-space ratios were very low. For instance, UNTSO, with fewer than 150 observers, had a border of over 620 kilometers to monitor in the Middle East.[39] UNMOGIP, with fewer than 50 observers, was charged with patrolling a cease-fire line of almost 800 kilometers through extremely difficult terrain in mountainous Kashmir.[40] UNOGIL's extreme force-to-space ratio is noted above. UNYOM deployed just over 100 observers to monitor a demilitarized zone (DMZ) of 15,000 square kilometers between Yemen and Saudi Arabia.[41] UNIKOM used 300 observers equipped with basic equipment, such as binoculars and passive night vision devices, to patrol a DMZ that was 200 kilometers long and 15 kilometers wide.[42]

It was noted that certain "force multipliers," such as air patrols and surveillance equipment, could compensate for a simple deficit of force to space on the ground. However, even in those few UN missions that had aircraft, the air power was usually hopelessly inadequate to accomplish the task efficiently. Consequently, with a restricted number of observers and modest material resources, fulfilling the mandate of an observation mission was almost totally dependent on the willingness of the belligerents to cooperate with the mission and to comply with the cease-fire agreement.

When that willingness failed, UN observers were not able to prevent minor or major violations of borders, DMZs, and cease-fire lines. Indeed, the catalog of recurring violence that happened in and around UN observation missions has led some to dismiss UN military observers as irrelevant. In UNTSO's area alone, five major cross-border wars have occurred along with hundreds of armed raids and reprisals. In another example, even with Iraq conclusively beaten by the 1991 allied coalition, UNIKOM reported regular Iraqi violations of the DMZ after the cease-fire.[43] The presence of UN observers might, at times, have had a deterrent effect on spontaneous local violations (and that is indeed one of their chief purposes). However, UN military observers have proven to be little hindrance to premeditated and concerted action.

Monitoring a Cease-fire, Truce, or General Armistice

This mission naturally overlaps with the first, as the monitoring of borders and DMZs is usually at the crux of a peace agreement. However, many cease-fire, truce, or armistice agreements include provisions applying to areas and installations away from borders, and these often are monitored by UN observation missions. In the missions to Central America, ONUSAL and ONUCA, small numbers of military observers concentrated their efforts on designated "security zones" and other areas of interest. There was no question that attempts to monitor the porous jungle and mountain borders of Central America would be fruitless. As it was, even without assuming border responsibilities, the 500 observers and support personnel of ONUCA were supposed to control 2,550 square kilometers of land in five separate security zones.[44]

In UNYOM, only part of the UN observation force was monitoring the demilitarized zone on the northern border of Yemen. The rest were deployed at ports and airfields and along major traffic arteries in Yemen to monitor the terms of the disengagement agreement. Because the force-to-space ratio in the UNYOM DMZ was so disproportionate, the small forces deployed at key points away from the border were more effective at spotting violations of the disengagement agreement.

In all observation missions, the physical ability to monitor a political settlement and all its sundry terms depended almost entirely on the cooperation of the belligerents. The handful of UNAVEM II observers assigned to Angola to monitor the accords of the Angolan civil war cease-fire were as stretched as their predecessors in UNAVEM I. Working in teams with members of joint commissions created by the Angolan peace accords, the UN observers were wholly dependent on the cooperation of the local observers with whom they traveled around the countryside. After all, the unarmed[45] UN observers had no military capability or mandate to control their environment or even operate somewhat independently. Unfortunately, in the fall of 1992, heavy fighting resumed in Angola, and the local observation system broke down. As their mandate was impossible to fulfill because of the lack of local cooperation, most of the UNAVEM II observers were quietly withdrawn in the summer of 1993.[46]

Supervising the Withdrawal of Forces

"Supervision," much like "border control," is a misleading term because it may imply that the UN military observers could regulate and control a belligerent troop withdrawal. Naturally, this has not been the case. In these missions, UN observers also were completely dependent on the belligerents for cooperation. The willingness of the Soviets to cooperate in Afghanistan and of the Cubans to do the same in Angola stands in stark contrast to the noncooperation of the Egyptians in Yemen in 1963. Like all observation missions, the goodwill and cooperation of the belligerents were the principal factors in judging UNGOMAP and UNAVEM I to be successes, and UNYOM a failure.

The mechanics of supervising a troop withdrawal required very close liaison between the small force of UN observers and the withdrawing forces. UNGOMAP observers had to monitor the withdrawal of over 100,000 Soviet troops from Afghanistan.[47] The Soviet representatives informed the UN observers of all scheduled movements and of all changes to withdrawal plans due to Mujahideen activity against their troops or bases. The Soviets also provided the UN observers with maps of withdrawal routes, detailed garrison information, and even transport. A similar situation existed in Angola in 1990–1991. The seventy UN military observers, covering a country of 1.2 million square kilometers, were kept precisely informed of Cuban operations to confirm the Cuban withdrawal. Had the belligerents wished to deceive the understaffed and underequipped UN observation mission, it would not have been difficult.[48]

Performing Quasi-Judicial Functions

This broad category of tasks is not a military objective per se but is considered briefly to show that a UN observation mission often involved supramilitary tasks. Most UN observation missions offered a quasi-judicial forum in which belligerents could air their official complaints. The experience of UNTSO offers good examples of how a mission has undertaken these roles. With the conclusion of the 1949 General Armistice Agreements between Israel and her Arab neighbors, four separate mixed armistice commissions (MAC) were established and staffed by three Israeli officers, three Arab officers, and one senior UN observer. Over the next fifteen years, the Israel-Syria MAC alone received over 60,000 complaints, split roughly equally between the two sides.[49] Naturally, the seven-member MAC had neither the time nor the resources to investigate all these complaints and make rulings.

The moral (not military) authority of the UN military observers often made a difference in these cases, however. For instance, in response to complaints that an organization such as a MAC did investigate, the decision mediated by the UN observer on the spot often was the end of the matter. Local disputes over the exact delineation of a cease-fire line, the transport of material through demilitarized zones, the positioning of belligerent settlements, and even the permission to grow crops in "no-man's-land" in Palestine were all settled on the spot by UN military observers working in mediation with the local parties. In 1958, the Security Council even gave the UNTSO force commander the authority to determine property ownership within the area surrounding Government House, the UNTSO headquarters in Jerusalem.[50] Quasi-judicial functions were not explicitly military missions, but remained a tacit responsibility of UN military observers. They reinforced the moral authority of the UN and contributed greatly to local efforts at sustaining peace.

Conclusion

Tangible evidence offering a direct relationship of causality between UN military observers and mission success (or failure) is hard to find. From a purely military standpoint, several factors undermined the direct military effectiveness of the observers sent to undertake these limited operations: their small size, inadequate equipment to enhance their effectiveness and compensate for lack of troops, the huge areas of difficult terrain in which they had to operate, and, most important, the mercurial cooperation often shown to UN observers by the belligerents on the ground. Most UN observation missions were militarily incapable of fulfilling their mandates without substantial cooperation. In the cases of UNTSO, UNMOGIP, UNOGIL,

UNYOM, MINURSO, ONUCA, and UNAVEM II, the failure directly and independently to affect the situation led to a failure to help deliver the political solution desired.

In other missions such as UNIKOM, UNGOMAP, UNIPOM, and UNAVEM I, the UN observers were still not militarily capable of efficiently carrying out their tasks, but the cooperation of the belligerents guaranteed mission success regardless. In many ways, UNIPOM reflects the characteristics of those observer missions regarded as successful. Although the ninety-six UN military observers could never hope to monitor effectively the border between India and Pakistan, according to UN scholar Alan James, their operations indirectly contributed to the peace process:

> The observers also engaged both sides in negotiation for a
> no-firing agreement, a limitation on aerial activity, and a
> ban on test firing in the vicinity of the front lines, with even-
> tual success in each case. In such ways as these the UN
> [observers] undoubtedly exercised a valuable cooling influ-
> ence, clearing the way for the parties to move on to the with-
> drawal of forces. [However], the affair also underlined the
> point that [these] measures are of full use only when all the
> immediately involved parties are anxious to maintain peace.
> In such circumstances, [UN observers] can play an impor-
> tant derivative role. But if that condition is not obtained,
> [UN observation] is at best of limited value—as a face-
> saver, maybe, or an impartial reporting body—and at worst
> is completely irrelevant.[51]

The strategy of observation missions relies on an indirect relationship between the handful of UN military observers and the political objective. One does not cause the other; there are many other players involved and the way in which the UN employs its observers reflects this imperative.

From the perspective of the United Nations as a strategic manager of military operations, UN observation missions were the simplest UN military missions to form, direct, and employ. This was because they were small, militarily innocuous, and deployed with the consent and cooperation of the belligerents, and they could improvise to overcome intractable political and military problems. However, these characteristics also made the missions less effective when considered as purely military enterprises.

When deciding on force structure, the United Nations relied heavily on political calculations rather than military requirements. This meant that the force often made good sense on paper, but much less sense when trying to operate as an effective unit in the field. In command and control, the United Nations used a loose interpretation of the chain of command and relied on improvised control procedures. This encouraged some competition from national chains of command and made for a UN chain of command that was at times unwieldy, unresponsive, ill-defined, and not very authoritative. It also gave rise to the practice of formulating ad hoc control procedures on the fly during field operations.

Last, UN reliance on an operational doctrine stressing consent and cooperation, impartiality, and the nonuse of force automatically put UN military observers in a peripheral and supporting role. The prime determinants of success were the belligerents and, although UN prestige was on the line, the amount of control the UN military observers could bring about to protect this prestige was minimal. Often UN military observers were hostage to their environment and had to suffer the capricious ebb and flow of belligerent goodwill and cooperation.

Because of this ancillary relationship between means and ends, it is indeed difficult to assess definitively the success of the strategy of UN observation missions. There is no doubt that in many cases their contribution to fostering trust and local negotiation among belligerents was invaluable. There also is no doubt that in many of the same cases the presence of a militant observation was almost irrelevant to the belligerent aims of some of the local parties. Alan James's assessment of UNYOM represents a reliable appraisal of many UN observation missions:

> There was, therefore, a clear sense in which the UN had failed in Yemen. However, as the concept of "failure" also implies a lack of capability and/or effort, the use of that term is not wholly appropriate for describing the UN's experience. For its servants did all they could to implement UNYOM's mandate— but ultimately its implementation was never up to them. Thus this case served to underline the point that [UN observation] is a secondary activity, dependent for its success on the cooperation of the principals.[52] [my emphasis]

In some UN observation missions, the political situation dissolved into an unsolvable stalemate (UNTSO, UNMOGIP), and there was conflicting opinion over whether the presence of the UN observation mission helped to solve the conflict. Indeed, some observers note that a UN presence could even sustain a simmering conflict. Professor James has written that "the existence of a peacekeeping body provides the parties with an excuse not to wind down their dispute—or at least is something of a discouragement to their doing so."[53] In other cases, the desired political solution came about (as in Central America), but resulted from many other factors than just the impact of a UN observation mission. Because a readily identifiable strain of causality is so difficult to discern, the overall assessment of UN observation missions is a matter of considerable debate.

What should be realized from this pattern is that UN military observation missions were undertaken for low stakes. In each case, the United Nations had a chance to reinforce and help a peace process already under way. The chosen vehicle for this reinforcement was a UN military observation mission. The United Nations stated that this technique was a "holding action . . . born of necessity, largely improvised, and a practical response to a problem requiring action."[54] The United Nations had no definitive resources, structures, procedures, or mechanisms confidently to address the management challenges of these missions. Therefore, the missions were thrown together from disparate resources and deployed to the field with no rehearsed structure, an inchoate chain of command, and a very restrictive modus operandi. UN observation missions did not have an ironclad political legitimacy, a coherent military strategy, or even effective military operations.

Thus the operations themselves gave rise to what has been outlined as some of the traditional foibles of UN military operations. These operational "weaknesses" were thrust on the United Nations by the fact that the institution was a many-membered international organization that lacked certain sovereign powers. Having sovereign powers, such as political authority and military legitimacy, could allow a political entity, even a multinational one such as the UN, the resources and dominion to competently mobilize, direct, and deploy international military forces. Without these powers, the United Nations was forced to improvise. Observation missions and the "principles of peacekeeping" evolved as a result. Given that the United Nations was essentially inventing a technique of conflict resolution for which it was poorly equipped to manage, it is a wonder that, despite military drawbacks, UN military observers were able to accomplish as much as they did in these twenty missions.

CHAPTER 3
The UN Observers in Iran and Iraq (1988–1991)

The experiences of the UN Iran–Iraq Military Observer Group (UNIIMOG) between 1988 and 1991 make a useful observation mission case study for several reasons. First, the mission was representative of most observation missions in terms of the operational aspects under examination. A study of UNIIMOG underscores both the capacity of the United Nations for managing military operations and the operational doctrine that evolved in light of the United Nations' attempts to form and command a group of military observers. The case study illustrates many of the traditional characteristics of UN observation missions, not only the common operational constraints, but the way in which those restrictions did or did not affect the success of the mission. Although all UN missions are sui generis to a great degree, the operational characteristics and limitations of UNIIMOG were indicative of most missions of this kind.

Second, this conventional observation mission took place in the post-glasnost era, where the atmosphere of cooperation at the Security Council gave rise to far more ambitious missions, such as second-generation peacekeeping. However, the Security Council in 1988 saw no need in the Iran–Iraq situation for anything other than a conventional mandate similar to those of limited observation missions that had been initiated since 1948. This reinforces the premise that Cold War Security Council politics were not the sole factor that determined the traditional restrictions under which UN military forces operated. The strengths and weaknesses of UN observation missions, even after the breaking of the superpower impasse, were derived from the immutable multinational character of the United Nations itself. The inherent moral strengths and military limitations of the organization, Cold War or post–Cold War, made traditional UN military doctrine, with its emphasis on consent, impartiality, and the passive use of force, just as relevant in the post–Cold War era.

Third, this mission illustrates the usual problems of directly analyzing the effectiveness of the military force used in pursuit of the political objectives involved. In political terms, the mission was a success. During UNIIMOG's deployment, there was no resumption of the war between Iran and Iraq that had been waged for eight years. The thousands of low-level border incidents that UNIIMOG military observers helped report and defuse undoubtedly spared the area some potential flare-ups of violence. However, the situation was ultimately resolved by political expediency on the part of Iraq, as it became involved in the struggle to preserve its annexation of Kuwait against a U.S.–led coalition.

It is not the purpose of this book to conduct a political analysis of this situation. However, it is relevant to ask how the military operations of UNIIMOG ultimately contributed to the political solution of conflict resolution. UNIIMOG operations undoubtedly helped foster an atmosphere more conducive to peace by helping the belligerents limit armed conflict. However, the fact must be borne in mind that these peace negotiations were fruitless until the Gulf crisis of 1990 forced a solution. Like many observation missions, the impact of UNIIMOG military operations was indirect, oblique, and perhaps even incidental to the eventual outcome. That pattern is supported by the experience of UNIIMOG.

Creating UNIIMOG

UNIIMOG was one of the few observation missions created as a direct result of Security Council and secretary-general initiatives. The United Nations, through the Security Council and especially the personal offices of the secretary-general, was involved in the Iran–Iraq crisis from its initiation. On 22 September 1980, Iraq launched a full-scale ground invasion of Iran, supported by air attacks. Volumes have been written on the origins of this crisis, but as analyst Brian Smith pointed out, the primary Iraqi motive was to "redraw its border at what appeared to be an opportune time, given Iran's political instability and evident military vulnerability."[1]

Within six days of the invasion, the UN Security Council passed Resolution 479, which called for an immediate end to the fighting and peaceful negotiation over the border and other disagreements.[2] However, the resolution had several weaknesses. First, its language was ambiguous and lacked recognizable guarantees for each side concerning the other's actions. Second, it had no tangible UN mechanism for ensuring that any cease-fire settlement would last. In essence, Resolution 479 did not offer either Iran or Iraq a better political situation than they could hope to achieve through continued fighting. The Security Council passed a similar resolution (540) in 1982, but it was once again unacceptable to Iran, which was increasingly intransigent about settling the conflict through negotiation.

On 20 July 1987, after almost seven years of war, the Security Council took more definitive action with the passage of Resolution 598. This resolution clearly called for an immediate cease-fire, the withdrawal of forces to the boundaries recognized by the 1975 Iran–Iraq treaty signed in Algiers, and, most important, the monitoring of these actions by a UN observer force. The UN force, which was to become UNIIMOG, was a key element of the cease-fire agreement, and its impartiality had to be absolutely unquestionable before the xenophobic regime of Iran, in particular, would accept its presence. On 8 August 1988, after Iran finally agreed to the provisions of the resolution, the Security Council unanimously approved the implementation plan for Resolution 598. The next day, a separate resolution (619) approved the creation and mandate of UNIIMOG.

The political atmosphere in which UNIIMOG was created was overwhelmingly characterized by the mistrust of the belligerents toward each other and the United Nations. Iran especially was reluctant to accept a UN–brokered and –monitored cease-fire agreement. However, Iran's international isolation had intensified throughout the crisis, and it could count on few supporters by 1987. In addition, the human and materiel expenditures of the war with Iraq had precipitated domestic angst and general war weariness among the Iranian rulers and public.[3] Nonetheless, the reluctance with which Iran accepted the deployment of UNIIMOG was later manifested in the restrictions it placed on the force's size and mandate. Iran's recalcitrance was also evident in the lack of cooperation it showed to UNIIMOG from its very inception.

There was no consensus in the United Nations for any sort of coercive operation to settle the Iran–Iraq war against the will of the belligerents, as happened a few years later when Iraq invaded Kuwait. The intention in the United Nations was to create, through negotiation and diplomatic processes, an atmosphere in which an unarmed UN force could operate as an honest broker with the cooperation of the belligerents. The degree of active cooperation from the belligerents would be the chief factor influencing UNIIMOG operations and would have daily implications down to the lowest tactical levels.

Forming UNIIMOG

Like almost all observation missions, the principal component of UNIIMOG was the unarmed military observer. The observers were officers contributed by twenty-six member states (see Table 4). As with most observation missions, military officers of some experience were required to perform the tasks specified in UNIIMOG's mandate. There was no question of using civilian verification teams. The technical tasks involved in daily UNIIMOG observations included the examination of fortifications, troop and logistic sites, supply routes, and other avenues for troop movement. The military

Table 4

The UN Observers in Iran and Iraq, February 1989

Contributing States	Military Personnel
Argentina	10 Observers
Australia	15 Observers
	4-Man Medical Team
Austria	6 Observers
Bangladesh	15 Observers
Canada	15 Observers*
Denmark	15 Observers
Finland	15 Observers
Ghana	15 Observers
Hungary	15 Observers
India	15 Observers
Indonesia	15 Observers
Ireland	37 Military Police
Italy	15 Observers
Kenya	15 Observers
Malaysia	15 Observers
New Zealand	10 Observers
	18-Man Air Unit
Nigeria	15 Observers
Norway	15 Observers
Peru	7 Observers
Poland	15 Observers
Senegal	15 Observers
Sweden	15 Observers
Turkey	15 Observers
Uruguay	12 Observers
Yugoslavia	11 Observers
Zambia	9 Observers
Total	**335 Military Observers**
	59 Support Personnel

Note: *Canada briefly deployed a Signals Battalion of over 500 troops between August and November 1988 to establish a preliminary communications network for UNIIMOG.

Source: S/20442, Report of the Secretary-General on UNIIMOG, 2 February 1989, p. 3.

expertise of the UN observers was crucial for determining the troop dispositions of the Iraqi and Iranian armies.

Another factor favored the use of experienced military officers as the basis of UNIIMOG force structure. UNIIMOG observers interacted almost exclusively with military officials of Iraq and Iran. As UNIIMOG was specifically tasked to carry out its mandate through observation and negotiation, it was thought that the professional military status of UNIIMOG observers was necessary to earn the respect of their counterparts from Iran and Iraq. Last, although UNIIMOG was deployed in an environment of consent and observers were unarmed, the operations did become dangerous at times. Although not directed at UN personnel, numerous hostile violations occurred throughout UNIIMOG's deployment and one UN fatality was incurred as a result.[4] Moreover, UNIIMOG operations took place in an arduous and inhospitable natural environment that ranged from swamplands to mountainous terrain. The formidable conditions of UNIIMOG's environment, regardless of hostile action from belligerents, required military personnel trained to work in such conditions.

The professional military observers of UNIIMOG were organized around the core element of the military observer team. The operations of these teams are detailed below. All nonobserver military elements of UNIIMOG served very specific support functions that did not entail observation duties. The four-man medical team from Australia provided for the group's medical requirements, the Irish military police provided security at group and sector headquarters, and the air unit from New Zealand manned a single Andover aircraft used for freight, passenger, and other logistic and administrative duties. The Canadian signals battalion, initially deployed to establish a communications network, was withdrawn within 90 days, by November of 1988.[5]

The original force structure of UNIIMOG called for the deployment of an air and naval unit.[6] This was a practical decision, made based on military factors alone, such as the mission, the terrain, and the troops available to UNIIMOG. The long-standing controversy between Iraq and Iran over the status of the Shatt al-Arab waterway and adjacent waters necessitated a UN naval component for patrolling. An operational air component would help to enhance the limited capability of 335 ground observers attempting to patrol a 1,400-kilometer border through difficult terrain.[7] However, the four UNIIMOG aircraft used between 1988 and 1991 were for administrative and logistic use only. Early in UNIIMOG's inception, the secretary-general had stated the requirement for "helicopters which the group urgently needs to enhance its patrolling capability."[8] Initial agreements with the belligerents had resulted in an ambiguous commitment from Iran and Iraq to provide aircraft and helicopters for observation.[9] This pledge was never honored, although the belligerents did occasionally provide air transport for administrative movement away from the cease-fire zone.

In February 1989, the secretary-general again emphasized the "urgent" need for air patrols, specifying the requirement of twelve helicopters.[10] In addition, the need for a naval element was reemphasized in every semiannual report to the Security Council. However, agreements for the use of UN air and naval assets to patrol the cease-fire zone were never reached with Iran and Iraq together. The secretary-general lamented this failure as "a major impediment to [UNIIMOG's] effectiveness."[11] This episode reflects the way in which the political conditions of the belligerents overrode the military requirements of the mission. Nonetheless, such a constraint was common for UN observation missions.

With no naval and air elements, UNIIMOG had a strictly ground-based force structure. The observer groups within UNIIMOG were an improvised and composite mixture of individuals from the twenty-six contributing member states. Unlike whole military units that were deployed in peacekeeping or enforcement operations, UNIIMOG personnel had neither worked nor trained together prior to their deployment. This ad hoc force structure was the norm for observation missions and was generally considered adequate for the mission, given the limited mandate of the force. Given the sensitivity of the belligerents, it was not considered feasible to deploy entire reconnaissance units from member states, such as the Yugoslav company that participated in the Yemen mission.

The actual numbers and composition of the UNIIMOG force structure were based on a planning report from a UN technical team that visited Iran and Iraq in July 1988. This team was led by General Vadset, the chief of staff of UNTSO in Palestine.[12] His planning was based on the military practicalities of the mission coupled with the agreements of Iranian and Iraqi officials as to size and operational mandate. However, this advance team, made up of General Vadset, a senior political advisor, a civilian logistics expert, and four military advisors from UNTSO, spent only a total of six working days in Baghdad and Tehran.[13] There was no reconnaissance of the cease-fire line and UNIIMOG area of operations, even from the air. The UNIIMOG force structure requirements were thus based solely on high-level political discussions conducted during that week.

This cursory military planning was necessitated by the political situation but is considered very superficial indeed from an operational military perspective. In short, it meant that the UNIIMOG force structure was not based on meeting the known operational requirements of the military task at hand. Instead, UNIIMOG was forced to stretch its politically mandated and understrength observer contingent in an attempt to cover the cease-fire line and fulfill its operational mandate. This enormous military challenge was all too often a common state of affairs for UN observation missions.

A more orthodox approach to force structure planning would have been based on military planning factors, such as the METT-T approach outlined in Chapter Two. Important actions to supplement this planning methodology would have been to conduct a thorough reconnaissance of the area of operations and to elaborate explicit rules of engagement worked out in cooperation with the belligerents. The planning staff could then have recommended a force structure that could accomplish the tasks given by the Security Council. Naturally, this force structure would ultimately be subject to Iranian and Iraqi review and approval. In contrast to this more deliberate procedure, however, UNIIMOG, like most observation missions, started with a force structure that was derived from political conditions even before specific operational tasks were determined. As a result of this somewhat backward planning, the UNIIMOG commanders then had to adopt their limited forces to military tasks once they were on the ground.

In keeping with another key tenet of UN military operations, impartiality, UNIIMOG was structured to reinforce this concept. Professor Alan James writes that the perception of strict impartiality was a critical component and that to "introduce more stability into the situation, [UNIIMOG had to] advertise its presence as an impartial body."[14] The five permanent members of the Security Council and regional powers were not represented in UNIIMOG, and the belligerents had a final veto over the composition of the force. This made for some force structure decisions based entirely on the political sensitivities of the belligerents. For instance, all Australian observers were exclusively deployed on the Iranian side of the cease-fire line due to the fact that Iraq had vetoed their presence on Iraqi territory. This decision apparently stemmed from Iraqi rancor over an Australian scientist who had led a UN inspection team in Iraq from 1984 to 1987. During three inspections over this period, this team had proven that Iraq had used chemical weapons in the war against Iran.[15]

To reinforce the multinational neutrality of the force further, the United Nations also planned its composition based on the self-imposed principle of equitable geographic representation. In his first report to the Security Council, the secretary-general stated that UNIIMOG was formed based on "the accepted principle of equitable geographical representation."[16] As a result, the national contingents from member states were finely balanced among contributors and no single country had more than a handful of observers involved at any one time. This principle was observed throughout the life of the mission. When the UNIIMOG force structure was reduced by 60 percent in late

1990, the primary operational concern of UNIIMOG was how to achieve its revised objectives with a smaller force. However, the major political concern of the secretary-general was to "adjust the size of national contingents which have become unbalanced as a result of the process of attrition used to achieve the reduction from 350 military observers to the current strength (184)."[17] This illustrates the primacy of the political considerations that determined force structure issues in UNIIMOG and most UN observation missions. Questions of military practicality were subsidiary.

In more orthodox military operations, the operational drawbacks of such force structure tenets are obvious. UNIIMOG was an ad hoc and unrehearsed formation, too diverse in its composition to attain any sort of cohesion as a military unit. Because the United Nations had to recruit from a broad spectrum of member states, all with different military traditions and capabilities, UNIIMOG had to accept that its members had neither trained together nor even trained separately under moderately similar military doctrines and to comparable standards.

To relieve the detrimental operational effects of this improvisation, UNIIMOG, like most observation missions, was organized into small observation teams. This served in some ways to limit the impact of poor unit cohesion and improvised organization. As the two-man observer team was the only operational element of UNIIMOG, there was no great need for rehearsed and reliable operations at higher levels. UNIIMOG was never meant to conduct small or medium unit–level operations. Thus, observation missions with a force structure such as UNIIMOG could accomplish their limited military operations without undue impact from an improvised organizational structure.

Command and Control in UNIIMOG

The command and control structure of UNIIMOG and other observation missions gave the United Nations only limited direction over its military forces. Although the United Nations could specify the observers' tasks, the UN commander could not decide when the observers came and went from the mission or how they were prepared on deployment, nor could he overrule challenges to his authority from national chains of command. The successful operation of this loose system of command—operational control—was predicated on voluntary cooperation from contributing member states, which was most often present in observation missions.

The second feature of UN command and control, improvisation in control procedures, was a fixture of UNIIMOG as well. Commonality is itself a control procedure, and a mission formed ad hoc from the individual officers and troops of twenty-six different member states would obviously experience problems in having common military control procedures. A military force must have common control procedures, such as rules of engagement, operations orders processes, standard operating procedures, reporting formats, modus operandi, training, and doctrine. This phenomenon is more fully examined in Chapters Four to Seven because it is more clearly evident in larger missions. It is helpful to note here, however, that, when deploying a disparate group of observers, such as UNIIMOG, to the field, these control procedures were usually improvised on the go to fit the unique characteristics of the UN force and its mission.

The chain of command in UNIIMOG ran directly from the secretary-general to the chief military observer (CMO) to the sector and team commanders on the ground (Figure 3). In practice, the under secretary-general for special political affairs was the principal manager at UN headquarters in New York. The secretary-general did have a personal representative to Iran and Iraq, Ambassador Jan Eliasson, but he was not in the operational chain of command for UNIIMOG. His responsibilities included the entire diplomatic process for the conclusion of the Iran–Iraq peace settlement, of which UNIIMOG was only one part. Thus, unlike some later missions where the UN military commander reported to a civilian representative of the secretary-general, the CMO of UNIIMOG was directly responsible to the secretary-general himself.[18]

UNIIMOG was commanded for most of its existence by Major-General Slavko Jovic of Yugoslavia. He had two brigadier generals to serve as assistant chief military observers (ACMO), one in Iraq and one in Iran. The CMO and his senior staff alternated their headquarters between Baghdad and Tehran. The ACMOs divided their areas of operations into sectors: four on the Iranian side and three on the Iraqi side. Each of these sectors had a headquarters and controlled a number of team sites from which the UNIIMOG patrols originated.

This chain of command looked fairly straightforward but, like many other aspects of the operation, was hampered by cases of belligerent recalcitrance. For instance, it took almost two months for the CMO to get permission to fly directly between Baghdad and Tehran. Before that, General Jovic had to take a circuitous route through neighboring countries. This hampered his command responsiveness to problems in the field that required his personal attention or negotiation with government officials. Responsiveness is an essential requirement for a military chain of command, and leaders and units throughout the chain have to be able to make well-informed and authoritative decisions in fluid military situations. This applies even in observation missions, such as UNIIMOG, where ACMOs were often called out to the cease-fire area on no notice to help defuse a tense situation. For instance, the most serious of these situations occurred on 11 December 1988 after an Iran–Iraq exchange of artillery, small arms, and rocket fire. Both ACMOs were immediately called to the scene.[19]

Figure 3

Chain of Command in the Iran–Iraq Mission

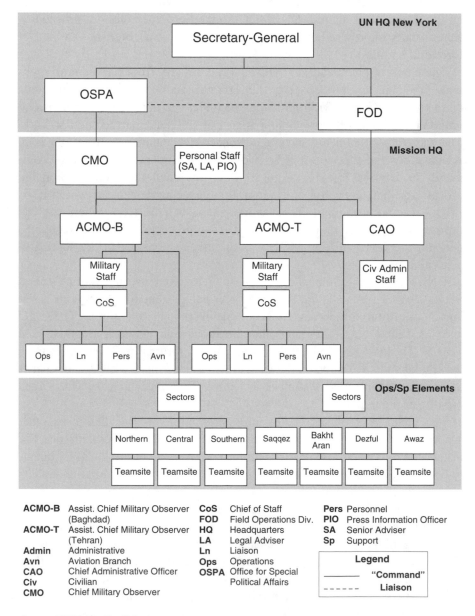

ACMO-B	Assist. Chief Military Observer (Baghdad)	**CoS**	Chief of Staff	**Pers** Personnel
ACMO-T	Assist. Chief Military Observer (Tehran)	**FOD**	Field Operations Div.	**PIO** Press Information Officer
Admin	Administrative	**HQ**	Headquarters	**SA** Senior Adviser
Avn	Aviation Branch	**LA**	Legal Adviser	**Sp** Support
CAO	Chief Administrative Officer	**Ln**	Liaison	
Civ	Civilian	**Ops**	Operations	
CMO	Chief Military Observer	**OSPA**	Office for Special Political Affairs	

ACMO-B Assist. Chief Military Observer (Baghdad)
ACMO-T Assist. Chief Military Observer (Tehran)
Admin Administrative
Avn Aviation Branch
CAO Chief Administrative Officer
Civ Civilian
CMO Chief Military Observer

CoS Chief of Staff
FOD Field Operations Div.
HQ Headquarters
LA Legal Adviser
Ln Liaison
Ops Operations
OSPA Office for Special Political Affairs

Pers Personnel
PIO Press Information Officer
SA Senior Adviser
Sp Support

Legend

———— "Command"

- - - - - Liaison

Source: UNDPI, *The Blue Helmets,* p. 415.

The lack of belligerent cooperation also hampered attempts to fully integrate UNIIMOG's operations and preserve the integrity of its single chain of command. Throughout UNIIMOG's existence, military observers who were not on the CMO's personal staff were assigned for their whole tour of duty to either the Iranian or the Iraqi side of the cease-fire line and responded to the chain of command (up to the ACMO) of their assigned country. UN patrols from opposite sides communicated by radio and even met in the cease-fire zone. However, negotiations with the belligerents for the opening of three crossing points to enable UN personnel and vehicles to cross the border were never fruitful.[20] Therefore integrated UNIIMOG operations initiated in concert from both sides of the border were not possible. In effect, UNIIMOG continued to operate with parallel chains of command in each country.

This forced separation of UNIIMOG into Iraqi and Iranian operations, whose only real planning and operational coordination was at the CMO level, spawned the de facto creation of two virtually separate observation missions. This complicated the efforts of UNIIMOG to appear as a single comprehensive mission that was not identified with one side or the other. In addition, the parallel chains of command on each side of the border restricted on-the-spot negotiations between UN military observers working with separate chains of command. This forced division of UNIIMOG greatly increased its operational requirements and even threatened its impartiality as each part of the mission became identified separately with its host country.

Yet another restriction placed on UNIIMOG's chain of command was the refusal of Iranian authorities to allow UNIIMOG to use its satellite communications. Over two years into the mission, UNIIMOG on the Iranian side was deprived of "the facility of instant communication with Headquarters New York and between its headquarters in Baghdad and Tehran."[21] In addition, Iranian customs officials even confiscated a consignment of radios intended for the team sites of the UN military observers.

A military command and control system is predicated on several principles, such as authority, responsiveness, effectiveness, integrity, and unity of command. Unity of command is considered an indispensable principle for any military operation. According to U.S. Army doctrine, it "means that all the forces are under one responsible commander . . . a single commander with the requisite authority to direct all forces in pursuit of a unified purpose."[22] The responsiveness and effectiveness of the two UNIIMOG operations differed enough to preclude an effective chain of command that ran directly from CMO to sector or team chief.

Because he could not achieve unity of command, the best the CMO could do from Baghdad or Tehran was to ensure that UNIIMOG had a "unity of effort" by coordinating the operations of his Iran-based and Iraq-based forces so that they were directed toward common objectives. The fact that UNIIMOG was restricted from complying with the principles of effective command and control made it less responsive and efficient as a military force. However, although deviation from accepted military doctrine in this modest military mission did signal military inefficiency, it did not necessarily hurt the overall success of the mission, which was, of course, principally dependent on others.

In addition to those problems in the field, command and control of UNIIMOG suffered from the basic organizational structure of UN headquarters in New York. As with all UN operations initiated before 1993, UNIIMOG had two parallel lines of command up to the secretary-general. The chain of command ran directly through the military force, but the UN Field Operations Division (FOD), which controlled UNIIMOG's logistic and administrative requirements, as well as UNIIMOG's civilian support staff (over 100 members), did not answer to anyone in UNIIMOG's military chain of command. Because this situation had existed for over forty years and was familiar to many, close coordination between the FOD and UNIIMOG was achieved.[23] This ensured that UNIIMOG suffered no major problems of the kind that had plagued many missions in the past. Nonetheless, it was an inefficient way to structure the command and control of any military mission.[24]

In 1988 when UNIIMOG was formed, the United Nations did not officially have a common operational doctrine on which to base its control procedures, but the seven UN observation missions that preceded UNIIMOG had given rise to some form of common practice. The conduct of six traditional peacekeeping missions (which perform many observation tasks) conducted prior to 1988 also had helped form something of an inchoate corporate wisdom at the United Nations about the modus operandi of observation missions. Some of this was codified as doctrine by member states, especially those with much peacekeeping experience, such as the Nordic nations. Peacekeeping conventions also were formalized by independent bodies, such as the International Peace Academy, which first printed the *Peacekeeper's Handbook* in 1978. However, because the field personnel were new to each mission, there always was a sense of "reinventing the wheel" in terms of control procedures that took place in each observation mission.

Like the loose chain of command, however, the military deficiencies caused by the improvisation of control procedures did not doom UNIIMOG to failure. The political influences that restricted UNIIMOG's command and control could be best characterized as irritants that hampered effective command and control rather than impediments that thwarted success. Because of UNIIMOG's modest operational mandate and its complete reliance on the belligerents, the less-than-optimum command and control structure that a nonsovereign political entity such as the United Nations was forced to use did not cause a breakdown in the peace process.

THE MILITARY OBJECTIVES OF UNIIMOG

The declared military objectives of UNIIMOG reflected the chief operational imperative of all observation missions, namely, that the full cooperation of the belligerents is a sine qua non for successful operations. UNIIMOG was given a mandate specifying seven military tasks:[25]

1. Establish with the parties agreed cease-fire lines on the basis of the forward defended localities occupied by the two sides on D Day but adjusting these, as may be agreed, when the positions of the two sides are judged to be dangerously close to each other.
2. Monitor compliance with the cease-fire.
3. Investigate any alleged violations of the cease-fire and restore the situation if a violation has taken place.
4. Prevent, through negotiation, any other change in the status quo, pending withdrawal of all forces to the internationally recognized boundaries.
5. Supervise, verify, and confirm the withdrawal of all forces to the internationally recognized boundaries.
6. Thereafter, to monitor the cease-fire on the internationally recognized boundaries, investigate alleged violations and prevent, through negotiation, any other change in the status quo, pending negotiation of a comprehensive settlement.
7. Obtain the agreement of the parties to other arrangements, that, pending negotiation of a comprehensive settlement, could help reduce tension and build confidence between them, such as the establishment of areas of separation of forces on either side of the international border, limitations on the number and calibre of weapons to be deployed in areas close to the international border, and patrolling by United Nations naval personnel of certain sensitive areas in or near the Shatt al-Arab.

These seven areas specified tasks that fall under each of the four mission categories examined in Chapter Two and were fairly standard for observation missions. The principal methods by which UNIIMOG carried out this mandate were observation (through patrolling) and negotiation. This approach required the full consent and cooperation of the belligerents on the ground. This was not always forthcoming, and, as Brian Smith has written, without *full* cooperation from the belligerents, UNIIMOG's mandate gave it "tasks that were beyond its power to perform."[26]

For the first two years of its existence, UNIIMOG operations were exclusively concerned with tasks 1 through 4 of its operational mandate because tasks

5 through 7 were predicated on withdrawal of Iraqi and Iranian forces to the international border recognized by the 1975 Algiers conference. This was the most important provision of the Iran–Iraq cease-fire settlement, but neither side made any moves to comply with this directive until August 1990. Consequently, most UNIIMOG operations did not entail operations directly connected with implementing the peace settlement. For the first two years, UNIIMOG patrols merely confirmed that the two sides were not trying to take further advantage from the cease-fire.

Monitoring Borders, Demilitarized Zones, Cease-Fires, Truces, or General Armistices

UNIIMOG's mandate for monitoring the cease-fire agreement was limited strictly to the cease-fire zone itself. As with almost all observation missions, the ratio of force to space in UNIIMOG's area of operations was so imbalanced as to make its objectives militarily unachievable. The 350 military observers (less with headquarters staff subtracted) were responsible for continuously monitoring a 1,400-kilometer cease-fire line (Map 2). This task was challenging in the extreme but was made even more unrealistic by the de facto split of UNIIMOG into two separate missions. The operational effect of this condition was that UNIIMOG had a de facto cease-fire line of 2,800 kilometers.

The initial agreements with Iran and Iraq indicated that at least three cross-border points would be available to UN observers to coordinate observation. The planning for UNIIMOG's modus operandi depended therefore on the fulfillment of agreements that were never concluded. As a result, a suspected violation on the Iranian side would have to be investigated by Iranian UNIIMOG observers, even if observers on the Iraqi side were just across the cease-fire line. The secretary-general reported to the Security Council that the UN patrols were limited to checking "that the side to which they are assigned is complying with the cease-fire."[27] Nonetheless, it was never proposed to double UNIIMOG's size when its operational area was effectively doubled. This situation left each active UN observer with over 8 kilometers of cease-fire line to observe continuously through difficult terrain that ranged from marshlands to mountains. In contrast, U.S. Army doctrine maintains that a reconnaissance platoon of thirty men can effectively observe only 5 kilometers of terrain. "If the [entire] platoon is spread out over more than 5 km, however, it quickly strains their ability to maintain command and control and accomplish the critical tasks." [28] Naturally, for the UN observer's purposes, not all parts of the cease-fire line needed to be under constant observation to monitor the agreement effectively, but it should be appreciated that UNIIMOG was under considerable strain in attempting to meet its operational mandate.

Map 2

The Observation Mission to Iran and Iraq

Source: UNDPI,*The Blue Helmets,* Appendix III, Map No. 3329.12

The initial size and operational mandate of UNIIMOG also were predicated on the introduction of air and naval assets to act as "force multipliers." Despite the importance that the secretary-general and UNIIMOG commander placed on the availability of these operational assets, Iran and Iraq never agreed on the details of their use, and they were never deployed. Neither the secretary-general nor the CMO ever proposed that UNIIMOG's strength or operational mandate be increased to compensate.

Understaffed, underequipped, and recognizing that it was quite impossible to monitor the entire cease-fire line on both sides, UNIIMOG adopted a logical operational doctrine. This doctrine was based on reaction, much like a fire or police emergency service. Because of the restricted size and mandate of UNIIMOG, the operation had little choice when it chose these methods:

> *Given the great length of the line of confrontation, the teams of observers will be attached to the relevant field headquarters of the two armies and will be sent out, on the initiative of the Chief Military Observer or at the request of one or other of the parties, to investigate incidents as circumstances demand. In certain particularly sensitive locations, static observation posts may also be established.*[29]

Despite this policy, restrictions on the operations of UNIIMOG observers consistently hampered operations. Certain sectors of UNIIMOG operations experienced greater restrictions on freedom of movement and others enjoyed a fair amount of cooperation from the belligerents.

UNIIMOG's freedom of movement differed greatly from sector to sector. Iran in particular hampered operations in some sectors, denying access to some areas and forcing cancellation of UN patrols on occasion by failing to provide liaison officers, interpreters, and/or transportation.[30] Iran would not even allow UNIIMOG to transport itself on patrol in the Ahwaz sector until July 1989, and in the other three Iranian sectors until January 1990.[31] Even after this breakthrough, UNIIMOG vehicles were denied freedom of movement throughout the cease-fire zone on a daily basis.[32]

On the Iraqi side, UNIIMOG divided the cease-fire line into three sectors, headquartered at Basra, Ba'quba, and As Sulaymaniyah, respectively. On the Iranian side, there were four UNIIMOG sectors operating out of Ahwaz, Dezful, Bakhtaran, and Saqqez. The patrol areas of team sites within these sectors ranged in length from 70 kilometers in the marshlands of the south to over 250 kilometers in the mountains of the north.[33] Patrols usually operated in groups of two UN observers, accompanied by Iraqi or Iranian interpreters, liaison officers, government officials, and local commanders. The patrols operated in wheeled vehicles, although they were sometimes conducted in boats, on foot, by muleback, and even on skis. The first day of UNIIMOG's deployment consisted of fifty-one patrols, and the daily operating tempo remained much the same (average of sixty-four to sixty-eight daily patrols)[34] until August 1990, when Iraq invaded Kuwait.

Minor violations of the cease-fire agreement were a regular event in the cease-fire zone, continuing throughout UNIIMOG's existence, and the secretary-general characterized the atmosphere as "inherently unstable."[35] Local reports of violations naturally far exceeded numbers of confirmed violations. Of the first 1,072 complaints investigated by UNIIMOG by 24 October 1988, only 235 incidents were adjudged to be cease-fire violations.[36] Some major violations did occur, most notably the attempt by Iran to flood a portion of the cease-fire zone in the Ahwaz sector to create a water obstacle between the two armies. This action continued from 13 September 1988 (despite the fervent and continuous protests of UNIIMOG) until Iraqi forces withdrew on 17 August 1990. Tension over this violation led to fatal shooting incidents in the area and artillery and rocket attacks.[37] However, the great majority of violations (eighty percent) were classified as minor by UNIIMOG.[38]

To maximize his limited resources and in accordance with the strategy of reacting to incidents as they happened, the CMO frequently shifted observers to areas that had experienced recent hostilities until the level of tension was reduced. In this way he hoped to deploy more observers to the critical areas and not use such resources on areas of little or no reported activity. The CMO of UNIIMOG chose this course of action in light of the fact that all his operational parameters were set by the cooperation of the belligerents. In analyzing the effectiveness of this course of action, it is necessary to recognize this operational imperative above all other factors.

As a result, UNIIMOG's patrolling and observation strategy was reactive and, by necessity, left the initiative of action solidly in the hands of the belligerents. Analyst Brian Smith noted that UNIIMOG operations and objectives could only "treat the symptoms of the conflict but not its underlying political causes."[39] The principles of peacekeeping, which emphasize the tenets of belligerent cooperation, impartiality, and the passive use of force, leave the initiative to the belligerents. That the conditions for the military success of UNIIMOG were largely out of UNIIMOG's hands was standard procedure in observation missions.

Supervising the Withdrawal of Forces

The most significant condition of the Iran–Iraq peace settlement was the withdrawal of forces to borders recognized in the 1975 Algiers agreement. This movement did not begin until late in UNIIMOG's existence. Once withdrawal commenced, almost all UNIIMOG operations were based on monitoring its progress. Only two years into its existence could UNIIMOG start to address the military objectives specified in paragraphs 5 through 7 of its mandate.

Throughout the period of UNIIMOG's mandate, Iraq had steadfastly refused to recognize the international Iran–Iraq border agreed upon at the 1975 Algiers conference. Even three days before its invasion of Kuwait in August 1990, Iraq had publicly reasserted its claim to the Shatt al-Arab waterway.[40] However, as the allied coalition cooperating with Kuwait in 1990 began to build in political and military strength against Iraq, Sadaam Hussein sought quickly to conclude a peace settlement with Iran. By 14 August 1990, Iraq had dropped almost every demand it had made since the conflict with Iran began in 1980, and it sued for peace with Iran. As Lawrence Freedman, professor of War Studies at King's College, London, and Efraim Karsh recognized, "the abruptness of the Iraqi initiative took the Iranian leadership by complete surprise."[41] On 17 August, Iraq began to pull its troops back to the recognized boundary, prisoners of war and deceased soldiers were repatriated the next day, and a lasting peace was at last brought to the area. UNIIMOG was informed of Iraq's intention to withdraw less than 48 hours before the operation commenced.[42]

After two years of stalemate, the desired political solution was in sight, and UNIIMOG's operational mandate was nearing completion. Cooperation from the belligerents was at its highest level, and the confirmation of the troop withdrawal was easily carried out by UNIIMOG patrols. The withdrawal to recognized boundaries, coupled with the increasing tension between the UN–approved coalition in Saudi Arabia and Iraq, caused the secretary-general to recommend to the Security Council that UNIIMOG be reduced in strength: "The Chief Military Observer has informed me that only about 60 percent of UNIIMOG's present strength of military observers would be required to perform these tasks [confirming withdrawal]."[43] The subsequent reduction of UNIIMOG lowered the operating tempo to an average of thirty-one daily patrols. However, because the latent conflict had essentially been terminated by the parties concerned, these patrols were more than enough to accomplish the mission. Some minor violations were still observed, but the atmosphere of excellent cooperation led to their quick resolution.

Although UNIIMOG's mandate continued to be renewed by the Security Council for brief periods of time (thirty to sixty days), the mission was effectively over. Some countries participating in the UN coalition against Iraq, such as Australia, Argentina, and Senegal, withdrew their forces from UNIIMOG. The military strength and operating tempo of UNIIMOG continued to decline until the opening of the coalition campaign against Iraq on 17 January 1991. At that time, all UNIIMOG personnel deployed on the Iraqi side were relocated to Cyprus or to Iran. Throughout the coalition operation against Iraq, UNIIMOG continued to deploy an average of three patrols per day on the Iranian side of the cease-fire line.[44] Iranian authorities reimposed tight restrictions on UNIIMOG freedom of movement for security considerations because of the "situation in the region."[45] The usefulness of UNIIMOG's operations were clearly in some doubt at this point, and the secretary-general declared an end to UNIIMOG on 28 February 1991.

Performing Quasi-Judicial Functions

In paragraphs 4 and 6 of UNIIMOG's operational mandate, the specific modus operandi of the force was clearly spelled out: UNIIMOG would establish its authority and credibility "through negotiation." Although this was the implicit approach for all UNIIMOG tasks (UNIIMOG could hardly accomplish its mission through force of arms), it applied in particular to quasi-judicial functions. The great majority of such UNIIMOG activities took place at the local level, where UNIIMOG military observers negotiated directly with the commanders on the ground. In many cases, mostly minor, UNIIMOG suggestions were implemented by the belligerents in the area. UNIIMOG personnel, like those in many other observation missions, found that the moral authority of their presence gave them tacit acceptance as fair arbiters of local issues.

As noted, most violations were minor. Major violations were taken up through the UNIIMOG chain of command to the ACMOs and the CMO in their meetings with Iraqi and Iranian officials. However, the lack of contact between the belligerents considerably hindered UNIIMOG's quasi-judicial functions at a high level. UNIIMOG officials could hardly arbitrate a major dispute with only one belligerent present at a time. Throughout UNIIMOG's existence, it tried to correct this situation by establishing a mixed military working group with officials from both sides. This failed to materialize until 6 January 1991, when Iraqi and Iranian officials met with the CMO in Tehran to discuss specific technical points of dispute.[46] That only one such meeting took place throughout UNIIMOG's mandate, and only after the conflict was effectively settled, emphasizes the local and sporadic character of negotiations that were permitted by the belligerents.

Conclusion

The experiences of UNIIMOG in 1988–1991 bear out the lessons of almost all UN observation missions conducted between 1948 and 1996. The force structure of UNIIMOG was predicated on the primacy of political requirements and conditions that overrode military necessity. The chain of command was neither responsive nor authoritative. Control procedures were created ad hoc in the field by a disparate group of observers. Military objectives were not only frustrated by the caprice the belligerents, but also somewhat hindered by the military deficiencies that were a result of the force structure and command and control system. In short, UNIIMOG exhibited all the traditional military failings of UN observation missions that were derived from the political-military improvisation of a mission by an organization not structured for managing military operations.

However, UNIIMOG also "succeeded." That success, of course, must be qualified when attempting to credit UNIIMOG directly. In comparison to orthodox military endeavors, UN observation missions must have very different standards for success, namely, that success ultimately depends on others. As analyst Brian Smith noted, the UNIIMOG "experience only reemphasizes the basic notion that local consent and cooperation are key to successful peacekeeping."[47] UNIIMOG in and of itself did not achieve military objectives that, in turn, delivered the political goal of the mission. Its contribution was considerably less direct, but important nonetheless. Professor Alan James noted in the summer of 1990 that UNIIMOG had

> made a very substantial contribution towards the firming-up of the cease-fire, which, after a long and extremely bitter war, was even more fragile than many such arrangements. Some escalatory developments have been nipped in the bud; calming-down action has been taken on numerous occasions; and a degree of stability has been fostered along much of the cease-fire line.[48]

This contribution was important, but ultimately UNIIMOG was considered a successful UN observation mission for the simple reasons that the Iran–Iraq war did not resume during its mandate and a peace settlement between the two countries was realized. The secretary-general implied that the August 1990 peace settlement between Iran and Iraq was the "result of a political process" initiated by the United Nations and maintained through UNIIMOG and other diplomatic activities and pressures.[49] It is apparent, however, that the quick conclusion of that treaty was a case of political expediency for Iraq, as it faced an absolutely overwhelming crisis that threatened its very survival as a state.

A UN observation mission is a very limited military enterprise, one that can afford a certain degree of political, strategic, and operational mismanagement and still "succeed." However, as UN operations become larger and more militarily complex, the stakes are raised and the need for strategic competence is correspondingly increased. It is to those larger missions that the book now turns.

CHAPTER 4

Traditional Peacekeeping

"Peacekeeping" is the military technique most often associated with UN military operations. As noted, most UN studies treat observation missions, traditional peacekeeping missions, and second-generation peacekeeping in the same elastic category of "peacekeeping." This book highlights the strategic and operational differences in these types of military operations and the different challenges they presented to the United Nations in terms of management. In addition to those distinctions, it is helpful to note that, much like UN observation missions, traditional peacekeeping missions themselves vary to some degree in their military characteristics.

In the main, however, these operations consisted of no more than a few thousand lightly armed troops, structured around light infantry battalions. These troops were generally deployed in linear buffer zones between belligerents and used military force only in a passive manner. Traditional peacekeeping forces were never intended to attain their military objectives through the use of coercive force. As Paul Diehl has noted, "one distinguishing attribute of peacekeeping is the performance of a noncoercive mission."[1] This "distinguishing attribute" was made possible by an important political precondition: traditional peacekeeping forces would be deployed only with the consent of all belligerents after a peace settlement had been reached.

At its core, peacekeeping is a military technique for controlling armed conflict and promoting conflict resolution. As such, the definitions for traditional peacekeeping abound, and there are differences in the actual wording of the definitions among various UN documents, the *Peacekeeper's Handbook*, and the doctrinal manuals of different nations and multinational military organizations. The British Army field manual *Wider Peacekeeping* lists thirteen separate definitions of peacekeeping and peacekeeping operations.[2] However, Paul Diehl offers a clear definition of traditional peacekeeping that is consistent with the definitions of most organizations and the actual conduct of traditional peacekeeping:

> *Peacekeeping is therefore the imposition of neutral and light-*
> *ly armed interposition forces following a cessation of armed*
> *hostilities, and with the permission of the state on whose terri-*
> *tory these forces are deployed, in order to discourage a renew-*
> *al of military conflict and promote an environment under*
> *which the underlying dispute can be resolved.*[3]

The Preface introduced these two principal goals of traditional peacekeeping. The first general objective was to limit armed conflict between the belligerents. For this reason peacekeepers were mostly deployed as an interpositional force to separate the belligerent parties. The second general objective of all UN military operations, including traditional peacekeeping, was to promote conflict resolution. However, as noted, this goal is most clearly understood as a diplomatic and political effort and has been thoroughly examined in political studies elsewhere. For this reason, this chapter concentrates on the analysis of traditional peacekeeping missions in light of the immediate military objective, to limit armed conflict.

To analyze the strategic and operational nature of these missions, this chapter examines their force structure, their command and control structure and procedures, and their military objectives and modus operandi. The missions that are surveyed in this chapter include the first United Nations Emergency Force in the Sinai, 1956–1967 (UNEF I), the United Nations Force in Cyprus, 1964–present (UNFICYP), the second United Nations Emergency Force in the Sinai, 1973–1979 (UNEF II), and the United Nations Disengagement Observer Force in the Golan Heights, 1974–present (UNDOF). The United Nations Interim Force in Lebanon, 1978–present (UNIFIL), also was a traditional peacekeeping mission, but it is examined in detail as a case study in Chapter Five.

Another traditional peacekeeping mission, the United Nations Security Force in West Irian, 1962–1963 (UNSF), will be noted. However, its operational characteristics were an anomaly. This mission was more akin to an observation mission with some additional armed forces for local security. In addition, some more recent peacekeeping missions, such as those in Namibia and Mozambique, had some superficial operational similarities with traditional peacekeeping but are examined elsewhere as second-generation peacekeeping missions because they were fundamentally different in their operational characteristics from traditional missions. The United Nations Operation in the Congo (ONUC), although initiated in much the same historical context as traditional peacekeeping missions, bears a much closer operational resemblance to second-generation missions and is thus treated in that category.

As with observation missions, the principles that governed the formation, direction, and employment of traditional peacekeeping missions were based on the tenets of peacekeeping. These principles were predicated on the impartiality of the Blue Helmets, the consent and cooperation of the belligerents, and the passive use of force by UN troops. These strategic tenets did act as operational constraints, but they also matched the strategic character of a voluntary multinational institution such as the United Nations. The United Nations simply did not have the political legitimacy or military authority that would allow it to build the systems and procedures it would need to mobilize, deploy, and direct large conventional military forces on missions that required the active or coercive use of force.

Thus the United Nations turned to the improvised military activity of traditional peacekeeping. These innocuous military endeavors reinforced the character of the United Nations as an international body that was operating in the military realm with neutrality, consensus, and a passive modus operandi. Despite the small size and humble nature of these military operations, they still posed a management challenge to an institution that had no formal structure or procedures for forming and managing military forces. Traditional peacekeeping operations were therefore often subject to the common foibles of UN military operations constructed ad hoc: improvisation, inconsistency, unresponsiveness, ineffectiveness, and helplessness in the event of unsupportive political environments. However, despite these "built-in" constraints, the United Nations' traditional peacekeeping missions enjoyed some notable successes when they were used in missions that suited their strengths and minimized their weaknesses.

Creating Traditional Peacekeeping Missions

Although peacekeeping as we know it was invented by the United Nations, its operational basis had some historical antecedents in imperial policing and some League of Nations actions, such as the League force in the Saar region following World War I. Nonetheless, creating UN peacekeeping operations was very much an improvised endeavor. Moreover, the lack of a regular and reliable security structure within the United Nations to create and form military operations was exacerbated by the fact that traditional peacekeeping missions were all initiated in response to an immediate crisis threatening international peace and security. This reinforced the frenetic and ad hoc nature of the political environment surrounding the creation of peacekeeping missions. As with observation missions, the political creation of traditional peacekeeping missions was characterized by improvisation on the part of the United Nations and the parties concerned to develop a method by which they could ease the volatile nature of immediate crises at hand.

To appreciate clearly the strategic character of traditional peacekeeping missions, it is critical to understand the political setting that surrounded their formation. Military missions are only a means to achieve greater political objectives, and, although they may have their own grammar (as Clausewitz has noted), their logic is the logic of politics. This chapter, like the rest of this book, recognizes this logic and then conducts a more specific examination of the grammar. Peacekeeping in particular is a military activity that is more political in nature than it is military. As William Durch has noted, "peacekeeping is primarily a political task that uses military symbols and some military tools, including force in certain circumstances."[4] It also has been noted that the military aspects of peacekeeping missions were only one facet of missions that most often included diplomatic, political, economic, and humanitarian elements as well.

Like observation missions, traditional peacekeeping missions find their political roots in three separate sets of circumstances with authorization from two separate UN bodies (the UN General Assembly authorized UNEF I and UNSF, and the Security Council authorized all other traditional peacekeeping missions). These three circumstances are UN initiatives, local initiatives, or brokered requests for assistance.[5] In the first category, the United Nations proper initiated the action that led to both missions in the Sinai (UNEF I and UNEF II), as well as the mission in Lebanon (UNIFIL). Of these, UNEF I had the distinction of being authorized by General Assembly resolutions, and not decisions of the Security Council, which was responsible for producing the mandates for all other traditional peacekeeping missions.

UNEF I (1956–1967) was the first traditional peacekeeping mission and the model on which all others would be built. Betts Fetherston writes that "UNEF I established a basic set of principles and standards which have served as the basis for the creation of all other missions which have followed."[6] The Suez crisis of 1956 presented a complex dilemma to the United Nations. It mixed ingredients of the volatile Arab–Israeli conflict, decolonization of the developing world, and the Cold War. Action through the Security Council was impossible because of vetoes by Britain and France, so the crisis was passed on to the General Assembly by authority of the "Uniting for Peace" resolution first used in the Korean crisis a few years earlier (Chapter Eight). Lester Pearson, the Canadian Secretary of External Affairs, was the driving force behind the concept of sending an armed UN emergency force to separate the belligerents in Egypt. This idea was a compromise of sorts between a small unarmed observation force such as that in Palestine (UNTSO) and a large and coercive collective security action such as the UN Command in Korea (UNC, 1950–1953). In this case, neither of those missions would suffice. Military observers would not constitute enough physical authority to deter renewed fighting in the Sinai, and there was hardly a consensus for action along the lines of the UNC in Korea.

The Canadian proposal for such a force set the pattern for traditional peacekeeping in all other missions. Because UNEF I and all other peacekeeping missions were initiated in times of extreme crisis, and because there were no regular UN mechanisms or procedures for dealing with such a crisis, the exercise was hurried and improvised. The proposal, adopted by the General Assembly on 4 November 1956, stated that the Assembly

> *requests, as a matter of priority, the Secretary-General to sub-mit to it* <u>within forty-eight hours</u> *a plan for the setting up, with the consent of the nations concerned, of an emergency inter-national United Nations Force to secure and supervise the ces-sation of hostilities in accordance with all the terms of the aforementioned resolution.*[7] *(emphasis added)*

The initial plan of the secretary-general for such a force was submitted to the assembly on the same day and was updated on subsequent days.[8] By 7 November, the General Assembly had approved the guiding principles for the formation, direction, and actual employment of the force. It is indeed extraordinary that a large and disparate body could so quickly approve a complex and untested concept for the use of armed military troops formed and controlled by the United Nations. In other situations, the United Nations sometimes acted with similar speed in its planning. The resolution that created UNEF II asked the secretary-general to submit an implementation plan within 24 hours,[9] as did the resolution creating UNIFIL. The deleterious operational effects of this political scramble are highlighted here and in the UNIFIL case study.

In contrast to those missions, the Cyprus operation (UNFICYP) fit in the second category of political inceptions: missions that were the result of a local initiative. In this case, the mission had the political and military planning advantage of being based on a British force that had an intimate local knowledge of the area of operations.[10] As the political situation worsened in 1964, the government of Cyprus requested UN assistance in keeping the peace. After consultation with the governments of Cyprus, Greece, Turkey, and the United Kingdom, the Security Council adopted a resolution establishing UNFICYP.[11]

Two missions fall in the last category of political creation: brokered requests for UN assistance. In both these cases, the United States mediated an agreement between the disaffected parties and crowned the agreement with the guarantee of an impartial UN peacekeeping force to help implement the settlement. In the case of UNSF, an agreement signed between the Netherlands and Indonesia in New York was endorsed a day later by the UN General Assembly.[12] In the case of UNDOF, a separate agreement between Israel and Syria was signed in Geneva and the mission was then legitimized by the Security Council later on the same day.[13]

As might be expected, the mandates of these traditional peacekeeping missions reflected the tensions of the political environment in which they were approved. Traditional peacekeeping was a relatively innocuous military activity largely because of larger political concerns in the United Nations and the world. All traditional peacekeeping missions were initiated during the Cold War, a time in which the tension between superpowers was the defining characteristic not only of the UN Security Council, but also of the international arena in general. As peacekeeping was an improvised exercise not agreed to in the Charter, it was viewed with some suspicion, especially by the Soviet Union.

To be approved by the Security Council during this time of Cold War friction, a peacekeeping mission had to be unambitious enough in its military characteristics and goals to fit below the threshold of tension on the Security Council. A large military mission with ambitious objectives did not stand much of a chance of approval. For instance, the UN Operation in the Congo (ONUC) received only intermittent support from powers such as France and the Soviet Union because of its large size, its ambitious mandate, and the active use of coercive military force by the UN peacekeepers.[14] The Congo experience in 1960–1964 seemed to prove to the United Nations that a nontraditional peacekeeping mission such as ONUC could not hope to enjoy the consensual support of the great powers because of its controversial goals and ambitious modus operandi.

Thus it was a sine qua non that a peacekeeping mission enjoy the full support of the Security Council, and the superpowers in particular, to be successful. Moreover, it was an operational prerequisite that traditional peacekeeping missions enjoy the full support of the local parties involved: the belligerents and the host states. As Durch noted, "peacekeeping operations require complementary political support from the Great Powers and local parties. If either is missing or deficient, an operation may never get underway or may fail to achieve its potential once deployed."[15]

Although the support of the great powers was reflected in the Security Council's mandate for the UN force, the support of the local parties was most clearly expressed through the strength of the local peace agreement, which in times of crisis most often was a temporary cease-fire agreement. A previously concluded peace settlement, such as a cease-fire, was necessary for the creation and deployment of a traditional peacekeeping mission. However, UN peacekeepers often were cause as well as effect in this diplomatic maneuvering. In many cases, the commitment of a UN peacekeeping force was itself a prerequisite to obtaining a cease-fire or peace settlement. This was true in UNSF, UNDOF, and UNIFIL.

In other cases, the cease-fire or settlement did not officially depend on the creation or functioning of the peacekeeping force. This was true in UNEF I, where the call for the cease-fire and the decision to create the force were established in separate resolutions.[16] In this case, the creation of a UN force often was eventually seen as necessary to induce a cease-fire, as the initial Security Council resolution (which did not mention a UN force) calling for a cease-fire was generally ignored in Egypt. There was a similar situation in UNEF II, where the Security Council established UNEF II on 25 October 1973, but Israel and Egypt did not sign a disengagement agreement until 18 January 1974. Regardless, a previously concluded peace agreement was absolutely critical to the deployment of a traditional peacekeeping force. Consequently, the continued observance of the provisions of such an agreement by the belligerents was the key to the success of the UN mission over the course of its existence.

In general, the more contentious the mission was among the Security Council powers or local belligerents, the more ambiguous the mandate. For example, UNEF II and UNDOF set out very clear operational parameters and military objectives for the peacekeeping forces. These missions were not particularly controversial to either the great powers on the Security Council or the belligerents. However, in the case of UNEF I and UNIFIL, more controversial missions, the mandate proposed only very broad objectives that did not specify any particulars of how the force would actually fulfill the mandate. In UNEF I, analyst Mona Ghali writes that "there was considerable controversy surrounding the interpretation of UNEF I's mandate."[17] Paul Diehl has written that, for controversial missions, "UN resolutions tend to be vague, a necessity to build the voting majority necessary to pass them."[18]

However, a clear and limited mandate was not necessarily a guarantee for success. As with all observation and traditional peacekeeping missions, the guarantee of success ultimately rested with the belligerents themselves. Having recognized the importance of this chief operational imperative, one must appreciate that the consent and cooperation of the belligerents stemmed in large part from the legitimacy and authority of the political process that created the mission itself. As former peacekeeper John Mackinlay noted,

> The important factor of success in a peacekeeping operation seems to be the effective nature of the political agreement which underpins the deployment and task of the peacekeeping force itself. If this agreement fails to provide for a workable armistice, cease-fire, or discontinuation of hostilities, then, no matter how well conceived and excellently conducted the peace operations may be, the peace force on its own cannot forestall or improve upon the conditions which may lead to its failure.[19]

This section now turns to an analysis of the military aspects of traditional peacekeeping, but the overwhelming influence of the political imperative should be borne in mind. The mandates of these missions were set through an improvised political process that was conducted in the frenetic atmosphere of crisis management. This resulted in ad hoc and hastily formed peacekeeping missions sent to areas of operation still volatile and unstable. As the political processes were themselves unfolding in the United Nations and in the mission area, the United Nations was attempting, through creative improvisation, to mobilize, organize, and deploy the military forces that would be needed for the operations.

Forming Traditional Peacekeeping Missions

The United Nations had to create military operations that were consistent with the restrictions on its political legitimacy and military authority. The principles of peacekeeping were therefore predicated on the notion that the peacekeepers would form a small, impartial, and passive force. The peacekeepers would be an "alert but inert" military presence.[20] This concept greatly determined the composition, size, and nature of peacekeeping force structures. The basic elements of these principles evolved into a UN doctrine that guided force structure decisions in traditional peacekeeping. The tenets of that doctrine that affected force structure were that the force (1) was constructed with the final approval of the belligerents; (2) would enjoy the consent and cooperation of the belligerents in carrying out its duties, therefore it need not have a coercive capability; (3) would be structured based on an equitable geographic representation of member states; (4) would be composed of national forces from neutral states and would not include great power participation; and (5) would be structured on the assumption that its use would be passive in nature and its arms used in self-defense only.

Composition

A UN peacekeeping force needed to be militarily large and robust enough to separate the belligerents through the occupation of an interpositional buffer zone. This occupation was itself a passive act, as there was no attempt to coerce the belligerents into separating. The interposition of UN forces came only after the belligerents had separated of their own accord. As the proposal for UNEF I noted, the passive nature of the force would be based "on the assumption that the parties to the conflict would take all necessary steps for compliance with the recommendations of the General Assembly."[21] However, in these environments there was always at least the danger of the occasional and isolated flare-up on the part of the belligerents, let alone more serious violations of the cease-fire. The almost 600 Blue Helmets killed in traditional peacekeeping missions are testament to the severity of even the small breaches of the peace in these missions and the frequency with which they have occurred.

A paradox of traditional peacekeeping missions was that their environments combined a physical danger from the heavily armed and aggressive belligerents with an assumption that these factions would cooperate with the UN force's wishes. The potential bellicosity of the environment made these missions unsuited for loosely organized teams of unarmed observers. However, the passive nature of the UN force's actions and the reliance on the cooperation of belligerents meant that a huge and aggressive collective security force was unsuited (and most often politically unattainable) for the mission.

It was recognized in the proposals for UNEF I that the force deployed to maintain a separation between four armies in Egypt must have at least a capacity to defend itself and also the capability of conducting unit-level defensive operations to deter further aggression. The first proposal for UNEF I, submitted by the secretary-general on 4 November 1956, proposed a force of observers only. However, the gravity of the situation in Egypt prompted his subsequent proposal to ask that the force "be more than an observer corps."[22] Even though a principal mission of traditional peacekeepers was still to observe and report, Diehl noted that "peacekeeping forces must also provide a visible deterrent, with the threat of defensive military actions, in patrolling buffer and other demilitarized zones; small, unarmed observer forces are generally considered inadequate for this task."[23] For this reason, the composition of traditional peacekeeping was always based on armed and complete units that had regular training in conducting unit-level combat operations.

The unit that was the basic building block for these operations was the light infantry battalion. The light infantry battalion was in many ways ideally suited for conventional UN peacekeeping. A battalion is the smallest level of military force that is essentially self-sufficient. It has its own staff, administration, communications, and logistics systems that are organic to the battalion. It also is the smallest level of military force that can conduct a full range of independent military combat operations. It is flexible and can conduct many types of operations in varying terrain. It also is inexpensive to transport and supply. And, as military analyst James Boyd noted, "the use of infantry battalions as opposed to composite units preserved the fundamental advantage of organizational integrity."[24]

Although an infantry battalion is a basic unit in all armies, there are many variations through the world. This diversity has been reflected in UN traditional peacekeeping. The light infantry battalions that were deployed as part of these missions varied in capability from a few hundred foot soldiers armed only with personal weapons to a motorized battalion that had some organic indirect fire support weapons (mortars) and crew-served heavy weapons (principally machine guns). However, the motorization of these infantry battalions was chiefly for mobility in their task of patrolling and occupying an inert buffer zone. Only in second-generation missions does one begin to see mechanized and armored forces used for self-defense and in limited offensive enforcement operations. The variation in capabilities in even these simple units led to problems of disparate and uneven force capabilities for UNIFIL and some second-generation peacekeeping missions.

Traditional peacekeeping missions have consisted of anywhere from two to eight infantry battalions and their supporting logistics forces. This basic force structure was, at times, supplemented by UN observers from other missions. For instance, the two Pakistani infantry battalions in the UNSF were deployed in concert with the operations of twenty-one UN military observers who were part of another mission, the UN Temporary Executive Authority.[25]

In addition, the traditional peacekeeping operations in the Middle East were all supplemented by observers from UNTSO. In fact, the initial headquarters of UNEF I was composed of observers assigned to UNTSO at the time.[26] The headquarters of UNEF II also was set up by UNTSO observers, and the peacekeeping mission itself was assisted in its duties by 120 observers of UNTSO.[27] UNDOF had the assistance of between seven and eighty-nine UNTSO observers,[28] and UNIFIL was similarly assisted. Although these observers complemented the peacekeeping forces, they also complicated command and control arrangements, which are discussed below.

The basic infantry battalion was sometimes supplemented by air reconnaissance assets or other "force multipliers." Because the ratio of force to space in these missions was almost as physically impractical as that in observation missions, these assets could help a smaller force observe larger areas of operation. In UNEF I, a small air reconnaissance element helped patrol a 187-kilometer-long stretch of Sinai coast from the Gulf of Aqaba to the Strait of Tiran.[29] UNFICYP and UNEF II also operated with small air components. In addition, UNEF II was supplemented by civilian surveillance teams from the United States operating sophisticated ground surveillance radars and U.S. air reconnaissance missions flown by SR-71A and U2 spy planes.[30]

To deploy peacekeepers rapidly, the force structure of traditional peacekeeping missions was supplemented in initial deployments by units deployed directly from other peacekeeping missions in progress. UNEF II's initial units were deployed directly from UNFICYP.[31] UNIFIL's initial components were deployed directly from both UNEF II and UNDOF. The ability to redeploy experienced peacekeeping units from one mission to another in the region helped the rapid planning being conducted in New York under the time constraints noted above.

Size

The size of traditional peacekeeping missions has varied, but a clear pattern is distinguishable. UNSF was composed of only 1,500 Pakistani infantrymen.[32] The UN Disengagement Observer Force (UNDOF) also was smaller than usual, 1,250 troops, its size the result of a compromise between Israel and Syria. As analyst Mona Ghali has written, "Israel preferred a large, well-defended force that could enforce the cease-fire if necessary and guarantee Tel Aviv's security interests. In contrast, Syria pressed for a small force of observers."[33] Alan James notes that "the outcome was a compromise, right down to the inclusion of both 'observer' and 'force' in the title of the peace-keeping group."[34]

However, all the other traditional peacekeeping missions had a peak strength of between 6,000 and 7,000 troops. In UNEF I, this precedent-setting number was established first by an estimation of the force commander, Canadian General E. L. M. Burns, who calculated that the equivalent strength of two small brigades would be needed to act as an interpositional force between the belligerents in Egypt.[35] The eventual peak strength of UNEF I was 6,073.[36]

This size precedent remained constant throughout most other traditional peacekeeping missions and came to represent the maximum size force that the Cold War United Nations was prepared to recruit, organize, and deploy. UNFICYP had a peak strength of 6,411, UNEF II of 6,973, and UNIFIL of 6,975.[37] This optimum size was based not so much on the mission planning of these sui generis operations as on the perceived military management capability of the United Nations itself. Whereas the size of UNEF I was based on the commander's estimate, his knowledge of the area of operations, and the mission, the size of UNEF II and UNIFIL was based on the past experience of UNEF I itself, as the size of these later missions was arbitrarily proposed within 24 hours of their political induction. There was no time in these latter cases for a thorough military planning cycle to be initiated that could have suggested a size more suited to the challenges of the mission on the ground. This process will be highlighted in the UNIFIL case study, and it will be seen in that case that the size of the mission was eventually revised after a reconnaissance of the area of operations.

In addition to precedent and management capability, the size of traditional peacekeeping forces was influenced by other political and financial reasons. In Cyprus, the force varied between a peak strength of 6,411 and a summer 1993 strength of less than 1,000.[38] UNEF I also fluctuated in strength over its almost eleven years of existence. As the mission environment stabilized in the early 1960s, contributing countries began to withdraw troops, and its strength in June of 1967, when Nassar asked it to withdraw completely, was only

3,378.[39] The financial state of peacekeeping missions is not surveyed in this book. However, this aspect also had a great impact on force levels in traditional peacekeeping missions, as these missions were habitually underfunded and in financial difficulty.[40]

Equitable Geographic Representation

The practical application of the principle of equitable geographic representation was noted in the examination of observation missions. Traditional peacekeeping missions followed this dictum as well, and the terms of reference for UNEF II are a good example of the planning guidelines of this principle. UNEF II's mandate stated that "the contingents would be selected in consultation with the Security Council and with the parties concerned bearing in mind the accepted principle of equitable geographic representation."[41] In addition, it had been articulated even earlier by the United Nations that "troops from the permanent members of the Security Council or from any country which, for geographical and other reasons, might have a special interest in the conflict, would be excluded."[42]

Two exceptions to this policy have taken place in traditional peacekeeping missions: in Cyprus, the British were allowed to play a central role in UNFICYP because of their heavy involvement in the non-UN peacekeeping mission that preceded UNFICYP. In addition, the logistic support system of UNFICYP was almost completely dependent on the British system that had been supplying its forces in Cyprus for years through the two large British bases on the island.[43] And, as will be examined in the case study on UNIFIL, the French were heavily involved in that operation.

Despite the great powers' general pattern of nonparticipation, their political concerns greatly influenced force structure, as was the case with UNEF II. In this instance the secretary-general had asked Canada to provide the logistics contingent for the entire mission, as it had ample experience in this field. However, the Soviet Union "insisted that a Warsaw Pact country should be included in the new force if a NATO member was."[44] Eventually a logistics unit from Poland was included, and the roles of these contingents were defined after two weeks of discussion on the matter. This delay and the resultant mix of logistics responsibilities made for a militarily impractical support structure. However, the case reinforces the point that political considerations at all stages of traditional peacekeeping planning and execution tended to outweigh purely operational requirements.

Naturally, the wishes of the belligerents themselves about the composition of the force were paramount. In UNEF I, President Nassar of Egypt objected to the inclusion of NATO members (Denmark, Norway, and Canada) because of his close relationship with the Soviet Union. He eventually acquiesced after long discussions with the secretary-general, but his right of veto over a national contingent remained in place.[45] In Cyprus the local government refused to agree to "troops of color" being part of UNFICYP.[46] Rosalyn Higgins also points out that Turkey made it clear to the secretary-general that it would not accept troops from developing countries, "lest the Turkish Cypriots be cast in the role of the Katangese" (in the Congo crisis).[47] As a result, UNFICYP had a distinctly European character, with military contingents coming from six West European countries and Canada.[48]

In another instance, Israel refused to let the UNEF II contingents from Poland, Ghana, Indonesia, and Senegal enjoy freedom of movement in areas under Israeli control because these countries had neither recognized nor opened diplomatic relations with Israel.[49] Alan James has pointed out that this Israeli ban affected three of five infantry battalions and one of two logistics battalions in UNEF II. He also states that because of the Israeli ban, "the flexibility of the force was considerably reduced."[50] The same policy applied to Polish units operating as part of UNDOF on the Golan Heights until Poland recognized Israel in 1990.[51]

In addition to the political whims of the great powers and the local powers, the secretary-general exercised the prerogative to accept some offers of national contingents and reject others to balance the principle of force neutrality with the desire to have a force that was not so multinational as to be operationally unwieldy. In UNEF I, the secretary-general received offers of troops from twenty-four countries, of which he accepted ten that met his criteria and were acceptable to the belligerents.[52] It will be seen that this luxury of choice was unfortunately not available when attempting to staff the large and complex missions of the second-generation of peacekeeping.

Examining observation missions and the UNIIMOG case study demonstrated that the United Nations attempted to adhere to the principle of equitable geographic representation even as missions fluctuated and changed. However, with traditional peacekeeping missions, the commitment of forces from member states was far greater than that of a few observers. This limited the number of member states that could contribute forces of a common standard for unit-level operations, and a balanced representation was sometimes harder to achieve than in observation missions. For instance, UNDOF started as a very politically balanced mission, with contingents representing Europe, the Americas, and Asia. However, with the withdrawal of the Peruvian contingent in 1975 and of the Iranian contingent in 1979, no replacement contingents from the Americas or Asia were offered. As a result, UNDOF remained a very European-looking force, manned by Canada, Poland, Austria, and Finland.[53] Former peacekeeper J. D. Murray records that in many other instances, the political requirement to have a force that appeared geographically balanced on paper often added peacekeeping units that were a "liability, not an asset."[54] This issue of "quality control" is examined at length in Chapters Five to Seven but was also present in traditional peacekeeping missions.

Interoperability

Ad hoc multinational forces that are hastily assembled for an immediate mission will meet interoperability problems. This term is used to denote the level at which a disparate force can perform coordinated and integrated operations. Interoperability is enhanced by common training and doctrine, compatible equipment and capabilities, well-defined command structures, common control procedures, and a similar modus operandi. The practical effects of interoperability issues are examined in the sections below on command and control and military objectives. However, it is important to note here that interoperability issues in a traditional peacekeeping force were the direct result of the political principles that influenced force structure decisions in the United Nations. As military analyst James Boyd noted,

> once the various countries decide to contribute units, an integrated United Nations operation does not automatically follow. There still remain the complex organizational problems of constructing a balanced military force and creating an adequate organizational structure. The efficiency of any military force cannot be measured merely by adding the sums of the capabilities of the component units.[55]

Because traditional peacekeeping missions were improvised and rapidly assembled enterprises, the disparity in national military capabilities, equipment, tactics, command and control systems, and operational procedures presented an interoperability challenge of the first order to a UN commander. If the UN commander could not coordinate and integrate the operations of his diverse forces, the total effect of the Blue Helmets could indeed be less than the sum of its parts.

Force structure decisions in traditional peacekeeping operations were greatly influenced by political imperatives and much less so by military requirements. As a result, peacekeeping forces rarely gave the appearance, on paper or in the field, of competently formed and well-drilled military formations. Traditional peacekeeping forces were small, lightly armed, disparate, and improvised military organizations that were subject to the political caprice of both the great powers and sometimes fiercely competing local factions. In addition, the political entity that had to manage these political whims and still build a military force around them was a multinational institution with limited political legitimacy, little military authority, and no rehearsed and reliable procedures for mobilizing and deploying military forces. However, despite these constraints, the United Nations did manage to recruit, organize, and deploy traditional peacekeeping missions in line with the principles of peacekeeping. This chapter now turns to their effectiveness and the United Nations' ability to manage their operations.

Command and Control in Traditional Peacekeeping Missions

It was seen in the examination of UN observation missions that a loose command structure and ad hoc control procedures were not necessarily a grave impediment to those UN missions. However, as missions move up the spectrum of operations in terms of the complexity and ambitions of their military operations, a more reliable, responsive, authoritative, and practiced command and control system is necessary for effective operations, especially when ambitious peacekeeping missions were conducted by UN forces in a contested environment where peacekeeping units might be threatened by organized hostilities. The UNIFIL case study highlights this phenomenon.

In the spectrum of operations, traditional peacekeeping missions were one step removed from observation missions in terms of the complexity of their military operations. Because they were closely related, the United Nations used a similar philosophy of command and control for both. As with observation missions, the principles of peacekeeping had two derivatives that characterized UN command and control. The first characteristic was that the UN chain of command was predicated on a loosely based definition of command. The second characteristic was that UN control procedures were marked by a lack of standardization that required improvisation in the field. Both of these characteristics combined to make the UN system of command and control much less responsive and authoritative than could be expected from the rehearsed and legitimate systems of nation-states or some established military alliances.

Chain of Command

The United Nations recognized as early as UNEF I that national contingents were not legally commanded by the United Nations, but only "under the operational control of the United Nations."[56] This distinction stems from the simple fact that the United Nations does not ultimately "own" the resources that it "commands."[57] Command of military forces "constitutes the authority to issue orders covering every aspect of military operations and administration."[58] Command is a nontransferable, sovereign, and total authority that draws its legitimacy directly from legislative acts, founding documents, or bodies of law. In the case of the United States, for example, command of military forces is based on the Constitution, federal law, and the Uniform Code of Military Justice. The total authority of command cannot be made available to the United Nations for two reasons.

First, as noted in Chapter One, a multinational organization that fully respects the sovereignty of individual member states cannot ultimately "own" the military resources of these same sovereign states. At no time has the United Nations asked a member state to surrender the legal sovereignty of any of its military forces to the United Nations. That sovereignty is legally not transferable. Second, there is no legal basis for command in the UN Charter or in the body of international law. The Charter only makes loose command provisions for the Article 43 forces that have yet to materialize in a UN context.

Operational control, however, is a subset of command designed temporarily to give over some aspects of command to another political entity. Two American officers writing on the subject described operational control as "the equivalent of long-term leasing."[59] This is somewhat accurate, although the lease does not necessarily have to be long term, just temporary. In addition, the powers that are leased are clearly enumerated in an operational control relationship. For instance, NATO defines operational control as

> the authority delegated to a commander to direct forces assigned so that the commander may accomplish specific missions or tasks which are usually limited by function, time, or location; further includes the deployment of units concerned and the retention or delegation of tactical control to those units; does not include authority to assign separate employment of components of concerned units; neither does it, of itself, include administrative or logistical control.[60]

When a unit is assigned to the operational control of another military unit or political entity, those functions, times, locations, and tasks are clearly spelled out so there is no confusion about which entity is responsible for what functions.

The key to understanding operational control is to appreciate that it is temporary and circumscribed.[61] Although the ability to assign missions is transferred, some powers and functions can never be transferred under an operational control relationship. These include the legal aspects of sovereignty guaranteed to the soldier (citizen) of a nation-state and the prerogatives of that nation-state to deploy its units when and where and in what capacity it sees fit. This means that, despite the United Nations' claim that the UN force commander should be able to "exercise the necessary disciplinary authority with members of his contingent," UN peacekeepers have always been subject only to the laws and administrative procedures of their nation-state.[62] The United Nations, as an organization whose charter explicitly recognizes the sovereignty of member states, can never overrule a member state in regard to the conduct of its soldiers or its units participating in a UN mission. All cooperation with the United Nations is strictly voluntary. When the United Nations and the many member states participating in a peacekeeping mission are in complete harmony about all aspects of the operation, this has not traditionally been a problem. When there are disagreements, however, the United Nations does not have the legitimacy or authority to overrule the nation-state.

One area where this phenomenon clearly shows is in the commitment of member state forces to traditional peacekeeping operations. Naturally, for the sake of operational consistency and continuity, the United Nations has preferred to have long-term commitments by member states to particular operations. The rapid and random turnover of forces, known in military parlance as "force turbulence," can prevent an operation from establishing momentum and force it to "reinvent the wheel" as new forces are inculcated into the mission. Because of the legal (and nontransferable) prerogatives of "command," however, member states always have reserved the sole right to decide when to deploy and redeploy forces.

As such, force turbulence always was a problem in traditional peacekeeping operations and did considerable damage to many a UN force's authority and legitimacy in its area of operations. This issue is highlighted in particular in the case study, but is replete throughout most traditional peacekeeping missions and especially troublesome in long-term missions. For instance, in UNEF I, two thirds of the initial infantry battalions stayed throughout the course of the mission. However, in UNFICYP the proportion was down to one half, and in UNEF II, only 30 percent saw the mission through to its conclusion.[63]

In UNEF I, when President Nassar of Egypt requested that the peacekeeping force be withdrawn in 1967, the secretary-general initially resisted the request to try and negotiate a less extreme action. However, his position was weakened by the unilateral decisions of India and Yugoslavia to redeploy their UNEF I contingents immediately in accordance with Nassar's wishes.[64] The failure of the secretary-general to have any control over the deployment and rotation policies of the national contingents greatly undermined the legitimacy and authority of the UN system of command and control. This problem was worse in the long-running missions, such as that in Cyprus, where Denmark and Canada decided in 1992–1993 to pull their infantry battalions out of UNFICYP after twenty-eight and twenty-nine years in the mission, respectively.[65] The United Nations could not order them to stay put.

The generic pattern for a UN chain of command in traditional peacekeeping missions is shown in Figure 4 and closely resembles that of observation missions. The secretary-general, advised by the under secretary general for special political affairs, had overall political authority for the mission. As an exception to this general rule, the General Assembly established an advisory committee for UNEF I. This committee was composed of representatives from Brazil, Canada, Ceylon, Colombia, India, Norway, and Pakistan. Five of these states had forces committed to UNEF I, and two did not. Five other states had forces participating in UNEF I but were not on the advisory committee. The lines of responsibility for this committee were ambiguous. It was to "undertake the development of those aspects of planning for the Force and its operation not already dealt with by the General Assembly and which did not fall within the area of the direct responsibility of the Chief of Command."[66] While the secretary-general "paid tribute to the indispensable services performed by the committee," this body never played any independent role in providing strategic direction to the force and consulted with the secretary-general only on matters of administration (such as the issuing of medals) and regulations governing the force's activities.[67]

The secretary-general's authority in the field was exercised by a special representative (SRSG) or the force commander. The SRSG was the strategic link, the man on the ground who translated the United Nations' political goals into the UN force's military objectives. However, the SRSG was not a regular appointment in most early UN missions. UNEF I was commanded by a force commander who answered directly to the secretary-general. This was also the case in UNEF II and UNDOF. UNFICYP, on the other hand, had both a SRSG and a force commander, both of whom answered independently to the secretary-general and were considered to have equal status.[68]

To add to this confusion about roles and authority at the political and strategic level, in some missions the force commander has had other responsibilities outside of his command. For instance, the commander of UNEF II, General Siilasvuo of Finland, was simultaneously chairing cease-fire negotiations. Indar Rikhye, a former UN peacekeeping force commander himself, has criticized this approach. He noted that "the presence of a commander in the early stages is always critical. Therefore Siilasvuo should not have been absent from his command until a routine had been established. Many of the subsequent weaknesses in command and control of UNEF II are attributable to the dual role which Siilasvuo was called upon to perform."[69]

As noted in Chapter Two, a last bit of confusion was served up by the traditional arrangement that split the operational chain of command from the logistic and administrative chain of command prior to 1993. This is also shown in

Figure 4

Chain of Command in Traditional
UN Peacekeeping Operations

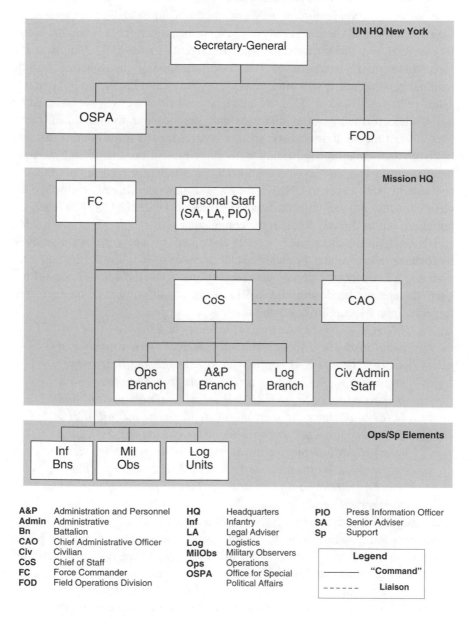

A&P Administration and Personnel
Admin Administrative
Bn Battalion
CAO Chief Administrative Officer
Civ Civilian
CoS Chief of Staff
FC Force Commander
FOD Field Operations Division

HQ Headquarters
Inf Infantry
LA Legal Adviser
Log Logistics
MilObs Military Observers
Ops Operations
OSPA Office for Special
Political Affairs

PIO Press Information Officer
SA Senior Adviser
Sp Support

Legend	
———	"Command"
- - - - - -	Liaison

Source: Based on UNDPI, *The Blue Helmets,* p. 409.

Figure 4. The effects of this split were felt most keenly in the administrative and logistics aspects of UN operations that are not specifically the purview of this book. However, it should be noted that the inefficiency of this system was prevalent, and its deleterious operational effects have been noted at length in the studies of several former peacekeepers.[70]

Another common feature of the chain of command in traditional peacekeeping missions is that there was only one level of headquarters between the secretary-general and the separate national contingents in the field. This was the force commander's headquarters. Because it was the only headquarters outside national contingents, it was often seen as top-heavy and having an unfavorable "staff-to-bayonet ratio."[71] This flat organizational structure was necessitated by the ad hoc formation of a disparate and unrehearsed multinational force. Moreover, it meant an unrealistic span of control for the force commander and his large and sometimes unwieldy staff. Principles of command and management maintain that one layer of command can efficiently control only three to five subunits. However, in UNEF I, the force commander directly controlled ten different battalion-size units, as was the case with UNIFIL. UNFICYP had six battalions report directly to the force commander.[72]

UNEF II, on the other hand, actually alleviated this span of control problem by forming intermediate "brigade" headquarters to split control of its nine contingents.[73] In other traditional peacekeeping missions, the span of control has been manageable because of the small size and small number of national contingents. John Mackinlay has noted that

> UNDOF [was] in many ways the least challenging as a command problem. This assessment is derived from a number of factors. In size and configuration it is the smallest peacekeeping force . . . and comprises units from only four countries as opposed to UNIFIL's initial force of nine nations and UNEF's thirteen. At the time of deployment its initial HQ staff were fortunate because the units chosen for the Golan were already deployed in the region. The HQ staff themselves were built up around a nucleus of UN staff officers who had already been working together as part of UNEF II's Northern Brigade.[74]

Thus, beyond the fact that UNDOF had a small span of control, it had an experienced staff who had instituted common control procedures in a previous mission. Common control measures could go some way to ameliorate the lack of authority and decisiveness in a loose and ad hoc chain of command. However, the fact remained in all traditional peacekeeping operations that the UN chain of command was predicated on incomplete and temporary powers of command. The powers of sovereignty that would allow a political entity to structure an authoritative and stringent chain of command were not transferable from member states to the United Nations. As will be seen, this would be a particular disadvantage for the United Nations in controversial and dangerous missions.

Control Procedures

The second characteristic of peacekeeping command and control was improvised control procedures. Common control procedures allow a force that has not rehearsed or trained together to undertake similar operations that can be coordinated and integrated. However, despite the growing body of institutional experience in UN peacekeeping throughout the 1960s and 1970s, the United Nations failed to formally codify most of its control procedures. In fact, standard operating procedures for UN forces, a critical component of command and control, were not officially documented until 1991 when the United Nations finally completed a *Guideline Standard Operating Procedures for Peacekeeping Operations (91-15137)*. The independent International Peace Academy had first published *The Peacekeeper's Handbook* in 1978 and various countries had documented tactical peacekeeping procedures, but none of these were promulgated by the United Nations itself before 1991. As a result, most control procedures were improvised in the field by the peacekeepers themselves.[75]

Control procedures for a military force can include headquarters and staff procedures, orders formats, planning procedures, reporting formats, rules of engagement, administrative policies, and standard operating procedures (SOPs). The importance of rehearsed and consistent procedures for the operations of a traditional peacekeeping force is highlighted in the UNIFIL case study. In the main, the lack of common military training among the disparate nations represented in traditional peacekeeping missions meant that these procedures frequently had to be reinvented and instituted as the missions progressed.[76]

In the absence of such common training and procedures, John Mackinlay noted that the traditional peacekeeping forces, "will usually have to resort to untried ad hoc procedures, and as a result the standard of command and control may suffer. Staff procedures may take on the lowest common factor of excellence, which in some cases will not be high enough to organize and control military operations in a consistently effective manner."[77] Another British peacekeeper noted that in UN operations,

> *time and again military officers in the field, as well as troop-contributor countries, have been obliged to devote time, ingenuity and energy to wrestling with problems that should never have arisen in the first place and in the meantime soldiers on the ground have suffered unnecessary hardship, resources have been wastefully employed and the success of the operations themselves have [sic] been jeopardized.*[78]

However, despite the inefficiency caused by the constant improvisation of control procedures, many have also noted that the military efficiency of a traditional peacekeeping force is not necessarily the key determinant of mission success. In an unambitious military mission whose success depends on the belligerents, ad hoc, inefficient, and unreliable control procedures may not unduly affect the mission outcome. However, in a more belligerent environment or in a mission with military operations of greater complexity, this is an entirely different story.

Military Objectives in Traditional Peacekeeping Missions

The military objectives and modus operandi of traditional peacekeeping were largely derived from the attributes of consent, impartiality, and the passive use of force that characterized the principles of peacekeeping. The following are the doctrinal tenets that were gleaned from these principles: (1) UN peacekeeping forces were given military objectives that reinforced their strict impartiality. No offensive or active military operations were conducted against any one local party. (2) The military objectives were undertaken with only the passive use of military force. This was limited to the use of force in self-defense or, by extension, the passive use of military force to defend the mandate of the mission if under armed attack. (3) The military objectives were predicated on the assumption that, in general, the force would enjoy the consent and cooperation of the belligerents in fulfilling their mandate.

There was some variation in missions, but traditional peacekeeping forces were primarily an inert interpositional force. Thus the principal operational military objectives of traditional peacekeeping centered on the occupation of a buffer zone to separate the belligerents. This section will examine the modalities of those buffer zones and the modus operandi used by peacekeeping forces in their establishment and occupation. Other ancillary tasks will also be noted, such as temporarily maintaining law and order, providing humanitarian relief, the repatriation of prisoners of war, or the monitoring of demobilization and disarmament agreements. Although these and other missions have been conducted through traditional peacekeeping missions, it is important to note that the overwhelming focus of traditional peacekeeping strategy was on occupying and maintaining an interpositional buffer zone.

Occupying an Interpositional Buffer Zone

The occupation of an interpositional buffer zone by traditional peacekeeping forces entailed several subsidiary operational tasks. First, there was the initial separation of the belligerents. This was not accomplished through coercion, but through the cooperation of belligerents in complying with the terms of the cease-fire agreement or peace settlement. Second, there was the continued separation of the belligerents through the physical occupation of the buffer zone by the peacekeeping force. Third, there was often the process of supervising subsequent withdrawals from the area of confrontation and the monitoring of treaty provisions that accompanied those withdrawals. These tasks often were seamless and many times had to be combined in one overall operational scheme.

The initial separation of belligerents was necessarily an anxious and critical time for traditional peacekeeping missions. In UNEF I the first peacekeepers were immediately interposed between Egyptian and Anglo-French forces. The first forces deployed to UNEF II were sent directly to an area between the Israeli and Egyptian armies. This dangerous phase of a traditional peacekeeping operation often evokes some unique and unrehearsed reactions from the peacekeepers themselves. In UNEF II, Finnish peacekeepers "put down their guns, linked arms, and invited the advancing [Israeli] forces to barrel through them." Other UNEF II peacekeepers were involved in fist-fights with belligerents.[79] These actions, despite their improvised nature, reinforced the operational character of the mission as one involving only the passive use of military force.

The initial deployment of peacekeepers was heavily influenced by the ad hoc nature of their political creation and the environment of improvised crisis management. As a result, the actual deployment of traditional peacekeepers was always staggered, unsynchronized, and somewhat incoherent by military standards. Because the United Nations had to recruit new forces for every mission and had no control over the time or fashion in which these contingents reported for duty, it could never plan for a coordinated and integrated deployment. Peacekeepers just reported to the area of operations as they became available, usually arriving without the benefit of advanced planning or a previously published and disseminated campaign plan. In many cases, some contingents arrived months after the initial deployments. Force commanders rarely had the chance to meet with staff prior to arrival in the field. In 1978, *The Peacekeeper's Handbook* noted that "pre-planning or advanced preparation has never been part of the UN policy with regard to international peacekeeping."[80]

While peacekeepers generally had to conduct military planning on the go, the political groundwork that was previously laid in initial negotiations between the United Nations, the contributing nations, and the belligerents or host nations greatly affected military operations. The traditional peacekeeping mission, a passive mission meant to assist conflict resolution, had to accept the operational inconveniences of the political constraints imposed by these negotiations. For instance, when traditional peacekeeping troops occupied a border region, the United Nations normally insisted that the force be allowed freedom of movement on both sides of the border. As noted in the UNIIMOG case study, this often was denied. Similarly, in UNEF I, Israel refused to let the UN forces deploy on its side of the border and they remained deployed exclusively on Egyptian territory for the duration of the mission.[81]

However, in most missions the UN peacekeeping force was given free run of an interpositional buffer zone. The difference between a demilitarized zone (as in UNIIMOG) and a buffer zone is simple, but militarily profound. A buffer zone is physically occupied and controlled by a military force.[82] The buffer zone in most traditional peacekeeping missions had several distinguishing characteristics. First, it was a neutral zone that was denied to the belligerents for movement within or transgression across. Second, it was usually linear in shape, often ending at international borders or significant physical features (the sea, for instance). Third, it was occupied by a small force, whose low force-to-space ratio would not permit the force to occupy the zone as for conventional defensive operations.

Buffer zones in traditional peacekeeping missions never had enough UN forces to defeat a concerted offensive action by one of the parties. The UN force's role in deterrence was based on its moral and political authority. This authority in turn depended on the legitimacy the UN forces had among the local factions. The United Nations hoped that this legitimacy and authority would be manifested in the good will of the belligerents in honoring the integrity of the buffer zone. The UN forces occupying the buffer zones served to prevent incidental flare-ups of violence that could occur between forces in close proximity to each other and ensured that no large-scale transgressions escaped the notice of the international community. The presence of a neutral and impartial force in the buffer zone fostered trust among the belligerents that the principal provisions of the cease-fire would be observed and recorded by a legitimate authority. As analyst Mona Ghali has written about the second Sinai peacekeeping mission, "UNEF II's presence was sufficiently useful in helping to build and maintain confidence on both sides so that their cautious steps toward peace could not easily be undone by random border incidents or unseen buildups of military force."[83]

The traditional peacekeeping force was not a military force that used its military power directly to arrest all armed conflict. Rather, the force's passive, firm, fair, and impartial operations served to defuse and de-escalate small incidents, as well as discourage major transgressions. As UN scholar Ramesh Thakur noted,

> *traditional peacekeeping operations were more akin to armed*
> *police work than standard combat. Success for the military*
> *means battlefield victory or surrender by the enemy.*

> *Peacekeeping forces had no [such] military objectives: they*
> *were barred from active combat, located between rather than*
> *in opposition to hostile elements, and required to negotiate*
> *rather than fight.*[84]

Bearing this in mind, one can appreciate the small size of traditional peace-keeping forces, who were not required in large numbers as they might be for combat. For instance, the UNEF I commander who asked for a brigade of peace-keepers estimated that he would need at least an infantry division, a tank brigade, and fighter aircraft to forcibly separate the factions in the Sinai in 1956.[85] Indeed, the force-to-space ratios in traditional peacekeeping missions would be considered dire if the peacekeeping force was to occupy and defend the buffer zone in a conventional military sense. In UNEF I, five battalions of infantry manned seventy-two observation posts along the 59 kilometers of the Armistice Demarcation Line around the Gaza strip. This was an adequate ratio of force to space in terms of the Blue Helmets' being able to control the territory under their mandate. However, the other two battalions of UNEF I had to patrol an international border some 214 kilometers long, running motorized patrols between only eight outposts. In addition, another 187 kilometers of international border were observed only by UNEF I aircraft.[86]

The buffer zone in Cyprus, in 1993 patrolled by less than 1,000 troops, extended 180 kilometers from coast to coast and varied in width from 20 meters in the streets of Nicosia to 7 kilometers elsewhere.[87] Since such a small force, even when it was at peak strength, could not physically defend such a zone, UNFICYP also had to rely on a system of mobile patrols and observation posts to monitor the buffer zone. By way of contrast, the U.S. Army estimates that a battalion of light infantry (some 500 soldiers) can effectively "defend" a front only some 5 to 8 kilometers long in ideal terrain.[88] This highlights once again that the legitimacy of traditional peacekeeping forces was not gained from being able to military defeat an armed transgression of the buffer zone. Such a mission might require three to four combat divisions for the Cyprus mission alone. As peacekeeper John Mackinlay noted,

> *Unlike a unit in a combat situation, the peacekeeping force*
> cannot therefore create the conditions for its own success, *it is*
> *acting rather in the role of an umpire or a referee. In this situ-*
> *ation, the referee's success is determined mainly by the consent*
> *of the players, only to a small degree by the quality of the rules*
> *which govern the game, and never by the pugilistic skills of the*
> *referee himself. [my emphasis]*[89]

Although traditional peacekeeping forces occupied a buffer zone, their powers were essentially limited to those exercised by observation missions. UNEF I's initial interpositional force between Egyptian and Anglo-French troops was "limited to investigating, reporting, and, if warranted, protesting to the relevant authorities."[90]

The buffer zone was an inert and physical barrier between belligerents, but traditional peacekeeping forces could also make their influence felt outside the area of occupation. The buffer zones in UNEF II and UNDOF made provision for zones of inspection just outside the buffer zone, where the belligerents were limited to a certain number and types of armaments, all of which were subject to inspection by UN peacekeepers or observers.

In some missions, particularly UNEF I and II, the buffer zone was expanded as belligerents withdrew their forces further from the area of confrontation. In these cases, the UN peacekeepers shadowed the movements of the withdrawing forces and incorporated the new areas into their operations. These missions essentially consisted of relief-in-place operations as the belligerents withdrew and the United Nations assumed control of the territory. Of course, these operations sometimes resulted in an even weaker ratio of force to space as the territory under UN control increased. For instance, a September 1975 agreement between Egypt and Israel made provisions for a further disengagement of their forces. This effectively increased the UN's area of responsibility by a third when the forces were reduced to almost half of UNEF II's peak strength.[91]

If the linear buffer zone is effectively controlled at its borders, the added territory in the middle is not likely to cause an operational challenge. This was especially true in the sparsely populated buffer zones of UNEF I and II. However, in the case of a more populated buffer zone, where the free movement of civilians must be allowed, this can be more problematic. This was a great problem for the mission to Lebanon as outlined in the subsequent case study. In general, a sparsely populated linear buffer zone provided the United Nations with a mechanism through which a small, lightly armed, and disparate group of peacekeepers could make a direct contribution to limiting armed conflict in the area.

Other Tasks

Secondary and other implied tasks of traditional peacekeeping missions are noted here but not explored at length. As this study focuses on the strategy of UN military missions, it will not provide a detailed tactical analysis of the military or nonmilitary tasks of traditional peacekeeping. The strategy of traditional peacekeeping missions is essentially defined by the operations of the interpositional buffer zone.[92] However, traditional peacekeeping forces also performed other very important tasks that contributed to continued stability in their area of operations and complemented their interpositional operations as well.

As noted, it was easiest for a traditional peacekeeping force to patrol a buffer zone in a nonpopulated or sparsely populated area. However, when that force was deployed in a populated area, it often performed other tasks that involved the local populace. For instance, when the initial contingents of UNEF I were deployed to the Port Said area to interpose themselves between the Egyptians and the British and French, they were given the mission to maintain civil order in cooperation with local authorities.[93] A few months later, upon moving into the Gaza strip to supervise the withdrawal of Israeli forces there, they also incurred other temporary responsibilities for maintaining civil order. UNIFIL also was tasked with duties in this area.

Providing humanitarian aid also was an implied task for traditional peace-keepers from the very beginning of peacekeeping. In UNEF I, the UN troops in the Port Said area were tasked with performing "administrative functions with respect to public services, utilities, and arrangements for the provisioning of the local population with foodstuffs."[94] UNEF II was specifically tasked with assisting the Red Cross in its humanitarian endeavors in the area.[95] UNFICYP conducted a whole range of humanitarian tasks, including the delivery of postal and other services to Turkish and Greek enclaves within southern and northern Cyprus, respectively.[96]

Other tasks frequently performed by traditional peacekeepers included clearing minefields (UNEF I, UNEF II, UNIFIL), assisting in prisoner of war exchanges (UNEF I, UNEF II, UNFICYP, UNDOF), and helping repair local infrastructure damaged by conflict (UNEF I, UNFICYP, UNIFIL).[97] The implied tasks of traditional peacekeeping have always complemented the principal objective of these operations, maintaining the physical separation of belligerents through the control of an interpositional buffer zone. In second-generation peacekeeping missions, the scale of these secondary and implied tasks greatly increased, as second-generation peacekeeping forces tended to deploy to heavily populated areas within deteriorating states.

Conclusion

With the collapse of the negotiations over Article 43 forces in 1947–1948, the United Nations lost any hope of becoming a direct player in international military affairs. Instead, the organization improvised a secondary military role in which it recruited small numbers of forces from member states and deployed them in modest military operations such as traditional peacekeeping. Because the United Nations did not have the political legitimacy and military authority to mount, direct, and employ large, complex, or active military operations, it needed to invent a military technique that, given its political constraints, it could manage. Alan James has noted that peacekeeping was exactly such a secondary activity, one that was "dependent, in respect of both its origins and its success, on the wishes and policies of others. In appropriate circumstances peacekeeping [could] make a valuable contribution to peace—but only if, and to the extent to which, disputants choose to take advantage of it."[98]

The United Nations (as an institution that managed military operations) and peacekeeping evolved together. This chapter has highlighted that the United Nations' ability to recruit, organize, deploy, and direct the operations of military forces was constrained by its very nature as a voluntary multinational institution with no dedicated military resources and very limited authority. As such, the politically influenced and militarily modest activity of peacekeeping was an operation well suited (along with observation missions) for the limited military management capabilities of the United Nations. The question remains however, did this experiment work? Did these missions contribute to the United Nations' charge to "maintain international peace and security?"

Of the traditional peacekeeping missions treated here and in the case study, only one can truly be labeled a failure in its efforts to limit armed conflict. That mission is UNIFIL, and the explicit analysis of this assessment is contained in Chapter Five. UNEF I, UNSF, UNFICYP, UNEF II, UNDOF, and UNPREDEP all contributed significantly to the easing of tensions in their area of operations and the continued maintenance of relative peace. "Relative" is used because throughout the history of these missions, there were many low-level incidents and minor transgressions against their mandate. Over thirty years after its inception, for instance, the mission in Cyprus is "still confronted with hundreds of incidents per year."[99]

In the strategic sense, however, these tactical breaches of the peace did not detract from the overall stability the peacekeeping forces helped to sustain. Some critics have argued that UNEF I cannot be considered a success, because Nassar ordered the peacekeepers removed in May 1967, to pursue military plans against Israel. As a result, the six-day war was waged in the Middle East unimpeded by UN troops. However, it has been recognized through this chapter and in the examination of observation missions that the consent and cooperation of the belligerents was the chief operational imperative of traditional peacekeeping. UNEF I helped keep the peace for over ten years before its removal, and its removal came as a result of political machinations that in no way reflected on its previous ability to limit armed conflict. James notes the qualified definition of success that must be used with such a modest operation.

> *What UNEF I did not do during its 10 years on the Egyptian-Israeli border, therefore, was to keep the peace. Rather, it helped these two states to implement their temporary disposi-*

tion to live in peace. It was a derivative rather than a substantive obstruction to the worsening of the situation, making a secondary rather than a primary contribution to peace. But that is not at all to say that it was of little importance.[100]

Here one sees the inextricable connection between the two missions of peacekeeping: to limit armed conflict and promote conflict resolution. As Mona Ghali noted, "a peacekeeping force that helps to preserve a cease-fire can give diplomats the time to find settlements that address the political problems that underpin a conflict."[101] As recognized in the Introduction, the vast bulk of literature in this area analyzes the latter objective of peacekeeping. Because that story is told elsewhere, this chapter has focused on the way in which the United Nations attempted to accomplish the first objective and on the political and military factors that influenced and framed those efforts.

In the planning and execution of traditional peacekeeping missions, the United Nations proved that, despite the need to improvise to overcome political stalemates and institutional limitations, it could manage successful, albeit limited, military missions. The keys to success in traditional peacekeeping missions were the impartiality of the force, the recognition by all sides of the moral authority and passive military capability of peacekeeping forces in a clearly defined linear buffer zone, and, of course, the cooperation of the belligerents. In short, success hinged on the separation of the willing belligerents through a buffer zone controlled by an "alert, but inert" UN presence.

Paul Diehl finds that his studies "clearly indicate that peacekeeping is most effective in disputes between state members of the international system" and that "interstate disputants are more easily identified and separated across internationally recognized borders or militarily defined cease-fire lines."[102] In the UNIFIL case study, it will be seen that well-intentioned traditional peacekeeping can founder in a nonsupportive political environment that does not fulfill Diehl's requirements. In a contested environment, especially one in which bellicose nonstate groups were key actors, the principles that formed the doctrine of traditional peacekeeping were found wanting. The principles of peacekeeping evolved as they did because, in large measure, they suited the unique nature and constraints of the United Nations as a military manager. However, they would not be equally germane to every crisis the United Nations would be called upon to address. The remainder of this book looks at those crises where the political preconditions that made UN military successes possible were not present.

CHAPTER 5

Peacekeeping in Southern Lebanon (1978–1996)

The United Nations Interim Force in Lebanon (UNIFIL) is a poignant case study of traditional peacekeeping missions for several reasons. On the one hand, UNIFIL was a good example of traditional peacekeeping because it was formed, directed, and employed based on the principles of peacekeeping. The political and strategic tenets that determined its force structure, command and control structure, and military objectives were derived from the practice of successful traditional peacekeeping missions. On the other hand, the mission took place in a contested and often bellicose environment. This greatly complicated UNIFIL's operations and severely tested traditional peacekeeping methods.

More important for this study, the challenges to UNIFIL also tested the United Nations' ability to manage military operations in unsupportive environments. These challenges of UNIFIL's operational environment proved too much for a traditional military operation that followed the principles of peacekeeping. Detailing the frustration and failures of UNIFIL not only provides insights on traditional peacekeeping, but also serves as a helpful transition to examining second-generation peacekeeping missions. In many respects, elements of UNIFIL's mission came to resemble those of second-generation missions. The presence of many warring and hostile nonstate factions in UNIFIL's area of operations, the ill-defined quasi-linear and heavily populated buffer zone, and the later focus on protecting humanitarian aid were all characteristics of second-generation peacekeeping missions. The inability of this traditional peacekeeping mission to deal with this nontraditional environment led to many of the changes in UN peacekeeping practice that are examined in Chapters Six and Seven.

Creating UNIFIL

The intensely complicated, destabilizing, and fractious politics that have characterized southern Lebanon since the early 1970s will not be recounted here. It is, however, important to note the principal factions that would exercise great influence on UNIFIL operations in southern Lebanon. Since the Cairo agreement of 1969, which (at least for Palestinians) legitimized a Palestinian Liberation Organization (PLO) presence in Lebanon, the PLO had been using southern Lebanon as a base from which to launch attacks on northern Israel. The Israeli Defense Force (IDF) frequently retaliated in kind and the situation was defined throughout the 1970s by sporadic aggression and heightened tension in the region. Despite attempts to reach cease-fire agreements (most notably in 1976), the situation remained explosive.

On 11 March 1978, the PLO seized an Israeli bus south of Haifa and in the ensuing clash with Israeli security forces, nine PLO guerrillas were killed along with thirty-seven Israeli citizens. With public hysteria running high in Israel, the IDF launched an invasion of Lebanon three days later, on the night of 14–15 March 1978. The IDF advanced to the Litani River (see Map 3) and occupied all of Lebanon south of the Litani with the exception of a strong PLO pocket around the city of Tyre. That day the government of Lebanon lodged a strong protest against the invasion with the UN Security Council. The Security Council met at Lebanon's request on 17 March to consider the issue, and the United States took the lead in drafting a resolution that could help ameliorate the situation.

The principal factor that motivated the urgent U.S. call for Security Council action was a desire to avoid damaging the Camp David peace conference between Egypt and Israel, scheduled to start on 21 March. There was therefore much U.S. pressure in the Security Council to create immediately a UN peacekeeping force for southern Lebanon. Brian Urquhart, then under secretary-general for special political affairs (and therefore entrusted with all peacekeeping missions) had strong reservations about placing a peacekeeping force in a contested environment where the consent and cooperation of the belligerents could not be ensured. He wrote,

> The hard facts of the situation militated against deploying such a force. Government authority, an important condition for successful peacekeeping, did not exist in southern Lebanon, where a tribal, inter-confessional guerrilla war was raging. The terrain of southern Lebanon was ideal for guerrilla activity and very difficult for conventional forces. The PLO, a dominating factor in the area, was under no formal authority. Another important element, the Israeli-sponsored Christian militia of the volatile Major Saad Haddad, though illegal, would certainly be supported by Israel. A force of the size and with the mandate necessary for the job was unlikely to be agreed upon by the Security Council.

Southern Lebanon would almost certainly be a peacekeeper's nightmare.[1]

Despite the misgivings of the United Nations' top peacekeeping official, the United States and its allies quickly drafted a Security Council resolution that was passed (with abstentions by the USSR and Czechoslovakia) as Resolution 425 on 19 March 1978. The resolution established a UN interim force for southern Lebanon. The broad mandate given to this force required it "to confirm the withdrawal of Israeli forces, restore international peace and security, and assist the government of Lebanon in ensuring the return of its effective authority in the area."[2] More important for operational considerations, the last paragraph of the resolution asked the secretary-general to submit a plan to implement this resolution within twenty-four hours.

Brian Urquhart and his staff had less than a day to propose an operational plan for UNIFIL that would include its area of operations, strength and composition, command structure, control procedures, military objectives, and modus operandi. Peacekeeper J. D. Murray observed that, "as is normal practice, [the UN] had no written contingency plan on which the establishment, deployment and support of UNIFIL could be based."[3]

In past UN missions, much of the planning work on such missions had been carried out by a technical team or some other advance contingent that could evaluate the situation on the ground before recommending the necessary operational parameters of the mission itself. However, with UNIFIL, UN scholar Bjorn Skogmo noted that "Resolution 425 did not ask the Secretary-General to carry out any feasibility study on the establishment of UNIFIL. Instead he was [only] requested through operative paragraph 4 of resolution 425 to report back to the Council within 24 hours."[4]

The operational drawbacks of this ad hoc method will become clear in this chapter. Mission planning is a deliberate process that is designed to eliminate as many operational uncertainties as possible, uncertainties that might jeopardize achieving a military force's mission once it is in the area of operations. To the greatest extent possible, a thorough study of the operational environment, the mandate, and the capabilities of the forces is undertaken to form the basic assumptions on which an operational plan can be formed. This deliberate planning process attempts to recognize all factors that could have an impact on mission effectiveness and plan for them accordingly. A thorough planning process for the UN Secretariat would have included analyzing the mission, issuing planning guidance to the staff, creating and thoroughly analyzing courses of action, choosing a course of action, making an estimate of the situation, drafting a concept of operations, and finally coordinating with all relevant parties to complete an operational plan.[5] Key elements in this deliberate planning process would include the participation of the actual force commander and his staff, a reconnaissance of the area of operations itself, and explicit negotiations with the local parties involved.

Naturally, none of these critical steps could be accomplished within twenty-four hours, and the "terms of reference" that were UNIFIL's operational basis reflected this rushed, ad hoc, and incomplete planning. As an operational guideline, the United Nations used the terms of reference for UNEF II and UNDOF, two traditional (and ongoing) peacekeeping missions considered "satisfactory" by the United Nations.[6] The effect of UNIFIL's terms of reference on force structure, command and control, and military objectives are examined below. What should be noted here, however, is that this initial plan for UNIFIL was, in reality, just further planning guidance for UNIFIL. Most of the planning would have to be worked out in the field and on the go. When the Security Council voted on UNIFIL, the area of operations was yet to be defined, a preliminary estimate of troop strength was proposed based on past missions, and only very broad and ambiguous military objectives and modi operandi were discussed.

The operationally vague terms of reference for UNIFIL could not be avoided if they were expected to be produced within one day at UN headquarters in New York. Therefore, UNIFIL's terms of reference represented only the first two steps of a military planning process: analyze the mission and issue planning guidance. In the meantime, UNIFIL's first contingents were deploying to southern Lebanon within days of the issuance of the terms of reference. The UNIFIL commander never even had the chance to meet with his contingent commanders for a dedicated planning session prior to their deployment.

This rush occurred as a result of the perceived political need to force a course of action through the Security Council and get UN troops on the ground in Lebanon. As Bjorn Skogmo noted at the time, "The Security Council can only act effectively if such moments of relative international consensus—which do not come very often in the Council nowadays—are exploited and transformed into decisions. There was therefore considerable satisfaction in the SC over the quick decision to establish UNIFIL."[7]

The terms of reference for UNIFIL listed three essential conditions for the success of the mission: (1) it must have the full backing of the Security Council; (2) it must operate with the full cooperation of the parties on the ground; and (3) "it must be able to function as an integrated and efficient military unit."[8] Some observers have argued that, despite the Security Council's rapid approval of UNIFIL (and continued extension of UNIFIL's mandate), the first condition has not always been present.[9] This study examines the second and third conditions in greater detail. It will be seen that neither condition was met to an extent where UNIFIL could be classified as an operational success.

The rush to establish UNIFIL ignored very important operational considerations that had always been key imperatives of peacekeeping missions. In particular, clearly defining the area of operations and ensuring that the UN force would have the consent and cooperation of the local factions were not explicitly addressed before initial elements of UNIFIL began deployment. The United Nations itself recognized that "these two questions weighed heavily on the operations of UNIFIL."[10] However, as Brian Urquhart recalls, these practical considerations were "swept aside" by the determination to push through a quick decision.[11]

It is doubtful whether UNIFIL might ever have been created in its present form if the deliberate planning process had been followed. In that case, one could assume that operational considerations would have been brought to the attention of the secretary-general, who would have to report two very important facts to the Security Council. First, the bellicosity and uncontrollability of the local factions in southern Lebanon were not conducive to traditional peacekeeping operations and the United Nations' emphasis on consent and cooperation. As Doran Kochavi noted, the operational environment in Lebanon was more akin to that confronting "the United Nations Congo Force of almost twenty years before."[12]

Second, and in relation to that environment, the terrain and military objectives of UNIFIL's mandate necessitated a force far larger than that considered "normal" by the Security Council for traditional peacekeeping missions. As is seen below, military requirements centered solely on meeting the mandate of Resolution 425 would have demanded a force closer in size and strength to that of the Congo operation (20,000) than that in the Sinai (7,000). However, the political imperatives and conditions that influence UN missions are paramount and could not be so easily dismissed. Because all the parties concerned with the situation in southern Lebanon were reluctant to accept a large force, UNIFIL was structured and employed as a small, traditional peacekeeping force. No one in the United Nations had a desire for a repeat of the Congo episode, one that William Durch said "was nearly as searing for the UN as the Vietnam War [was] for the United States."[13]

Despite Under Secretary-General Urquhart's concerns and the lack of advanced political or military planning, UNIFIL was quickly established. The broad parameters and hopeful assumptions of the terms of reference were necessary for the mission to gain even token approval by the Security Council and the local states concerned. This political expediency, conducted in the face of operational reality, had a lasting effect on the development, direction, and conduct of UNIFIL's operations.

Force Structure of UNIFIL

Composition

The force structure of UNIFIL was based initially on the light infantry battalion, the basic unit for peacekeeping since UNEF I in 1956. UNIFIL's terms of reference specified that the forces would "be provided with weapons of a defensive character."[14] As such, UNIFIL's initial infantry contingents had only personal firearms and some light crew-served weapons such as machine guns. However, as the mission evolved, considerable disparity in organization, equipment, and capability grew in UNIFIL. For instance, as the bellicosity of UNIFIL's area of operations became apparent, the French and Irish battalions deployed with heavier machine guns, light mortars, and one French antitank recoilless rifle.[15]

The heaviest weapon in UNIFIL's inventory was the 120-mm mortars that were an organic fire support component of the Dutch battalion. These mortars were not used by UNIFIL, even in cases of self-defense, because of the fear that a stray shell might cause collateral damage in the heavily populated UNIFIL buffer zone. However, some contingents eventually used heavier weapon systems. In particular, the Dutch contingent used antitank guided missiles (TOWs) in self-defense and the incursion of armed belligerents in their sector decreased markedly.[16]

In addition, some UNIFIL contingents deployed infantry battalions equipped with armored personnel carriers and armored reconnaissance vehicles. This change came about in 1979, as hostile incidents directed against UNIFIL forces increased.[17] In response to the belligerency of the environment, UNIFIL formed a "Force Mobile Reserve" composed of armored platoons from several different nations.[18] For some countries, such as NATO members that trained almost exclusively for heavily armored battles in Europe, this sort of armored component was standard in infantry units. For other components, especially from developing countries, light infantry included no armored vehicles at all. The inclusion of "heavy" units into a traditional peacekeeping structure was undertaken in UNIFIL for force protection. However, it should be noted that such a change in composition has major ramifications in logistics, administration, interoperability, and finances. Such a move also greatly increases the challenge to the United Nations, as a strategic manager, of recruiting and organizing peacekeeping forces. The more militarily sophisticated the national forces, the harder it was to recruit and form ad hoc operations that were neutral, representative of all UN member states, and capable of integrated and coordinated operations. This phenomenon is examined in detail in the chapters on second-generation peacekeeping missions.

Realizing that the ratio of force to space was too great to provide efficient observation of the UNIFIL area of operation, in 1979 some UNIFIL contingents introduced sophisticated surveillance devices. These included night-vision devices and ground surveillance radars that could multiply the effectiveness of the limited number of troops sent to observe and control the area. UNIFIL did not use its air component for reconnaissance, which meant observation was purely a ground-based activity. Throughout its mandate, UNIFIL experienced problems receiving flight clearance from the IDF, which controlled the air space over southern Lebanon.[19]

Although UNIFIL infantry battalions formed the core of the mission, other units were deployed in support of these battalions. Medical, logistics, maintenance, aviation, administration, and signal detachments not organic to battalions were part of UNIFIL and generally remained consolidated at UNIFIL headquarters. In addition, a multinational guard detachment of about 100 Blue Helmets from eight countries maintained the only UNIFIL presence in Tyre.[20] This detachment served a purely symbolic function in the PLO-dominated area and eventually was reduced in strength and manned by rotations of small elements from UNIFIL's infantry battalions.

In addition to those UNIFIL units, elements of other UN missions in the area were used to complement and supplement UNIFIL. In the initial stages of the deployment, these included a Swedish infantry company from UNEF II in the Sinai and an Iranian infantry company from UNDOF in the Golan Heights. In addition, a Canadian movement control team and a signals unit were sent to the area from UNEF II.[21] These units were already in the Middle East and already under UN authority and could be immediately deployed to southern Lebanon. Like other traditional peacekeeping missions, UNIFIL's force structure was reinforced by unarmed observers attached to UNIFIL from the UNTSO observation mission. Last, UNIFIL had operational control of some Lebanese Army personnel. In April 1979, 500 Lebanese soldiers enhanced the force structure of UNIFIL. This number grew to 1,350 in June 1982 but was soon rapidly depleted by the crises in Beirut and the relative lack of authority associated with the Lebanese government and, by extension, these forces. By 1983, there were only 100 Lebanese army personnel assisting UNIFIL in their mission.[22]

Size

The initial terms of reference for UNIFIL specified a force of approximately 4,000 peacekeepers. As noted, this figure was based on overnight planning by the staff of the under secretary-general for special political affairs in New York. They specified that "in order that the Force may fulfill its responsibilities, it is considered, as a preliminary estimate, that it must have at least five battalions each of about 600 all ranks, in addition to the necessary logistics units."[23] Once UNIFIL officers were on the ground in southern Lebanon, however, it was quite obvious that five battalions would not make much of an impact in the still-to-be-defined area of operations.

On 1 May 1978, the secretary-general requested that the Security Council increase the force by three battalions and some additional logistics support, to a total of 6,000 [Table 5]. He wrote,

> During my tour of the area of operations with the Force Commander, I met all the contingent Commanders and they reported to us that the present inadequate strength level of the Force resulted in an exceedingly thin deployment of their troops on the ground. Taking all these factors into account, it is my considered opinion that it is necessary to increase the strength of UNIFIL to the level of about 6,000 for this very crucial stage of the operation if the Force is to be in a position to carry out fully and effectively the tasks entrusted to it by the Security Council under resolution 425.[24]

The Security Council approved this change two days later in Resolution 427, and UNIFIL continued with approximately 6,000 troops until the Israeli invasion of 1982, when the Security Council approved a final ceiling of 7,000 for the rest of UNIFIL's mandate.[25]

The size of the UNIFIL force structure, like most observation and peacekeeping missions, was more a factor of political requirements than military practicality. As noted earlier, one planning method used by military force planners is the METT-T formula: considerations of mission, enemy, terrain, time, and troops available. By just using the military planning formula of METT-T, one can appreciate the operational limitations of a force this size.

The *mission* tasked UNIFIL with confirming Israeli troop withdrawal, preventing a recurrence of fighting, restoring peace and stability to the area, and assisting the government of Lebanon in a return to authority. The *"enemy"* forces in this case were the belligerents involved in the fighting and consisted of thousands of PLO guerrillas,[26] the whole of the Israeli invasion force of several divisions, and the thousands of Christian militia of Major Saad Haddad (known to the United Nations as the "de facto forces (DFF)."[27] The *terrain* consisted of over 650 square miles of rugged hills extending down to the sea.[28] As military planning measures, these three factors mitigated against a small force and pointed to the need for a much larger UN mission.

In contrast, *time* and *troops available* were factors that limited UNIFIL's size. The political urgency for deployment demanded a rapid UN presence, easier to achieve with a small force. In addition, although finding contributing member states was not a problem at the outset, available troops soon became an issue.

Table 5

The UN Peacekeepers in Lebanon, December 1979*

Unit	Number of Troops
Fijian Infantry Battalion	658
Ghanaian Infantry Battalion	300
Irish Infantry Battalion	653
Nepalese Infantry Battalion	644
Dutch Infantry Battalion	865
Nigerian Infantry Battalion	700
Norwegian Infantry Battalion	659
Senegalese Infantry Battalion	591
Irish Headquarters Company	47
Ghanaian Headquarters Company	57
French Engineer Company	94
French Logistics Battalion	524
Italian Air Contingent	33
Norwegian Medical Company/Maintenance Company	301
Total	**6,126**

Note: *Typical Force Structure for UNIFIL, 1978–1993.

Source: S/13691, Report of the Secretary-General on UNIFIL for the Period 9 June–10 December 1979.

By 1979, "Canada and Austria were aware of the dangers inherent in the Lebanese crisis and with so many unpredictable forces fighting one another advised the Secretary-General that they would be reluctant to contribute units until an effective cease-fire agreement was reached. Both Mexico and Bolivia promised troops but withdrew their offer to provide them because of the danger of renewed fighting."[29]

However, the luxury of planning in an operational vacuum was not available to the United Nations. Traditional UN peacekeeping, with its emphasis on consent, cooperation, impartiality, and passive operations, was very much a diplomatic activity that required quasi-military tools. In consequence, and like all such missions, UNIFIL's size was influenced more by the political atmosphere of its creation than by the military necessities of its mission. The operational requirements of peacekeeping missions had to be subordinated to the political and diplomatic conditions at hand.

The successful peacekeeping missions of the past had been conducted with forces of no more than 7,000. Those operations set a precedent that became an important standard for the Security Council. Politically, creating a much larger force would have undoubtedly unnerved an already reluctant Israel and a hesitant USSR. The number 7,000 also came to be considered a de facto limit for the size force that the small staff on the UN secretariat could recruit, organize, deploy, and control through its improvised procedures. William Durch, among other observers, postulates that this was due to both the perceived successes of similarly sized missions in the Sinai and the abject failure of the very large mission in the Congo.[30] Thus, despite an environment and mission that seemed to require a larger force, UNIFIL's size would remain consistent with accepted peacekeeping standards. Only a buoyant mood in the post–Cold War Security Council and an aggressive secretary-general would see this standard broken some fourteen years later.

That the strength of UNIFIL did not change throughout the rest of its operational life is an important characteristic of traditional peacekeeping. Once the initial impotence of UNIFIL became evident, military logic would have insisted that the force be increased to meet the challenges of the operations (or at least the mandate be reduced to match the capabilities of such a small force).[31] To struggle on with a small force in a mission with large challenges was a self-inflicted concession to the principles of peacekeeping. There was no thought of putting together a large military force bent on coercing the belligerents into an accepted pattern of behavior (as in the Congo).

The size of the military force for a particular mission can be determined in three ways: first, upon deciding the mission requirements, one can structure forces specifically to accomplish that mission. Second, if one has a strict limit on the number and type of forces involved, one can limit objectives to meet the capabilities of that force. Third, one can fix requirements and fix force levels in a degree of exclusion from one another and then hope that one can meet the other. Unfortunately for UNIFIL, its force structure planning reflected the third case. The political assumptions in the planning process that created UNIFIL were all important to its structure. The crux of those assumptions was that UNIFIL would receive the cooperation of the belligerents on the ground. When that cooperation did not come about, UNIFIL was forced to soldier on with a greatly understrength force.

Equitable Geographic Representation

As with all observation and traditional peacekeeping missions, this long-standing principle greatly influenced the international composition of UNIFIL. The secretary-general, in assembling the force, told the Security Council that "the contingents of UNIFIL would be selected in consultation with the Security Council, and with the parties concerned, bearing in mind the accepted principle of equitable geographic representation."[32] In following this principle, the secretary-general requested units from member states in Western Europe, Asia, Africa, the Americas, and Oceania.

All the contingents initially represented in UNIFIL were from so-called middle powers, in keeping with the fourth principle of peacekeeping. Sweden, Canada, Fiji, Ireland, Nepal, Nigeria, Norway, and Senegal all seemed excellent candidates for the role of honest broker in that their national governments were not connected with the fractious political struggles in the Middle East. Even the Iranian contingent, then serving the government of the Shah, was not seen as a political player in the area. Naturally, this changed after the fundamentalist revolution of the Ayatollah Khomeini in Iran, and the Iranian contingent was withdrawn.[33] The one exception to the apparent neutrality of all the contingents was the participation of the French in providing both an infantry battalion and a logistics detachment to UNIFIL. However, as noted in the previous chapter, France, as a former colonial power, had a precedent in this action because of British participation in UNFICYP.

It was not the intention of "equitable geographic representation" to have tactical repercussions beyond supporting the unquestioned impartiality of the UN force, but the tactical and operational decisions taken by UNIFIL were influenced by the geopolitical force structure of the mission. As Doran Kochavi noted,

> Realizing the diverse interests among the protagonists, the political/religious composition of contingents was taken into consideration by the force commander during the early stages of the deployment of the various contingents of UNIFIL.

> *Therefore, the Shia Moslem Iranian battalion was deployed in*
> *the Shia Moslem dominant area. Likewise, Irish and French*
> *forces were deployed on Christian dominant areas.[34]*

In addition to this policy of trying to enhance operational success by politically savvy deployments, the mission was responsive to political sensitivities that were manifested as a result of hostile actions. For instance, in 1988, after the kidnapping of an American Marine officer, UNIFIL agreed with the U.S. government request that all American UNTSO observers assigned to support UNIFIL be reassigned to other UNTSO areas.[35]

Another effect of equitable geographic representation was the effort needed to maintain this desired balance of forces throughout a long-running (and dangerous) mission. UNIFIL, more so than other traditional peacekeeping missions, was beset by force turbulence, with forces coming and going in line with the decisions of national governments and many times in contravention to the United Nations' preference. This phenomenon is examined in detail below as a ramification of the United Nations' restricted ability to command national military forces. However, in terms of force structure, the constant turnover of forces, coupled with the principle of equitable geographic representation, meant that a continual effort was needed in the UN Secretariat to recruit new forces from the world over for UNIFIL. All in all, managing the force structure of a peacekeeping mission such as the one to southern Lebanon would have been a difficult enough challenge without having to factor in global and local political requirements and sensitivities. Adding those ingredients to the pot made it a complicated stew indeed.

Interoperability

The force structure of UNIFIL was a product of political requirements such as the consent of the belligerents and the policy of equitable geographic representation. As such, it was an extremely diverse force in terms of training, doctrine, tactical methods, equipment, planning procedures, command and control processes, and even intangible factors such as soldiers' perspectives about and attitudes toward their mission. This was the norm for UN military operations because they were formed from scratch.

UNIFIL was no exception, and the problems of an ad hoc formation were exacerbated by the urgency to deploy a force into the volatile environment of southern Lebanon. Once on the ground, the contingents had to try and invent the control procedures and modus operandi that are discussed below. The UNIFIL force commander complained that there were no "staff college or other textbook solutions for the sort of operational difficulties that confronted us from day to day."[36] With no common UN training program, staff school, or even standard operating procedures produced and circulated by the United

Nations until 1991, every UNIFIL contingent brought its own methods, procedures, and perspectives to the mission.

Light infantry battalions were the simplest components of most armies, but
they did differ in capability, training, organization, equipment, and techniques
throughout the world. As a consequence, the battalions in UNIFIL had a fairly
high degree of disparity in their operational capabilities and organization. Some
contingents came with well-trained and professional soldiers, fully equipped
with all manner of modern equipment and organic support. Other units arrived
with poorly trained conscripts who had only personal weapons. Many of these
contingents needed the equipment and supply contributions of other countries to
perform even the most basic operations.

Transforming the diverse contingents of UNIFIL into a cohesive and efficient military force would be challenging in almost any operational environment. Doing it in the bellicose and chaotic setting of southern Lebanon
exacerbated the traditional foibles of UN force interoperability. The problems
of interoperability that were brought about by the force structure of UNIFIL are
discussed in two areas examined below: command and control, and military
objectives and operations.

Command and Control of UNIFIL

Chain of Command

The chain of command for UNIFIL was typical for that of most UN missions up
to 1978 (Figure 5). As such, it was subject to many of the same problems that
had been features of the United Nations' traditional peacekeeping and observation missions. Because of the loose and temporary operational control relationship, the United Nations could not authoritatively control how and when
national contingents came and went from the mission. In addition, UNIFIL was
plagued by competition between the UNIFIL chain of command and national
chains of command. This problem became more prevalent and more serious
when UNIFIL was confronted with significant challenges to its mandate in
southern Lebanon. UNIFIL's chain of command also suffered from a series of
tactical problems caused by its rushed deployment and lack of local authority in
its ill-defined area of operations. Overall, UNIFIL found it difficult to achieve
unity of command, a military condition characterized by a responsive and
authoritative chain of command that confidently directs the integrated and coordinated efforts of its forces. In simple and innocuous UN military missions, the
lack of concrete authority over national contingents in UN missions was not a
critical factor. However, in a bellicose atmosphere, such as southern Lebanon,
effectively directing peacekeeping operations was a far more challenging task.

Figure 5

Chain of Command in the Mission to Lebanon

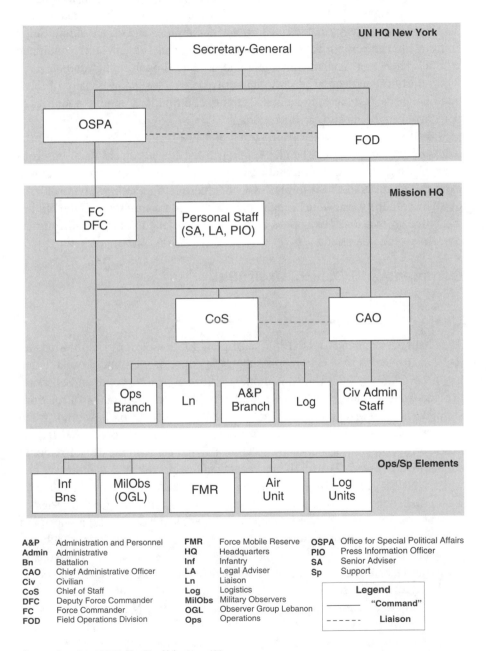

A&P	Administration and Personnel	
Admin	Administrative	
Bn	Battalion	
CAO	Chief Administrative Officer	
Civ	Civilian	
CoS	Chief of Staff	
DFC	Deputy Force Commander	
FC	Force Commander	
FOD	Field Operations Division	

FMR	Force Mobile Reserve
HQ	Headquarters
Inf	Infantry
LA	Legal Adviser
Ln	Liaison
Log	Logistics
MilObs	Military Observers
OGL	Observer Group Lebanon
Ops	Operations

OSPA	Office for Special Political Affairs
PIO	Press Information Officer
SA	Senior Adviser
Sp	Support

Legend

——— "Command"

- - - - Liaison

Source: Based on UNDPI, *The Blue Helmets*, p. 409.

The usual problem of UN force turbulence greatly affected UNIFIL's attempt to establish an authoritative and locally respected military presence in southern Lebanon. Force turbulence was constant and heavy. For instance, the French infantry battalion was first withdrawn in March 1979 and then redeployed in May 1982. Months later, this French battalion was moved by its government to Beirut, where it took part in the non-UN–sponsored Multinational Force. Finally, France withdrew its infantry battalion altogether in 1986 out of frustration over UNIFIL's stymied mandate and continued conflict with the PLO elements in its area of operations.[37] Along similar lines, the Dutch battalion deployed in 1979 was withdrawn from UNIFIL in 1985. The reasons given by the Dutch government were clear: "The government of the Netherlands has informed the Secretary-General that it has reluctantly decided to withdraw its contingent at the end of the present mandate because UNIFIL, in its view, has not been able to fulfill its mandate and the situation is not likely to improve in the near future."[38]

The Iranian battalion was withdrawn in March 1979 because of Khomeini's revolution. The Nigerian contingent was withdrawn in February 1983. The Senegalese gave up on UNIFIL in 1984. The government of Nepal withdrew its initial battalion in May 1980, redeployed the following year, withdrew in November 1982, and was back for the duration in 1985. The initial withdrawal of the Nepalese battalion left a gap in the UNIFIL area of operations over which the UN never reassumed control.[39]

In addition to this force turbulence in national contingents, UNIFIL operations experienced an uncoordinated and somewhat haphazard personnel turnover within national contingents caused by the wholly different and uncoordinated soldier rotation policies followed by the different nations. Some rotated after six months, some after one year. Some rotated their battalions whole, and some rotated soldiers in and out of UNIFIL from within battalions. The fact that these widely varying rotations were national and not UNIFIL force structure decisions gave an uncoordinated and turbulent appearance to UNIFIL. Institutional experience, built up by the hard work of peacekeepers, was either lost or kept and passed on within national contingents, not within UNIFIL proper, because of the uncoordinated personnel turnover within the mission as a whole.[40]

The wholesale departure and arrival of completely new contingents had serious operational ramifications for UNIFIL. The concern for UNIFIL was that, every time a contingent left, it needed to shift units, reestablish sectors of responsibility, and, more important for peacekeepers, reestablish liaison and relations with the local parties. In most areas, the period immediately following unit rotation was subject to increased violence before the new troops could establish their authority and contacts with the local belligerents.[41]

Although over the long period of UNIFIL's mandate there has been some continuity in forces, every unit that left and was replaced represented a break in operational continuity that did not help the mission. The United Nations, however, did not have the authority to counter the administrative decisions of member states. It could only give the national contingents operational missions during their temporary duty with UNIFIL (however long the member state decided that might be).

Another effect of a loose chain of command was that UNIFIL often had to compete with national chains of command that extended from member states directly to their contingents in southern Lebanon. John Mackinlay noted that those member states, such as France, who regularly deployed forces overseas, had established and rehearsed command and control links to their contingents that operated more regularly than those from UNIFIL headquarters.[42] The UNIFIL commander recognized the pervasive influence of national command and control systems and concluded that he had no choice but to accept his (and the UN's) restricted authority. On paper, the UN chain of command looked straightforward and authoritative. In the field, however, General Erskine wrote that "all contingent commanders take instructions from home, and some are instructed to report daily to their home authorities. This practice is tantamount to interference in command."[43]

This situation was aggravated by the isolation of UNIFIL headquarters (HQ), which could not regularly make staff visits to contingents to check that standard operating procedures were being adhered to by the diverse contingents. In the early days of the mission, after temporarily working out of three headquarters simultaneously,[44] UNIFIL established its headquarters at Naqoura for the duration of the mission. The UNIFIL commander himself wrote that "Naqoura was, in tactical terms, the worst possible site in which to locate UNIFIL HQ."[45] The command problems of this headquarters centered on the fact that Naqoura was not only physically removed from the UNIFIL area of operations, but also subject to further isolation from UNIFIL contingents by the hostile actions of local factions.

Throughout the course of UNIFIL's mission, the headquarters was shelled, attacked, blockaded, and even had its telephone communications cut off on several occasions.[46] John Mackinlay noted that "the location at Naqoura was vulnerable not only to the hazards of war but also to the capricious behavior of the Israelis and the DFF in whose area it lay."[47] The competition from national chains of command was exacerbated by this isolation of UNIFIL HQ from its contingents. For instance, the Norwegian battalion was not only isolated from UNIFIL HQ, but also from the rest of UNIFIL, over 90 kilometers from the force HQ, through "enemy" territory. Because units were often isolated, national command and control systems were many times more responsive. Some contingents, especially those with advanced communications equipment, had links with national chains of command that were established more rapidly and maintained more efficiently than communications links to UNIFIL headquarters. This not only made national chains of command more important, but as will be shown, it also had an important effect on the different operational approaches of the various UNIFIL contingents.

Another problem in the UNIFIL chain of command that was typical of UN peacekeeping missions was the lack of single manager control in the early stages of UNIFIL. Major-General Emmanuel A. Erskine of Ghana, the UNTSO chief of staff, was appointed the UNIFIL force commander. However, another important participant in UNIFIL's initial command and control was Lieutenant-General Ensio Siilasvuo, who was the UN chief coordinator of peacekeeping operations in the Middle East. In the early stages of UNIFIL's deployment, both General Erskine and General Siilasvuo were in separate contact with different elements of the belligerents.[48] Although there was unity of effort and close coordination in their work, there was no clear single-manager control of UNIFIL because General Siilasvuo was not in the UNIFIL chain of command going up to the secretary-general. Observer J. D. Murray wrote that the "potential for duplication, misunderstanding and even conflict between the two generals [was] obvious."[49]

Last, the chain of command in UNIFIL was bothered by the usual UN problems of the span of control necessitated by the immediate activation of an ad hoc and composite mission. UNIFIL headquarters at Naqoura exerted direct control over up to eight infantry battalions and two to three battalion-size support units. This represented an unrealistic span of control for one headquarters. UNIFIL headquarters was set up, in both size and composition, along the lines of a brigade-size command, which would ideally control no more than three or four battalions. In reality, UNIFIL headquarters was trying to command and control a small division-size operation. No attempt was made to subdivide the operation into "brigades," as was done in UNEF II. This excess of subordinate units all reporting to one staff overwhelmed the isolated headquarters staff at Naqoura. The more immediate result however, was for the contingents just to exercise greater autonomy at UNIFIL HQ's expense.[50] From the perspective of some line battalions, there was no unity of command in the initial stages of UNIFIL, and these battalions "reacted differently and complained about unclear orders."[51] As a result, clarification was many times sought through national chains of command instead of through the United Nations.

Control Procedures

UNIFIL experienced great difficulty in forming, promulgating, and supervising the application of common control procedures. As a result, UNIFIL's operations generally were viewed as inconsistent, unsynchronized, and uncoordinated. Much of this was caused by the lack of thorough prior planning and the slow process of establishing an authoritative and functioning headquarters that could issue control procedures and enforce their application.

Because there was no effective military planning staff in New York, the initial planning was undertaken by the civilian-staffed Office for Field Operational and External Support Activities. As Mackinlay noted, this was

> an organization better equipped to deal with political problems, administration, and funding [rather] than day-to-day military operations. As a result, there was no staff at UN HQ anticipating these military problems, nor was there perhaps anyone to represent with much conviction the organizational procedures that were needed to overcome them.[52]

General Erskine, who was appointed UNIFIL force commander only three days before the first UNIFIL troops deployed in the theater, had no time to organize his staff, reconnoiter the area, analyze the situation, and establish long-term command and control procedures for the operation.

Instead, the officers assigned from other missions to help start UNIFIL initiated short-term solutions that temporarily satisfied the rush to establish a UNIFIL presence but did not augur well for the continued operations of the force. The officers who established UNIFIL HQ and served as quartering parties for the initial deployment of UNIFIL contingents were not assigned to UNIFIL. In most cases they were not from UNIFIL contributing nations either.[53] Once permanent UNIFIL officers did arrive in theater, staff officers estimated that "it took 3–4 weeks to get the nucleus of the HQ staff operative to such a degree that it could assume the functions of interim command."[54]

The commander's staff is a crucial extension of the commander's ability to control his forces. The protracted manner in which General Erskine's staff established control over the operations of UNIFIL was not due to a lack of dedicated and professional staff work by the competent UNIFIL officers. The problem was that units were deploying to the area well ahead of established, rehearsed, and fully operating control procedures. Mackinlay has written that "a headquarters staff must arrive in advance of the units under their command, as a working group, with an agreed modus operandi, a common language, some experience, and a developed group ethos."[55] Although that is the ideal, each of UNIFIL's contingents had to establish a separate modus operandi out of necessity, while the HQ staff rushed to establish control procedures for the force as a whole.

Synchronizing military operations facilitates command and control. The operational tenet of synchronization maintains that a force should attempt to arrange its activities in time and space to achieve an effect that promotes a deportment of coordination, cohesiveness, and effectiveness.[56] The piece-meal deployment of UNIFIL was not synchronized in any sense. As UNIFIL's units arrived, they were deployed immediately to areas and set up operations without the benefit of comprehensive guidance or common control procedures from headquarters. Most contingents went about their initial tasks individually and differently.[57] Mackinlay noted that, when he visited UNIFIL after its initial deployment, at least two battalions had still never received written operations orders from UNIFIL HQ:

> *It seems, and this is still the case, that battalion commanders did not receive a written operation order translating the bare statements of the Secretary-General's terms of reference into a directive which was relevant to the local situation they faced with the AO. This obliged them to make on-the-spot decisions about important tactical and political issues. The result of this was that from the opening phase of the UN force's deployment there was an uneven profile to the behavior of the various nations.[58]*

For instance, a study done by the Norwegian Institute of International Affairs documented the different operational attitudes of the various contingents. The study classified some battalions (such as the French and Fijians) as "aggressive" because they attempted to prevent the deployment of any armed elements in their area of operations. In contrast, "passive" battalions actually had strong IDF or DFF elements operating within their area of operations.[59] Another study noted that the French and Fijians were considered tough with everyone and especially the PLO, while the Senegalese were sympathetic with the PLO and the Nepalese were overly affable with the DFF.[60]

One result of this disparity of operational approaches was that belligerents naturally began to operate in areas where UNIFIL contingents were perceived to be more sympathetic to the belligerents' agenda. The United Nations might claim that in the strategic sense it maintained one attitude toward the belligerents. In practice, as one observer has noted, "the interpretation of UNIFIL's SOPs varies with the temperament and dispositions of the national units and the nature of their respective areas of operations."[61] What is more important, however, is that the local factions perceived very different tactical approaches to UNIFIL's mandate from its different units.[62]

For instance, in the mid-1980s, the Muslim elements in southern Lebanon perceived the French as being pro-Lebanese Christian (because of historical reasons and the recent MNF activities in Beirut) and anti-Iranian (because of support for Iraq in the ongoing war with Iran). Consequently, attacks increased on the French contingent, which responded aggressively. Kochavi noted that "the French policy concerning self-defense was to shoot to kill if fired at, and so provoked angry and hostile reactions from the Palestinians who were reported to have said that the French were in Lebanon not as a peace force, but as a force of intimidation."[63] By the end of 1986, both UNIFIL and France thought it best that the French infantry battalion be withdrawn, as it had lost all claims to neutrality. Alan James noted that "not everyone was sad to see the French infantrymen go, as they sometimes seemed ill-attuned to the restrictive demands of peacekeeping."[64]

The failure of UNIFIL to promulgate and apply common control procedures quickly encouraged differing national attitudes as well as competition from national chains of command. Ironically, the integration of UNIFIL as an efficient military unit had been specified as one of the prerequisites of success spelled out in UNIFIL's terms of reference. However, this integration never took place. Several observers noted that, even in UNIFIL headquarters, the UNIFIL staff was more likely to group in national enclaves than together.[65] Although this facet of human nature does not preclude operational effectiveness in itself, John Mackinlay noted that, "when considered with the idiosyncratic interpretation of the mandate, the nationally determined fissures within the force assume a greater significance."[66] Mackinlay also noted how the lack of common control procedures applied to integrated operations undermined operational success.

> In previous and later examples of peacekeeping deployments, the sudden arrival of large numbers of well-disciplined international troops in an area of conflict has been seen to cause a momentary lull in the tempo of violence which allows the peacekeepers to establish themselves as a credible presence before the local combatants grow accustomed to their presence and restart hostilities. For UNIFIL there was no such honeymoon period.[67]

The traditional shortcomings of UN command and control were exacerbated by the operational challenges to UNIFIL's authority in southern Lebanon. It had been axiomatic that UN command and control would be characterized by a loose chain of command and improvised control procedures. This was always accepted by UN missions because it reflected the political characteristics of the United Nations as an organization of occasionally cooperating member states, who kept for themselves the vestiges of sovereignty that included command of their military forces. What became apparent in UNIFIL was that, although this traditional UN command and control system worked adequately in supportive political environments, it was a significant operational drawback in missions that were contested by local factions.

The Military Objectives of UNIFIL

The political objectives of UNIFIL were to confirm Israeli withdrawal from southern Lebanon, restore peace and security to the area, and assist the government of Lebanon in ensuring the return of its effective authority.[68] In turn, the military contingents of UNIFIL had military objectives that supported each of those goals. These military objectives were derived from traditional peacekeeping practice, which maintained that the objectives and modus operandi should be determined in light of several conditions: the strict impartiality of the UN force, the use of force in a passive manner and of force of arms only in self-defense, and, most important, the assumption that the UN force would enjoy the cooperation of the local factions.[69]

Had this last assumption held, then the task of UNIFIL would have been infinitely easier, especially in its early stages when it was rushing to establish a cohesive and organized military presence in southern Lebanon. As noted above, UNIFIL started to deploy units within days of the issuance of its terms of reference, and its commander and staff were left scrambling to produce coherent and detailed operational plans to catch up to the troops already operating on the ground. As John Mackinlay noted,

> It was left to the General officer commanding UNIFIL, Major-General E.A. Erskine, to translate the bare statements of the mandate and its qualifying set of instructions into a military operation which could succeed in south Lebanon. The Secretary-General had given him terms of reference which set out a list of objectives for the force, without specifying in too much detail how he saw them being carried out.[70]

In other words, strategy was developed on the go.

The rushed and poorly executed deployment might have had little negative impact had the local factions been as cooperative on the ground as the UN Security Council hoped they would have been. However, the collapse of that crucial assumption, coupled with UNIFIL's imprecise plan of operations, helped cripple military effectiveness from the start. As a result, UNIFIL was given unrealizable objectives for a peacekeeping force that was operating with a traditional peacekeeping modus operandi. In addition to UNIFIL's seemingly impossible tasks, the military mismanagement of the force contributed even further to its ineffectiveness.

Confirming the Withdrawal of Israeli Forces

Several military objectives were involved in the task of confirming the withdrawal of the IDF from southern Lebanon. The first was to observe and report on the status of the IDF in southern Lebanon. The second was to occupy the former IDF positions with an eye to returning them to the proper Lebanese authorities. For the UNIFIL battalions in the field, this entailed conducting observation operations through stationary observation posts, traffic control points, and patrols and conducting relief-in-place operations of IDF positions. The intention was to occupy a traditional interpositional buffer zone (as in the Golan Heights) to keep the local factions separated.

This task required the complete cooperation of the IDF more than any other local faction. Since the 1970s, Israel had maintained that it had to have some measure of control over PLO-occupied southern Lebanon to guarantee the safety of its northernmost cities and settlements. By driving up to the Litani River in the 1978 invasion, Israel effectively established a security zone that it has held to the present day. However, in April 1978, Israel seemed willing to cooperate in full with Resolution 425 and submitted plans for a three-phase withdrawal of the IDF from Lebanon.

The modus operandi of UNIFIL was to conduct relief-in-place operations with withdrawing IDF units. The UNIFIL forces in the area coordinated for the handover of IDF positions and then occupied the positions as the IDF left. As UNIFIL was a small force and could not occupy all IDF positions, it attempted at least to deny the use of former IDF positions to other armed factions through observation and patrolling. Other related UNIFIL tasks in this objective were to observe, record, and report on the exact progress of the IDF withdrawal through liaison with the IDF and direct observation of the withdrawal from observation posts, mobile patrols, and traffic control points.

However, UNIFIL encountered two significant problems in these operations. The first stemmed from the fact that the UNIFIL area of operations had never been officially defined and agreed to by all the parties concerned. By the end of the third phase of Israeli withdrawal in June 1978, UNIFIL had occupied the maximum amount of territory it physically could, although that was only 45 percent of the Lebanese territory occupied by the IDF south of the Litani River. In addition, the UNIFIL territory was effectively split into two zones, divided by a gap some 15 kilometers wide in which UNIFIL was able to maintain only four isolated positions.[71] The area of southern Lebanon under the control of the IDF through its de facto forces (DFF) proxy became known as "the enclave" [Map 3].

The terms of reference for UNIFIL had stated that the area of operations was "to be defined." It was indeed eventually defined—not by the United Nations, but by the IDF and its Lebanese Christian allies, the DFF (led by Major Haddad). As UNIFIL began its relief of IDF units, the IDF turned over as many positions to armed DFF elements as it did to UNIFIL. Most of these were in the enclave. In addition, the Israelis kept control (largely through the DFF) of many strategically important sites actually in the UNIFIL area of operations.[72] An important consequence of the Israeli decision to turn over many positions to its DFF ally was the appearance of the large gap in the UNIFIL area of operations that was occupied by the DFF after the 13 June 1978 IDF withdrawal. As Bjorn Skogmo noted,

> *The existence of the gap, which encompasses Major Haddad's*
> *headquarters in Marjayoun, meant that UNIFIL's deployment*

Map 3

The UN Mission to Lebanon

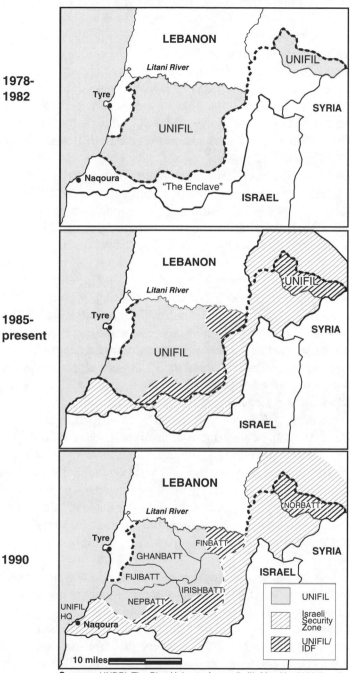

1978-1982

1985-present

1990

Sources: UNDPI, *The Blue Helmets,* Appendix III, Map No. 3329.5; and
Alan James, *Peacekeeping in International Politics,* pp. 342, 346.

*did not form one uninterrupted zone across Southern Lebanon
and that UNIFIL had no possibility of controlling infiltration
from the Palestinian positions north of the Litani through this
area. The existence of the gap also meant that UNIFIL could
not control Israeli incursions into Southern Lebanon, particularly across the Litani to Palestinian concentrations around
the Beaufort Castle, Nabatiya, and Aichiyeh.*[73]

The existence of the gap and the lack of a UNIFIL presence in the enclave meant that UNIFIL could never effect an interpositional buffer zone, the operational mechanism deemed essential to the success of most traditional peacekeeping missions. This greatly reduced the authority of the UNIFIL and the opportunity for UNIFIL to execute its mandate.

The IDF continued after 1978 to maintain control of the enclave through the DFF, which it controlled, equipped, and funded.[74] UNIFIL continued throughout the 1978–1982 period to lodge complaints with Israel about the presence of these regular IDF forces in southern Lebanon. During this peri-od, Israel and the PLO fought a "camp war" over, around, and (in some cases) in southern Lebanon. By 1981, Israel became increasingly concerned about PLO activity in southern Lebanon, and the United Nations admitted that, "given the limited size of UNIFIL and its lack of enforcement power, it was virtually impossible to prevent all infiltration attempts."[75] Because of these infiltrations, the United Nations also estimated that the PLO population in southern Lebanon had increased over threefold since 1978.[76] By April 1982 the tensions between Israel and the PLO were acute, as Israel respond-ed to terrorist and rocket attacks by conducting massive air raids on PLO camps and villages in Lebanon.

On the morning of 6 June 1982, the IDF chief of staff told the UNIFIL commander that a full-scale Israeli invasion of Lebanon would commence through UNIFIL territory in 28 minutes.[77] The IDF expected UNIFIL to stand aside and provide no resistance. General Callaghan, who had succeed-ed General Erskine as the UNIFIL force commander, ordered the UNIFIL troops to stay in their positions and defend their mandate unless their safety was imperiled. This spawned some creative attempts by some UNIFIL con-tingents to slow the Israeli invasion forces, but they were overcome relative-ly quickly.

The UNIFIL response, like most of its operations, was not consistent and varied greatly by national contingent. Some contingents put up a brief fight with arms, some merely stood aside, and some tried passive measures such as constructing obstacles for roadblocks. Much of this varied response was due to the ambiguity about the concept of "self-defense." Officially, UNIFIL's peacekeepers were authorized to use force "when attempts are made to prevent them from performing their duties under the mandate of the Security Council."[78] This was interpreted as a rule of engagement that allowed the peacekeepers to use force of arms not only in personal self-defense, but also in self-defense of their mandate when under armed attack.[79] However, when confronted with an overwhelming force such as an Israeli armored column, the futility, ambiguity, and subjectivity of these "rules of engagement" became evident. They left too much room for interpretation, and, given the traditional lack of a unified approach to UNIFIL operations, they were interpreted differently. Traditional peacekeepers do not have the capabilities or mandate for a backup plan when the assumptions of consent and cooperation are violated in such blatant fashion.

By 8 June 1982, the entire UNIFIL area of operations was under IDF control. Since 1982, the IDF and its new proxy, the South Lebanese Army (SLA), have maintained virtual control over almost all of southern Lebanon. This left UNIFIL operating in occupied territory and, as Alan James noted, made "the terms of its original mandate even less applicable than they had ever been to the situation on the ground."[80] In 1985, the IDF again carried out a three-phase withdrawal that left most of the old enclave and some more territory north of the Litani in the hands of the IDF and the Israeli-supported SLA. The Israelis saw this zone as vital for providing security to their borders, a goal that Israel maintained UNIFIL was unable to accomplish. Even after Israeli "withdrawal," the security zone included over seventy armed IDF/SLA positions in the UNIFIL area of operations.[81]

The "camp war" between Israel and opposing factions has continued with varying degrees of hostility since 1985. In July 1993, the IDF launched another large operation principally consisting of air and artillery attacks against the PLO in response to rocket attacks on Israel.[82] The Israeli authorities replied to UN criticism by insisting that the security zone was only a "temporary arrangement."[83] However, no withdrawal of the IDF or its active proxies from southern Lebanon is likely as long as elements that threaten Israel could use the UNIFIL area of operations and surrounding area as a base for hostile actions against Israel. The United Nations has been forced to accept this and conceded that Israel does not consider UNIFIL capable of ensuring peace and security in southern Lebanon.[84]

The failure of UNIFIL to establish a clearly recognized and respected interpositional buffer zone doomed the mission. The force commander wrote that he "did not anticipate the hard-line attitudes of the Israelis, which were to determine the progress, or lack of it, in the fulfillment of our mission."[85] Traditional peacekeeping forces simply could not effectively operate as intended without the political cooperation of the local factions and a credible interpositional buffer zone.

Restoring Peace and Security

The military objectives involved in this broad goal centered on "preventing the recurrence of fighting, ensuring the peaceful character of the area of operations, and to that end, controlling movement into and out of the zone."[86] The UNIFIL operations undertaken to achieve these goals also would be achieved principally through the occupation of its buffer zone, no matter how imperfect. In this buffer zone UNIFIL would attempt to (1) occupy observation posts and checkpoints on roads and conduct mobile patrols; (2) detect, halt, and disarm armed infiltrators of the area of operations; and (3) deny movement in the area of operations to belligerent parties intent on the conduct of hostile actions.[87] General Erskine, the force commander, stated that the main objective in this phase of operations was "to prevent contact between the two groups [IDF/DFF and PLO]."[88]

Most successful conventional peacekeeping missions had well-defined and sparsely populated buffer zones. In contrast, the indeterminate and volatile nature of UNIFIL's area of operations effectively passed the initiative of setting UNIFIL's operational agenda to the belligerents. In fact, the IDF was still expanding its area of operations as the terms of reference for UNIFIL were being completed in New York. When the UNIFIL area of operations had solidified by September 1978, the headquarters at Naqoura, the guard detachment at Tyre, the Norwegian and Nepalese battalions in the northeast sector, and five permanent observation posts on the Lebanese/Israeli border were all isolated from the main body of UNIFIL's six infantry battalions.

All of these isolated positions were subject to attacks and harassment by the belligerents in southern Lebanon. None of them could be mutually supported by other UNIFIL elements. As such, these isolated detachments, including the UNIFIL HQ, were subject to constant harassment, virtual states of siege, and attack. The French detachment in the Tyre area fought a running gun battle with PLO elements in May 1978, resulting in three French soldiers killed and fourteen wounded, including the battalion commander.[89] The Norwegian and Nepalese battalions were similarly isolated and harassed. The disjointed deployment of UNIFIL not only prevented it from attempting to achieve its mandate fully, but also greatly endangered the units that were isolated from the main body.

In the most benign peacekeeping environment, this would not be a completely unacceptable state of affairs. In such a situation, the cooperation of the belligerents would not prevent UNIFIL from placing its units where they could mutually support one another in a seamless buffer zone. In Lebanon, the hostility and noncollaboration of the belligerents meant that "the UNIFIL area constituted an imperfect buffer between the opposing forces."[90] The hostility of the UNIFIL area, characterized by its commander as a " semi-war zone," was obviously far from being benign.[91] Therefore, to continue operations in such an incoherently occupied zone of operations was beyond the pale of military logic. However, such difficulties often were part and parcel of the strategic environment for the peacekeeper.

In attempting to "restore peace and security" to the area, it was essential that the UNIFIL contingents have a common purpose and a continuity of operations. Both of these objectives were hampered by the variety of operational procedures and the differing rotation policies of the contingents. Considerable force turbulence occurred when member states pulled out their contingents. For example, the pullout of the French and Iranian battalions in 1979 necessitated a "significant change in the deployment of the Force."[92] Another major redeployment weakened the UNIFIL force posture when it was undertaken just before the 1982 Israeli invasion.[93] In the northeast area of UNIFIL operations, the 1982 withdrawal of the Nepalese battalion meant that the Norwegian contingent had to expand its area of operations substantially. UNIFIL never recovered any control over this gap in its area of operations, and when the Nepalese rejoined UNIFIL in 1985, they were sent to an entirely different area in the southeast.[94]

Nonetheless, UNIFIL did what it could, and operations settled into the occupation of observation posts and traffic control points and the conduct of mobile patrols to prevent a recurrence of fighting in southern Lebanon. When belligerents were determined to carry on with their actions, they either circumnavigated the understrength UNIFIL force in small numbers or, as in the case of the IDF, merely ignored the UN presence entirely. The atmosphere remained hostile, and veteran peacekeeper General Indar Rikhye noted that "the number of shooting incidents against UN troops was comparable to the worst of the Congo experience."[95] By April 1996, 209 UNIFIL peacekeepers had lost their lives.[96] It remains the costliest UN military operation with the exception of the Congo.

The virtual control of the UNIFIL area of operations by the IDF/SLA after 1982 sharply reduced UNIFIL's chances of restoring peace and security to the area, after failing to see Israel cooperate in the first task. Throughout the mid-1980s UNIFIL reduced its number of positions throughout the area, especially those isolated in the security zone. This was a tacit admission of failure in maintaining an authoritative presence in pursuance of the task. But, as Alan James has noted, "if one is simply in the business of flag waving, a lot of flags are not required."[97]

Assisting in Restoring Lebanese Authority

UNIFIL military objectives to support this political goal included assisting Lebanese government forces to occupy positions in the area and supporting their military operations to restore local authority. UNIFIL operations in this regard included (1) protecting the movement of Lebanese government forces in the UNIFIL area of operations and (2) conducting combined operations with the Lebanese government forces to man observation posts and traffic control points and conduct patrols.

The operations undertaken to support this task need less examination than the other two above, largely because they were never seriously implemented. This was mainly due to the failure to make progress in the first two objectives, which were mostly preconditions for the fulfillment of the third. The continued instability of the area, the continued presence of Israeli forces in the enclave and later the security zone, and the lack of authority of the Lebanese government in Beirut all contributed to hamper this mission. UNIFIL attempted to help deploy Lebanese gendarmes and army troops to the area but were frustrated by repeated attacks on the Lebanese columns by the various factions in southern Lebanon.[98]

Starting in the mid-1980s, UNIFIL's humanitarian efforts increased greatly, as did the population of southern Lebanon. In 1978, the United Nations estimated that the population of southern Lebanon was at most a few thousand. By the time of the 1982 Israeli invasion, it had increased to 150,000.[99] UNIFIL still works closely with UN relief agencies and other nongovernmental organizations to help coordinate and deliver humanitarian aid to a population that is growing larger still and approaching half a million. The lack of Lebanese authority led UNIFIL to assume many of the Lebanese government functions concerning the security and welfare of the population.

UNIFIL continues to remain deployed in southern Lebanon largely because the government of Lebanon does not appear capable of assuming these responsibilities from UNIFIL. In fact, if one reads the language in Security Council reports since 1982 that ask for the renewal of the UN force's mandate, UNIFIL's responsibility for facilitating the provision of humanitarian aid has become its primary justification for existence. This implied mission, which was not specifically part of the original mandate, has made the disengagement of UNIFIL even more problematic. As one observer noted,

> the Force has been sucked into the economic and political fabric of the wider society in which it operates and of which it has become an integral part. UNIFIL increasingly has come to function as a pseudo-government for the south whose chances of being replaced by the appropriate authorities in the foreseeable future seem remote.[100]

The UN peacekeepers in southern Lebanon are now part of the problem—and perhaps not so much of the solution.

Conclusion

Traditional peacekeeping was a passive and limited military technique, one that relied on the cooperation of accountable belligerents in order to succeed. As such, consent and cooperation were always an assumption when peacekeeping missions were being planned. However, as the United Nations noted after UNIFIL's initial difficulties, "the assumptions on which UNIFIL was set up have not been fulfilled."[101] As a result, throughout the course of its existence, UNIFIL was left to hope for cooperation from the belligerents.[102] As the secretary-general noted, "When an operation is mounted in an emergency with ambiguous or controversial objectives and terms of reference, and on assumptions which are not wholly realistic, it is likely to present far greater difficulties. This is undoubtedly the case with UNIFIL."[103]

It was noted that some at the United Nations had great doubts about the potential success of UNIFIL during its very inception. These doubts gave way to a resigned outlook of impending failure as it became apparent that the belligerent factions in southern Lebanon were not intent on cooperating to help fulfill the UNIFIL mandate. The Security Council's continued renewal of that same unachievable mandate is an expression of political perseverance more than the prospects of operational success.

By 1978, when UNIFIL was created, the United Nations had initiated eleven observation or traditional peacekeeping missions based on the principles of peacekeeping. These operations suited the political nature of the United Nations by taking advantage of its moral legitimacy and impartial standing as the most well-represented international organization in the world and one specifically dedicated to international peace and security. Traditional peacekeeping and observation missions were innocuous enough militarily to reflect this passive authority and were, at the same time, a small enough management challenge for an organization with little of the political legitimacy, military authority, or management capabilities needed to recruit, mount, direct, and employ large, complex, and coercive military operations. Years of experience had proven to the United Nations that the principles of peacekeeping suited the institutional capabilities (and constraints) of the United Nations and vice versa. Thus, the military forces of UNIFIL were structured and deployed based on traditional peacekeeping doctrine.

However, that doctrine demanded a supportive political environment (internationally and locally) to succeed. The strength of that political support was especially important, given the almost unavoidable military deficiencies of a traditional UN peacekeeping force. The volatile and contested environment of southern Lebanon greatly challenged and exacerbated the traditional foibles of UN military operations: rushed, incomplete, and ad hoc planning; a force structure influenced more by political requirements than military necessity; a loose chain of command and improvised control procedures; and a passive modus operandi that left the force hostage to its environment. However, in these sorts of quasi-military missions, the success of the UN force in a diplomatic context was much more important than its military prowess. Conversely, skill at arms on the part of the peacekeepers could not compensate for the local political failings. As the first UNIFIL force commander noted, "UNIFIL's major difficulty has been a political one."[104]

UNIFIL proved, without a doubt, that the tenets that guided the formation, deployment, and direction of traditional peacekeeping missions were successful only in certain supportive political environments. As such, there was little desire after 1978 to launch other operations like UNIFIL. This changed with the thawing of Cold War tensions in the late 1980s. Then, with an unprecedented attitude of consensus on the Security Council, the United Nations once again began to consider peacekeeping involvement in volatile environments such as southern Lebanon. These new challenges, however, would change the traditional parameters that had guided force structure, command and control, and military objectives decisions since 1948. It is to this second generation of peacekeeping that this book now turns.

CHAPTER 6

Second-Generation Peacekeeping

The end of the Cold War and the success of the UN–sanctioned coalition in the Gulf War of 1990–1991 led many to think that the United Nations could be more active in international security affairs—managing more ambitious military operations to pursue international peace. Perhaps the inherent restrictions and constraints on the United Nations' capacity for military management could be overcome by the unprecedented spirit of cooperation on the UN Security Council between 1989 and 1994. During this time there was a strong belief from many international leaders that the Security Council could address more contentious threats to international peace and security through UN–managed military operations. This mood was reflected in the Secretariat as well, and in 1992, Boutros Boutros-Ghali, the UN secretary-general, proposed a more ambitious approach for the United Nations in creating and employing UN military operations.

In *An Agenda for Peace*, the secretary-general opined now that political consensus was easier to achieve on the Security Council, the United Nations could undertake more complex operations in the international arena. These missions would require larger and more sophisticated military components that might deploy to bellicose and contested environments. The secretary-general noted that the expanded and more muscular UN peacekeeping units might deploy without the traditional assurance of local consent[1] and could even be authorized to use force when the traditional UN rules of engagement were "no longer sufficient" to accomplish the task at hand.[2] This represented a sea change in thinking from the accepted practice of UN military operations conducted over the previous forty-four years.

This chapter first briefly recounts the analytical method for defining and examining second-generation peacekeeping operations. This is necessary because of the conceptual confusion that still exists in most literature over the parameters of post–Cold War peacekeeping missions. It then details the political forces behind the creation of second-generation peacekeeping operations.

This is principally an explanation of how consensus on the Security Council and a contested environment on the ground in many missions combined to give these missions their unique and unprecedented military character. The chapter highlights how the traditional UN approaches to force structure, command and control, and military objectives, rooted firmly in the principles of peacekeeping, were not appropriate as a doctrine for managing second-generation peacekeeping operations. The crux of this section is an examination of the United Nations' attempts at working through that dilemma.

Mats Berdal noted in a 1993 study of the UN Protection Force in the Former Yugoslavia (UNPROFOR) that "the operational restraints character-istic of traditional peacekeeping . . . may substantially undermine the ability of [UNPROFOR] forces to accomplish their assigned tasks."[3] This observa-tion is repeatedly borne out in this study of managing second-generation peacekeeping missions. An important observation in this chapter and the sub-sequent case study is that the United Nations, when undertaking more ambi-tious and complex military operations in bellicose and contested environments, often had to abandon the political precepts that guided obser-vation and traditional peacekeeping missions. Many times, it did this in favor of military requirements that contradicted the principles of peacekeeping. In second-generation peacekeeping operations, the United Nations found itself with an entirely new set of political and military challenges. In the end, the strain of trying to meet these new challenges by managing large, complex, and, many times, active military operations served to further highlight the institutional shortcomings of the United Nations as a political entity seeking to form and direct military operations. Conversely, these episodes brought out the comparative advantages of some other multinational political or mil-itary organizations, such as alliances or coalitions-of-the-willing led by a major military power.

Second-Generation Peacekeeping Operations

Traditional peacekeeping operations and second-generation peacekeeping oper-ations span somewhat elastic categories that overlap and can be considered seamless. However, although the spectrum of UN military operations is pro-gressive, there are some distinctive characteristics that clearly separate the cat-egories of peacekeeping in two respects. The first is the environment in which peacekeeping missions have operated. The second is the nature of the UN forces' military objectives and modus operandi.

The environments of second-generation peacekeeping missions were, in the main, considerably more bellicose and complex than those of traditional peace-keeping, where most missions were deployed in clearly delineated linear buffer zones between consenting nation-states. In contrast, the environment of second-generation peacekeeping was characterized largely by unstable intrastate conflicts. These often were hostile environments where a virtual state of war existed or was in temporary remission. In addition to these characteristics, the lack of a definitive and reliable peace settlement before and during UN involvement in these conflicts plagued almost all second-generation peacekeeping missions. As Richard Haass noted, "Intra-state conflicts are qualitatively different and often pose more difficult policy questions than inter-state conflicts. [They] are essentially civil wars, fought along ethnic or sectarian lines, tend to be more violent, long-lasting, zero-sum struggles. There are often multiple protagonists, usually with no clear, authoritative leaders, making diplomatic efforts that much more difficult."[4]

The second aspect that helps to define second-generation peacekeeping concerns their complex character. These were multifunctional missions in which the military component was only one part of a comprehensive political, diplomatic, humanitarian, and economic effort. The objectives of these missions included supporting civilian components and nongovernmental organizations in the provision of humanitarian aid, the organization and protection of elections, the supervision of government functions, the disarmament and demobilization of large numbers of belligerents, the repatriation and rehabilitation of refugees, the protection of safe areas, restoration of national government and institutions, and other missions. These tasks were also done as ancillary missions in many traditional operations, but on a much smaller scale and with much less emphasis than in second-generation peacekeeping. The actual military missions of second-generation peacekeeping are examined later in this chapter, but in general, they were a great deal more challenging and complicated than those of their buffer zone predecessors, even when conducted in a permissive environment.

Attempting to carry out ambitious multifunctional operations in these dangerous environments led the United Nations after the Cold War to form and employ much larger and militarily complex military forces. Some forces even were authorized to conduct limited enforcement operations under Chapter VII of the UN Charter to achieve objectives under difficult circumstances. Taken together, these factors gave second-generation peacekeeping operations a radically different military character compared to traditional peacekeeping.

The combination of ambitious tasks and the often dangerous and unstable environment of second-generation peacekeeping missions gave a new "look" to peacekeeping after the end of the Cold War. In the simple terms of military force size and composition, a few second-generation missions resembled traditional peacekeeping: UNTAG in Namibia and ONUMOZ in Mozambique were relatively small missions.[5] However, other second-generation missions were significantly different in terms of their military structure, both quantitatively and qualitatively. Although ONUC in the Congo foreshadowed larger operations in a time of traditional peacekeeping, UNTAC in Cambodia, UNPROFOR in the former Yugoslavia, and UNOSOM II in Somalia all represented a dramatic transformation in the pattern of UN military operations as they were significantly larger and more complex military enterprises than any of their traditional peacekeeping predecessors. Two of these large missions (UNTAC excepted) were specifically given very limited mandates authorizing the active use of force to coerce belligerents into compliance with UN resolutions.

Many recent studies have preferred to make a clear analytical divide based on the use of force in UN military operations. This places those missions that used passive force on one side of the divide and those that were authorized to use active force on the other. As noted in Chapter One, the former often are somewhat loosely referred to as Chapter VI missions and the latter as Chapter VII missions. Alternatively, many studies refer to the former category of missions as peacekeeping and the latter as peace enforcement. This analytical method is inflexible and unhelpful. It forces missions into categories based on legal provisions and unfulfilled political mandates and gives less attention to an examination of events themselves.

This common categorization of UN operations does not accurately reflect an empirical operational study of the second-generation missions themselves between 1989 and 1996. There are several reasons for this: First, as this chapter will show, a pure concept of peace enforcement was never achieved in practice—it was largely theoretical. The distinction between peacekeeping, Chapter VI, and peace enforcement, Chapter VII, is overly legal and breaks down in the conduct of the missions themselves. ONUC, UNPROFOR, and UNOSOM II, although authorized to undertake some limited enforcement actions, were overwhelmingly peacekeeping missions in the strategic nature of their operations. As Berdal noted, the missions to the former Yugoslavia and Somalia were "established in the framework of traditional peacekeeping operations."[6]

For instance, although UNPROFOR had enforcement provisions authorized by specific resolutions,[7] no enforcement actions were carried out by UNPROFOR forces until May 1995, over three years into the mission. It was at this time that UNPROFOR crossed the so-called "Magadishu Line" by undertaking offensive actions against local factions. Even then, it was not UNPROFOR troops per se who undertook the offensive combat actions, but NATO air forces that were acting in support of the UN mission. Prior to that episode, the NATO air forces patrolling the no-fly zone and offering combat air support acted offensively on only eight occasions in the first 710 days of

Operation "Deny Flight"—this out of over 36,500 combat sorties.[8] On the ground, hundreds of operations every day were conducted by UNPROFOR in the first two and one-half years of its mandate, and seven air missions were the only enforcement actions taken. Despite the limited actions of the NATO air forces, UNPROFOR could hardly be characterized as a coercive peace enforcement mission.

General Sir Michael Rose, the UN commander in Bosnia-Herzegovina 1993–1994, was always quick to remind the public that his UN force was neither structured for nor, in his mind, authorized to use coercive force to create an atmosphere in which his UN force could succeed. He constantly emphasized the passive nature of UN operations in the former Yugoslavia and stated that "patience, persistence, and pressure is how you conduct a peacekeeping mission. . . Hitting a tank [in self-defense] is peacekeeping. Hitting infrastructure, command and control, logistics, that is war, and I'm not going to fight a war in white-painted tanks."[9] In addition, the deputy commander of UNPROFOR in 1993–1994, Canadian Major General J. A. MacInnis, stated that, despite the resolutions authorizing the use of force and the combat air support from NATO, "UNPROFOR is not involved in the forceful imposition of peace nor in so-called peace enforcement. It is a peacekeeping force mandated for humanitarian purposes operating amidst ongoing conflicts. Apart from some increases in size, it remains configured, equipped, and mandated for peacekeeping."[10] A. B. Fetherston also notes that, despite UNPROFOR's Chapter VII mandates, "in practice it has not had the operational capability to enforce and has, therefore, continued to operate under traditional peacekeeping principles."[11]

It was a similar situation with both ONUC and UNOSOM II, missions that were occasionally mislabeled as peace enforcement when both missions were overwhelmingly peacekeeping in character. This was reflected in the structure of their forces, their military objectives, and modus operandi.[12] Both were authorized limited enforcement provisions that were used sparingly, but with traumatic effects and great media attention. The effect of mixing limited enforcement mandates with peacekeeping is explored in this chapter and the case study.

The point to be made here, however, is that peace enforcement is largely a concept that has never been tried, and it is misleading and inaccurate to refer to missions such as ONUC, UNPROFOR, UNAMIR, and UNOSOM II as peace enforcement because of a few limited enforcement provisions applied to a mission overwhelmingly peacekeeping in character. To treat these operations separately as peace enforcement missions and therefore doctrinally different from peacekeeping would be an attempt to try and bend reality into line with the theory. John Gerard Ruggie noted in 1994 that the conceptual debate raging about peacekeeping versus peace enforcement certainly did not help UN units in the field, as "nearly half of all ongoing UN peace operations find themselves in this gray area between classical peacekeeping and enforcement, however, they are currently condemned to make up things as they go along."[13] This chapter shows that an unused or rarely used political mandate does not an enforcement mission make.

The second way in which the peacekeeping/Chapter VI and peace enforcement/Chapter VII divide is misleading is in its very legal nature. Such a method has to treat missions such as ONUC, UNPROFOR, and UNOSOM II in the same analytical framework as the UN–sanctioned efforts in Korea in 1950–1953 and Kuwait in 1990–1991.[14] This legal distinction also would put UNIKOM, an observation mission with a small security component mandated under Chapter VII, in the same category as Korea, UNPROFOR, and UNOSOM II. It is quite obvious that the strategic character of UNIKOM bears no resemblance to second-generation peacekeeping or enforcement actions.

That distinction is helpful if one is conducting a legal or political examination of the use of force by UN–formed or –sanctioned troops. However, in a strategic analysis where the United Nations is examined as an institution that manages military operations, this legal distinction does not enlighten and can in fact obscure helpful analysis. The challenges to the United Nations of mounting, directing, and employing 20,000 troops for "muscular" peacekeeping in Somalia were radically different from those involving 550,000 troops for war in Korea. From a strategic manager's perspective, it is unhelpful to think of them both as Chapter VII operations.

Even so, there are no universally accepted definitions for the new generation of UN operations. Although there is general agreement among professional and academic analysts about the defining characteristics of traditional peacekeeping, the characteristics of second-generation peacekeeping are in some doubt, and the continued evolution in the nature of these missions has not helped. In fact, the attempt to label second-generation peacekeeping has seen these post–Cold War multifunctional missions referred to as aggravated peacekeeping, wider peacekeeping, expanded peacekeeping, enhanced peacekeeping, broader peacekeeping, muscular peacekeeping, protected peacekeeping, peacemaking, and even inducement operations. The confusion over an exact set of strategic and operational parameters for these missions is reflected in the profusion of terms.

Boutros Boutros-Ghali recognized this in *An Agenda for Peace* and detailed a conceptual framework that recognized traditional peacekeeping and the greater challenges of second-generation peacekeeping missions. He also proposed peace enforcement units that would be separate from peacekeeping units, constituted differently, and "warranted as a provisional measure under Article 40 of the Charter."[15] No such units have come to pass, and it would be a dramatic analytical leap to rationalize peacekeeping missions such as UNPROFOR and UNOSOM II as ones fulfilling this vision.

Therefore, a strategic study of UN military operations must recognize that by 1996, the United Nations had not achieved, on the ground, a clear divide between peacekeeping/Chapter VI and peace enforcement/Chapter VII missions. The "enforcement" in so-called peace enforcement missions (ONUC, UNPROFOR, UNOSOM II, UNAMIR) was greatly limited and did not change the overall nature of these missions in a way that would bring them closer to enforcement missions than to other second-generation peacekeeping missions.[16] They will therefore be considered in the same flexible category as other complex multifunctional post–Cold War peacekeeping missions. From the perspective of the United Nations, as a strategic manager of military operations, the challenges of UNTAC were similar to those of UNPROFOR, much more so than to the UN command in Korea. It will be recognized here, however, that enforcement provisions did have important effects on the way in which these operations were managed.

To highlight the difference between second-generation peacekeeping operations and their traditional predecessors, this chapter focuses on those second-generation missions that marked the clearest departure from the traditional principles of peacekeeping. As such, ONUC is occasionally noted as it can rightly be considered a historical antecedent of second-generation peacekeeping.[17] However, the great majority of the explicit analysis focuses on UNTAC and UNPROFOR, leaving the UN mission in Somalia for the subsequent case study. UNOSOM II marks the most significant departure from the principles of peacekeeping and is instructive as it represents the upper range of the scale of second-generation peacekeeping (or the lower range of the scale of peace enforcement, depending on one's perspective). The smaller second-generation peacekeeping operations are also noted, but less so than the larger and more complex military enterprises that gave the United Nations so much political and operational angst in 1992–1995.

Creating Second-Generation Peacekeeping Operations

Three important factors combined to shape the political milieu in which second-generation peacekeeping operations were created. The first factor was the consensus for action on the Security Council made possible by the end of Cold War tensions. This spirit of cooperation resulted in an explosion of UN peacekeeping and the ambitious mandates under which the new peacekeeping missions operated. The second factor was the lack of support for UN operations from belligerents on the ground, often in dangerous and intractable intrastate conflicts. The third factor in this nexus concerned the institutional capabilities of the United Nations itself. Despite the new management requirements caused by the increase in the number, size, and complexity of missions, the UN Secretariat (even when reorganized and reinforced) was still greatly restricted by its intrinsic political constraints and lack of sovereign military authority. It therefore continued to rely on the improvised planning and ad hoc procedures common to observation missions and traditional peacekeeping.

The "New" Security Council

The thaw of Cold War tensions on the Security Council from 1988 had an absolutely remarkable effect on the creation of UN military operations in the following years. The Security Council became a body of action and consensus, tackling with determination issues that would have never been approached during the Cold War. Between 1945 and 1990, 279 vetoes were cast in the Security Council, a poignant indication of the inability to achieve consensus in that body. Between 1990 and the publication of *An Agenda for Peace* in 1992, there were none, and there was only one (later reversed) up to 1994.[18] This spirit of cooperation first became possible in the late 1980s when Soviet President Mikhail Gorbachev introduced the concept of glasnost to the Soviet Union's foreign relations.

Consensus on the Security Council had three immediate effects: (1) a dramatic increase in the number of missions; (2) a radical increase in their size and complexity; and (3) the authorization of ambitious and complex mandates. In the seven years following 1988, the Security Council increased its output of new missions by more than 150 percent over what it had authorized during the previous forty years.[19] In mid-1990 there were some 10,000 UN field personnel conducting eight observation and small traditional peacekeeping missions, and by 1993, this number had risen to almost 80,000 in eighteen observation, traditional peacekeeping, and second-generation peacekeeping missions.[20]

In addition to the increase in the number and size of missions, the consensus on the Security Council also was manifested in ambitious political mandates that often were unachievable on the ground or at least were poorly matched to military resources and operational methods in operations such as UNPROFOR, UNOSOM II, and, later, UNAMIR. Most of the second-generation peacekeeping missions during this time had far more challenging objectives than observing a cease-fire or containing armed conflict through the occupation of a passive interpositional buffer zone. Many had humanitarian, nation-building, economic, and civil tasks that at times amounted to taking complete responsibility for a failed state. This phenomenon is also examined below in the section on military objectives.

The first UN military operation to profit from the spirit of consensus on the Security Council was UNTAG in 1989, which, like all post–Cold War second-generation peacekeeping operations, was a brokered request for UN assistance. The political underpinning for UNTAG was provided by a negotiated and previously concluded peace settlement that charted Namibia's path toward becoming a stable and democratic state. The political settlement, over ten years in the making, called for a UN military force to help monitor the cease-fire, the phased withdrawal of South African troops, the dismantling and disarmament of paramilitary and guerrilla groups, and several other major tasks. The agreement enjoyed wide international support and, with the exception of ONUC some 30 years prior, it was the most complicated mandate for a UN force to date.

The spirit of cooperation reflected in the approval and implementation of UNTAG, the first force-level UN mission since 1978, was boosted by the international cooperation shown in the Gulf War of 1990–1991. This cooperation also saw, in late 1991, the United Nations approve a small advance mission to Cambodia, UNAMIC, which would pave the way for UNTAC in 1992, a much larger and even more complicated peacekeeping operation than UNTAG. In short order, during 1992 the Security Council created UNPROFOR for the former Yugoslavia and ONUMOZ in Mozambique, authorized a U.S.–led task force in Somalia (UNITAF) that would give way in 1993 to UNOSOM II, and created another mission in Rwanda (UNAMIR) that would come to fruition and prove controversial in 1994. All these missions were approved for deployment in environments characterized by ongoing or simmering intrastate civil wars and, in addition, were given complex and multifunctional mandates. It was a heady and optimistic time on the Security Council.

Many studies have noted that the success of a UN military operation depends in large part on a clear political mandate.[21] Ironically, these same studies and others have highlighted how missions steeped in political controversy often may have ambiguous mandates to support the "fragile political consensus behind the operation."[22] In other words, a critical component of success often was ignored just to get a mission to happen. This phenomenon was noted in the UNIFIL case study and was also indicative of ONUC. Conversely, the political atmosphere of consensus surrounding the creation of second-generation peacekeeping missions gave rise to a different strategic problem: ambitious political mandates approved by the Security Council that were unachievable on the ground. For instance, between September 1991 and March 1994, the Security Council passed fifty-six separate resolutions concerning UNPROFOR, the mission to the former Yugoslavia. These resolutions enlarged the mandate of UNPROFOR twelve times after it had been deployed, a phenomenon known to military professionals as "mission creep."[23] This sort of disconnection between political objectives and military means, so exasperating for the commander on the ground, is examined in the section on military objectives below.

The Belligerent Environment

The second factor surrounding the creation of second-generation peacekeeping missions relates to the environment in which they were deployed. Although great power support was ensured from the Security Council, local support for second-generation missions often rested on very tenuous peace settlements. In traditional peacekeeping, a legitimate and observed peace settlement was considered a sine qua non for the operations of a UN force. Given the ambitions of the military (and civil) tasks involved in second-generation peacekeeping, such a settlement should have been even more of a prerequisite. However, that was not often the case. In Cambodia, the Khmer Rouge, one of four local parties to the Paris Peace Accords, ceased to comply with the Accords' provisions almost from the start. In the former Yugoslavia, not only were UN troops deployed before there was any sort of definitive peace settlement, but they also remained as the local environment became one characterized by unreliable cease-fire agreements that only occasionally and sporadically halted fierce fighting.

The character of second-generation peacekeeping is thus a result of the combination of the first factor, an eager and united Security Council passing ambitious mandates, and the second factor, environments often described as contested, semipermissive, nonpermissive, bellicose, or downright hostile. Throughout the United Nations' existence, the entire basis of peacekeeping as a viable military technique rested on a political environment that was supportive, both in the United Nations and on the ground. This environment shaped the size, structure, strategy, and operations of the force. It was a technique that had limitations, but limitations that suited the political legitimacy, management capabilities, and military authority of the United Nations. However, these limits of traditional UN techniques would be exposed by the volatile environment of second-generation peacekeeping missions. Because of this, traditional doctrine was revised by the United Nations when directing larger, more militarily complex, and sometimes actively cohesive missions.

Mechanisms and Procedures

The third factor influencing the creation of second-generation peacekeeping missions was outlined in Chapter One, which addressed the mechanisms and procedures used by the United Nations in managing a mission. During the beginning of the explosion in UN peacekeeping, the United Nations continued to approach the political (and subsequently military) planning and execution of missions with ad hoc procedures and methods. The United Nations had never maintained rehearsed and reliable mechanisms when creating peacekeeping missions, as it had no trained and ready military forces. Naturally, the necessity for improvisation somewhat hampered the formation and employment of the small and innocuous missions of the Cold War.

These traditional shortcomings of UN mission planning and management were aggravated by the ambitious and innovative nature of second-generation missions, their size and complexity, and the number taking place simultaneously. The secretary-general noted this continued reliance on improvisation and stated that "peace-keeping has to be reinvented every day."[24] However, A. B. Fetherston wrote that the Secretariat could not quite improvise quickly enough and the "ad hoc system of peacekeeping [could] not meet the demands posed by the post–Cold War world."[25]

Throughout the time in which most second-generation missions were initiated, the capability of the small staff in the Secretariat to manage this explosion in UN operations was stretched to the limits.[26] As Berdal noted in late 1993,

> *The UN machinery for organizing and sustaining peacekeeping missions has not changed fundamentally since the revival of UN field operations in 1988. Indeed the case of the former Yugoslavia has shown that the management of field operations continues to rely heavily on improvisation, ad hoc solutions, and the cultivation of close personal relationships among members of UN Departments.*[27]

Indeed, the weaknesses of this traditional system were exacerbated between 1992 and 1993 by two factors: the great number of large missions being created and deployed together (UNTAC in Cambodia, UNPROFOR in the Balkans, and UNOSOM II in Somalia were all operating together in 1993) and the sheer complexity of the missions themselves.

The quantitative and qualitative change in the breadth and depth of peacekeeping in such a short time overwhelmed the United Nations' ability to manage such operations. During that time, the United Nations tried to reinforce its management capabilities through the reforms undertaken by the Secretariat in 1993. These were intended to make the United Nations a more competent institution for managing military operations. However, the "pace and pressure of events in 1992–3" overwhelmed the marginal improvements in management capabilities.[28] In particular, the institutional reforms in the Secretariat could not overcome some of the fundamental shortcomings of political legitimacy and military authority that had always existed in UN operations. Problems in small observation and traditional peacekeeping missions were always a challenge, but the strategic character of the missions themselves ameliorated these weaknesses somewhat. In contrast, the United Nations' limited powers of sovereignty became a much more serious handicap for a strategic manager attempting to form, direct, and deploy the large and ambitious military operations of 1992–1993.

Forming Second-Generation Missions

Chapters Two through Five highlighted how political requirements most often overrode military requirements when it came to structuring a UN military force. Most missions were small, lightly armed, neutral, and fairly well balanced by geographic distribution. These forces did suffer from military inefficiencies gained as a result of hasty assembly, but the innocuous, passive, and unchallenging nature of their operations somewhat offset this condition. In the immediate aftermath of the end of the Cold War, the United Nations attempted to use these same principles to guide the formation of second-generation peacekeeping missions. There really was no other blueprint for putting together UN military operations. As Fetherston noted in 1994, "peacekeeping still has no conceptual base beyond a certain set of principles developed in reference to managing inter-state conflict."[29]

However, the demanding nature of second-generation peacekeeping, characterized by UN troops attempting to achieve ambitious objectives in dangerous and contested environments, would naturally change the factors that influenced force structure. By 1993, all the tenets that guided UN force structure planning in the past had been significantly revised by the experience of second-generation peacekeeping operations. Several missions had large, heavy, complex, and joint combat forces—missions with more than one component of air, ground, or sea forces. Some missions had certain objectives contracted out to non-UN organizations to take advantage of more significant military capabilities outside of UN control. Furthermore, the great powers were heavily represented in second-generation missions.

Finally, and deriving from the three innovations just listed, some missions had forces structured for active enforcement operations within an overall peacekeeping context. The challenges of second-generation peacekeeping missions and the bellicosity of the environments in which they operated meant that purely military requirements would assume far greater significance than they had in the past and would significantly alter the classical tenets derived from the principles of peacekeeping.

Composition

The dangerous nature of the environments in which many second-generation missions operated was, of course, most readily apparent to the UN soldiers on the ground. In many ways, the impetus for moving to heavier UN force structures to cope with this environment came from the bottom up instead of being directed by UN headquarters from the top down. For instance, in UNPROFOR, the United Nations initially gave contributing nations specific guidance about the composition of UNPROFOR contingents. Canadian Major General Lewis Mackenzie, the former commander of UN forces in Sarajevo, noted that UN headquarters initially placed a limit on the number of tracked armored personnel carriers per contingent for budgetary reasons. However, the individual contingents, more concerned with protecting their soldiers in a dangerous environment, "cheated" when they had the chance and brought more than "allowed."[30]

Given the lack of tension on the Security Council and the hostility of the environments to which they deployed, national contingents in second-generation missions quickly began to deploy heavier armored units for UN peacekeeping. There was no longer international political pressure to look innocuous, and, in these new environments, the cooperation of the belligerents was tenuous at best. The United Nations allowed this with the intention of constructing a UN force that was heavy enough to provide adequate self-defense in a contested environment but light enough to reinforce local perceptions of the United Nations' role as an impartial party.[31] The secretary-general stated in a report that "a positive response has been given to those contributing Governments that wish to strengthen the equipment of their contingents in order to reinforce their self-defense capability."[32] Some contingents even were allowed to bring main battle tanks—painted white—a first in UN military operations. Some of these tank units used their main armament under their mandate of acting in self-defense, the most notable instance occurring in 1994, when a Danish/Swedish unit fired seventy-two main gun tank rounds at Bosnian-Serb positions that had attacked the UN force.[33]

The introduction of mechanized and armored forces into some second-generation peacekeeping operations was very much a factor of military requirements. It was noted in the study of observation missions and traditional peacekeeping that the considerations of METT-T or other military planning formulas very often were overruled by the unique political imperatives and considerations of those UN missions. However, in second-generation peacekeeping operations, military necessities had more influence. After all, the Security Council was united in support of ambitious military missions, and there was little need to secure the consent of the local factions if they were generally intransigent already. In essence, the more challenging the military task and the more bellicose the environment, the greater the perception that it was necessary to abandon the precepts of the principles of peacekeeping. As might be expected, however, moving to much larger and heavier force structures had enormous financial, logistical, administrative, and management repercussions. Although finances are not covered in detail here, it should be noted that second-generation peacekeeping missions were many times more expensive per Blue Helmet than traditional missions. The total financial effect was even greater given their huge size. In 1988 the UN peacekeeping budget was $230 million. In 1994 it was $3.16 billion.[34]

Because the improvised and ad hoc procedures of the United Nations had not changed significantly to deal with the huge challenges of forming second-generation missions, the United Nations still had to go through a time-consuming process of seeking voluntary contributions from member states and then weaving the disparate responses into a coherent force. Naturally, this was even more difficult given the large size, complex operations, and dangerous environments of second-generation forces. As in traditional operations, the forces needed to be recruited ad hoc, and the force commander had little choice over the composition of the force. The deputy commander of UNPROFOR noted that "it remains a fact that the force commander must use the force he is given and has little influence over its composition."[35] In one instance, the UNTAC commander, hoping to exert some influence over the process, traveled uninvited to New York to try to influence the force structure and planning of UNTAC.[36]

Although UN methods stayed the same, the Blue Helmets changed greatly. Besides the UN forces themselves looking more and more like heavy combat units, another significant break with traditional peacekeeping doctrine occurred when the United Nations decided to contract out certain military missions in second-generation peacekeeping to non-UN forces. The four instances of this were the former Yugoslavia, Somalia, Rwanda, and the UN Mission in Haiti (UNMIH). The contracting out of military tasks in UNPROFOR is explored below, and the case study covers the experience of the U.S.–led task force (UNITAF) in Somalia. The French operation in support of UNAMIR and the U.S. intervention to start UNMIH both occurred late in 1994 and further illustrated both the advantages and disadvantages of using non-UN–managed forces in second-generation peacekeeping missions.

UNPROFOR contracted out two major operational tasks to combat air forces operating under NATO command. In 1995, UNPROFOR also used the services of French, British, and Dutch combat troops from a NATO rapid reaction force (nominally under UN control) to shell Bosnian Serb forces with 155-mm artillery and 120-mm mortars stationed on Mount Igman, overlooking Sarajevo. These tasks, to protect peacekeepers under attack in safe areas and enforce the no-fly zone, are examined below. In terms of UNPROFOR's force structure, the inclusion of NATO combat aircraft, although not technically part of UNPROFOR, gave the mission a strategic composition not unlike that of a joint warfighting coalition. In the strategic sense, UNPROFOR was a large and joint combat force with significant fighting capability. It had a corps-sized mechanized ground force, a large and sophisticated supporting air force, and even a fleet of advanced warships in the Adriatic enforcing the UN sanctions against the former Yugoslavia. This represented a radical departure from the force composition seen in observation and traditional peacekeeping missions. [37]

Most second-generation peacekeeping operations also had large nonmilitary forces that, although they are not covered in this book, did impact on the military structure, command and control, and objectives. For instance, UNTAC had seven separate components, of which the military, although by far the largest, was only one. The others were human rights, electoral activities, civil administration, civil police, repatriation, and rehabilitation.[38] In addition, second-generation peacekeeping operations worked closely with nongovernmental organizations (NGOs) and private volunteer organizations that provided much of the humanitarian aid in these conflicts. The relationship between NGOs and the UN force has been problematic at times and is explored further in the case study and below. The integrated presence of so many other UN agencies and NGOs added to the very different composition of second-generation peacekeeping missions.

Size

The largest traditional peacekeeping operation had eight light infantry battalions and supporting logistics units. In contrast, UNPROFOR in February 1994 was operating with twenty-seven combat arms battalions—either light, motorized, or mechanized infantry, as well as armored reconnaissance units. In addition, there were engineer, transportation, signals, medical, aviation, and general support battalions.[39] All told, UNPROFOR was as large as a corps-size operation, reaching almost 39,000 military personnel by November 1994.[40] Naturally, an operation of this tremendous size and military complexity complicated the management of such a force greatly. These complications and their impact on the missions are examined in the sections below on interoperability, command and control, and military objectives.

In the more challenging military environments of second-generation peacekeeping missions, there was a tendency for military requirements to have greater influence on force structure than in the more politically sensitive UN missions of the past. Despite that operational imperative, the political constraints inherent to a multinational body such as the UN still hampered military planning greatly. Much of this stemmed from the fact that the United Nations still had to recruit the voluntary contributions of member states and hastily put them together for an operation. This intrinsic constraint was exacerbated by huge demand for heavy forces and the subsequent scarcity of resources accompanying the growth in UN military operations of 1992–1993. This situation was highlighted in UNPROFOR, when in 1993 the UN commander in Bosnia-Herzegovina estimated that he would need 34,000 more peacekeepers to protect both humanitarian aid convoys and safe areas.[41] The estimate of 34,000 was made based on military requirements and without regard to political constraints on resources.

However, knowing that it would be impossible to secure that number of troops from member states (UNTAC with almost 15,000 troops and UNITAF with almost 35,000 troops were competing with UNPROFOR for member states' resources at the time), the secretary-general recommended implementing a "light option" with only 7,600 troops. This was a best-case scenario plan that "represented an initial approach [and] limited objectives. It assumed the consent and cooperation of the parties and provided a basic level of deterrence."[42] However, even after the light option was chosen, some nine months later only 5,000 of the 7,600 authorized troops had deployed to Bosnia.[43] This episode highlighted the fact that, although second-generation peacekeeping missions broke with years of traditional UN force structure planning in terms of size and composition, they were still subject to some of the same political constraints inherent to the UN as a strategic manager. Among the most obvious of these was the inability of the institution authoritatively to recruit and simultaneously organize many thousands of well-equipped troops in eighteen different missions around the globe.

Equitable Geographic Representation

The multinational composition of any UN force can be, at the same time, its political strength and its operational weakness. A diverse multinational force reflects consensus and cooperation among many member states. However, as missions grow in size, ambitions, and military complexity (not to mention when operating in a belligerent environment), the ad hoc multinational character of a UN force has, at times, become a severe military handicap. The potential military weaknesses of the UN multinational formations were ameliorated by the small and uncomplicated missions the United Nations conducted before the end of the Cold War. However, in complex and dangerous second-generation operations, a hastily assembled, geographically balanced, and unrehearsed multinational force often had its inherent weaknesses exacerbated and exposed. This was especially evident in the former Yugoslavia and Somalia.

In the advantage column, the post–Cold War United Nations had more freedom when recruiting to staff second-generation peacekeeping operations. The end of superpower tensions and the rise of nonstate belligerents that were not member states (and could therefore not veto a contingent in the Security Council or any other UN group) freed the UN staff from having to seek out neutral troop contributors acceptable to both the superpowers and the belligerents. However, even with this constraint lifted and more countries contributing, demand for peacekeepers began to far outstrip supply by 1993. The huge military requirements of the many second-generation peacekeeping missions forced the United Nations in many cases to forsake a politically balanced force on paper in favor of one that could simply accomplish the military mission.

On the one hand, there was an unprecedented number of member states participating in UN operations. In 1988, twenty-six countries contributed UN troops. In 1994, seventy-six member states had Blue Helmets employed in UN military operations.[44] Brunei, Bulgaria, Germany, Japan, Namibia, and Uruguay were all participating in UNTAC, their first UN mission.[45] Such a diverse group of newcomers and the end of Cold War blocs around the world would appear to make wide political balance in UN forces even easier to achieve. On the other hand, complex second-generation missions required more than simple light infantry battalions and first-line logistical support units. These new missions often required the advanced military capabilities possessed by only a few nations—usually the major powers and other industrialized nations. These forces were in considerable demand in these missions and the contributions of the major powers played a much greater role than in traditional missions.

This was evident in UNPROFOR. While military contingents from thirty-six member states were represented in UNPROFOR in March 1994, Britain and France alone provided almost 25 percent of the total force. Other NATO or European nations made up another 50 percent, and the rest of the world represented less than one quarter of the force.[46] In addition, although many nations could deploy light combat units of a certain standard, reliable logistics, medical, engineer, communications, transportation, and aviation units are largely restricted to First World countries. All the units of this type in UNPROFOR were from European or other NATO countries.[47] A mission structure such as that of UNPROFOR accentuated the disparity in capability between nations, which was further exacerbated by the challenging environments and complex military operations. This is highlighted in the section on interoperability below.

It was considerably harder to achieve political balance on paper in a complex mission of over 30,000 troops, especially when it was operating concurrently with two other large missions and fifteen smaller ones. The UN system for obtaining troops was always slow. When coupled with greatly increased requirements, it became even slower. It was one thing to deploy two to six light infantry battalions to an agreed-upon area of operations where they could expect the support of the UN member states hosting the mission. It was quite another to throw together a force of between twelve and twenty-five heavier battalions (plus heavy logistics support); deploy the force to a contested environment with little or no support from reliable local factions; and integrate the force's operations with other components in a comprehensive humanitarian, electoral, economic, and nation-building operation. The challenges of these circumstances meant slow going at times. In UNTAC, for example, no formal troop contributors' meetings were held until April 1992, two months before full deployment was scheduled. This delayed the deployment of the force considerably and undermined the mission.[48]

The frantic scramble for resources from member states led to a disproportionate reliance on some First World nations and a marginalization of other member states. Having to recruit from so many disparate member states also led to problems of quality control in some missions. The luxury of choosing troop contributors that the United Nations enjoyed in forming observation and traditional peacekeeping missions meant that, during the limited operations of the Cold War period, the United Nations could accept or dismiss offers of contingents. In addition, in traditional peacekeeping missions the standard of military forces required was not high (in terms of military capabilities) given the simple nature of the missions. However, the need for *quantity* in 1992–1993 deprived the UN of the ability to set binding criteria on the *quality* of the forces involved. As one senior UN official remarked, "beggars can't be choosers."[49]

Because so many UN troops were needed, second-generation peacekeeping missions were many times staffed with forces that spanned the entire spectrum of experience and proficiency in terms of doctrine, training, equipment, discipline, and operational capability. The United Nations did not have the luxury of turning down offers of troops when attempting to recruit over 80,000 troops for eighteen missions. The effects of this phenomenon are examined below and in the case study, but some examples are worth noting here. They are by no means unusual and can even be said to characterize second-generation peacekeeping missions. For instance, when forming UNPROFOR, the United Nations accepted an offer of troops from Pakistan, which, by 1994, could not manage to deploy the 3,000 troops promised because of a lack of basic equipment.[50] In UNTAC, all units were told to arrive with enough organic support to supply themselves for sixty days. Only a few were actually capable of this.[51]

Beyond operational capabilities, which are examined below, maintaining a high standard of behavior, professionalism, and discipline in these large and disparate forces was a problem. In UNPROFOR, the United Nations censored Russian, Ukrainian, and Nigerian units for racketeering, illegal dealings in weapons and fuel, prostitution, drug dealing, and other charges.[52] In UNTAC, the Bulgarian contingent contained only one English speaker; the troops, many of whom were recent convicts, had only one to two months of rudimentary military training; and a few even threatened the UN force commander with death unless he increased their pay![53] In a short time, fifty-six members of the battalion, including eight officers, were sent home for disciplinary reasons.[54] Quality control was a consistent problem in second-generation missions for force commanders and the UN staff in New York.

Although the traditional tenet of equitable geographic representation was challenged by the human capital needs of these operations, nowhere was it so clearly repudiated as in the United Nations' decision to contract out some missions. These included the initial entry into Somalia by a U.S.–led task force, the use of NATO to enforce the no-fly zone over the former Yugoslavia, the intervention into Rwanda by a French force in 1994, and the U.S. entry into Haiti in September 1994, which kick-started the moribund UN mission that had been approved on paper a year earlier. Nothing refutes the principles of equal geographic representation and neutrality in force structure more than the use of great power–led alliances or coalitions subcontracted for certain UN missions.

Interoperability

It is axiomatic from a military standpoint that interoperability between forces of different member states working together assumes greater and greater importance as forces become larger and attempt more complex and challenging operations. Interoperability, if not commonality, is considered critical for a well-functioning multinational force. Any degree of common doctrine; common training; common command, control, and communication procedures; common equipment; and common standards of professionalism can make it infinitely easier for a thirty-six–state ad hoc force to operate with a sense of cohesion.[55] Interoperability becomes even more important to the effectiveness of a multinational peacekeeping force trying to present a common front of stern impartiality to recalcitrant belligerents.

Interoperability was always a challenge for UN military operations, as noted in the case study of UNIFIL. Naturally, the challenges of interoperability were considerably lessened in smaller multinational forces, especially when only a few states were conducting relatively simple operations. A large, diverse, many-membered force, operating with different training, equipment, procedures, and tactics can aggravate these differences, especially in second-generation peacekeeping environments. In second-generation missions, the local factions often used the lack of interoperability among UN troops to their advantage. One U.S. government report noted that a Khmer Rouge general maintained that his troops knew how the UNTAC contingents differed greatly in their interpretation of the UNTAC mandate. The Khmer Rouge knew "which troops should be respected and which could be taken advantage of."[56] Many times, this bred resentment and distrust in the UN force. One senior UNTAC officer described the behavior of the French contingent in Cambodia as "treasonous!"[57] As Trevor Findlay noted in regard to UNTAC, "in the more demanding circumstances of second generation missions there needs to be a more appropriate trade-off between multilateralism and efficiency."[58] In other words, as military challenges increase, a successful force would wish to err on the side of efficiency, not multinationalism for its own sake.

Accordingly, a force such as UNPROFOR could be said to have been politically unbalanced in favor of military interoperability. The NATO or European character of UNPROFOR was noted above. However, even with that practical advantage, the integration of up to twenty-seven light, mechanized, and armored battalions in a dangerous environment (while conducting complicated military missions) was an enormous management challenge. Quite a gap opened up in UNPROFOR's military capabilities, which were relatively standard among light infantry battalions but extraordinarily different in heavier formations that were supported by sophisticated combat support and combat service support units.

For instance, in terms of equipment alone, the NATO contingents in UNPROFOR came with top-of-the-line armored and mechanized forces, with all the support trimmings to match (indirect fire support, fire detection radar, engineers, logistics, transportation, etc.). In contrast, some contingents from developing nations came with no winter clothing, no shelter, no individual protective gear, and even no arms! This was the unfortunate case of the only partly armed Bangladeshi battalion that was unable to protect itself after deployment to the Bihac safe area and was subsequently besieged and had to be relieved in the Bihac crisis of October–November 1994.[59] This situation forced second-generation peacekeeping operation commanders to "play favorites" by assigning less capable or reliable forces to secondary and peripheral roles. The former deputy commander of UNPROFOR noted that "the great variance in unit capabilities becomes, of necessity, a key factor in one's appreciation of the situation."[60] The alternative was to assign tasks equally, thereby preserving the customary UN principle of equal representation. As with the Bangladeshi troops at Bihac, this often put the less capable unit at risk or endangered the mission. With seventy-six member states contributing forces to complicated UN military operations in 1994, interoperability could not help but be a problem in missions where the stakes were so much higher than the innocuous missions of the past.

Command and Control

The greater military burdens of second-generation peacekeeping operations challenged the command and control tenets derived from the principles of peacekeeping. Ad hoc UN chains of command that were by necessity based on the United Nations' limited political legitimacy and military authority were overwhelmed when trying to command such large, ambitious, and complex multifunctional missions. In addition, as might be expected, the more dangerous and complex the UN military operations became, the more the traditional interpretation of UN "command" was called into question and challenged by national systems. As a result, UN contingents with difficult and dangerous military missions tended to fall back on rehearsed, authoritative, and responsive national chains of command.

Another traditional UN characteristic, the improvisation of control procedures, also was found wanting in many second-generation missions. The ambitious operations of these missions, which sometimes entailed offensive military operations in support of limited enforcement provisions, demanded practiced and common control procedures. Naturally, attempting to undertake these operations in a contested environment and with a large and diverse UN force greatly complicated matters. As a result, some tasks were contracted out to coalitions operating with the control procedures of a framework state or a rehearsed military alliance. Inventing and implementing control procedures on the go simply did not work and was dangerous in the near-combat environments of some second-generation missions.

The Chain of Command

The chain of command in second-generation peacekeeping operations was more complex in both depth and breadth than that of traditional peacekeeping. This greatly complicated the command of these missions, resulting in confusion and inefficiency. In some operations the United Nations had to contract out missions because it simply could not command large military operations undertaking limited enforcement operations. In many of these same missions, the UN chain of command was already overwhelmed with trying to direct the operations of large multifunctional operations with many different components. Berdal wrote in 1993 that "command, control, and communications arrangements in the field and between the force headquarters and the UN headquarters in New York have been unable to meet the requirements and coordinate the activities of multicomponent missions."[61]

Although this book deals with the military components of these missions, it is important to note that many military tasks in second-generation operations were undertaken to support and enhance the work of civilian groups. Therefore, the military chain of command was greatly affected by the many semiautonomous civilian components, other UN agencies (UNHCR, WHO, etc.), and NGOs. For the United Nations as a strategic manager, the addition of these groups and their nontraditional military requirements greatly expanded the layers of management and the number of actors involved.

To ensure unity of effort among these groups, the UN chain of command needed to effectively coordinate and integrate their operations at all levels, in New York and in the field. This was achieved to some extent in smaller missions such as UNTAG and ONOMUZ, but not in the larger and more ambitious missions. Trevor Findlay noted that "a clear lesson of UNTAC is the need for better strategic coordination between the components of large multipurpose UN missions. In what has been described as a managerial stovepipe, each component reported to its own headquarters in Phnom Penh rather than to UNTAC HQ."[62]

Although the chain of command increased in breadth to accommodate other mission components and in depth to accommodate larger and more military forces, the command relationship at the top remained the same. The secretary-general was invested with the responsibility for the mission by the Security Council, which provided strategic direction through mandates for the mission. The interaction between the Security Council and the secretary-general and his Secretariat staff represented the political level of command. As Berdal has written, their role together was to "translate the political will of member states into practicable mandates and provide continuous political/strategic guidance to missions."[63]

A small Secretariat staff was able to handle UN operations throughout the Cold War period, given the simple military nature and small size of most of these missions. Even then, there were notable problems in managing UN military operations at the strategic level of command. After 1991, this situation was aggravated by the sudden advent of many missions, some of which were of a size and complexity never before imagined by UN planners. As Berdal noted, "DPKO, and especially the Military Advisor's Office, was hopelessly understaffed to cope with the explosion of UN operations in 1992."[64] Adam Roberts noted that "the UN's lack of serious institutional machinery for long-term strategic planning of particular operations only reinforced the weakness of this process."[65]

The results of this dilemma were manifested in several areas. First and most important, there was the strategic coherence of the missions themselves, that is, how well the UN bodies in New York matched political objectives to the military resources at their disposal (and the modus operandi that these forces used). This is examined below. Second, it caused delays in forming the force, planning its operations, and deploying it in the field. These delays greatly affected some missions, such as UNTAC, where some nine months passed between the signing of the Paris Peace Accords and the "almost complete" deployment of the UNTAC battalions.[66] Trevor Findlay noted that

> the delay in deploying UNTAC led to a serious deterioration
> of the situation in Cambodia. . . . By the time UNTAC finally
> arrived, the peace settlement was in considerable jeopardy. . . .
> A second cause of the delay (the first being budgetary prob-
> lems) in UNTAC's deployment was that the UN Secretariat
> lacked the experience, resources and qualified personnel to
> organize a mission of such complexity, magnitude, and novel-
> ty at short notice. There were no organizational precedents on

> *which the Secretariat could draw for any of the civilian*
> *aspects of UNTAC and even some of the military aspects, such*
> *as those related to cantonment, were new to the UN.*[67]

Third, there were the problems created by the loose chain of command. These concerned the actual direction of the force in the field, in the day-to-day command and control between the strategic level in New York, and the operational level of command in the field.

The key link between these levels of command was the special representative of the secretary-general (SRSG). Although this position had been used only occasionally in past missions, it was standard for second-generation peacekeeping missions. This was a reflection of the need to separate the strategic level of command in these complicated missions from the political (Security Council/secretary-general), the operational (force commander), and the tactical (contingent commanders). The SRSG's strategic responsibility was to link the actions of the military forces in his mission to the political objectives mandated in New York. In addition, and more important from the perspective of the whole mission, the SRSG was tasked to coordinate the overall diplomatic, humanitarian, economic, and political efforts along with the military enterprise. It was therefore a surprise that in UNPROFOR, a mission that needed this leadership and coordination more than most, a special representative of the secretary-general did not arrive until January 1994, twenty-two months after the mission had been authorized in Croatia and nineteen months after its mandate had been extended to Bosnia-Herzegovina.[68] A subsequent report on UNPROFOR noted that this lack of an overall strategic leader led to "inconsistent responses [that] undercut the authority of UN forces in the eyes of the factions."[69]

The SRSG's task for strategic coordination was particularly hard in missions that had strategic actors other than the United Nations proper, such as the subcontractors who answered to other political entities (such as NATO, the French force in Rwanda, or the U.S.–led forces in Somalia and Haiti). The addition of a non-UN force working with a UN military operation at times greatly complicated the overall command and control of the mission. This was especially the case in UNPROFOR, where the NATO air forces were prepared to use active and coercive military force in support of passive peacekeepers on the ground. In this situation, it remained to NATO and the United Nations to work out a reliable and responsive command and control system whereby the extensive NATO air operation over the former Yugoslavia could coordinate effectively with the many thousands of peacekeepers on the ground.

In June 1993, in Resolution 836, the Security Council authorized NATO to perform close air support strikes in support of peacekeepers under attack in designated safe areas. For the next eight months, the command system for such NATO strikes required the UN force to call for close air support up through the UN chain of command to the SRSG, who would then take the request to the North Atlantic Council, the political forum of NATO.

This system proved to be overly complex, unresponsive, and unwieldy (Figure 6). After some negotiating, it was decided in February 1994 that the SRSG would have the final authority to call for NATO close air support in Bosnia-Herzegovina. In addition, he would have to call only the commander in chief of NATO's Southern Region.[70] The system still proved unresponsive, as evidenced by an incident on 12 March 1994, when it took four and one-half hours for UN officials to approve NATO air strikes against Bosnian Serbs shelling French UN peacekeepers. Although NATO planes were on the scene and ready to strike, the Serb force had disappeared by the time the United Nations approved the air strikes.[71] Consequently, the military representatives of thirty-two nations met in Britain for an international workshop on cooperation in peacekeeping. At this workshop, one observer noted that the best description that could be given to the UN-NATO command and control arrangements in Bosnia was "a shambles."[72]

The confusion over the chain of command that included subcontractors or executive agents mandated for UN–approved enforcement actions revealed the problems of integrating new actors into the UN chain of command in second-generation peacekeeping operations. Even without the dynamic introduced by subcontractors, multinational command and control structures—especially ad hoc ones—tended to weaken as the environment and mission became more dangerous. So, too, do improvised command structures weaken as the mission expands. Berdal noted that "the command and control structure that evolves ad hoc will be unable to accommodate subsequent mandate enhancements."[73] It was noted in Chapters Two through Five that the United Nations faced many institutional constraints, both political and technical, in attempting to command a mission. However, in observation and traditional peacekeeping missions the inability of the United Nations to command a mission while retaining a measure of operational control was ameliorated by the simple nature of those small missions.

In contrast, these constraints can vitiate large and ambitious missions that take place in dangerous environments. Berdal noted that in these cases "the relative impact of the [United Nations'] constraints will be intimately related to the nature of the environment in which a peacekeeping force is deployed; in hostile/complex settings, where the issue of the use of force naturally arises, both technical and the political constraints invariably tend to be more pronounced."[74]

In addition, in volatile environments, where complex operations have a much greater degree of risk to UN troops, there was more competition to the United

Figure 6

Command Relationships in Operation Deny Flight

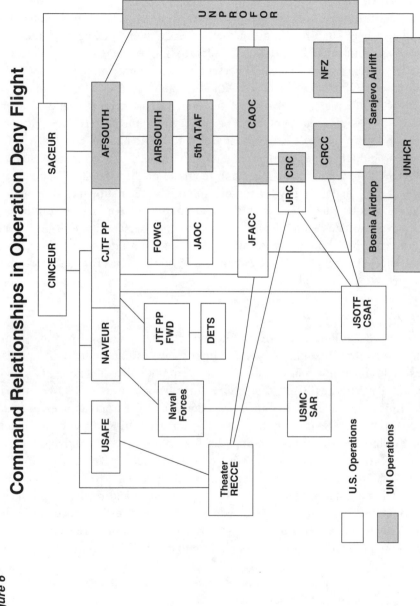

Source: Albert and Hayes, *Command Relationships for Peace Operations*, p. 63.

Nations from national chains of command. This phenomenon, colloquially known as the "phone home" syndrome, is highlighted in the case study. Needless to say, the increased propensity of national contingents to challenge the ad hoc UN chain of command threatened the command integrity of many second-generation peacekeeping operations. A U.S. GAO report noted the example of a UN troop contingent that, after double-checking with national authorities, refused a UNPROFOR order to move its troops to protect a UNHCR warehouse in Zenica. Other contingents sometimes questioned the authority of UNPROFOR to redeploy their troops.[75] As Berdal noted in regard to UNPROFOR, the "greater risks of such operations increases national interference in UN missions, not least because governments have a legitimate responsibility for their nationals. Many UNPROFOR nations constantly refer home for guidance on operational tasks."[76] A U.S. government study of UNPROFOR recognized the legal ramifications of this and stated unequivocally that the "final authority for command lies with the national contingent."[77] A similar report stated that "each national contingent commander ultimately has the right to decide on whether to execute an order and commit his troops to action that he deems to be harmful."[78] When the going got tough in these UN missions, the tough looked in many different directions for guidance—and not usually to the United Nations.

Control Procedures

This tendency to look to the rehearsed and reliable systems of national command and control also highlighted the importance of common control procedures in large, ad hoc multinational forces. Commonality is a key component in control procedures. Units that trained together (such as NATO countries) with similar doctrines and control procedures had great advantages over ad hoc coalitions of disparate contingents. The former UNPROFOR commander, General Philippe Morillon, noted that basing his initial command and control arrangements on the core framework of a rehearsed organization, NATO's recently defunct NORTHAG headquarters, helped UNPROFOR considerably.[79] The national military forces of member states and rehearsed alliances had common control procedures, such as operations order processes, staff operations, reporting formats, standard operating procedures, rules of engagement, communications procedures, interpretations of the laws of war, and codes of conduct.

Because the United Nations always had to recruit and form ad hoc forces from many disparate member states for each different mission, it never was able to implement and promulgate common control procedures. During the Cold War years, a conventional practice evolved in observation and peacekeeping missions that approached some form of common control procedures.

In addition, the simple military tasks of these missions meant that disparities over control procedures often could be worked out on the ground and did not generally have ramifications serious enough to undermine operations. As a result, until 1992–1993, the United Nations never attempted to institute procedures that would bring a measure of institutionalized continuity to its military operations.

However, as is examined in the case study, it became obvious during the conduct of complicated second-generation peacekeeping operations that a disparate coalition of forces could not improvise effective control procedures for complex operations in dangerous environments. As a result, the United Nations foundered in operations such as UNPROFOR and UNOSOM I and had to turn to subcontractors who could provide an off-the-shelf force package with rehearsed and reliable control procedures. The military requirements of second-generation peacekeeping demanded more professional command and control structures, methods, and procedures. As Berdal noted in his study of second-generation missions, "the lack of UN joint doctrine, or a minimum of published guidance, makes it impossible to run cohesive operations."[80]

Military Objectives

The military objectives of traditional peacekeeping could generally be understood in the context of the linear buffer zone. This was a strategic and operational mechanism that allowed a small, impartial, and passive force to limit armed conflict in certain (favorable) circumstances. The operations of second-generation peacekeeping missions did not feature this critical precondition for successful traditional peacekeeping. Second-generation operations usually took place in large and many times indeterminate areas where warring belligerents were not separated by recognized cease-fire lines, demilitarized zones, or buffer zones. The lack of a clearly defined mechanism that would encourage the separation of aggressive belligerents greatly complicated the environment and missions of second-generation peacekeeping operations. In addition, the combination of political cooperation on the Security Council and, conversely, little cooperation from local parties on the ground, gave these second-generation UN peacekeepers ambitious military objectives to accomplish in contested environments.

The case study of UN peacekeeping in southern Lebanon noted the deleterious effects on traditional peacekeeping when the assumptions of consent and cooperation failed. The experience in traditional peacekeeping made it clear that peacekeeping was a technique that could help only those who were willing to help themselves. This basic assumption also held true for second-generation peacekeeping missions. Belligerent cooperation was needed, expected, and factored into all planning and operations. Trevor Findlay noted in his study of UNTAC that the UN continued in second-generation missions to "organize military components on the basis of 'best-case' rather than 'worst-case' assumptions."[81] Mats Berdal also has noted that UNPROFOR "was conceived firmly within the framework of traditional peacekeeping operations with the implementation of the mandate contingent upon the continued consent of all parties."[82]

In the main, the critical assumption that underlined traditional peacekeeping also was the chief strategic imperative for second-generation peacekeeping. What determined the objectives and modus operandi of second-generation UN forces was largely the consent and cooperation of the belligerents. When that cooperation was not forthcoming in several large missions, second-generation missions differed from their predecessors in that they sometimes took limited actions to circumnavigate the missing consent. The challenge to second-generation peacekeeping operations in the field was how to deviate from the principles of peacekeeping and still be effective. The challenge to the United Nations was to attempt to manage the changing dynamics of these nontraditional mission objectives and modus operandi.

These challenges spawned a functional and theoretical debate in 1992–1995, sometimes known as the "consent debate." The debate existed between two schools of thought: one school characterized by a traditionalist approach to UN peacekeeping on one hand,[83] and on the other by a more robust approach to second-generation missions and the use of coercive force.[84] The crux of the debate, as seen below in the Somalia case study, was to what extent the UN forces should have changed their modus operandi to accomplish their missions in contested environments.

The traditionalist school maintained that peacekeeping was impossible without the consent of the belligerents. Once a UN force attempted to use active force to compel belligerents into a pattern of behavior, it crossed a Rubicon into enforcement missions in which the impartiality of the UN force was compromised and peacekeeping in its traditional form was impossible. Shashi Tharoor, assistant to the under secretary-general for peacekeeping, wrote that "mixing peace enforcement with peacekeeping is the military equivalent of having one's cake and eating it too."[85] The traditionalist school drew much of its conceptual support from the experience of missions that attempted at times to mix passive and active measures in the same missions, or, in other words, to move back and forth at will across the boundary of consent. Traditionalists were supported by officers such as the former deputy commander of UNPROFOR, who stated, "Peacekeeping and peace enforcement do not mix. Any attempt to overlap and produce a gray area within which a peacekeeping mission attempts to operate, creates a condition of such dissonance that the mission is in danger of collapse. There can be no grey area, no overlap of peacekeeping with peace enforcement."[86]

However, the robust peacekeeping school of thought maintained that in contested environments, it was sheer folly to operate based entirely on the traditional tenets of consent, impartiality, and the passive use of force. A peacekeeping force operating in these environments, such as happened in the former Yugoslavia and Somalia, was hostage not only to the environment, but also to its modest modus operandi. The robust school maintained that a second-generation force could use some limited coercive measures to shape consent and exert some influence over the environment, but fell far short of launching a full-scale enforcement mission. This school recognized that a robust second-generation force hoped for consent and was traditionally passive if such consent and cooperation were present. However, a robust force would also identify consistent transgressors, and, through operations using proportional active force, use the "lightest touch possible in the hope that the parties on the ground will, in the end, assent to the UN's mandate." [87]

It is helpful to keep this debate in mind when examining operational tasks, especially in the case study. The debate over consent remained unresolved throughout this period as soldiers and analysts attempted to create a doctrine in which an impartial force could operate with the minimum use of active force in a contested environment and still accomplish something. What was more certain, based on empirical evidence, is that the application of traditional peacekeeping doctrine in contested environments such as the former Yugoslavia and Somalia represented the mistaken application of an apparently sound (albeit limited) technique developed to meet other contingencies. As Berdal has noted in reference to UNPROFOR, "the very insistence on adhering to the normative principles of consent, impartiality, and the non-use of force except in self-defense have, with the exception of Macedonia, undermined the military effectiveness of UNPROFOR operations."[88]

However, attempts to revise traditional peacekeeping doctrine and undertake more muscular operations undermined some second-generation peacekeeping missions. As Adam Roberts wrote in 1994, "there is as yet little sign of the emergence of a satisfactory doctrine or practice regarding operations which have an essentially hybrid character, involving elements of both peacekeeping and enforcement."[89] Traditional UN peacekeeping was not appropriate for many new missions; yet muscular peacekeeping managed by the United Nations backfired. More important for this study, regardless of which technique was more effective, the United Nations could manage the military operations of the traditionalist school but did not have the institutional competency to form, direct, and employ larger and more complex military forces in the more robust operations. The challenges associated with managing that military muscle were better faced by credible and rehearsed military alliances or small groups of states than by a disparate multinational body such as the United Nations. It was for this reason that a NATO implementation force (IFOR) replaced UNPROFOR in Bosnia in December 1995. When the Dayton peace accords provided a political framework for Bosnia that needed to be enforced by a large and robust combat force with the ability to intimidate factions and perhaps conduct coercive operations, it was patently obvious that the United Nations was not a suitable manager for this type of operation.

The process of contracting out certain parts of a UN military operation to other political or military entities allowed the United Nations to undertake complicated military tasks it might otherwise not have attempted. An organization such as NATO could bring to the United Nations advanced weapon systems, established and rehearsed multinational command and control structures, common operational procedures, extensive infrastructure and communications systems, and readily available trained forces because NATO's focused and limited defensive mission caused the interests of its few members to converge. This gave NATO a political legitimacy, military authority, and functional credibility not found in large and disparate collective security organizations. Roberts noted that "NATO's greatest advantage over the UN, historically, has been agreement on some clearly defined defensive purposes, whereas the UN has an almost infinite range of responsibilities.[90] Moreover, beyond NATO's operational advantages, its political military structure was more conducive to a coherent matching of political goals to military means, a problem that plagued the United Nations in many second-generation missions.

Strategic Coherence

Strategic coherence is a phrase used to measure the feasibility of the connection between the political ends and the military means of a mission. Second-generation peacekeeping missions, especially the larger and more ambitious ones, were often characterized by poor strategic coherence. In most of these operations an enormous gap existed between the expectations raised by Security Council resolutions and the available resources and modus operandi of the forces in the field. In UNPROFOR, especially, the numerous and ambitious Security Council resolutions were seen to be created almost in complete seclusion from the intractability of the operational environment and the limited resources of UNPROFOR. As Berdal noted in 1993, "this has placed impossible demands on UNPROFOR and has generated legitimate criticisms from field personnel to the effect that the Security Council treats resolutions as if they were 'self-executing.' "[91]

The seeds of this sort of discontent were rooted in the language of UNPROFOR's mandate, which described the force as an "interim arrangement to *create* the conditions of peace and security required for the negotiation of an overall settlement to the Yugoslav crisis"[92][my emphasis]. Given the intractability of the crisis, one should read this statement of purpose not as naïveté, but as a reflection of the confidence on the Security Council in early 1992. What is misleading at best, and deceptive at worst, is the use of the word "create" to describe the strategy of the operation. As noted, no second-generation peacekeeping operation was structured, trained, or mandated for the active and coercive operations required to "create" the conditions of peace and security in an environment such as the former Yugoslavia.

During the first two years of UNPROFOR, the mandate was enlarged over a dozen times.[93] After the initial mission was established in Croatia, it then became successively responsible, inter alia, for greater peacekeeping functions in the protected areas in Croatia; the security and functioning of Sarejevo airport in Bosnia-Herzegovina, including the delivery of humanitarian aid through the airport; the assumption of monitoring functions in the "pink areas" of Croatia; the performance of immigration and customs functions on Croatia's borders; the delivery of humanitarian assistance to Bosnia-Herzegovina and protection of UNHCR convoys performing such missions; the monitoring of military withdrawals, heavy equipment removal, and the demilitarization of the Prevlaka peninsula; the passive monitoring of a flight ban over Bosnia-Herzegovina; the establishment of a preventive deployment in the former Yugoslav republic of Macedonia; the active enforcement (by NATO) of the no-fly zone over Bosnia-Herzegovina; the successive establishment of Srebrenica, then Sarejevo, then four other Bosnian towns as "safe areas"; and the authorization of the use of active airpower to protect these safe areas. [94]

It is not damning in itself that the mandate of a UN mission may be enlarged. All political situations shift constantly, and military missions must change accordingly. However, the problem in UNPROFOR, UNAMIR, and UNOSOM II was that the mandates were enlarged with apparent disregard for the resources of the UN force in the field, the will of the international community to provide more, and the environment in which the UN force operated (as well as its ability to affect that environment). Coherence would dictate, as Berdal noted, that "the political aspirations which a mandate embodies must be capable of translation into a set of realizable military objectives."[95]

In UNPROFOR, the apparent disconnection between the ambitions of the Security Council and the situation facing the UN commander in the field led one UNPROFOR commander, Belgian LTG Francis Briquemont, to remark that "I don't read the Security Council resolutions anymore because they don't help me." Indeed, upon announcing his resignation as UNPROFOR commander, Briquemont pointed to a widening rift between the United Nations in New York and peacekeepers on the ground. When asked what advice he would have for his replacement, Briquemont suggested the new commander "constantly remind those politically responsible about the difficulties in which they put us [UNPROFOR] because there is no coherence in their strategies."[96] As a result, and as in Korea (see Chapter Eight), UNPROFOR commanders would often reinterpret their mandate to match their available resources—approaching strategy backward.[97]

The UN Secretariat recognized this problem of widening and unachievable mandates as UNPROFOR evolved but appeared to have little influence in convincing the Security Council to pay it more heed. A report of the secretary-general stated,

> *The steady accretion of mandates from the Security Council has transformed the nature of UNPROFOR's mission in Bosnia-Herzegovina and highlighted certain implicit contradictions. The increased tasks assigned to UNPROFOR in later resolutions have inevitably strained its ability to carry out [its] basic mandate [delivery of humanitarian aid]. The proliferation of resolutions and mandates has complicated the role of the force.[98]*

Thus the gap between means and ends in UNPROFOR (and, as will be seen, in UNOSOM II) was characteristic of several large and ambitious second-generation peacekeeping missions. In Cambodia, the former Yugoslavia, Rwanda, Haiti, and Somalia, the UN missions were faced with the possibility that noncompliance from large groups of belligerents would prevent the fulfillment of their mandate. In a situation such as this, the UN force faced three choices: (1) revise its mandate to reflect more limited goals and a recognition that ultimately the pace of the peace and reconciliation process rested with the belligerents; (2) soldier on in the hope the belligerents would eventually be persuaded to cooperate; or (3) reinforce the mission and commit new resources and/or extend its mandates to give it a greater probability of success.

As is seen below, UNTAC chose a combination of the first and second paths and was fortunate that the Khmer Rouge did not disrupt the elections after the abandonment of the plan to disarm that faction. UNOSOM II in Somalia and UNAMIR were not so lucky. UNMIH was moribund for a year until it choose the third path through getting an American military task force to kick-start the international effort in Haiti. UNPROFOR chose a combination of persevering and limited reinforcement in both force size and mandates. Unfortunately for UNPROFOR, a huge gap still existed between expectations and reality, between the mandates and the military resources of UNPROFOR. In a situation such as that faced by UNPROFOR, the operational method left to the United Nations was "soldiering on in hope," which was judged to be preferable to "withdrawing in abdication."[99] The strategy did not reflect a logical connection between ends and means. Rather, objectives were determined in a degree of isolation from military resources and requirements, and the gap was left to be filled by hope.

Disarming and Demobilizing Local Belligerents

Second-generation peacekeeping missions were often conducted in an intrastate environment where legitimate governments did not have a reliable monopoly of control over armed groups. In these missions UN forces were therefore often tasked to disarm and demobilize militias, paramilitary groups, guerrilla forces, or even well-organized forces such as the Khmer Rouge. In every case where the United Nations attempted such a mission (Namibia, Cambodia, Mozambique, the former Yugoslavia, Somalia, and Haiti), the cooperation of the belligerents was the principal operational imperative. The UNOSOM II case study highlights the deleterious effects of attempting to disarm even loosely organized paramilitary groups through coercion and without their cooperation.

In UNTAC, the most comprehensive UN attempt to disarm and demobilize belligerents, the process was faced with the dilemma raised by the intransigence of the Khmer Rouge. The UNTAC plan had been to deploy its twelve infantry battalions to cantonment sites and checkpoints where the factions could gather and turn in their weapons to UN officials. The scale of the operation was immense and the original plan called for eighty-four cantonment sites and twenty checkpoints. Statistically, that left only one platoon of UN infantry (25–35 troops) per site to prepare for the disarmament of an estimated 550,000 regular army and militia forces.[100] When the Khmer Rouge refused to cooperate and denied UN forces access to areas under its control, the UNTAC hierarchy (up to the secretary-general) faced three choices: to abandon this crucial mission, to carry on without the Khmer Rouge, or to coerce the reluctant party into compliance. The third option would have required a new mandate and a force structure above and beyond the loose multinational mix of disparate forces in UNTAC. It was never a realistic option to seek an enforcement mandate. In fact, French General Loridan, the deputy military commander of UNTAC, was relieved of his position after advocating the use of active force against the Khmer Rouge.[101]

In addition, it was felt in UNTAC that to seek enforcement provisions against even one clearly recalcitrant party would cause the UN mission to compromise its impartiality. This decision was pragmatic in that it recognized that an enforcement operation designed to coerce 12,000 Khmer Rouge guerrillas in the jungles of Cambodia would take an absolutely immense military effort.[102] It would also introduce the United Nations to the conflict as merely another party instead of an impartial and honest broker. This might repeat what was viewed as a critical mistake by ONUC in the Congo, some thirty years before. There, in what Alan James called a "double departure from the basic values of peace-keeping," the United Nations authorized limited enforcement action and squandered its status as an impartial actor.[103]

In the end, the United Nations disarmed and demobilized only one fifth of the armed belligerents in Cambodia.[104] There was much debate about whether to hold elections as planned, as "the failure of the cantonment and disarmament phase of the peace plan"[105] threatened the neutral environment that the successful completion of disarmament was to provide. However, UNTAC kept its nerve, hoped the Khmer Rouge would not cause full-scale disruption of the election, redeployed its forces to provide electoral security, and rode its luck. Trevor Findlay has listed "serendipity" as a factor behind UNTAC's success.[106] UNTAC, like most peacekeeping missions, was a mission with neither the mandate nor the forces to create or shape the environment in which it operated. In light of the instability of the peace accord, it was left to hope that belligerents would cooperate. The use of the word "hope" itself is common in UN documents related to peacekeeping, verifying that UN troops had to accept their capricious environments as they came, an extremely uncomfortable operational method for a soldier, but de rigueur for the peacekeeper—traditional or second generation. In this way peacekeeping refuted a classic soldier's dictum, "Hope is not a Method," often stated to reflect the desire of the soldier to have the resources and mandate necessary to create the conditions for his success and eliminate or minimize the impact of variables not under his control.

Protecting Humanitarian Aid

This mission will be examined in greater detail in the case study; however, it is instructive to note here the important role it assumed in other second-generation peacekeeping missions. In UNPROFOR, it is not unfair to say that the delivery and protection of humanitarian aid became, in light of its failures to limit armed conflict, the de facto raison d'être of the UN mission. In fact, because of the failure of UNPROFOR to limit armed conflict and promote conflict resolution throughout its first three years, humanitarian aid achievements were virtually the sole measure of success identified by UN officials in the various reports on the effort in the former Yugoslavia. Tonnage of aid delivered measured success. The effort was substantial, indeed, and in 1993 alone UNPROFOR protected almost 5,000 UNHCR convoys, as well as administering Sarajevo airport and the airlift, which delivered 71 percent of Sarajevo's food.[107]

The protection of humanitarian aid in a bellicose environment would imply that the UN force was prepared to use force of arms if necessary. The Blue Helmets could use force passively, within the traditional authorization of self-defense (which allowed self-defense of their mandate when under armed attack). These provisions could easily be applied to convoys under UN protection. Alternatively, it could use force actively to guarantee that corridors for the delivery of humanitarian aid were free of threatening belligerents. Naturally, a force such as UNPROFOR, structured and mandated for a peacekeeping mission predicated on consent, impartiality, and the passive use of force could not realistically choose the latter course. The UNOSOM II study examines a case of humanitarian aid operations undertaken with a more aggressive philosophy.

In UNPROFOR, although the Security Council initially authorized UN member states in Bosnia to "take all measures necessary" under Chapter VII of the Charter to deliver aid,[108] none undertook enforcement operations. This resolution was an attempt to avoid giving UNPROFOR proper any enforcement provisions and yet authorize those member states concerned to take it upon themselves to push through humanitarian aid, even if it meant using active military force to coerce recalcitrant belligerents. The United Nations later withdrew this authorization and assigned UNPROFOR proper to protect aid convoys with passive force,[109] the secretary-general noting that this "new dimension" in peacekeeping did not "require a revision of the [traditional] rules of engagement."[110]

Humanitarian aid operations in contested environments had three important effects on second-generation peacekeeping operations. In terms of force structure, the protection of humanitarian aid was an expensive mission—one that required great amounts of manpower for the security of storage sites, supply bases, main supply routes, air- and seaports, and distribution sites. These sites could all be separated by hundreds of miles of hazardous terrain, poor roads, and bad communications infrastructure, all controlled by well-armed belligerents with pernicious intentions. The UN operations therefore required mobile and well-armed forces with reliable command, control, and communications arrangements, as well as transportation and engineering support. As noted above, the military demands of these operations were reflected in the UNPROFOR commander's initial estimate of the large military forces he would need to accomplish his mission in Bosnia.

Second, the provision of humanitarian aid in second-generation peacekeeping missions was carried out principally by civilian components of the mission as well as NGOs, many of which required UN military protection (and some of which wanted nothing to do with the UN military forces at all). The effort needed to coordinate the actions of these very disparate groups was tremendous. In UNPROFOR, there were over 150 NGOs operating in the UN area of operations, of whom only forty-one regularly coordinated their operations with UNPROFOR. In the words of UN peacekeeping consultant

Sir David Ramsbotham, this led to over 100 "loose cannons" operating independently in what belligerents perceived as an overall UN effort.[111] In many missions, the impartiality of the NGOs was very suspect at times, as some aligned themselves with particular factions.[112] Overall, the management of this facet of a humanitarian aid mission was, at the very least, an ordeal for military commanders.

Third, there was the perverse strategic dilemma that arose when humanitarian aid was provided without being tied to a coherent strategic plan that revolved around the political resolution of the conflict. Humanitarian relief was most often the result of public opinion, especially in the West, that demanded immediate action. As such, it was usually an instant reaction not often integrated into the overall political and military strategy. One U.S. government report noted that, "according to senior managers in Bosnia," the lead UN agency for humanitarian relief "did not have a concept of operations that linked military and humanitarian actions."[113] Ironically, the immediate goals of humanitarian aid (to provide relief to as many suffering people as possible as soon as possible) did not always contribute to the long-term goal of conflict resolution. Even more tragically, the immediate goals of humanitarian aid could be at complete variance with the goals of conflict resolution and even prolong the conflict itself.

It has been noted throughout this book that the goal of "limiting armed conflict" (which is what all other UN military objectives were ultimately designed to do) could contribute directly and indirectly to conflict resolution. However, in both UNPROFOR and UNOSOM II, the provision of humanitarian aid did not appear to even indirectly contribute to conflict resolution. As Berdal noted, the immediate provision of humanitarian aid without regard to how it affected the objectives of the United Nations and the local belligerents could have an adverse effect:

> The point here in terms of future peacekeeping is that when humanitarian operations serve as a substitute for dealing with the root cause of conflict or as compensation for diplomatic failures, formulation of realizable military objectives becomes extremely difficult. More seriously still, it may prolong the conflict by drawing attention away from its underlying sources.[114]

Thus, other than the immediate benefits to recipients, the effects of providing humanitarian aid as a reaction, rather than a strategy were twofold. On the political level, it could substitute for more substantial and concrete diplomatic actions, even providing conditions that enabled all belligerents to concentrate on continued fighting rather than peace.[115] On the operational military level, these missions required enormous troop strength to protect ports of entry, convoys, supply routes, distribution centers, and storage bases. Berdal noted that "the chief lesson of UN military operations in Bosnia is that in the midst of continuing civil war, humanitarian support operations (in this case, armed protection for convoys) are exceptionally difficult."[116]

Ensuring the Security of Protected or Safe Areas

In the course of second-generation peacekeeping mandates, the United Nations set up protected areas, safe areas, and semiprotected areas known as "pink zones" in an attempt to ensure that certain peaceful conditions existed in specified areas. In UNPROFOR's Croatian protected areas, the UN troops "were required to ensure that the protected areas (and 'pink zones') remained demilitarized and that all persons residing in them were protected from fear of armed attack."[117] This included general monitoring of the temporary and capricious cease-fires, verifying the withdrawal of the Croatian Army and irregular militia groups from the "pink zones," supervising the restoration of authority by the local governments, and monitoring the maintenance of law and order as well as the rights of minority groups. In February 1993, UNPROFOR had twelve infantry battalions assigned to this mission, an enormous number by UN standards (almost 14,000 with support troops),[118] but far too few to do the mission properly without significant belligerent cooperation. By 1995, the United Nations was considering abandoning some safe areas entirely because of the lack of resources to carry out the mandate adequately in an increasingly belligerent environment.[119] A final series of humiliations occurred in May 1995 when almost 400 UN peacekeepers were taken hostage by Bosnian Serbs after NATO air strikes and in July 1995 when Bosnian Serb forces overran the UN safe areas of Srebrenica and Zepa.

UNPROFOR peacekeepers on the ground failed to guarantee the security of protected areas, pink zones, and safe areas for three principal reasons. First, they did not have the required cooperation from the belligerents. This could almost be expected for, as James Schear noted, "the safe area mission tended to cast UNPROFOR in a partisan light."[120] In some safe areas, such as Bihac, the impartiality of the safe area mission was damaged further when they were used by Bosnian Muslim forces to shield their own military operations. All told, the UN forces guarding the safe areas hardly seemed like honest brokers to any of the parties concerned and were ripe for manipulation.

Second, and stemming from that failure, the Blue Helmets were too limited in number to form a deterrent presence around the areas, which were large tracts of land in extremely difficult terrain. The secretary-general stated that "militarily, in order for UNPROFOR to deter attacks against the safe areas, it would need to have a substantial number of troops, equipped adequately to counter the besieging forces and defend UNPROFOR positions. Without such resources it is impossible to defend the safe areas, not least because they are totally surrounded by hostile forces."[121] As mentioned above, the UNPROFOR peacekeepers did not have a mechanism such as a buffer zone that could extend their resources and compensate for a small number of troops by freeing them from physically occupying all areas at once. Third, the force structure, modus operandi, and resources of UNPROFOR did not support the use of active force by the peacekeepers to protect the areas.

The first phenomenon, noncooperation, need not be explored further here. However, the second phenomenon is instructive. An important lesson that came out of UNPROFOR's experience with these protected or safe areas was that, if there was no legitimate, clearly recognizable, and inviolable separation of belligerent factions, the operation would not succeed. This seemingly obvious observation[122] reinforced the profound importance of a clearly defined buffer zone to traditional peacekeeping techniques. Like their predecessors in traditional buffer zones, second-generation peacekeepers also were "alert, but inert." The difference between the two situations was that in traditional peacekeeping, the legitimate buffer zone was the mechanism through which a mission could apply passive techniques to the environment and succeed.

The buffer zone extended limited resources and enabled the peacekeepers inside to exert some measure of authority and control over recognized UN territory. It also allowed UN soldiers to use a passive operational technique that uniquely suited the limited military authority of the United Nations. The technique suited the institution and vice versa. In the absence of such a zone, the passive techniques of traditional peacekeeping were applied without a control mechanism. This often left second-generation peacekeepers as spectators to the fighting between inextricably mixed belligerents in difficult terrain. The separation of forces cannot be underestimated as a necessary precondition in which passive peacekeeping can succeed.

In response to the dilemma posed by the third reason for failure, the United Nations authorized the use of NATO air strikes to "support UNPROFOR in the performance of its mandate."[123] The same resolution authorized UNPROFOR troops on the ground to "take all necessary measures, including the use of force" to defend the safe areas against bombardment or armed incursion. As noted above, the ground forces of UNPROFOR never moved to take advantage of this authorization, for much the same reason that UNTAC did not seek enforcement powers against the Khmer Rouge. UNPROFOR was not structured for peace enforcement, and it was felt that any such attempts would have jeopardized UNPROFOR's impartial standing and left the peacekeepers vulnerable and exposed to immediate retaliation. It was felt that, if UNPROFOR acted actively against one side in the conflict, it would endanger the entire diplomatic, humanitarian, and military effort, which was of course predicated on the classic precepts of peacekeeping—consent, impartiality, and the use of force in self-defense only.

Although UNPROFOR gave good reasons for not using its enforcement powers, it did experiment with using active force from the air in combination with passive force on the ground. The use of NATO close air support happened on seven occasions between 1992 and 1994, twice in defense of UNPROFOR ground forces, four times against Bosnian Serbs threatening safe areas, and once against a Bosnian Serb surface-to-air missile site.[124] The most dramatic episode in this plan to mix passive force on the ground and the threat of active force in the air to protect safe areas in Bosnia happened in November 1994. NATO jets bombed Bosnian Serb artillery and tank positions attacking Bihac. The measure was treated as a success initially, but the operation had no lasting effect and the Bosnian Serbs took retaliatory actions such as denying UNPROFOR freedom of movement and activating surface-to-air missile batteries.[125]

When the smoke had cleared, the entire episode had left both NATO and UNPROFOR with extreme doubts about the efficacy of this approach to the gray area between peacekeeping and peace enforcement. The NATO secretary-general was critical of the seeming contradiction between active enforcement directed principally at one side in the air and passive impartiality on the ground: "I do not believe, however, that we can pursue decisive peace enforcement from the air while the UN is led, deployed, and equipped for peacekeeping on the ground. If we have learned anything from this conflict, it is that we cannot mix these two missions."[126]

In addition, the authorization for active enforcement by UNPROFOR on the ground once again exposed the gap between strategic guidance and operational reality in UNPROFOR. As the former deputy commander has stated,

> The Council's reference to Chapter VII of the UN Charter in several of its Bosnia-related resolutions, conveying compulsory authority for certain actions, has created unrealistic expectations that UNPROFOR is postured to repel attacks against safe areas by force . . . such a condition, the grey area, was produced by certain interpretations of resolution 836. . . . My point is that there can be no grey area, no overlap of peacekeeping with peace enforcement.[127]

This fear came to fruition when NATO air strikes on the Bosnian Serb capital of Pale precipitated the shelling of Tuzla (71 civilians killed) and the taking of hundreds of UN peacekeepers as hostages in May 1995.[128] As a result, in June 1995 Britain, France, and a few other NATO nations deployed a heavily armed combat rapid-reaction force to Bosnia (under titular UN command) more aggressive rules of engagement than their UN counterparts. This force engaged in some artillery duels in defense of the safe area of Sarajevo, even though nobody was ever quite sure under whose command (national, NATO, or the United Nations) they were operating.[129] As one report noted, "the British–French rapid reaction force seems at least as inclined to take its cues from London and Paris as from UN officials."[130]

Denying Movement

The clearest example of a second-generation peacekeeping mission's task to deny movement was the no-fly zone instituted over parts of the former Yugoslavia. Technically, the no-fly zone was not part of UNPROFOR per se and was patrolled and enforced by NATO, under the authorization of Security Council Resolution 816 (31 March 1993). NATO itself could also be said to have instituted another movement-denial operation in Bosnia when it established its own exclusion zones for heavy weapons around Sarajevo and Bihac. These exclusion zones were not explicitly authorized by the UN Security Council.[131] The UN no-fly zone, authorized in October 1992 by Security Council Resolution 781, declared a ban on all military flights in the airspace of Bosnia-Herzegovina. It was originally intended that UNPROFOR would passively monitor this ban through the efforts of approximately seventy-five military observers placed at airfields around Bosnia-Herzegovina.[132] It soon became apparent that the ban was not easily enforced through passive measures, especially in light of the lack of cooperation from belligerents. That was when NATO was brought on board.

In the first six months of the no-fly zone, the United Nations reported over 540 violations of the ban on military flights.[133] After the passage of Resolution 816 and the active enforcement of the ban by NATO combat aircraft, there were only two verified exceptions to the no-fly zone over the next ten months. In the first a Bosnian Serb combat aircraft heeded a NATO warning to land immediately. In the second incident, NATO fighters shot down four Bosnian Serb jets that refused to land.[134] It was the first use of active military force by NATO in the history of the alliance.

The mission to deny movement, whether it is on the ground or in the air, would seem to be one that implies enforcement. A passive interpositional buffer zone was supposed to deny movement through that zone to all parties. The legitimacy and authority of the buffer zone was predicated on the moral authority of the United Nations and made possible through the cooperation of the local factions. In contrast, the denial of movement presupposed noncooperation and required a deterrent as well as a credible use of proportional force when the deterrent failed. The possible use of this amount of force, especially in an air operation, required a sophisticated and complex military capability. For

UNPROFOR, this meant that the United Nations had to contract out the enforcement mission to a military alliance with well-rehearsed procedures, reliable command and control mechanisms, and advanced combat, support, and intelligence-gathering aircraft.

"Nation Building"

The environment to which second-generation peacekeeping missions were deployed was often that of the failed state. In every second-generation peacekeeping operation, the "host" state experienced some degree of deterioration in terms of the effective functioning of all levels of government, the control of the military and police, the provision of basic services to its citizens, and the disintegration of all manner of national infrastructure. As such, a significant feature of second-generation peacekeeping operations was "nation-building" functions, such as the organization and protection of elections, the supervision of government functions, the restoration of law and order, the rebuilding of national infrastructure, mine clearance, and the repatriation and rehabilitation of refugees. Naturally, in a strategic sense these missions were not always in the purview of the military component. However, they did require the support of the UN military component. This mission is explicitly highlighted in the case study of UNOSOM. Along with Haiti and Rwanda in 1994, Somalia in 1992 represented the classic candidate for a failed state that many felt needed UN nation-building activities.

Conclusion

Many challenges of the post–Cold War world, such as those in the former Yugoslavia, Rwanda, Haiti, and Somalia, did not lend themselves to the technique of traditional UN peacekeeping. Nonetheless, the consensus enjoyed on the Security Council following the end of the Cold War led members of that body to authorize peacekeeping operations in the clear absence of a supportive local political environment. To tip the balance in favor of the peacekeepers, the military components of these missions were made larger, heavier, more sophisticated, and given ambitious objectives that might help the UN force shape the environment into one that benefited the UN presence. It soon became clear, however, that the local political environment was still very much the most influential factor in determining the ultimate success or failure of these reinforced missions. As Berdal noted in his study of UNPROFOR, "The conflict in the former Yugoslavia has never been amenable to resolution through the 'peacekeeping treatment.' 'Peacekeeping' cannot by itself serve as a means of resolving violent conflict and ought not to become a substitute for addressing structural sources of conflict as it has in the former Yugoslavia."[135]

When in missions such as UNPROFOR this new and more muscular approach to UN peacekeeping failed to produce dividends, an even more radical departure was made. Some peacekeeping missions were given limited enforcement measures, which at times were executed by the well-armed and organized combat formations of non-UN organizations. On several occasions, these subcontractors acted without the explicit authorization of the UN Security Council, although they maintained that their operations were within the spirit of vague and overly ambitious UN mandates. This was most clearly evident in NATO's decisions to impose its own heavy weapon exclusion zones and in the American attempts to capture General Mohammed Farah Aideed in Somalia.[136] Needless to say, managing these large, dangerous, and ambitious operations—in which other military actors were involved in the United Nations' cause—greatly challenged the limited powers of the United Nations as it attempted to form, direct, and employ these military forces.

The political and military requirements of second-generation peacekeeping operations forced the United Nations to abandon the traditional principles of peacekeeping that had evolved from over forty years of trial and error. In 1989–1992, many hoped that the active consensus on the Security Council could surmount the new challenges of these missions: surely peacekeeping could evolve over time as a political-military technique and grow to meet these new challenges? To help in that cause, the Secretariat was reorganized and reinforced to manage these complex missions more effectively. However, by 1995, the United Nations was seeking to scale back these ambitions.[137]

Of the second-generation missions completed to date, only UNTAG in Namibia and ONUMUZ in Mozambique, both relatively small missions, can be considered successes. UNPROFOR in the former Yugoslavia, UNOSOM II in Somalia, and UNAMIR in Rwanda can be considered abject failures in the strategic sense: they all failed, after enormous sacrifice, to limit armed conflict enough to promote a stable environment that could conceivably lead to conflict resolution. UNTAC in Cambodia was considered only a qualified success because, although the conflict was temporarily resolved, UNTAC ultimately failed to accomplish its primary mission of disarming the various factions. Recent turmoil in Cambodia may make "qualified success" an overly kind judgment of UNTAC's legacy. ONUC in the Congo also can be considered a qualified success in that it ultimately achieved its goals, but at the cost of traumatizing the United Nations about large and active missions for another thirty years.[139]

Ultimately, the increase in the size, military capabilities, and ambitions of peacekeeping in its second generation was more than offset by the recalcitrance of the belligerents in many of the areas to which these peacekeepers were deployed. The challenge of conducting these complex missions in these environments was aggravated by the inherent constraints on the United Nations as an institution attempting to manage military operations. The limited military operations of observation missions and traditional peacekeeping were more suited to the limits on the United Nations' institutional capabilities.

This leads to the conclusion that in the case of many second-generation missions, the United Nations applied a good (albeit limited) technique to the wrong environments. John Mackinlay wrote in 1994,

> *Although the UN experts had developed a valuable understanding of the political and institutional components of the UN, many were ignorant of existing military requirements and techniques. They had lost touch with operational developments on the ground and symbolism had become reality. The token, Cold War-era peacekeeper, they believed, could cope in internal conflicts. No real effort had been made to distinguish between the certainties of the buffer zone and the pressures and challenges of dealing with armed factions in a large, ill-defined area of responsibility.* [140]

Boutros Boutros-Ghali had given notice that this was appreciated in the United Nations when he noted, after two years of frustration in the former Yugoslavia, that "UNPROFOR is willing to help to facilitate peace, but it does not have (nor does it seek) the mandate or the resources to impose peace upon those who do not desire it."[141] Nonetheless, the United Nations tried a more robust approach in all these missions, but the incremental addition of marginal and limited enforcement provisions in ONUC, UNPROFOR, UNOSOM II, and UNAMIR merely pushed the peacekeepers slowly into the gray area between peacekeeping and enforcement without providing the resources or techniques used in full-scale enforcement missions. As John Gerard Ruggie noted, "It is in the gray area between peacekeeping and all-out warfighting that the United Nations has gotten itself into serious trouble. The trouble stems from the fact that the United Nations has misapplied perfectly good tools to inappropriate circumstances."[142]

Traditional peacekeeping precepts, ones with which the United Nations was familiar, could not succeed in many of these missions. More important, the new muscular military approaches that broke with peacekeeping conventions required an entity with the political legitimacy and military authority to rapidly mobilize, deploy, and direct the operations of large, complex, and coercive military forces. As Berdal noted, large second-generation forces required "better coordinated deployment, redefined rules of engagement, and above all, higher standards of command and control."[143] The UN, even when reorganized and reinforced, could not be the authoritative framework institution needed to organize such efforts.

Other entities could, however, and it was for this reason that NATO replaced the United Nations as the strategic manager of choice when the Dayton peace accords necessitated the deployment of some 60,000 heavily armed peacekeepers to Bosnia in December 1995. It was also for these reasons that a U.S. military task force preceded the United Nations into an uncertain situation in Haiti in 1994. In answering the question of why this step was not taken earlier in Bosnia, one can appreciate the fundamental dilemma of second-generation peacekeeping politics. Large, ambitious, complex, and dangerous second-generation peacekeeping missions managed by the United Nations were not truly seen as a policy by the great powers on the Security Council—they were seen as a way of avoiding policy. The half measures of UNPROFOR were preferable for years to the alternative of the great powers having to take concerted action themselves in the morass of the former Yugoslavia.

As James Schear noted at the time,

> In UN field operations, as in life, you get what you pay for. A weak and divided international response to a conflict, such as the one in Bosnia and Herzegovina, is going to breed a cautious, self-constrained field operation. It is unrealistic to expect that an operation like UNPROFOR could fill a void created by political disagreements among UN member states on how to maneuver the Bosnian parties toward a peace settlement. The operation was, and remains, a stopgap measure, not a solution to the conflicts of Bosnia.[144]

Thus, in the tradition of "let's ask Mikey, he'll try anything," the United Nations—an organization manifestly unsuited for such a mission—was given the job. The great powers compounded the situation by then making it harder by stages for the United Nations to get anything accomplished by increasing UNPROFOR's mandate at every turn. It is indeed ironic that the great powers, especially the United States, blame the United Nations for the failures in the former Yugoslavia and elsewhere considering that they themselves proposed and passed all the resolutions setting its tasks in the first place. This plot line is even more blatantly repeated in the subsequent story of the United Nations in Somalia.

CHAPTER 7

The Mission to Somalia

There are several poignant reasons for selecting the United Nations Operations in Somalia between 1992 and 1995 as the second-generation peacekeeping mission case study. All of these reasons highlight the strategic challenges that second-generation peacekeeping missions presented to the United Nations. First, the UN military operations in Somalia were comprehensive and ambitious in their goals. Unlike observation or traditional peacekeeping, the UN objectives in Somalia were supported by complex military operations ultimately centered on rebuilding a failed state in an environment of chaos and near civil war. Second, these ambitious military objectives were thought to require authorization for the possible use of coercive military force and were thus mandated under Chapter VII of the UN Charter. In this sense, the UN operations in Somalia can truly be called the only peace-enforcement mission. It is helpful to have a case study of this particular phenomenon as a transition in the spectrum of operations before an analysis of large-scale enforcement missions. Last, the UN operations in Somalia highlight the unique dynamics of combining ambitious UN–sponsored and –managed operations with those of a UN–sanctioned but non-UN–managed subcontractor. A direct comparison between the experiences of these two entities is instructive.

Three separate operations combined to make up UN military involvement in Somalia. They illustrate the strategic challenges of managing ambitious second-generation peacekeeping operations. The first United Nations Operation in Somalia (UNOSOM I) was initiated in response to the widespread death and destruction from famine and civil war that gripped Somalia in 1992. The operation eventually consisted of only fifty observers and 500 Pakistani infantrymen based at the airport in the capital, Mogadishu. The Pakistani unit was tasked with providing security at the port and in the immediate area of Mogadishu, where the security situation was deteriorating on a daily basis.[1]

Because the small forces of UNOSOM I could do nothing to break the cycle of clan violence and banditry that was sustaining the famine, the United Nations authorized an American-led coalition, the Unified Task Force (UNITAF), to intervene to protect the delivery of humanitarian aid to the famine belt. This operation deployed quickly and rapidly grew to a strength of over 38,000 troops from twenty-three countries. After only a few months, UNITAF handed the operation back to the control of the United Nations in the form of the second United Nations Operation in Somalia (UNOSOM II). UNOSOM II attempted to undertake more ambitious operations with an expanded mandate and a UN-managed force of around 28,000 troops.

The nature of UNOSOM II's mission changed sharply in June 1993 when the United Nations responded aggressively to attacks on its troops from one Somali faction. This marked the beginning of a period in which limited enforcement actions were mixed with traditional peacekeeping tenets in the same mission. Four months of aggressive UN action directed against one Somali faction culminated in a U.S.–initiated raid on 3 and 4 October 1993 that ended in a substantial number of American and Somali casualties and some American and UN prisoners taken as well. The United States immediately announced that it was withdrawing from the mission, and several other nations followed suit. Faced with intransigent opposition and a weakened force, UNOSOM II moved into what one observer called an "accommodative phase,"[2] in which it ceased to use coercive force against Somali belligerents. The situation in Somalia continued to deteriorate throughout 1994, and UNOSOM II was eventually withdrawn in March 1995, ending UN intervention in Somalia.

The individual efforts of these three operations combine to make the UN operations in Somalia one of the most unique and complex UN military operations. Although not the largest peacekeeping operation undertaken by the United Nations since its inception, it was the most comprehensive and multifarious operation undertaken short of the UN–sanctioned enforcement actions examined in Chapter Eight. This chapter, like the other case studies, examines the UN experience in mounting, directing, and employing the military forces that conducted operations in Somalia. It addresses the issues and concerns that influenced force structure, command and control, and military objectives in Somalia and contrasts these with the principles of peacekeeping that influenced earlier UN military operations. As was shown in the previous chapter, when conducting complex military operations in a bellicose environment, the United Nations' second-generation peacekeeping missions often abandoned the classic political tenets of peacekeeping for a more robust approach to military operations in these ambitious and dangerous operations.

More important, this case study examines how the challenges of managing a large mission with Chapter VII enforcement authority proved beyond the political and military capabilities of the United Nations. This conclusion leads into the next chapter, which illustrates the institutional advantages of the powerful nation-state or coalition of nation-states in terms of managing much more significant and active military enterprises.

Creating UNOSOM I, UNITAF, and UNOSOM II

Naturally, given the very different nature of these three missions, the political context in which they were created was also very different. Chapters One and Six noted the post–Cold War enthusiasm for peacekeeping missions that was evident in the Security Council in 1992 and 1993. The conflict in Somalia benefited less than other crises from this trend because it came under Security Council consideration while the UN mission in Cambodia (UNTAC) and the mission to the former Yugoslavia (UNPROFOR), two other large and complex second-generation peacekeeping missions, were also getting under way. Consequently, the enthusiasm for immediately launching another large operation in 1992 was somewhat muted. In addition, UNOSOM I and UNOSOM II were subject to the same slow ad hoc mechanisms and improvised management procedures used by the United Nations since 1948 and charted throughout this book. The combination of these factors contributed to the ineffectiveness of UNOSOM I, the need for a subcontractor to undertake the UNITAF mission, and the delay in the eventual deployment of UNOSOM II.

Throughout 1991 and 1992, Somalia was racked by civil war, clan violence, and widespread lawlessness, which combined to exacerbate a serious famine. Hundreds of thousands of Somalis had died, and the United Nations estimated that another 1.5 million lives were at risk in the spring of 1992.[3] Early UN efforts to mediate the civil conflict ended with a local cease-fire agreement. The Security Council adopted a resolution establishing UNOSOM I and requesting the secretary-general to "immediately deploy a unit of 50 United Nations Observers to monitor the cease-fire in Mogadishu."[4] The political preconditions of this mission were firmly in keeping with the military tenets of traditional observation missions. The UN military personnel would be deployed after the cease-fire had been reached, they would remain strictly impartial, they would be passive observers only, and the belligerents would bear the responsibility for policing the cease-fire agreement.

Despite the Mogadishu cease-fire and the presence of UN observers, the security situation in Somalia continued to deteriorate and the famine worsened in the large areas of central and southern Somalia outside Mogadishu. In response to these predicaments, the United Nations negotiated with Somali clan leaders for a larger deployment of UN forces and grudgingly won approval for the deployment of 500 Pakistani infantrymen to Mogadishu in September 1992. The operation at this point could not be characterized as traditional peacekeeping, but, rather, an observation mission with an enhanced security force, much like the relationship between UNTEA and UNSF discussed in Chapter Four.

Well aware that these small efforts in Mogadishu had done nothing to alleviate the man-made famine in the countryside, the Security Council authorized an increase in the strength of UNOSOM I, and the secretary-general introduced a plan to deploy four separate UN units to protect humanitarian convoys and distribution centers throughout Somalia.[5] However, the United Nations could never secure local agreement to deploy these additional forces, and the general situation in Somalia deteriorated further. The Pakistani forces, unsure of the way in which they should go about providing security in the dangerous streets of Mogadishu, remained virtual hostages at the airport. In the meantime, the United Nations estimated that as many as 3,000 persons a day were dying of starvation in Somalia.[6]

This was the political context that generated the creation of UNITAF and UNOSOM II, about which most of this case study is written. In late 1992, the United Nations was frustrated by a combination of local intransigence and the institutional inability to form and deploy what would have to be an active intervention force. By necessity, this force would have to be armed with the mandate and capabilities needed to coerce reluctant belligerents into allowing the delivery of humanitarian aid to the famine area. In a November 1992 report analyzing the United Nations' options, the secretary-general stated that, although such an action would be philosophically "consistent with the recent enlargement of the Organization's role in the maintenance of international peace and security . . . the United Nations Secretariat did not currently have the capability to command and control an enforcement operation of the size required."[7]

There was another option open to the United Nations, one in which it would sanction such a large enforcement action but leave the strategic management of the operation to a coalition of member states. This option was realized in late November when the outgoing president of the United States, George Bush, offered to lead an international force that would attempt to break the hold of the famine on south and central Somalia.[8] Much like the U.S.–led coalition in the Persian Gulf War, this multinational Unified Task Force would be authorized under Chapter VII of the UN Charter to "use all necessary means to establish as soon as possible a secure environment for humanitarian relief operations in Somalia."[9] The day after the resolution passed, the United States announced the immediate deployment of a large and combat-ready force to Somalia. On 4 December 1992 U.S. Defense Secretary Richard Cheney said, "There will be no question in the mind of any of the faction leaders in Somalia that we would have the ability to *impose* a stable situation if it came to that, *without their cooperation*"[10] (my emphasis). Meanwhile, the United Nations postponed the further deployment of UNOSOM I troops and left the decisions about force structure, command and control, and military objectives of UNITAF to the United States and the other members of the multinational task force.

The political creation of UNOSOM II was a direct result of the U.S. plan for UNITAF. It was not an initiative of the secretary-general or other members of the Security Council. The UNITAF operations order issued by the U.S. Central Command (the American military agency that would carry out mission planning and execution) specifically listed a transfer of responsibility to UN peacekeeping forces as the closing phase of UNITAF operations, and the commander stated that he wanted a "rapid transition to UN control."[11] U.S. officials thought that "clearly UNITAF was a transition to the long-term, broader UN operation that was expected to follow."[12] However, there was no indication in Resolution 794 or in discussions with UN officials that the UN planned a second UN peacekeeping operation in Somalia. The American envoy to Somalia, Robert Oakley, noted in a meeting with the secretary-general and his assistants on 1 December 1992 that "the top UN officials rejected the idea that the U.S. initiative should eventually become a UN peacekeeping operation."[13]

However, the U.S. idea of a rapid transition to a UN operation was such a determined American policy goal that the secretary-general was soon forced to acquiesce. On 4 December 1992, the U.S. defense secretary also had announced that, once the famine situation had stabilized, Somalia could "return to a state where the normal UN peacekeeping forces can deal with the circumstances." All other U.S. pronouncements addressed the need to hand over the operation to a "traditional" or "conventional" UN force. President Bush stated that, "once we have created that secure environment, we will withdraw our troops, handing the security mission back to a regular UN peacekeeping force."[14] The chairman of the joint chiefs of staff even raised the possibility of handing over the operation to "UN observer forces."[15]

There were some inherent contradictions in these American statements, however, principally concerning the nature of the follow-on UN force that would become UNOSOM II. Despite the public pronouncements about handing over responsibility to traditional UN peacekeepers or observers, the American policy actually envisaged a UNOSOM II that would be similar in capability to UNITAF: large and armed with a Chapter VII mandate to use active force against belligerents should the need arise. The secretary-general became aware, after meetings with U.S. officials, that they expected the follow-on UN force to be "little different [from] the Unified Task Force itself" with the same "concept of operations, level of armament, and rules of engagement."[16]

However, Boutros Boutros-Ghali correctly maintained that "traditional," "conventional," and "regular" UN peacekeeping forces were not large, heavily armed, or provided with an unprecedented Chapter VII mandate. From the United Nations' perspective (and from that of the misleading U.S. pronouncements), a traditional UN force that would follow UNITAF could be smaller and provided with a traditional peacekeeping mandate with little need for Chapter VII authority to undertake coercive operations. Consequently, the secretary-general resisted the American concept of a muscular UNOSOM II and on 19 December grudgingly reported to the Security Council that he would consider such an operation but would defer the decision until it was evident to him that UNITAF had accomplished an ambitious series of tasks such as establishing a reliable cease-fire, controlling heavy weapons, disarming lawless factions, and establishing a new Somali police force.[17]

However, throughout the short life of UNITAF (five months), the United States continued to resist implementing the tasks that were not part of their limited mandate to "establish a secure environment for humanitarian relief operations." The United States also continued to push Boutros Boutros-Ghali to quickly establish UNOSOM II before the secretary-general thought a UN force could be effective. This policy debate over two very different visions of UNOSOM II "raged out of public view" for the next few months, resembling, according to one observer, "bargaining in a bazaar."[18] The United Nations was uncomfortable with rapidly establishing and controlling an unprecedented peace-enforcement operation and deploying it to a belligerent environment where security concerns had been only partially addressed by UNITAF's more limited actions.

Given American influence in the Security Council, the debate ended on 26 March 1993 in the United States' favor with the passage of Security Council Resolution 814 establishing UNOSOM II. In this resolution, the Security Council proposal, sponsored by the United States, gave UNOSOM II an expanded mandate and, in theory, "decided to empower UNOSOM II with essentially the same military powers, rules of engagement, and command and control" as UNITAF.[19] The resolution authorized, for the first time, Chapter VII enforcement authority for a UN–managed military force. More important, the resolution greatly expanded the mandate of UNOSOM II beyond what UNOSOM I and UNITAF were expected to accomplish. One former U.S. ambassador to Somalia characterized the UNOSOM II mandate as "a bolder and broader operation intended to tackle underlying social, political, and economic problems and to put Somalia back on its feet as a nation."[20]

It was unfortunate and ironic that this expanded mandate would have to be undertaken by a UN military force that was smaller and less capable than

Map 4

UN Mission to Somalia, November 1993

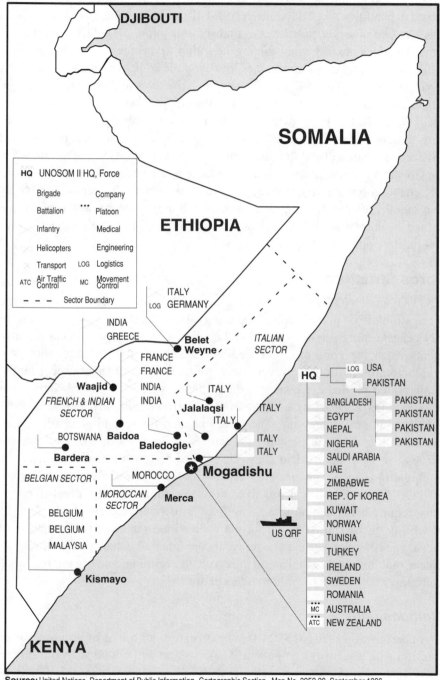

UNITAF. This issue is fully explored in the section on military objectives below, but it is also a theme that will be evident throughout the examination of force structure and command and control. Compared to the limited objectives and robust capabilities of UNITAF, UNOSOM II had to do much more with much less. As one observer noted at the time of transition, "[UNITAF] leaves the United Nations peacekeeping contingent with a first act few could follow."[21]

The rest of this chapter examines this dynamic in light of the way in which UNITAF and UNOSOM II were formed, the structures and procedures through which they received their direction, and the military objectives that they pursued. However, this brief review of their creation reveals the roots of the problems that the UN operations in Somalia eventually experienced. A hostile local environment emasculated the traditionally created UNOSOM I at a time when the UN proper was reluctant to manage a large peace-enforcement force. A non-UN coalition temporarily relieved the pressure for forceful action, but barely five months after expressing doubts about handling such an intervention, the United Nations was pushed into managing UNOSOM II, the most ambitious UN military operation to date.

Force Structure

UNITAF and UNOSOM II are good examples of the dramatic changes in the force structure of peacekeeping operations. In the past, the force structure of UN peacekeeping missions had been heavily influenced by political requirements, such the consent of the belligerents, neutrality, and equitable geographic representation. However, these political imperatives of peacekeeping could not be applied in a contested environment where the United Nations (or its appointed agent) was attempting to undertake complex and sometimes coercive military operations. The forces needed for second-generation tasks had to follow different planning guidelines in order to have any chance for success, or even survival in some cases. The following examination of the composition, size, geographic representation, and interoperability of UNITAF/UNOSOM II is instructive in this regard. It not only reveals the military requirements behind these new force structures, but also highlights the capability of the United Nations as an institution to manage the formation of these types of units. Ultimately, it reveals the inherent disadvantages for a volunteer multinational organization in recruiting, forming, and organizing large, complex, and dangerous military enterprises.

Composition

The composition of UNOSOM I was consistent with that of an observation mission with a security component. That mission will not be analyzed further here. Instead, the composition of both UNITAF and UNOSOM II will be examined. UNITAF was a multinational combat force based on two American combat formations, a marine expeditionary force and an Army infantry division. Because both these units could be deployed within days to Somalia, they were considered "light" by normal combat standards, being predominately light infantry with some mechanized support and extensive aviation assets.

However, "light" is a relative term, and U.S. forces were among the most heavily armed in Somalia. Combat air support played a key role in American strategy, and helicopter gunships were used to engage and neutralize hostile Somali "technical" vehicles posing an early challenge to UNITAF. Other UNITAF contingents also brought what heavy armaments they thought were necessary, including tanks and armored personnel carriers. In addition, UNITAF was initially supported offshore by a U.S. aircraft carrier, cruiser, and destroyer. UNITAF also had some very specialized units that were force multipliers in such a mission environment, including special operations forces that included psychological operations and civil affairs teams. These types of units were considered critical for retaining the confidence of the Somalis and stressing the limited nature of UNITAF's humanitarian mission. Most of these "small, yet vitally important parts of UNITAF were not replaced" by UNOSOM II forces.[22] In the strategic sense, however, UNITAF looked very much like a conventional and potent combat force.

The composition of UNOSOM II was influenced to some extent by UNITAF, as many of the UNITAF units were committed to continuing the mission under the rubric of UNOSOM II. There were some notable exceptions, however, and the replacement of some heavy-combat First World forces with lightly armed Third World forces is discussed below in the section on equitable geographic representation. The planning for the exact composition of UNOSOM II was delayed by the policy imbroglio between the United States and the secretary-general mentioned above. Throughout the life of UNITAF, Boutros Boutros-Ghali continued to insist that UNITAF widen the breadth and scope of its limited mandate so that the follow-on UN operation could resemble traditional peacekeeping in a supportive local environment. In December 1992, the secretary-general insisted that the composition and size of UNOSOM II need not be well armed and large but could vary and would "depend on the success of UNITAF in establishing a secure environment throughout Somalia before it withdrew, and cannot therefore be estimated at this early stage of its operations."[23]

By March 1993 it was apparent that UNITAF was not going to expand its mandate in either breadth (to cover the other 60 percent of Somalia) or depth (to aggressively seek to disarm all Somalia factions) and that UNOSOM II would need to be fairly robust in size and composition. The secretary-general estimated that "the strength of the forces required to implement [the] mandate would have to be substantial in the early stage in order to minimize the risk of any deterioration in the security conditions and to ensure a secure environment as quickly as possible."[24] This was clearly a departure from his original wish to move to a more traditional peacekeeping force structure. However, given that the force structure tenets that derived from the principles of peacekeeping could not be applied to an environment such as Somalia, and given the ambitious mission that UNOSOM II would have in that environment, there was clearly a practical need for a nontraditional UN force.

Consequently, the secretary-general recommended that UNOSOM II include "combat forces" that would need the capability for operations that could include close combat, patrolling, indirect fire, antiarmor fire, all-weather night and day operations, and combat air support.[25] The United Nations had come a long way indeed from the days of a few light infantry battalions that left their heavier weapons at home. However, even with these atypical UN requirements listed, many of the contingents reporting for UNOSOM II were still structured more for traditional peacekeeping and humanitarian missions. One Somalia veteran noted that "it is fair to say that the vast majority of the contingents that remained after the start date for UNOSOM II were better suited to peacekeeping than enforcement."[26] As is examined below, most were not equipped for a mission with coercive authority. In addition, UNOSOM II did not have the air mobility of UNITAF, which had predicated its operations on extensive aviation assets used for both transport and combat support.[27] Finally, as noted below, the ratio of combat troops to lightly armed peacekeeping or logistics troops was much lower for UNOSOM II in its crucial first months than for the combat-heavy UNITAF.

Jonathan Howe, the special representative of the secretary-general to Somalia, also noted that UNOSOM II was in practice poorly structured for its ambitious mission. Instead of being structured based on a rational calculus of military planning considerations, it was composed of the disparate leftovers from UNOSOM I, UNITAF, and whatever volunteers the secretary-general could mobilize during UN peacekeeping's busiest year.[28]

To try and offset this disadvantage, UNOSOM II subcontracted support in the form of the U.S. Quick Reaction Force (QRF), which, although technically not part of UNOSOM II, was in Somalia to provide combat support to UNOSOM II should it be needed. The QRF consisted of an American infantry battalion, a composite aviation battalion of thirty-one helicopters, and support assets that brought the QRF total to 1,175 soldiers.[29] An early request to add heavy armored support to the QRF was turned down by Les Aspin, the U.S. secretary of defense, much to the later consternation of the U.S. military.

Later, a special operations task force of U.S. Army Rangers and counter-terrorist squads were added to the QRF. As might be expected, this arrangement complicated the command and control systems greatly, a phenomenon examined in that section below. After the 3 October 1993 battle in Mogadishu, the United States greatly reinforced the QRF, adding tanks, armored personnel carriers, combat air support, and additional troops to bring it to a strength of almost 18,000.[30] These troops were deployed principally to provide security for the U.S. withdrawal, which was complete by 31 March 1994.

As a final point on composition, it is important to note here the advantage of having prepackaged force structures and plans. Those military plans that have been rehearsed in a base form can later be added to or revised in light of mission requirements. The U.S. Central Command, which had geographic responsibility for the horn of Africa, based its initial operations plan on humanitarian relief exercises that had been rehearsed and evaluated.[31] This was a great advantage, as it allowed UNITAF to design its force structure on an existing model and enabled CENTCOM to distribute functional military plans within three days of notification.[32] UNOSOM II had no such template, an advantage usually reserved to nation-states or well-rehearsed military alliances with permanent planning bureaus, such as NATO.

Size

As in all past UN missions, the constraints inherent to a disparate multinational institution meant that the political considerations surrounding the Somalia mission often overruled military requirements. This routine situation was complicated further by the United Nations' small planning staff and ad hoc mechanisms and procedures. This was reflected again in the initial planning for the operation in Somalia. UNOSOM I, with all its attendant political difficulties, was planned for a top strength of 3,500.[33] Even that could not be achieved because of local intransigence and the lack of troops volunteered by member states. In contrast, initial estimates of UNITAF's American military planners, not hampered by the constraints built into the system of UN peacekeeping, put the minimum number of troops needed at 12,000 to 15,000 (over 25,000 were eventually used).[34]

UNITAF was a twenty-three–nation force based on two American combat formations. The American light infantry division consisted of around 10,000 soldiers, and the marine expeditionary force was of similar size. At peak strength, the United States had 25,400 service members from all four services either in Somalia or just offshore in a naval task force.[35] In addition, other major combat formations (battalion- or brigade-size) were present from Australia, Belgium, Canada, France, Italy, and Pakistan. The smaller contributions of sixteen other nations brought the non-U.S. coalition total to a peak of 12,555.[36] The integration of these many forces into UNITAF is examined below in the sections on interoperability and command and control.

As noted above, the size of the UNOSOM II force was not immediately established by UN planners because of the uncertainty about the success that UNITAF might have throughout Somalia. In late 1992, the United States envisaged a force that would be similar in size and composition to that of UNITAF, but the secretary-general preferred a smaller force with a more traditional size and structure.[37] When it became clear that UNOSOM II would have both an ambitious mandate and a dangerous operational environment, the need for a large mission became self-evident. The first planning recommendation of the secretary-general was put forth in March 1993 and called for a force of 28,000: 20,000 Blue Helmets for the mission itself and 8,000 other multinational troops to provide logistics support (the core of which would be American). This estimate closely matched the number of UNITAF soldiers actually deployed ashore in Somalia.[38]

UNOSOM II eventually peaked at a strength of 29,284 in November 1993,[39] but fluctuated well below full strength for most of its existence (Table 6). This was due in part to the slow deployment of UNOSOM II forces, which was heavily affected by the explosion in peacekeeping around the world. For instance, by 31 July 1993 (four months after Resolution 814), UNOSOM II was at less than 75 percent strength and missing almost half of its promised nonlogistics forces.[40] This greatly affected deployment plans and caused UNOSOM II to revise its operations considerably in that it had to abandon completely the thought of expanding outside of south and central Somalia. This situation can be contrasted with the rapid deployment of the UNITAF forces, which had over 38,000 combat-ready forces from twenty-three nations in the area and operating within six weeks of the implementing resolution.[41]

Throughout the early life of UNOSOM II, the secretary-general continued to push for more troops, recommending an additional brigade to reinforce UNOSOM II in August 1993.[42] However, as the security situation continued to deteriorate throughout 1993 and the United States announced its imminent withdrawal after the battle in Mogadishu on 3 and 4 October 1993, it became apparent that member states would not commit enough troops to bring UNOSOM II up to its mandated strength. By November 1993, the secretary-general noted that there were "unmistakable signs of fatigue among the international community" and was resigned to a UNOSOM II that would have to carry on with fewer than 20,000 troops for the foreseeable future of its mandate.[43] As is examined below in the section on military objectives, the mission was subsequently revised to reflect the greatly weakened force structure of UNOSOM II after March 1994. Instead of the mission determining the force structure, it was largely a case of the available resources determining a more limited mission.

Table 6

The UN Peacekeepers in Somalia, July 1993

Country	Description	Strength
Australia	Movement control unit	30
Bangladesh	Infantry battalion	25
Belgium	Brigade headquarters	
	Infantry battalion	
	Total, Belgium	998
Botswana	Infantry company	204
Canada	Headquarters staff	5
Egypt	Infantry battalion	540
France	Brigade headquarters	
	Infantry battalion	
	Aviation unit	
	Logistics battalion	
	Total, France	1,130
Germany	Logistics unit	772
Greece	Field hospital	110
India	Headquarters staff	5
Italy	Brigade headquarters	
	Infantry battalions	
	Aviation unit	
	Logistics/engineering	
	Medical unit	
	Total, Italy	2,538
Kuwait	Infantry company	108
Malaysia	Infantry battalion	873
Morocco	Infantry battalion	
	Support unit	
	Total, Morocco	1,341
New Zealand	Supply unit	43
Nigeria	Recce battalion	561
Norway	Headquarters company	137
Pakistan	Brigade headquarters	
	Infantry battalions	
	Signal unit	
	Supply and transport company	
	Engineer squadron	
	Medical unit	
	Electrical and mechanical engineering workshop	
	Ordnance company	
	Total, Pakistan	4,973
Republic of Korea	Engineer battalion	61
Romania	Field hospital	236
Saudi Arabia	Infantry battalion	678
Sweden	Field hospital	130
Tunisia	Infantry company	143
Turkey	Infantry battalion	320
United Arab Emirates	Infantry battalion	763
United States	Logistical unit	2,703
Zimbabwe	Infantry battalion	928
Headquarters staff		284
Provost Marshal section		68
Grand Total		**20,707**

Source: S/26317, Further Report of the Secretary-General Submitted in Pursuance of Paragraph 18 of Resolution 814, 17 August 93, pp. 2–3.

Equitable Geographic Representation

In forming the observation force of UNOSOM I, the UN Secretariat was able
to adhere to the traditional UN guideline of equitable geographic representation. UNOSOM I's observers were drawn from middle powers to reinforce
their neutrality: Austria, Bangladesh, Czechoslovakia, Egypt, Fiji, Finland,
Indonesia, Jordan, Morocco, and Zimbabwe.[44] UNITAF, on the other hand,
had a broad geographic, but hardly "equitable," representation (the United
States wanted to include at least three regional and three African countries).[45]
The United States dominated the coalition much as it had done in the enforcement actions in Korea and Kuwait. For practical military reasons, UNITAF
divided the non-American contingents into two groups: those that were self-
sustaining and able to operate independently and those that were too small to
support themselves or operate on their own. This meant that larger contingents, such as those of France, Belgium, Australia, and Canada, were able to
operate with tactical autonomy, whereas smaller contingents, such as those
from Botswana, Kuwait, and Zimbabwe, were grouped into a composite unit
under U.S. control.

With the handover to UNOSOM II and the withdrawal of the great majority
of U.S. forces, the force structure of UNOSOM II represented a more strictly
equitable grouping. However, the geographic composition of the two coalitions
differed to such an extent that it became impossible to entirely avoid the perception that UNITAF was a first-rate professional Western military force and
that UNOSOM II was composed of less capable forces from developing nations.
For instance, Canada and Australia, two experienced peacekeeping countries,
both deployed elite combat units for service in UNITAF (the Canadian Airborne
Regiment and the Royal Australian Regiment)[46] but withdrew the units upon
the transition to UNOSOM II. Both countries were committed to other large UN
missions running at the time, Canada in UNPROFOR and Australia in UNTAC.
In addition, a racial incident involving Canadian troops and local Somalis
increased domestic pressure on Canada to withdraw its troops.[47] These units
were replaced by troops from developing nations. Some military observers
noted outright that the replacement units (even when from the same countries)
"were much less able to operate effectively in a combat environment and to execute the rules of engagement with the same reserve and accuracy as the
UNITAF forces."[48]

At the same time that the United States announced its planned withdrawal from UNOSOM II, the governments of Belgium, France, and Sweden
decided to withdraw their contingents as well. By April 1994, every
European, NATO, and Arab nation had withdrawn. Those that remained in
strength were from Bangladesh, Botswana, Egypt, India, Malaysia, Nepal,
Nigeria, Pakistan, and Zimbabwe.[49] This prompted the secretary-general to

offer publicly a rejoinder to accusations that UNOSOM II was suspending the aggressive pursuit of its mandate because of the inferior military capabilities of the troops from developing nations that were replacing North American, European, and forces from other wealthy nations: "I would like strongly to reject the insinuations made in some circles that only the troops from Europe and North America have the necessary qualities to implement the mandate given to UNOSOM II."[50] More important, none of this went unnoticed by Somali factions. U.S. envoys John Hirsch and Robert Oakley noted that "there was a widespread Somali perception that UN-led forces would be weaker than UNITAF."[51] Other veterans and observers of operations in Somalia noted that warlords were looking to take advantage of the "weaker" units in UNOSOM II—picking out (rightly or wrongly) the Nigerians and Pakistanis in particular.[52]

The disparate capabilities of the UNOSOM II forces were as much a handicap to UN planners as to commanders in the field.[53] For instance, the reliability of some nations to deploy their contingents in full strength and on time was in great doubt. As noted in earlier missions, the United Nations had no control over these matters and did not have the power to guarantee that the contingents would stay for the length of the mission. Boutros-Ghali articulated this sense of helplessness in November 1993 when he noted that it was hard to anticipate UNOSOM II's continuing capabilities because of uncertain commitments from member states. He warned that "it would be prudent not to discount the possibility of substantial delays or even review of such decisions as well as of additional withdrawals taking place."[54]

The special representative of the secretary-general also noted the impossibility of undertaking comprehensive mission planning when resources were so unreliable.[55] In short, the United Nations felt that it could not trust member states to honor their commitments in light of the increasing dangers posed by the Somalia mission. Howe later noted that this problem was rooted in the institutional character and constraints of the United Nations:

> The UN has all the disadvantages of a volunteer organization. Troop contributors rotate their units at short intervals and withdraw them altogether with little notice. Nations want to dictate where their contingents will serve and what duties they will perform. The UN does not have the authority to hold individual nations to a fixed contract. The result in Somalia was a significant loss of time due to constant reassignment and readjustment of the forces.[56]

Interoperability

The operational repercussions of interoperability are reflected most clearly in an analysis of command and control and military objectives. However, it is important to note here the impact on force structure. This study has highlighted how observation and traditional peacekeeping missions have experienced some interoperability problems due to the ad hoc nature of the way in which the United Nations mounted military operations. The requirement of having to solicit voluntary commitments from member states greatly restricted the United Nations in attempting to piece together a military force that had similar equipment, doctrine, training, and operational methods. Naturally, as seen in the preceding chapters, these problems were an irritant in small traditional missions but were greatly exacerbated and made more consequential when trying to mount a complex 28,000-troop operation that required a measure of offensive combat capability.

UNOSOM II had great problems in this regard, mainly because of the disparity in equipment, training, and modus operandi of the forces. UNITAF fared better because it was heavily dominated by a framework state that was a major military power. In addition, other major UNITAF partners were America's close military allies with similar doctrine and capabilities, such as Belgium, Italy, Canada, France, and Australia. Alliance structures such as NATO gave these nations vehicles through which to plan and rehearse their interoperability and identify problems. As one military expert has noted, "training and doctrine within a coalition need not be uniform for true integration, but it must be compatible."[57] As is examined below in the section on command and control, UNITAF contingents that did not have compatible training and doctrine were given separate missions or grouped in composite units where their individual contributions were somewhat marginalized.

Unlike UNITAF, UNOSOM II had no framework force on which to establish its doctrine or modus operandi. As in many UN military operations, this led to different operational approaches from the various contingents and inevitably, a reduced tempo of operations.[58] In addition to this problem, which was aggravated by the overall size and large number of UNOSOM II contingents, the United Nations had trouble equipping those contingents with the military apparatus needed to accomplish an ambitious mission in a bellicose environment. The secretary-general accounted for some of the interoperability delays in UNOSOM II by stating that some member states "found it difficult to provide their soldiers with adequate weapons and equipment. In some cases, the provision of weapons and equipment from third countries had to be arranged, causing further delays."[59] Some countries even made the availability of their UNOSOM II forces contingent on receiving additional materiel that would give their soldiers equipment that was comparable to that of many UNITAF contingents.[60] This caused accusations that some states were volunteering for UN peacekeeping solely to outfit their units.

It had always been a difficult management challenge for the United Nations to build an interoperable military force from voluntary contributions requested for an ad hoc military operation. During the Cold War period, while it was managing a limited number of military operations, the United Nations was able to pick and choose to some extent. However, that was not possible in attempting to fill out UNOSOM II during the explosion in peace-keeping of 1992–1993. The interoperability problems of UNOSOM II were exacerbated by the fact that the decisions about what forces to send and for how long were national decisions, not those of UN planners organizing UNOSOM II.[61] As Jonathan Howe later noted, the military challenges of UNOSOM II's mission and belligerent environment required a legitimate central authority that could definitively organize a much more capable and integrated force.

> When dealing with general lawlessness, the need to integrate contingents is not particularly apparent, but when troops must work closely in mutual defense to combat organized opposition, practical problems of interoperability, insufficient armament, and widely varying states of training come into sharp focus. Such a challenge also increases the difficulty of creating an effective integrated force out of small units from some 20–30 nations that have not previously worked together.[62]

Command and Control

The differences in the command and control problems experienced by UNITAF and UNOSOM II are best summed up as a combination of differences in the organic capabilities of the organizations and differences in the military challenges of the operations (and *to* the operations). UNITAF, based on a large American military chain of command and control procedures, had an institutional advantage that has never been available to the United Nations. UNITAF's political and military command and control arrangements were rooted in the significant capabilities and rehearsed institutions of a major military power. In addition, UNITAF's Operation Restore Hope did not face any significant or organized military challenge from factions in Somalia. Even with the United States providing the authoritative command and control framework, serious resistance to the mission could have caused some fraying in the multinational and ad hoc command links of UNITAF. This did not happen, however, partly because of the limited nature of the mission and the deterrent effect of so much available military force (and a coalition leader come straight from the successes of the Persian Gulf War).

In contrast, even the post–*Agenda for Peace* United Nations did not have those vestiges of sovereignty that would allow it to authoritatively command significant military forces. Its constraints in this area limited it to control over small missions with simple military objectives. As a result, the United

Nations proper and UNOSOM II lacked a trained and rehearsed chain of command and did not have the benefit of a common set of control procedures. To complicate matters, UNOSOM II also was the first UN–commanded mission with a Chapter VII mandate for enforcement actions. The tasks to be undertaken by UNOSOM II forces often prompted different interpretations from member states about the division of command responsibility among the United Nations proper, UNOSOM II, and national contingents. As one Somalia veteran noted, "UNOSOM II was the first instance wherein a UN staff attempted directly to command and control a force whose primary mission was to bring combat power to bear should diplomatic peacemaking efforts fail."[63] When UNOSOM II faced a meaningful military challenge, these problems were greatly exacerbated and the frailty of an ad hoc coalition with no real command authority was exposed. Former U.S. ambassador Chester Crocker summed up this double disadvantage for UNOSOM II in this observation: "The United Nations' attempt at a militarily challenging 'peace enforcement' operation shows that it cannot manage complex political-military operations when its own structure is an undisciplined and often chaotic set of rival fiefdoms that resist unified command and control in the field and at both civilian and military levels."[64]

Ultimately, the failure of UNOSOM II's command and control arrangements was rooted in the exposure of its improvised organization to significant military opposition. Improvised structures and procedures rarely survive under fire—except when backed by a strong and legitimate military framework state or credible alliance structure. The pressures of such a chaotic and dangerous environment, unmitigated by the leadership of a strong and recognized central authority, inevitably led to different approaches to operations and different interpretations of the mandate. In UNOSOM II this inauspicious situation was exacerbated even further by an ambiguous mandate from the start. This cycle of confusion was aggravated by other problems and weakened the command structures and control procedures of UNOSOM II to the point of breakdown.

Chain of Command

Much like most multinational operations, UNITAF's military chain of command structure also was improvised: both as a temporary U.S. Joint Task Force (JTF) formed just for operations in Somalia and as a multinational command that needed to accommodate the military contributions of twenty-three other nations. However, such a JTF could be characterized as semipermanent, or off-the-shelf, as it had the benefit of being part of a regular U.S. combat command, the U.S. Central Command, and it had a permanent staff and units that trained together (and, indeed, had recently fought together in the Persian

Gulf conflict). The first task for the CENTCOM staff was to select the right mix of forces from among various U.S. services and combine them into an efficient military force. This was a command challenge for which the United States had rehearsed and reliable command and control structure and procedures. These types of joint operations had been greatly emphasized in the U.S. military since the invasion of Grenada in 1983, and this type of joint training was even required by law under the Goldwater-Nichols Defense Reorganization Act of 1986.

Beyond purely national military concerns, the challenge of directing an ad hoc multinational force was more problematic. U.S. commanders knew that UNITAF would require a responsive and authoritative chain of command that would preserve unity of effort and approach unity of command as far as the national laws of contributing states would allow. Therefore, all UNITAF contingent commanders were asked to place their units under the operational control of a U.S. commander (unlike Desert Storm).[65] Because "command" in its strictest sense was a nontransferable sovereign authority established by law, UNITAF exercised only varying degrees of operational control over coalition partners, the details of which changed and were worked out bilaterally with coalition members.

These decisions were prompted by practical military concerns about the efficiency of a multinational command. Like the coalition enforcement actions in Korea and Kuwait, the size and operational capability of a national contingent determined its degree of autonomy in the UNITAF chain of command. Brigade-size or larger units were placed directly under the UNITAF Joint Task Force or an intermediate-level commander, such as the U.S. Army forces commander (Figure 7A). Smaller units were grouped into a composite unit in Mogadishu that eventually grew to a five-battalion-size mechanized regiment from nine separate nations under the operational control of a U.S. Marine lieutenant colonel.[66] Units as large, diverse, and unwieldy as this composite unit usually are considered anathema to efficient and responsive chains of command, but this unit was braced by sufficient U.S. support to ensure that it did not encounter any significant operational difficulties. The use of intermediate-level commands and the division of operations into nine humanitarian relief sectors helped alleviate any span-of-control problems that could have resulted from one headquarters attempting to manage directly the forces of twenty-three countries.

The command problems inherent in any ad hoc voluntary multinational coalition were less of a problem in UNITAF than in UNOSOM II for several reasons. First, UNITAF had the overwhelming and recognized leadership of the United States as the main coalition partner. The unilateral capacity of the United States was great enough to guarantee mission success and allow the

Figure 7A

Chain of Command in UNITAF Somalia

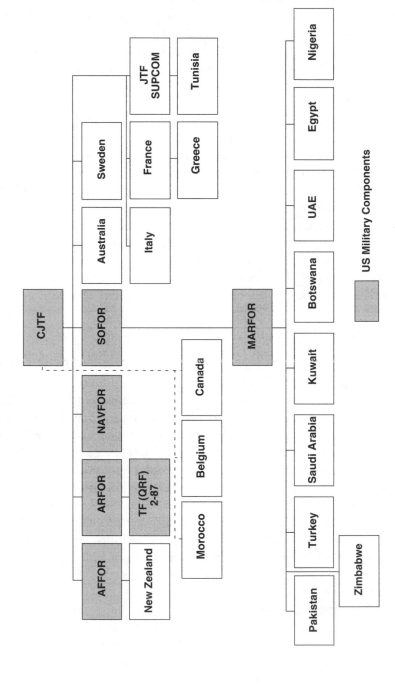

Source: Allard, *Somalia Operations: Lessons Learned*, p. 27

Figure 7B

Chain of Command in UNOSOM II

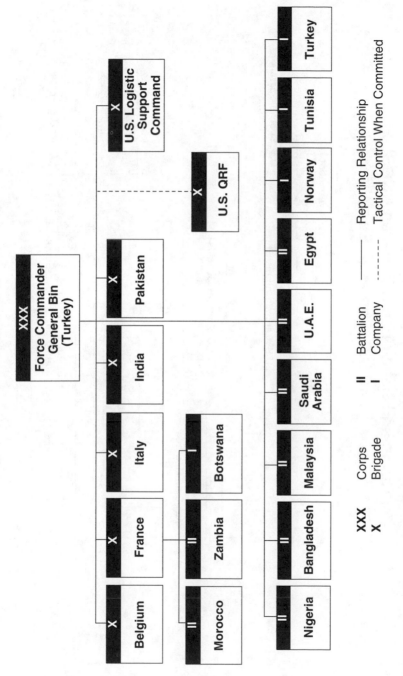

Source: Albert and Hayes, *Command Relationships for Peace Operations*, pp. 43, 45.

Figure 7C

Command Relationship Between UNOSOM II and U.S. Forces in Somalia

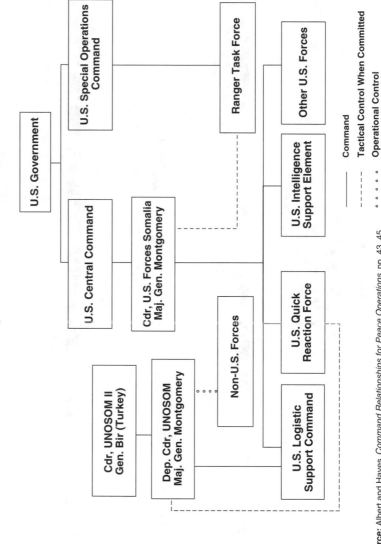

Source: Albert and Hayes, *Command Relationships for Peace Operations*, pp. 43, 45.

UNITAF planners to factor in national political and military requirements within the framework of the overall mission. For instance, contingents that insisted on double-checking for separate guidance from national chains of command were given separate preplanned missions so there would be no competition between chains of command working together on the same missions. Other contingents were given clearly delineated geographic areas in which only they would operate.[67] In essence, if a state wanted some degree of operational autonomy, it was given its own task or its own space in which to work. This helped ameliorate potential command friction arising from the need for two or more units that had not trained together to jointly take decisive action in a crisis situation.

Second, and largely because of its overwhelming combat capabilities, UNITAF never faced a substantial military challenge that could test such a multilateral system. However, when the security situation threatened the mission of UNOSOM II more directly, these weaknesses were aggravated and exposed. When the military dangers of the Somalia mission grew during UNOSOM II's tenure, the tolerance of many nations to the risks involved dropped accordingly. This pressure caused the improvised chain of command of UNOSOM II to fracture. Some units unilaterally reinterpreted the mandate as requiring a permanent withdrawal into defensive positions, others conducted secret negotiations with some Somali factions, and there were even accusations of individual contingents buying off faction leaders or making other deals. Still others blatantly refused to follow UN orders and precipitated widely publicized bickering between UN headquarters and various state capitals. The most publicized imbroglio was between the United States and Italy over the Italian commander, General Loi. After reports that the Italian contingent was negotiating separately with clan leader Mohammed Farah Aideed and refusing to follow UN orders, the United Nations (under U.S. urging), requested that Italy relieve its commander. Italy refused, prompting analyst Kenneth Allard to note that the episode was "a useful demonstration of both the fundamental existence of parallel lines of authority and the fundamental difficulties of commanding a coalition force under combat conditions."[68]

A brief look at UNPROFOR and UNTAC in Chapter Six also highlighted the fact that when a mission involved greater risk and the possibilities of casualties or other setbacks, national contingents tended to invoke their national chains of command to compete with the improvised, loose, and voluntary UN chain of command. In Somalia, the "phone home" problem was very serious and one observer noted that this "made the entire operation almost hopeless from a command and control perspective."[69] The secretary-general also noted that competition from national chains of command was a "serious and sensitive problem" and the actions of some contingent commanders had the effect of "weakening the integrity of UNOSOM's military command structure."[70]

The hostile environment that followed the 5 June attack on Pakistani peacekeepers aggravated the confusion over command roles in a mission under fire. The resulting fracture in the UNOSOM II command structure made the problem worse and gave encouragement to the hostile factions in Somalia. As one report noted,

> *Confusion regarding policy and command and control responsibilities in a combat environment under Chapter VII for the first time meant unclear relations between the troop contributors and UNOSOM II. These and other problems reinforced the Somali perception that after most U.S. forces left UNOSOM II would be vulnerable, and that there was once again a tempting vacuum of power.*[71]

In addition to the problems posed by having an ad hoc and loose chain of command in dangerous conditions, UNOSOM II had command problems posed by the use of a subcontractor in the form of the U.S. QRF and ranger task force. Like UNPROFOR's confused command structure vis-à-vis NATO, this arrangement gave UNOSOM II's already substantial command problems an added and woeful twist. In one sense, it was similar to traditional UN practice—merely another form of an improvised and confusing temporary command arrangement. However, it was even more confusing than usual given the many players involved and their occasional reluctance to talk to one another. As one observer noted, "UNOSOM II clearly suffered from the UN's Byzantine bureaucratic structure, *a problem compounded by compartmentalization within the U.S. military command*"[72] *(my emphasis)*.

The QRF was never under UN control, even at the level of operational control with which UN military forces usually operated. During UNITAF's deployment, the QRF was part of the regular U.S. military chain of command and operated, along with all other U.S. forces, under the combatant command (the strictest sovereign level of command authority) of the U.S. Central Command. With the transition to UNOSOM II, the United States maintained the commitment of the QRF to support UNOSOM II operations in special circumstances. The QRF was not permitted to undertake regular UNOSOM II operations, but was supposed to be an emergency back-up force that had combat capabilities that UNOSOM II could not muster.[73] Although the U.S. logistics contingent in UNOSOM II was under the operational control of the UN commander (like all the other UNOSOM II units), the QRF remained under the command (and operational control) of the U.S. Central Command in Florida. As a concession to the United Nations and the need for a local commander, the deputy UN military commander, an American general, was given tactical control (the most limited form of temporary command authority)[74] over the QRF. Complicating matters further was the fact that neither UNITAF nor UNOSOM II controlled the offshore units of the U.S. Navy and Marine Corps, which were "still under the operational control of CENT-COM" in Florida.[75]

Although confusing, this arrangement appeared to satisfy several conflicting policy dilemmas. The United States wanted to show its strong support for UNO-SOM II and therefore had to place some of its forces in the UN chain of command. On the other hand, the United States was aware of strong public and congressional sentiment about placing troops under foreign command. If an operation went awry, there was no way under U.S. or international law to hold the UN commander accountable. This violated an important political and legal convention for the Americans. Thus, as part of the compromise, the logistics forces, who were unlikely to be put in harm's way, were placed in the UN chain of command. However, the combat forces of the QRF, which by the very nature of their mission in Somalia were more likely to see combat, were kept out of the United Nations' operational control but had a limited official relationship through the deputy UNOSOM II commander.

In essence, the QRF was therefore subject to three lines of influence, all with varying degrees of command authority. The secretary-general's special representative, a retired American admiral (Jonathan Howe), had informal influence with the U.S. military and political authorities in Washington, as well as formal UN authority over the U.S. commanders in UNOSOM II. This formal authority did not extend to the QRF, except through the limited tactical command authority enjoyed by Admiral Howe's deputy military commander, the American General Thomas Montgomery. Last, and most tangibly, was the formal command relationship between General Joseph Hoar in Florida and the QRF, which was part of his combatant command. This structure definitely violated an old military aphorism: "If you cannot clearly explain the command structure in 10 seconds or less, it is not likely to work."

Like many overly complex military plans, this system did not survive first contact with the enemy. After the attack on the Pakistanis of 5 June 1993, the QRF began to play a much more aggressive role in operations against the Aideed faction deemed responsible (see the disarmament section below). Meanwhile the deployment of the ranger task force to Somalia added yet another layer to an already confused command and control picture. The ranger task force, deployed in August 1993 to capture Mohammed Farah Aideed, was from the Joint Special Operations Command in North Carolina and under the operational control of U.S. CENTCOM in Florida. No UNOSOM II officials in Somalia (even Montgomery) were officially in the ranger task force chain of command.[76] When the great debacle of 3 October 1993 occurred, UNOSOM II authorities, including Admiral Howe, were among the last to know about the operation.[77] Even General Montgomery was told of the 3 October operation only forty minutes before its launch.[78]

These particular problems with the U.S. military elements in the command structure of UNOSOM II complicated the command arrangements considerably and Allard wrote that "the greatest obstacles to unity of command during UNOSOM II were imposed by the United States on itself."[79] However, the other problems raised earlier were not unusual for an ad hoc coalition thrown together under the restricted authority of a large and voluntary multinational organization. As noted throughout this book, the lack of authoritative institutional command structures, both legal and functional, doomed the United Nations to seeking cooperation in its chain of command. The UNOSOM II force commander, Turkish General Bir, "cited his lack of command authority over the assigned forces as the most significant limitation of [UNOSOM II] or any other one organized under Chapter VII."[80] More often than not, this gave UN military operations command problems. More important, in a large, complex, ambitious, and dangerous operation with Chapter VII enforcement authority, those problems of friction in the chain of command could bring down the mission.

In operations that called for a greater sacrifice of both human and material resources, firm, clear, competent, and recognized authority was needed to hold together the chain of command. Ultimately, the difference in the capabilities of the chain of command between UNITAF and UNOSOM II was in their inherent ability to handle a significant military challenge. UNITAF never had such a challenge but could have fallen back on the U.S. chain of command, on which it was heavily based. UNOSOM II did have such a challenge and, lacking a legitimate and authoritative command "backbone," crumbled accordingly. The subcontracting relationship with the various U.S. forces only made things worse. The loose interpretation of command necessarily used by a voluntary multinational organization such as the United Nations could not be effective in complex and controversial missions. Divergent views about the mission from the participants destroyed this loose system. These sorts of missions required a chain of command that satisfied the political and legal requirements of command in a way that UN–managed military operations never enjoyed.[81]

Control Procedures

Given the disparity in the nature of UNOSOM II's military forces, inventing common control measures for UNOSOM II was a challenge regardless of the mission. Given that those same forces faced a challenging mission in a bellicose environment, the need for thorough and competent control of the operation was paramount. It was a critical military necessity for such a complex enterprise.[82] For such a large and diverse multinational force to succeed with an ambitious mandate in a dangerous environment, there had to be a basic agreement on some common control measures: staff operations, orders processes, rules of engagement, standard operating procedures, reporting formats, and other control measures discussed throughout this book.

UNITAF's control procedures were, on the strategic and operational levels, based on American doctrine and modus operandi, which also was fairly standard for its NATO and other military alliance partners in UNITAF. As noted above, on the tactical level, differences in control procedures were ameliorated by assigning specific and limited tactical tasks or geographic areas to certain units. In this sense, and because it was an ad hoc coalition, UNITAF operations were, for the most part, "coordinated" as opposed to "combined." Coordinated operations did not require the same level of tactical interdependence that necessitates the use of common control procedures. Some units shared common tactical control procedures with the Americans, and this allowed for some very successful combined operations between the U.S. and other contingents, notably operations involving the U.S. Army's 10th Infantry Division and Belgian paratroops. However, for the most part, small tactical differences were absorbed within the operational and strategic framework laid down by the large American command and control system.

This practical advantage was not available to UNOSOM II, which did not have a recognized and authoritative framework doctrine on which to base common control procedures. Moreover, the control procedures that had evolved over years of UN peacekeeping practice were not applicable to peace-enforcement missions. The slow evolution of military procedures common to UN operations occurred in observation and traditional peacekeeping missions. For peace enforcement, the United Nations had no institutional expertise on which to draw in an effort to guide its UNOSOM II contingents toward common goals. Because of UNOSOM II's composite nature at the strategic and operational level, it could not present a common face to its Somalia operations. Because it lacked a standard base, one could fairly characterize the total effect of UNOSOM II operations as less than the sum of its parts.

It has been noted elsewhere that the exposure of this improvised system to significant military challenges precipitated even more disparate interpretations of UNOSOM II's operational mandate. This included the widely publicized accusations of unilateral deal making. This inconsistency with which contingents operated was preyed on by certain Somali factions. Further problems were caused by various interpretations of the accepted coalition rules of engagement by the force contingents of UNOSOM II.[83] For instance, for historical and legal reasons, the German contingent operated under different rules of engagement entirely. Some of this disparity was the result of UNOSOM II's having inherited the same rules of engagement as UNITAF, but without the same capabilities. UNOSOM II contingents were therefore forced at times to revise and interpret the rules of engagement differently, making their actions commensurate with their military capabilities. However, as one military analyst noted, the root problem was that "because the United Nations lacks standard doctrine, tactics, and equipment, command and control is a problem for all but small operations in generally peaceful environments."[84]

Thus the lack of a common doctrine and control procedures for complex and dangerous military operations hurt UNOSOM II considerably. The absence of a common modus operandi was exacerbated by the vagueness of the mandate, which offered no concrete functional guidance. Having a clearly defined mission statement and a clearly defined and common modus operandi is a control measure in itself, as reflected in the standard operating procedures, rules of engagement, and other control measures. UNITAF had a narrowly defined mission and was able to delineate a clear unity of purpose in the coalition. This allowed all the nations in UNITAF, even with their disparate capabilities and experiences, to work within any national limits and still accomplish the mission.

In contrast, UNOSOM II's mandate was so open to interpretation that this prompted a divergent sense of purpose. The United States noted that this divergence stemmed from separate interpretations of the mandate itself and that "more problematic has been the fact that some countries have arrived in Somalia with clearly differing perspectives on what would be required of them."[85] Unity of effort as a control measure was never achieved in UNOSOM II. This was a result of the greatly enlarged mandate, the simultaneous reduction of forces, the confusion over standard operating procedures and rules of engagement, and the lack of a competent and recognized political-military authority to propose a solution.

This problem first became apparent in the transition from UNITAF to UNOSOM II. Early planning by the United Nations could have gone some way to proposing common control procedures that would have addressed future problems, such as the interpretation of the mandate and actions taken in the face of a military threat. However, because the United Nations resisted the very idea of a large and ambitious UNOSOM II for so long, planning for the mission did not start until March 1993, less than six weeks before taking over from UNITAF. UNOSOM II staff were notoriously slow in arriving and the staff was formed, for the most part, from personnel who were individually selected from contingents as they arrived in Somalia.[86] This reinforced the lack of a common operational base on which to plan control procedures. On 4 May 1993, the day of transition from UNITAF to UNOSOM II, the UNOSOM II staff was at only 30 percent strength.[87] The UNITAF commander described the UN approach to transition as inept: "The UN has known for eight months they're coming to Somalia and there's still no game plan."[88]

As will be noted, many critics maintained that the United States pushed the United Nations into a hasty transition for which UNOSOM II was not prepared. There were others who maintained that UNOSOM II would probably never have been prepared, for what the secretary-general labeled a "daunting prospect," given the paucity of its resources and challenge of its environment and mission.[89] There is substantial evidence to support both charges. Regardless, UNOSOM II had no game plan because the United Nations was not an institution that kept one or could create one at short notice. Common control procedures for ambitious military enterprises must be rooted in rehearsed military formations that are, for the most part, the sovereign province of nation-states or highly bureaucratized military alliances. The United States or an alliance such as NATO could deploy such a strategic package at almost no notice, one that could encompass and absorb the disparities of some of its coalition partners. The United Nations could not.

Military Objectives

This examination of the strategic military objectives of UNITAF and UNOSOM II explores further how these operations linked their military missions with their political mandates. Ultimately, the mission to Somalia was a strategic failure for the United Nations because military forces did not achieve the political objective. Under the same narrow formula, the UNITAF mission could be said to be a success. Chester Crocker writes, "The Somalia 'failure' was less a failure of either humanitarian intervention or muscular peacekeeping than a failure to apply them steadily and wisely. The failure was of another order: strategic confusion followed by a collapse of political will when the confusion led to combat casualties."[90] In keeping with the military focus of this book, this section examines the strategic confusion of operations in Somalia and leaves the story of political will to others.

Strategic Coherence

The section on the creation of UNITAF and UNOSOM II highlighted the fundamental policy disagreements between the United States and the United Nations over the nature of UNOSOM II's mission and the transition from UNITAF. This policy imbroglio caused a strategic imbalance in both missions: favorable in the case of UNITAF and very unfavorable in the case of UNOSOM II. This section considers the strategy of the missions, matching means to ends. In essence, the need for UNOSOM II to accomplish more ambitious objectives with a smaller, less capable, and more disparate set of military resources gave UNOSOM II a strategic incoherence similar to that of UNPROFOR and some other second-generation peacekeeping operations.

In the foreword to the memoirs of UNITAF envoys John Hirsch and Robert Oakley, a former U.S. ambassador wrote of the "coherence and dramatic success" of the UNITAF mission.[91] Most observers attribute this to the use of enormous resources to accomplish a carefully delineated and limited strategic objective: provide a secure environment for the delivery of humanitarian aid. This was to be achieved with overwhelming military force if necessary. The U.S. Central Command's commander-in-chief wrote that a "clear and precise mission statement which defines measurable and attainable objectives is paramount [as is] the application of decisive, rather than just sufficient force."[92]

UNITAF diplomats worked hard to ensure that the Somali factions knew of the very limited nature of their operations, and they encouraged local dialog and cooperation with faction leaders. However, UNITAF also used "implicit threats of coercion" and pointed reminders about the robust military capabilities of the U.S. military, fresh from Operation Desert Storm in Iraq.[93] National credibility was engaged and at stake, particularly for the United States. Had there been a significant local challenge to the overwhelming military might of UNITAF, the coalition could have responded quickly with even more forces. In short, the means were calculated to make sure that the ends would be achieved in short order and with minimal disruption.

This strategic coherence was lacking in UNOSOM II, which had exactly the opposite imbalance between means and ends. UNOSOM II had a much more ambitious mission and yet was equipped with an ad hoc composite force that had much less cohesion and more disparate military capabilities. If the UNITAF plan was to do less with more, then the UNOSOM II mandate was the opposite.[94] As noted in the section on force structure, the SRSG was resigned to working with only "half a loaf" and never felt that UNOSOM II had sufficient strength to undertake its full mandate, especially considering the growing resistance from some Somali factions.[95] To complicate this equation, Resolution 814, establishing UNOSOM II, was vague in setting out the strategy for accomplishing its tasks. Resolution 814 called for UNOSOM II to take on tasks associated with "nation building" and yet gave no indication of how UNOSOM II would go about accomplishing this unprecedented mandate. One observer remarked at the time of the mandate that UNOSOM II was "proven to be seriously weak just where Restore Hope was strong: its objectives were vaguely defined, its reach is exceedingly ambitious, and its results are difficult to measure."[96] Jonathan Howe characterized the resolution as "overly ambitious given its inherent complexity, the limited means available to the UN, the tenuous commitment of key nations, the amount of arms already loose in the country, and Somali unreadiness for self-government."[97]

Thus the strategic incoherence of UNOSOM II stemmed from the same cause as that of UNPROFOR. An overly ambitious Security Council Resolution was passed without proper consultation with the secretary-general or his representatives in Somalia, who were left with the duty, in the words of Jonathan Howe, to "salute the flag and carry on."[98] Given the security situation in Somalia, the recent tradition of resistance by Somali faction leaders to UN initiatives, and the scarcity of competent military resources available to UNOSOM II, it was incredible to many involved that the Security Council could pass such an overreaching resolution. The U.S. Institute of Peace wrote that "the far reaching goals of Resolution 814 would have required staffing and supplies far beyond those that were readily available or en route."[99] Resolution 814 mandated UNOSOM II to undertake these tasks as well as accomplish less specific goals centered on "nation building." The initial military tasks for UNOSOM II were to:

1. Monitor the cessation of hostilities.
2. Prevent any resumption of violence and, if necessary, take action against violators.
3. Maintain control of heavy weapons pending destruction or transfer to new national army.
4. Seize the small arms of unauthorized armed elements and assist in arms registration and security.
5. Maintain the security of all ports, airfields, and lines of communications for delivery of relief aid.
6. Protect UN and NGO personnel and equipment and take action against threats if necessary.
7. Continue mine-clearing programs.
8. Assist in repatriation of refugees.
9. Carry out other functions assigned by Security Council.
10. Tasks to be accomplished throughout all of Somalia.[100]

As has happened to UN forces many times in the past, the United Nations was left to hope that an unexplained and unanticipated upsurge of peaceful cooperation from the Somalis would help their small forces undertake UNOSOM II's ambitious plans successfully. Chapter Six showed that UNTAC, when faced with a similar situation vis-à-vis the Khmer Rouge, took the chance that the elections would not be disrupted by the yet-to-be-disarmed Khmer Rouge. UNTAC rode its luck and it held, making UNTAC a temporary success. UNOSOM II also rode its luck, but it did not hold. The security situation in Somalia continued to deteriorate and UNOSOM II's attempt to use a small and disparate force for an active and ambitious mandate was unsuccessful.

UNOSOM II, by using limited means to accomplish an ambitious mandate, planned only for a best-case scenario. As Chester Crocker has noted, when that unlikely scenario did not occur, one could only conclude, "The United Nations overreached in Somalia when they expanded the initial mandate without providing the means to carry it out."[101] However, other factors complicated the issue, making UNOSOM II's failure much more complicated than the simple failing of not providing adequate military means for a complex enterprise. These complications were rooted in the policy disagreement between the United States and the United Nations over the exact objectives and criteria for success that would define the goals of UNITAF. This would in turn exert considerable influence on the environment in which UNOSOM II would have to try to achieve the goals above.

Protecting Humanitarian Aid

As noted, UNOSOM I was incapable of protecting humanitarian aid in Mogadishu and, as a result, was kept under a virtual state of siege at Mogadishu airport. UNITAF approached a similar mission with the assumption that it could be opposed by armed Somali factions and was prepared to use offensive combat operations to accomplish the mission. In accordance with the contemporary American military doctrine, overwhelming forces would be available to UNITAF should the need arise. U.S. Envoy Robert Oakley, who was personally preceding UNITAF into specific areas and talking with all the Somali faction leaders, noted that the "demonstrated readiness to respond with overwhelming force caused the faction leaders to avoid confronting UNITAF."[102]

The UNITAF mission statement ordered it to:

> conduct joint and combined military operations in Somalia, to secure the major air and sea ports, key installations and food distribution points, to provide open and free passage of relief supplies, to provide security for convoys and relief organization operations and assist UN/NGOs in providing humanitarian relief under UN auspices.[103]

The mission was to be a four-phase operation that would first establish control over relief supplies in Mogadishu and secure the famine-racked town of Baidoa. Next, UNITAF would expand operations to other ports, airfields, and towns in the interior while securing the lines of communication to central Somalia and the major arteries along which aid would flow. The third phase envisaged expanding these operations further into central and southern Somalia, including setting up operations in the southern port city of Kismayo. The fourth phase was the "transition from a U.S.-led to a UN-controlled effort."[104]

At every stage of the UNITAF operation, the U.S. planners had decided on criteria that would be used to measure the success of operations in the present stage to assess the feasibility of moving on to the next phase. For instance, a summary of these criteria for the end of Phase III read: "Phase III is considered complete when sufficient control over the relief network has been established to allow for the delivery of enough food to arrest the famine, to break the cycle of looting, and UNOSOM forces are ready to relieve JTF forces in zone."[105] The United States maintained throughout its operational planning that its military forces would address only the security of the *local* environment vis-à-vis the delivery of humanitarian aid. As is discussed below, armed and/or warring factions that did not immediately threaten the delivery of humanitarian aid in the nine relief sectors were not a concern to UNITAF. However, as noted above, the secretary-general had very different criteria for satisfying the overall goal of "providing [throughout all of Somalia] a secure environment for the conduct of humanitarian operations." The day after Resolution 794 passed, a report noted that, "in the interest of expediency, diplomats [on the Security Council] tried to gloss over the question of what constitutes a 'secure environment.'" The failure to define this would come back to haunt UNITAF and UNOSOM II.[106]

It is here that the fundamental policy differences between the United States and the United Nations were exacerbated. Boutros Boutros-Ghali had not been able to resist the U.S. insistence that there should be a UNOSOM II, but he did, throughout late 1992 and early 1993, resist the idea that UNOSOM II would be a peace-enforcement force. The United States maintained that with the transfer of many UNITAF units to UNOSOM II and the progress made by UNITAF on the local security situations in south and central Somalia, UNOSOM II should be more than capable of carrying out its mandate. One observer noted that the United States was eager to declare its mission ended and was supported by the perception that "the five month UNITAF occupation of south-central Somalia created an appearance of normalcy."[107] Meanwhile, as noted above, the secretary-general did not wish even to start planning UNOSOM II until his broader requirements for "providing a secure environment" were met. On 3 March 1993, three weeks before the resolution establishing UNOSOM II was passed, the secretary-general wrote that "it is clear to me that the effort undertaken by UNITAF to establish a secure environment in Somalia is far from complete and in any case has not attempted to address the situation throughout all of Somalia."[108]

This disagreement stemmed from the fact that the strategic objective was ambiguous. Once an attempt was made to define it more clearly through the specific criteria selected by UNITAF planners, it was still profoundly different from the preferred criteria of the secretary-general. At the root of the failure and strategic incoherence of UNOSOM II was the failure of the United States and the United Nations to reach an agreed-on definition of success in this mission for UNITAF. The United Nations, for its part, knew that UNOSOM II had little chance of succeeding in UNITAF's definition of a "secure environment" unless the concept was expanded in both breadth and depth. On the other hand, the United States was exceptionally wary of expanding its very limited mandate or staying in Somalia any longer than absolutely necessary. In the fall of 1992, the U.S. ambassador to Kenya had warned Washington, "If you liked Beirut, you'll love Mogadishu."[109] This sentiment highlighted deep U.S. insecurity over deployments that might drag on with no clearly discernible end state in sight. The disagreement was carried through into the transition between UNITAF and UNOSOM II, causing the U.S. CENTCOM commander to note, "efforts to effect an expeditious and seamless turnover were delayed by differing views that arose in part over the UNITAF success."[110] The situation was further complicated by the change in U.S. administration's in January 1993.

Some UNITAF observers noted that the criteria for UNITAF's success were too narrow to represent a starting point for UNOSOM II's mission, thus giving the weaker, but more ambitious, UN mission a shaky foundation upon which to build. Some have strongly criticized UNITAF for not undertaking the "implied" tasks of its mission, such as a more comprehensive disarmament plan.[111] The special representative of the secretary-general in command of UNOSOM II also maintained that the United States left too soon, leaving too much of a mission challenge to a much less capable UNOSOM II force.[112]

However, it was the explicit policy of the United States that it would not undertake issues such as those "more related to long-term efforts to bolster Somalia's future as a nation." These sorts of nation-building tasks "offered no measurement criteria . . . and diluted the [U.S.] command's focus [of] ensuring that relief supplies could be moved."[113] From the U.S. perspective UNITAF had to be a success, and if the only criteria for clearly measuring that success were in limited objectives, then that was fine. Jonathan Howe noted that the United States was "determined to prevent mission-creep, [and] was unwilling to accept critical but complex complementary tasks urged by the UN such as disarmament."[114]

The United Nations, for its part, based all its planning on one flawed assumption of this UNITAF mission: that "during its presence in Somalia, the Unified Task Force will have brought about an effective cessation of hostilities throughout the country and will have established the secure environment called for in resolution 794."[115] When it became obvious that this secure environment would not exist beyond the confines of the ports, supply lines, and distribution sites for humanitarian aid in south and central Somalia, there was no attempt to revise UNOSOM II's mandate. As UNOSOM II deployed to Somalia with its ambitious mandate, the security situation deteriorated in the capital and the attention of the world shifted from the successful, but limited, humanitarian aid effort in the Somali countryside to the violence in the streets of Mogadishu.

Disarming and Demobilizing Local Belligerents

The mission to disarm and demobilize the local factions in Somalia can be considered as a subset of the mission to provide a secure environment. As such, the various interpretations of this particular mission are easily derived from the mandates of UNITAF and UNOSOM II and from the disagreement outlined above. UNITAF saw disarmament in the narrow and temporary context of providing security for the immediate delivery of humanitarian relief supplies. UNOSOM II saw disarmament in the much broader and permanent context of restoring the failed state of Somalia. One analyst has therefore characterized UNITAF's policy as "arms control" and UNOSOM II's mandate as "disarmament" proper.[116]

The narrow context of UNITAF's disarmament policy centered on what was colloquially known as "The Four No's": no bandits, no technical vehicles with crew-served weapons, no Somali-manned checkpoints, and no visible weapons.[117] This disarmament program was selective in the sense that UNITAF did not aggressively pursue comprehensive disarmament outside of this rudimentary guidance. Disarmament was largely reactive, undertaken with overwhelming force when needed and only to protect the larger mission of providing a secure environment for the delivery of humanitarian aid. The UNITAF envoy to Somalia noted that the UNITAF mandate focused on putting weapons out of circulation primarily to facilitate the movement of the relief convoys. "[The mandate] deliberately excluded disarmament [and] there was no need to confront [faction leaders] over the disappearance of weapons as long as they posed no threat to UNITAF forces or humanitarian operations."[118] Because of the overwhelming military capability of UNITAF and the clearly limited and less intrusive nature of the policy, resistance was very limited.

The United States resisted the urging of Boutros Boutros-Ghali in expanding the disarmament mandate of UNITAF because of concerns on both political and military levels about the feasibility of an ambitious disarmament program. Politically, there were very real fears in the United States that a more intrusive disarmament policy would drag UNITAF into the intra-Somali conflict as another local party. There were also fears about such actions being perceived as having "colonial" or "imperial" overtones.

UNITAF had no desire to confront the power base of local factions aggressively and lose its standing as a neutral entity on a humanitarian mission. Chester Crocker wrote that, "realizing the more open-ended time frame, the additional resources required to disarm the Somali factions, and the possible negative fallout on the home front, both U.S. administrations strongly opposed it."[119] Militarily, comprehensive disarmament was an expensive operation, requiring much greater military resources and an extended combat deployment. The U.S. CENTCOM commander-in-chief wrote,

> Disarmament was excluded from the mission because it was neither realistically achievable nor a prerequisite for the core mission of providing a secure environment for relief operations. Selective "disarming as necessary" became an implied task which led to the cantonment of heavy weapons and gave UNITAF the ability to conduct weapons sweeps.[120]

During the transition to UNOSOM II, it became difficult to define UNOSOM II's approach to disarmament, which, given its nation-building mandate, could hardly be as selective as UNITAF's. Security Council Resolution 814 provided little guidance on the operational methods to be used and only reiterated the long-standing UN observation that UNOSOM II would need a more comprehensive disarmament program to succeed.[121] In addition, the United Nations had no common operational plan for disarmament because of the failure of the organization to form a UNOSOM II staff that would seriously consider the question should the assumption about the efficacy of UNITAF's operations prove flawed. As one report noted, "the UN never undertook the type of planning for the demobilization and reintegration of the military that it had done in such previous peacekeeping operations as Namibia and El Salvador. The UN essentially refused—both through passivity and overt rejection—to plan for a hand-off."[122]

As an ironic consequence, the UNITAF staff set up the UNOSOM II disarmament plan, including timetables, cantonment sites, and all other operational details. One analyst emphasized that UNITAF had a "central, not supportive role in establishing the [UN] national disarmament plan."[123] Aware of the perceptions of its military weakness (vis-à-vis UNITAF), UNOSOM II began its disarmament program aggressively, initiating show-of-force operations throughout Somalia and in Mogadishu on the day after the transition from UNITAF.[124] However, the resolve of UNOSOM II was soon tested. The very next day the forces of Ahmed Omar Jess launched a planned and coordinated attack against the UN force in Kismayo.[125] The violence escalated, and the turning point came on 5 June 1993, when Somali forces from the faction of Mohammed Farah Aideed attacked and killed twenty-four Pakistani peacekeepers on a disarmament mission.

As a consequence, the UN Security Council passed Resolution 837 calling for the apprehension of those Somalis responsible. This started a U.S.–led manhunt for General Aideed and put UNOSOM II in direct conflict with a major Somali faction. There is no need to revisit the subsequent events here, but it is important to note that this started a period of aggressive UNOSOM II action, in which the hunt for Aideed and the disarmament program were carried out by UNOSOM II through offensive combat operations. This period precipitated much of the divergence of views noted in this chapter and great concern at UN headquarters and among the NGO community about the efficacy of mixing coercive actions with a peacekeeping mission.

These operations ended with the disastrous battle in South Mogadishu on 3 and 4 October 1993 and the subsequent announcement by the United States of its unilateral withdrawal. UNOSOM II then abandoned its aggressive policy of disarmament and resorted to a passive program that sought the cooperation of the local belligerents. The mix of limited enforcement measures with a peacekeeping operation had failed. Regardless of the military capability of UNOSOM II, the ultimate decision to disarm and cooperate was voluntary and relied for success on the belligerents.

There were great differences in the UNITAF and UNOSOM II approaches to disarmament, but there was one constant: civilian and military planners in both the United States and the United Nations knew it would be a difficult and potentially costly operation. The United States excused itself from this intricate challenge by setting a limited strategic objective that required only selective disarmament. In this it ensured success by using overwhelming force to achieve a clearly circumscribed goal. The United Nations, because it was hoping (in vain) that UNITAF would expand its goals, neglected to plan for the comprehensive disarmament plan needed to support UNOSOM II's ambitious mandate. As a result, the UNOSOM II disarmament plan went off half-cocked and precipitated a violent backlash from local factions that UNOSOM II did not have the military resources to contain.

Conducting "Nation-Building" Activities

"Nation building" itself is a catch-all phrase that refers to political processes much more than to military operations. For instance, the nation-building mandate of UNOSOM II tasked it to "assist the Somali people in rebuilding their shattered economy and social and political life, re-establishing the country's institutional structure, achieving national political reconciliation, recreating a Somali State based on democratic governance, and rehabilitating the country's economy and infrastructure."[126] Security Council Resolution 814 had similar, but more ambiguous, language, tasking UNOSOM II to help "create conditions under which Somali civil society may have a role in the process of political reconciliation."[127]

Other missions included supporting economic, humanitarian, police, refugee, and civil programs designed to make Somalia a self-reliant state. As such, the military missions involved in supporting these activities and creating supportive conditions were generally the same as those outlined above in the sections on protecting humanitarian aid and disarming and demobilizing local factions. For instance, the United Nations called disarmament a *"conditio sine qua non* for other aspects of UNOSOM II's mandate."[128] In this mission, the military worked to provide a secure and generally peaceful environment so that other programs could proceed without disruption from armed and organized resistance. The civil missions that involved administrative or logistical military support to civil, police, economic, electoral, and humanitarian programs are beyond the scope of this book.

The implied tasks in nation building were complex indeed when undertaken in a contested and bellicose environment. Even less ambitious strategic goals have many diverse tasks contained within their mandate. For instance, UNITAF's mandate gave it the implied tasks of

> *Opening up a secure environment for relief while keeping the warlords more or less sweet and somewhat off balance; maintaining and demonstrating military primacy without making a permanent adversary or national hero of any local actor; pushing the military factions towards a locally led political process while opening up that process to civilian elites, without advocating precise formulas, removing heavy weapons from areas of conflict while fostering the restoration of police and government functions—these are undertakings of the highest order of delicacy and complexity in a militarized and fragmented society such as Somalia's. These UNITAF accomplishments in fact went far beyond the one-line goal of creating a secure environment for humanitarian relief.[129]*

Although UNOSOM II existed for twenty-three months, the active military operations in support of its nation-building mandate were in effect only between May and October of 1993. During this period, UNOSOM II attempted to impose its mandate on Somalia while facing well-organized resistance from one faction and sporadic resistance from others. This situation gave rise to differences among contingents about how best to implement the UN mandate. One observer noted,

> *Some UN military advisors attributed this problem to the varying interpretation of UN Resolution 814 which authorized the rebuilding of Somalia as a nation. While the U.S. saw the need to marginalize the warlords, the Italians saw a strictly humanitarian UNOSOM II mission. The purposefully*

> *vague resolution caused a failure in translating UN (strate-*
> *gic) guidance into operational and tactical guidance.*[130]

After the debacle of 3 October and the U.S. decision to withdraw, the mission moved into an accommodative phase for the rest of its existence, effectively ending this debate in favor of passively accommodating Somali factions resisting the mandate.

To continue its goal of nation building but without using any coercive means, the United Nations was forced to revise its mandate. In February 1994, the Security Council passed Resolution 897, which lowered the expectations for what UNOSOM II's large military contingent could accomplish and placed more emphasis on traditional passive tasks that would "encourage and assist" the local parties "to achieve disarmament and to respect the cease-fire."[131] For the rest of its existence, UNOSOM II took only passive actions in Somalia while attempting to carry out its mandate. In the meantime, the security situation in Somalia worsened and the military resources available to UNOSOM II were reduced even further. The secretary-general reported in May 1994 that, "under the prevailing security conditions, the ability of the force to achieve its mandated tasks has become limited."[132] As the patience of the international community steadily waned, all UNOSOM II forces were eventually withdrawn by 31 March 1995. Somalia steadily fell back into a familiar pattern of civil war and chaos.

The failure of UNOSOM II's nation-building mandate is not a separate phenomenon, but one that is deeply rooted in the strategic incoherence highlighted above and the failure of the long-term efforts to achieve a secure political environment in Somalia. UNITAF strenuously chose to avoid such a mandate, seeing only the potential for a protracted commitment with no guarantee for success. American leaders were always quick to emphasize that "at no time have U.S. forces been tasked with such missions as 'nation building.' "[133] Given the bellicose environment, the resources available, and the complexity of the missions, one diplomat concluded that UNOSOM II should have reached a similar conclusion and that "either the nation-building mandate should have been drastically scaled down or the means to implement it should have been mobilized."[134] Unfortunately for Somalia, neither choice was available. The great powers wanted to make a bold move in Somalia but were unwilling to pay the costs themselves of a protracted military intervention that required great sacrifice on their part (as they did in the Persian Gulf War). Led by the United States, the Security Council therefore thrust the mission on a reluctant United Nations in another failed attempt to do such an ambitious mission on the cheap.

Conclusion

At its core, the UN operations in Somalia were an attempt to impose a humanitarian aid operation and comprehensive peace settlement on a community that was reluctant enough to resist successfully. As the international community began to conduct the inevitable postmortems on UN operations in Somalia, U.S. Envoy Robert Oakley noted that "there is a growing recognition that in many [such] situations, the United Nations must be perceived as having the military capability, the will to use it, and the decisiveness to win armed confrontations."[135] In its operations in Somalia, the United Nations proper had none of these three capabilities and characteristics. Military capability, political will, and the ability to be decisive in armed combat are characteristics usually associated with nation-states or rehearsed military alliances, not 185-member voluntary international organizations whose military expertise lies in running small, impartial, and passive operations.

Because it recognized this fact, the United Nations turned to UNITAF, a coalition led by a major military power. UNITAF brought tremendous institutional advantages to its military operations: it was based on a combat capable, ready-made, and readily deployable force package. This formation was capable of absorbing other force contributions and yet still performing complex military operations within a cohesive command framework and with a common modus operandi. To maximize its inherent military advantages, the political leaders of UNITAF gave the coalition finite and limited objectives that could be measured and achieved with a decisive force that would deter organized resistance and a mission that would not include an extended presence in Somalia.

In quite the opposite fashion, UNOSOM II was created in accord with traditional ad hoc methods used in UN observation missions and peacekeeping practice. As such, it was subject to the same problems of force structure, command and control, and military capability that had plagued other UN military formations. Although these inherent military foibles had not significantly undermined limited and innocuous UN missions in the past, they hurt UNOSOM II greatly. UNOSOM II was given an ambitious mandate that included the authorization to use active force in pursuit of its goals. When UNOSOM II encountered organized and violent resistance to its operations, the fallacy of managing large combat operations in the way that the UN managed small observation missions was exposed.

An analysis of UN operations in Somalia casts doubt on the efficacy of peace enforcement as a technique of conflict resolution. As noted in the survey of the debate on peace enforcement in the preceding chapter, to date the concept had yet to be fully proven in practice. The experience of UNOSOM II would seem to support the traditionalist notion that once the Rubicon of consent has been crossed through coercive action, the UN force has lost its status as an honest broker in the conflict. As Adam Roberts noted, "this hybrid of enforcement and peacekeeping achieved very mixed results, and was riddled with disagreements between different participants over the purposes of the operation and its command structure."[136]

However, the principal theme of this book does not concern the competence of the technique itself. This book is concerned primarily with the ability of the institution to manage the military operations of several different techniques of conflict resolution (including observation missions, traditional peacekeeping, and large-scale enforcement actions). In this sense the story of UN operations in Somalia reinforces the central theme of this examination. The United Nations, as an institution, was ill suited for managing complex military operations in bellicose environments.

The United Nations recognized this several months into UNOSOM II's existence, and the secretary-general wrote that UNOSOM II's problems were "symptomatic of the inadequacies of the present structure and procedure [of the UN] for coping with the heavy demands of the new generation of UN peacekeeping operations."[137] Because of the limited political legitimacy and military authority inherent in a voluntary multinational institution, the United Nations could not command the resources and authority needed to manage ambitious military operations in contested environments—especially when missions became costly and dangerous. The story of UNITAF and UNOSOM II shows the advantages and disadvantages of attempting to work around that dilemma through the partial use of subcontractors. The next chapter illustrates situations that required even more significant moves in the direction of contracting out military tasks to political entities with characteristics and resources more suited to running dynamic military operations.

CHAPTER 8

Enforcement: Korea and the Persian Gulf

Between 1948 and 1996, the United Nations was associated with two large-scale enforcement actions that were undertaken by UN–sanctioned multinational coalitions engaged in war against a state. In both the Korean conflict and the Persian Gulf conflict, the United Nations acted principally as a political forum for cooperative approaches to these conflicts, an institution that could formulate and legitimize the political goals of the coalitions. The United Nations itself was not directly engaged in managing these military forces. The strategic management of both these coalitions was left to the United States, the power most heavily engaged. In both conflicts, this fact led many observers to dismiss the UN–sanctioned efforts as merely U.S. wars with international window dressing. More important, as Adam Roberts noted after the Persian Gulf conflict, "the UN involvement in sanctioning force without controlling it left a legacy of concern within the organization, and beyond, that will have to be addressed."[1]

This brief chapter notes the way in which the United Nations was involved in the strategic management of these two large-scale enforcement actions and the military challenges of managing the operations. It does this to help explain why the United Nations itself could play little functional role in the military efforts of the coalitions. This short survey is necessary to fully understand the need for political legitimacy and military authority when a political entity attempts to form, direct, and employ a coercive military operation that consists of hundreds of thousands of troops conducting complex air, sea, and land operations against an intransigent enemy. In both conflicts, there never was any doubt that a multinational organization such as the United Nations could be a useful political forum, but could play only a supporting role in military affairs.

The UN Relationship to the Military Coalitions

The founders of the United Nations actually envisaged circumstances in which a UN coalition similar to the victorious wartime alliance could cooperatively engage in large-scale enforcement actions. It was hoped the forces would be available to the United Nations under Article 43 agreements and managed through the Military Staffs Committee. Chapters Two through Seven examined the way in which the United Nations improvised different types of military operations in the absence of the fulfillment of those provisions of the Charter. As with these lesser UN military operations, the large-scale enforcement operations in Korea and the Persian Gulf had to be improvised as well. In both cases, the United Nations ceded the strategic management to a coalition of member states that was managed by the chief military power in the coalition, the United States. In both instances, only the United States had the political legitimacy and military authority to mobilize and organize enormous military resources, provide a responsive and effective command and control structure, and direct the combat operations of these coalitions.

In Korea, the coalition was officially known (and still is for the troops deployed there today) as the United Nations Command (UNC). The UNC was mandated by a Security Council resolution passed on 7 July 1950, twelve days after North Korea invaded South Korea. Two previous resolutions passed immediately after the invasion of 25 June 1950 had identified North Korea as the aggressor, insisted it withdraw troops from South Korea, and recommended that "members of the United Nations furnish such assistance to the Republic of Korea as may be necessary to repel the armed attack and to restore peace and security in the area."[2] The United States had rushed troops to the area from Japan and was soon followed by air and sea support from Britain, Australia, and other states. President Truman made a decision immediately after the invasion to work through the United Nations to garner unqualified international support for the U.S.–led military response.[3]

This response was perfectly legitimate under Article 51 (the right of states to individual and collective self-defense) of the UN Charter and was indeed sanctioned by the Security Council Resolution of 27 June 1950. However, because the Soviet representative to the Security Council was boycotting its sessions (because of the issue over Chinese representation), the United States and her allies were able to push for a more explicit Security Council mandate. Resolution S/1588 of 7 July 1950 recommended that those member states assisting South Korea make their forces available to a unified command under the United States, asked the United States to appoint a commander, and authorized the UNC to use the UN flag (the UNTSO flag from the Palestine peacekeeping mission was even presented to General Douglas MacArthur).[4] Thus the United Nations officially made the United States its executive agent for carrying out the military operations necessary to expel North Korean forces from South Korea. Although the United States had already responded militarily to the crisis at hand, the UN resolutions gave the United States what UN scholar D. W. Bowett called an *"ex post facto* justification" from the United Nations for American actions taken in defense of South Korea.[5]

Political events concerning the Iraqi invasion of Kuwait in August 1990 followed a similar pattern. The UN Security Council responded immediately to the Iraqi invasion, passing a resolution condemning the invasion and demanding immediate withdrawal.[6] In June 1950 the UN Security Council was able to act with speed and decisiveness because of the absence of the Soviet Union. In 1990 the end of Cold War tensions between the United States and the USSR made a speedy resolution once again possible. However, Iraq did not withdraw in the face of a united Security Council and even continued to threaten Saudi Arabia. The Security Council then passed several further resolutions imposing economic sanctions on Iraq and giving member states permission to enforce a blockade. In the meantime, King Fahd of Saudi Arabia had requested military assistance from many nations, including a huge military commitment from the United States.

Throughout the fall of 1990, a military coalition of thirty-one member states gathered in the Gulf region to defend Saudi Arabia from Iraqi aggression and enforce the UN sanctions on Iraq. The coalition was organized under the political and military direction of the United States but, unlike in Korea, was not authorized as a UN command. The United Nations recognized the legitimacy of the coalition under Article 51 of the UN Charter and referred to the coalition as "those member states cooperating with the government of Kuwait."[7] As will be seen below, the United Nations legitimized the political goals and use of force by the coalition but was not involved in any way in the strategic management of the Persian Gulf force. This arrangement was sought by the United States, which, as Lawrence Freedman and Ephraim Karsh wrote, "wanted clear UN authorization, but without the encumbrance of a United Nations force with a United Nations Command, which was judged unwieldy and impractical."[8] Naturally, while meeting the requirements of the United States, some UN members protested the arrangement and sought a tighter relationship between the United Nations and the American-led coalition. Yemen's ambassador to the United Nations called the loose affiliation "a classic example of authority without accountability."[9]

Force Structure

The force structures of the coalitions in both Korea and the Persian Gulf were overwhelmingly dominated by the United States. In Korea, the United Nations received fifty-three offers of contributions for the UNC from member states, and the United States eventually assimilated the military forces of sixteen nations into the force structure.[10] Because of practical military requirements, the United States rejected token offers from some member states and insisted on combat units that had organic artillery, engineer, administrative, and logistic support. The United States alone was responsible for organizing the force structure of the coalition and, after receiving notification of an offer from a UN member state, formalized the relationship through bilateral agreements, not the United Nations. There was an attempt to have wide representation, but principles such as equitable geographic representation were subordinated to questions of military cohesion, interoperability, capability, equipment, and training standards.[11]

At its peak in June 1951, the UNC consisted of over 550,000 soldiers, 61 air squadrons, and over 250 naval vessels. The United States contributed over 50 percent of the ground forces (another 40 percent were South Korean), 94 percent of the air squadrons, and 86 percent of the ships.[12] Although this did represent an extreme imbalance in a political sense, it was a direct reflection of the military response to the crisis in June 1950. At the time of the North Korean invasion, the largest concentration of American troops outside of North America was in Japan. The United States was able to respond quickly with sea, air, and ground forces in 1950. Britain was heavily engaged in Malaya (and elsewhere) at the time, and France had over 65,000 troops fighting the Vietminh insurrection in Vietnam.[13] The Inchon landing of September 1950 was conducted with a multinational air and sea force but only U.S. ground troops. By the time the small forces of other countries arrived in Korea, the United States was conducting intensive combat operations with three Army corps, a Marine division, and two corps from South Korea. Consequently, the forces of other UN member states were integrated into American units as they arrived. Only when the battlefield stabilized in 1951 were some other national contingents able to function autonomously at the operational level.

The UN–sanctioned coalition in the Persian Gulf had a broader representation of member states, although the United States still overwhelmingly dominated the force structure. In the Gulf, however, political representation that challenged purely military logic (such as interoperability concerns) was tolerated. The broad nature of the Persian Gulf coalition was necessary to isolate Sadaam Hussein. The participation of Arab and Islamic nations (especially Syria) was seen as critical for success. The Gulf coalition therefore included small and underequipped units from Bangladesh, Senegal, Niger, Pakistan, Afghanistan, and elsewhere. The United States did not regulate the contributions of coalition members, as American leadership was informal and shared with Saudi Arabia. However, the United States ensured that the broad representation of thirty-one contributing member states did not dilute the military cohesion of the attack into Kuwait and Iraq. For instance, only British and American naval forces directly participated in the 1991 offensive, and only British and American ground units were assigned to defeat the Iraqi Republican Guard, the centerpiece of the campaign.[14]

Of the over 750,000 ground troops in the Persian Gulf coalition, more than 70 percent were American. Of the 1,820 combat aircraft, 76 percent were from the United States, and two out of three warships were U.S. naval vessels, including all of the six coalition aircraft carriers that participated in the attack on Iraq.[15] In addition to this numerical domination, the sophisticated nature of this complex campaign reinforced American dominance in the coalition force structure. For instance, only American warships and a few British frigates could electronically integrate air defense screens and were subsequently the only warships deployed in the northern Persian Gulf. In addition, although eleven nations provided combat aircraft, none could make an air strike without U.S. air support. The intelligence, targeting information, command and control, electronic warfare, and tanker aircraft were almost exclusively American. For instance, every electronic warfare aircraft in theater on 20 January 1991, the third day of the air campaign, was American.[16] The interoperability requirements of a large and complex warfighting coalition precluded the token participation of most member states in the main operations of the coalition and made the American domination of a politically broad force structure a military necessity.[17]

Command and Control

In the Korean conflict, there was some initial confusion over the UN role in the UNC's chain of command. Trygve Lie, the UN secretary-general, attempted to formalize an agreement that would reduce the purely American character of the UN chain of command. Lie wrote that this agreement proposed a committee of contributing nations that would "keep the United Nations 'in the picture.' The delegates of the UK, France, and Norway liked the idea . . . the United States turned thumbs down."[18] The United States felt that decisions by committee in a campaign of war would ultimately be self-defeating, producing a confused and ambiguous chain of command that was neither unified, focused, authoritative, nor responsive.[19] Consequently, UN scholar Evan Luard noted that there was no suggestion that "the UN commander should report to the Security Council or the Secretary-General."[20] The UNC commander, General MacArthur, testified before the U.S. Congress that his connection with the United Nations was "nominal. . . . I had no direct connection with the United Nations whatsoever."[21]

As a result, the chain of command and control procedures of the UNC in Korea were principally those of the U.S. Department of Defense and the

American Far East Command (Figure 8). The United Nations was kept informed of operations, but the chain of command was almost completely American. The representatives of the other UN contingents had the right of direct access to General MacArthur (and later General Ridgeway) on matters of policy, but this did not represent any meaningful influence in providing strategic direction for the UNC.[22] The heavy American dominance of the chain of command marginalized the UN proper and other UNC contingents but was a result of the political and military weight with which the United States had responded to the invasion of South Korea. As Robert O'Neill noted, "the way in which a war commences inevitably influences the command relations which result."[23]

It was a slightly different case in the Gulf conflict. There, the United Nations made no attempt at a formal command relationship with the U.S.–led coalition. As a result, there was no confusion about the UN role, but the United Nations was still marginalized in terms of strategic influence. The predicament of the United Nations was highlighted in January 1991, when Secretary-General Perez de Cuellar hinted that his eleventh-hour diplomacy was essentially moot, because he had no working control over the coalition.[24] As in Korea, and for many of the same reasons, the chain of command in the Gulf was dominated by the United States (Figure 9). However, the broad political coalition in the Gulf necessitated a looser framework for the chain of command. This was manifested in the decision to treat General Schwarzkopf, the American commander, and General Khalid bin Sultan, the Saudi commander, on equal terms in the coalition chain of command.

This political arrangement had little military meaning, but it eased political sensibilities and encountered no military threats that would have called its efficacy into question.[25] In addition, there was no attempt in the Gulf to thoroughly integrate the operations of such a disparate coalition. To ensure that the necessary political accommodations did not unduly affect operations, many coalition units were given specific tasks or independent areas of operation (as in UNITAF's Somalia operations) that ameliorated the possible command problems arising in a disparate thirty-one-nation ad hoc military coalition. The United States, as the framework state for the coalition, provided an authoritative and responsive system of command and control at the strategic level that allowed smaller contingents to work within their own structures and procedures at tactical levels.

Military Objectives

In both Korea and the Persian Gulf, the military objectives of the UN–sanctioned coalitions centered on countering the armed invasion of an aggressor state. In Korea, the three immediate resolutions of the Security Council autho-

Figure 8

Chain of Command of the UNC in Korea

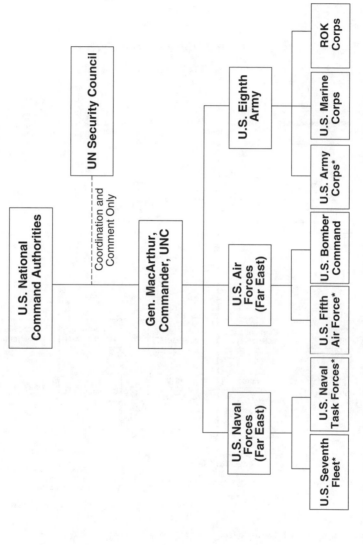

* Allied units attached at small unit levels with the exception of certain Commonwealth units after 1951.

Sources: Various sources compiled by author.

Figure 9

Command Relationships in the
Persian Gulf Coalition

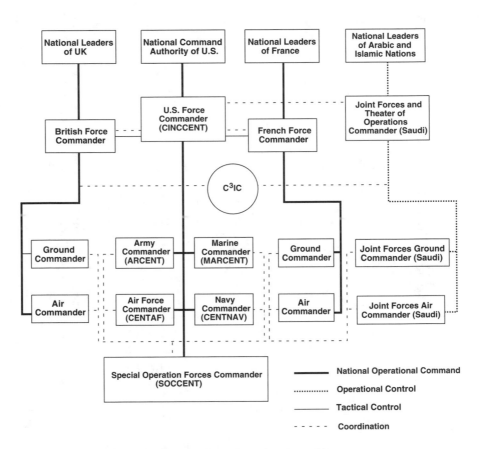

Source: Alberts and Hayes, *Command Arrangements for Peace Operations*, p. 54.

rized the UNC to take such military action necessary to restore the status quo ante. The United States made this the political objective of its Korean strategy, and the U.S. secretary of state stated soon after the invasion that U.S. action was "solely for the purpose of restoring the Republic of Korea to its status prior to the invasion."[26] General Douglas MacArthur's bold military plan intended to bring about this objective centered on a "deep envelopment, based on surprise . . . the most decisive maneuver of war."[27] This would be accomplished through an amphibious landing in the rear of the North Korean lines at Inchon. The plan was successful, and the UNC drove quickly to the North Korean border, effectively restoring the status quo ante by the end of September 1950.

However, due to the success of the attack, President Truman and his advisors in Washington (as well as General MacArthur) began to entertain ideas of continuing the attack into North Korea to unite the peninsula. A U.S. National Security Council document of the time recommended to President Truman that this was in keeping with three UN General Assembly Resolutions of 1947, 1948, and 1949, all of which called for the independence and reunification of Korea.[28] Using this as a pretext, the United States proposed a General Assembly resolution (the USSR had since resumed its seat on the now-moribund Security Council) authorizing the UNC to use military force to unify Korea.[29] Within days of the passage of the resolution, UNC troops crossed the border and subsequently advanced to the Yalu River, prompting a Chinese intervention and eventually a retreat back to the 38th parallel. By early 1951, in the face of the military challenges presented by the Chinese forces in Korea, the United States had scaled back its goals and replaced General MacArthur. The conflict was concluded with a cease-fire in 1953 negotiated not by the United Nations, but by a committee of the sixteen nations that fought as the UNC in Korea. While the United Nations contributed to the effort to regain momentum in stalled peace talks throughout 1952–1953, it had little direct influence in the strategic resolution of the conflict.

In the Persian Gulf conflict, Security Council resolutions also set the initial political goals for the UN–sanctioned coalition. And, as in Korea, the United States worked to gain UN legitimacy before changing the near-term objectives and methods of the coalition. Unlike in Korea, the United States was not hampered by great power tensions on the Security Council and had no need to seek ex post facto legitimacy for some phases of the campaign through other bodies, such as the UN General Assembly. The Security Council resolutions concerning Iraq and Kuwait supported the passive actions of Operation Desert Shield, the U.S.–led coalition that was intended to deter further Iraqi aggression and enforce the sanctions imposed on Iraq by the Security Council. However, in October 1990, President Bush began to consider the option of offensive military operations to achieve the UN resolutions centered on restoring the sovereignty of Kuwait. Such military actions were not, at the time, explicitly mandated by the UN resolutions and would require a significant international consensus for political, operational, and domestic reasons.[30]

After considerable campaigning by the United States, on 29 November 1990 the UN Security Council passed Resolution 678, which "authorized Member states co-operating with the government of Kuwait . . . to use all necessary means to uphold and implement resolution 660 and all subsequent resolutions." The exact form that "all necessary means" would take was left up to the coalition. The Yemeni ambassador to the United Nations, who cast one of the two votes against the resolution, mocked that the ambiguous resolution permitted "persons unknown to use means unspecified to achieve goals unstated."[31] However, although some believed that offensive action was not explicitly mandated by the United Nations, there was no ambiguity in the U.S. campaign plan intended to restore the sovereignty of Kuwait. In January 1991, the U.S.–led coalition began a six-week campaign that attacked Iraq by air throughout the depth of its strategic defenses (including Baghdad and other targets not in the Kuwait theater of operations) and culminated in a massive enveloping ground attack that comprehensively defeated the Iraqi army in and around Kuwait. The coalition was a tremendous success in achieving the United Nations' stated political goals. The United Nations itself, however, played no role in determining the military objectives, modus operandi, or strategy that would make those political objectives possible.

Conclusion

In the absence of functioning political-military mechanisms and procedures such as the Military Staffs Committee and Article 43 forces, the United Nations was doomed to be marginalized in the management of large-scale enforcement actions. Although it could serve as a forum for gaining international consensus and setting political objectives, the United Nations could not provide the institutional framework for executing the military operations needed to realize its resolutions. In the conduct of lesser military operations, the United Nations had used, with some successes, ad hoc and improvised procedures that suited its political and military constraints. However, these restricted methods could never be used to recruit, organize, deploy, and direct the sophisticated combat operations of hundreds of thousands of troops.

Only a major political and military power, or perhaps a credible military alliance, could provide the framework needed to mount, direct, and employ such operations. In both Korea and Kuwait, the United States was asked to provide a rapid and massive military response to an overwhelming threat. The military requirements of both crises could not be met by any other nation. As Robert O'Neill noted, in military situations "need creates its own priorities."[32] This thrust the United States into the position of taking responsibility for reversing aggression. However, the United States shared the "needs" of these crises by seeking international cooperation through the United Nations in both instances. Working through the United Nations was exclusively a political exercise, one in which the United States had enormous influence, too much for many critics. The functional military decisions, on the other hand, were kept out of the United Nations and shared only to a small extent with allies in the U.S.–led coalitions. The military requirements of these enormous and complex operations required a major power able to provide a legitimate and authoritative framework that could mobilize, organize, command, control, and employ the combined efforts of those states involved in these combat operations.

Conclusion

Four brave men who do not know each other will not dare to attack a lion. Four less brave, but knowing and trusting each other well, will attack resolutely.
— Charles Ardant du Picq, *Battle Studies* (1880)

To manage military forces, a political entity must have certain means. These means are manifested as institutions, organizations, structures, and procedures. Moreover, the more difficult the military mission, the more the means must be grounded in legitimate, authoritative, accountable, fully functional, and well-rehearsed political or military institutions. These means to undertake military operations first enable the political entity to recruit, organize, train, and equip personnel as military forces. Additional means allow the political entity to make plans, deploy military forces, and direct their operations. The means and capabilities necessary to carry out these tasks ultimately derive from the legitimacy and authority of the political entity. Political legitimacy and military authority allow a political entity to build the institutions, structures, and procedures necessary for undertaking military action.

Those sorts of political or military legitimacy and authority does not exist between international organizations and the world's citizenry. It is a vestige of sovereignty that remains the province of the state (and, in increasing cases, lesser political entities). As Professor Innis Claude recognized, sovereignty is inherent in states because there is no "government of governments."[1] Ronald Steel wrote similarly that "the UN was not designed to be a world government, nor the collective conscience of mankind. Rather, it is a market place where deals are struck and interests protected."[2] Paul Kennedy and Bruce Russett carried the corporate analogy even farther and noted that the United Nations is not "an embryonic world government, but an international corporation so to speak, with the nation-states as shareholders."[3] Moreover, in this corporate system, each shareholder can mobilize military forces as a matter of sovereign right, but sharing them under unwieldy corporate control— the concept of pooled sovereignty—is a completely voluntary exercise.

Attempting to replicate sovereign political or military means in a multinational organization that recognizes the sovereignty and preeminence of the state in the international order (as stated in Article II of the UN Charter) can be ultimately self-defeating. Without the sovereign relationships of legitimacy, authority, and accountability between itself and its "citizenry," a political entity such as the United Nations cannot competently form the means necessary for significant military actions. In a few cases, a credible military alliance of a few nation-states, focused on a common and cohesive cause (such as NATO during the Cold War), can share these means to some extent. As peacekeeping scholar Andrei Raevsky noted, "only individual countries and some military alliances have comprehensive military means."[4] Comprehensive, reliable, credible, and rehearsed military means are especially necessary for a military force undertaking large and complex combat operations (attacking the lion).

Between 1948 and 1996, the United Nations, regional organizations, other military alliances, and states have all mounted, directed, and employed military forces in various operations. The successes and failures of these organizations in managing different types of military activities provide much evidence for analysis. In particular, the experience of the United Nations in managing the large, complex, and sometimes active military operations of second-generation peacekeeping missions recently brought into sharp focus the institutional capabilities that a political entity must have to manage military force competently. In 1993, as UN efforts in Somalia and Bosnia were getting under way, Adam Roberts noted with some prescience that

> *military actions require extremely close coordination between intelligence-gathering and operations, a smoothly functioning decision-making machine and forces with some experience of working together to perform dangerous and complex tasks. These things are more likely to be achieved through existing national armed forces, alliances, and military relationships, than they are within the structure of a UN command.*[5]

This book concludes that, if applied to the operations such as those in Bosnia and Somalia, Professor Robert's observations were correct: the UN simply has not had the institutional competence to manage military forces engaged in what he labels "dangerous and complex tasks." However, the existing "structure of a UN command" has shown over the years that it could accommodate some military operations that are managed through the United Nations proper. In the main, these operations were small and simple, as they were kept limited by the constraints and restrictions inherent to a multinational organization such as the United Nations. To paraphrase Clausewitz, UN military operations had their own grammar, but not their own logic. Their logic was the logic of the United Nations' politics and the organization's multilateral character. The grammar of UN military operations closely reflected the character and limitations of the United Nations, what Israeli diplomat Abba Eban has called "not the parliamentary, but the diplomatic principle" of the organization. Eban notes that the United Nations is not "an instrument for solving conflicts, [but] an arena for waging them."[6] As a result, most UN military operations had characteristics uniquely suited to the "diplomatic principle," a principle that reflected the limited political legitimacy and circumscribed military authority of the organization.

The principles of peacekeeping that codified these characteristics therefore stressed the need for small and innocuous UN military forces that would work only with the consent and cooperation of the belligerents, that would be conspicuously impartial in appearance and action, and that would use force of arms only in the most passive of ways. Following these principles, the United Nations could mobilize and manage, through voluntary cooperation with member states, the small resources needed for relatively simple military operations such as observation and traditional peacekeeping. However, as the Congo experience taught the United Nations, the organization did not have the legitimacy and authority to muster, organize, and direct large and active military operations that sought to impose the United Nations' will on belligerents through force of arms. In 1992, William Durch noted the enduring trauma of ONUC for the United Nations and stated, "The Security Council is unlikely to ever again dispatch such a sizable force under UN command with such a similarly undefined initial mandate."[7]

Durch was proven tragically wrong (twice over) only a few months later when the United Nations attempted to manage large, complex, and occasionally active military missions in Somalia and the former Yugoslavia. These missions were a result of a Security Council consensus enjoyed in the aftermath of the thawing of the Cold War and the international cooperation of the Persian Gulf conflict. During this brief period, many prestigious observers maintained that the inherent political constraints of the United Nations were purely a product of the Cold War rivalry between the great powers on the Security Council. David Hendrickson noted that "these developments have produced an unprecedented situation in international society. They have persuaded many observers that we stand today at a critical juncture, one at which the promise of collective security, working through the mechanism of the United Nations, might at last be realized."[8]

The secretary-general's *An Agenda for Peace* and numerous other reports championed this idea and proposed steps to institutionalize the structural reinforcements and managerial changes needed in the United Nations to manage more significant military operations. Thomas Weiss, one of the scholars involved in such projects, wrote that *An Agenda for Peace*

> *is perhaps the most spectacular indication of just how signifi-*
> *cant the UN's role could be in international peace and securi-*
> *ty as the twenty-first century dawns. . . . The United Nations is*
> *the logical covener of future international military operations.*
> *Rhetoric about regional organizations risks slowing down or*
> *even making impossible more timely and vigorous action by*
> *the UN, the one organization most likely to fulfill adequately*
> *the role of regional conflict manager.[9]*

Yet only two years later, following the failures of UNOSOM II and UNPRO-FOR, Weiss wrote that the United Nations' "diplomatic and bureaucratic structures are inimical to initiating and overseeing military efforts when serious fighting rages, and where coercion rather than consent is the norm."[10] Despite consensus on the Security Council, structural and procedural reinforcements to the UN Secretariat, and unprecedented cooperation from member states throughout the period following *An Agenda for Peace*, the United Nations still could not manage military operations other than those small, simple, and innocuous missions that adhered to the principles of peacekeeping. Progress was made in smaller second-generation missions, such as those in Namibia, Mozambique, and even Cambodia. However, the organization simply could not assume the vestiges of sovereignty necessary to manage large and ambitious military forces engaged in dangerous and complex operations like those in the former Yugoslavia and Somalia. The legitimacy, authority, and accountability (as well as funding) needed by a political entity to manage significant military missions were not transferable, even temporarily, to the United Nations.

In 1995, after the debacle in Somalia and the impending failure of UNPRO-FOR, Boutros Boutros-Ghali reaffirmed this and noted in a speech that "the imposition of peace requires military, financial, and political resources that member-states are simply not willing to provide for operations other than war; and these resources require a capacity to manage them which the United Nations Secretariat does not possess and is unlikely to be granted."[11] Subsequently, in a 1995 supplement to *An Agenda for Peace*, Boutros Boutros-Ghali "trimmed his sails"[12] and downplayed the central role that the United Nations could play in managing large and ambitious military efforts. The United Nations, after an attempt at forming, directing, and employing comprehensive and sometimes coercive military missions, realized it could not provide the political and functional framework for significant military operations.

That framework was necessary to mobilize the great resources needed for these large and complex operations. The framework also could be relied on to steer a steady direction in the conduct of costly and dangerous military missions. Coalitions of the willing, led by a powerful nation state, or credible military alliances with a clearly defined unity of command and effort could provide such a framework within a multinational context. The United Nations could not. However, as Harvey Sicherman noted, "the assertive multilateralists [of 1992–1993] placed more weight upon the UN than it could bear, while ignoring NATO and other regional coalitions."[13]

The United States (led by then-ambassador to the United Nations Madeleine Albright, who is credited with coining the strategy of "assertive multilateralism") and the other great powers pushed missions on the United Nations that it could not hope to handle and then refused to support its efforts. It was convenient to fob off the Bosnias and Somalias on the United Nations despite the warnings of then-Under Secretary-General for Peacekeeping Koffi Anan, who noted that any plans to further expand the size, scope, and nature of UN military operations were "building on sand."[14] It has been shown that Somalia was definitely such a case. UN diplomat Shashi Tharoor writes that Bosnia, too, fit this bill. He noted that "it is sometimes argued that the peacekeeping deployment to Bosnia-Herzegovina reflected not so much a policy as the absence of policy; that [UN] peacekeeping responds to the need to 'do something' when policy-makers are not prepared to expend the political, military, and financial resources required to achieve the outcome that the press and opinion leaders are clamoring for."[15] Ronald Steel agreed and noted at the time that "the current enthusiasm for multilateralism results in large part from the unwillingness of states to make serious sacrifices to establish order."[16] This was especially so when a multilateral intervention promised much human and material sacrifice in areas of little direct interest to the great powers. For, as John Mearsheimer wrote, "war is a deadly business and few countries want to commit themselves in advance to paying a huge blood price when their own self-interests are not directly involved."[17]

Managing UN Military Operations

Because the United Nations lacked the political legitimacy and military authority necessary to competently form, direct, and employ significant military forces, it improvised its management of military operations. While this was an ad hoc approach, over a period of years a series of conventions evolved, conventions that uniquely suited the political character of the United Nations itself. These conventions, manifested in the principles of peacekeeping, were not merely a reflection of the Cold War impasse on the Security Council; they more clearly reflected the enduring character of the United Nations and the structure of an international arena predicated on the sovereignty of the nation-state. The Cold War exacerbated the problems of trying to work through voluntary international structures such as the United Nations, but this great power struggle was not solely responsible for keeping the United Nations from functioning as the preeminent collective security structure in the world, as some observers suggested. This was quickly affirmed within a few years of the end of the Cold War when, despite consensus on the Security Council and unprecedented cooperation and resources from nation-states and the great powers, the United Nations proved that it was not, as Weiss suggested above, "the logical convener of future international military operations." [18]

Much as water will flow around obstacles, the principles of peacekeeping evolved to flow around (and work within) the United Nations' natural lack of political legitimacy and military authority. Although constraining from a military perspective, the principles evolved to suit the immutable character of the United Nations. In terms of force structure, this meant that the United Nations would recruit and organize military force based principally on political requirements, not military stipulations. Regardless of the functional requirements for interoperability or military effectiveness, the force structure of most UN missions had to be politically acceptable to the Security Council and, more important, to the local belligerents. In addition, the force structure needed to reinforce the perception of strict impartiality and equitable geographic representation. As Andrei Raevsky noted,

> the arrangements of most peacekeeping operations are shaped with prevailing political rather than military considerations. This is, in fact, almost inevitable because most UN peacekeeping operations are highly political in their nature and, thus, the military forces involved are operating in an environment in which military considerations are secondary to political priorities.[19]

Indeed, one of the chief reasons that most UN peacekeeping operations were "highly political in nature" was because they were not very military in nature. The UN military operations that were conducted in consonance with the principles of peacekeeping were small and innocuous quasi-military missions. Although these missions used military tools, they were diplomatic in their purpose, a self-help technique for belligerents who had to be willing to help themselves. The noncoercive nature of most UN operations meant that military efficiency was not a prime determinant of mission success. Thus, although the traditional constraints of UN force structure considerations made most UN missions somewhat impractical from a military standpoint,[20] they did not unduly cripple these missions that relied overwhelmingly on success in the diplomatic and political realm.

However, in challenging missions, such as the former Yugoslavia and Somalia, military requirements sometimes overrode traditional political sensitivities as the missions became larger, more militarily sophisticated, and more ambitious, coercive, and costly. When the enormous military requirements of second-generation peacekeeping missions and enforcement actions were realized, it became apparent that the United Nations could not be the institution that could recruit and organize such forces, nor could the United Nations command and control the operations of large, complex, and offensive-minded military forces. The United Nations had directed most of its military missions through an improvised system of command and control. The system that evolved was based on a loose definition of command that recognized the prerogatives of the nation-state in regard to its troops in UN service. In addition, because the United Nations always formed and commanded sui generis and ad hoc forces, the control procedures of UN forces were improvised as the mission proceeded. This worked to some extent in small and simple missions that were executed in a supportive military environment. In contrast, these conventions of UN command and control were disastrous in large, complex, and ambitious military missions operating in contested environments.

The United Nations' inability to command and control significant military operations was rooted in its lack of sovereign legitimacy and authority. The fact that these characteristics were not transferable from the United Nations' member states locked the United Nations into a self-defeating cycle in terms of its ability to command military forces authoritatively. As Charles Lipson noted, institutions such as the United Nations have the power only to call for the "decentralized cooperation of individual sovereign states, without any effective mechanism of command."[21] Although "cooperation" as an organizing imperative could work in small and simple missions, it quickly broke down in dangerous, costly, and controversial missions. When that lack of an effective mechanism for command became apparent in military missions such as UNPROFOR and UNOSOM II, Professor Ramesh Thakur noted that "states [were] reluctant to transfer control over their national armed forces to the UN because of doubts over its managerial capacity for military operations."[22] Having to operate based on voluntary cooperation severely limited the United Nations' command and capacity for challenging military initiatives.

The military objectives of traditional UN missions (observation and traditional peacekeeping operations) suited the constraints of the organization and its ability to form and direct military forces. The innocuous military objectives of most UN military operations were based on the United Nations' "diplomatic principle," that is, the ability of the organization to construct, through diplomatic and political means, a supportive political environment for UN military. As such, the environment to which Blue Helmets were deployed was the key to success in UN military operations, not the operations or objectives of the force itself. Moreover, preserving the political environment was more important than competent military operations. As Emmanual Erskine, the former commander of UNIFIL, wrote in his memoirs, "the main difficulty is that there are a lot of things which a [UN] force commander cannot do on his own because of political constraints, even though militarily they may be sound."[23] Nonetheless, politics and preserving the political environment were everything in UN peacekeeping—and provided for some absurd violations of good military practice. As John Mackinlay noted, "it is true to a certain extent that all military activity has an underlying political motive which influences its success in varying degrees, but peacekeeping is more influenced by the success of the preceding political arrangements than any other."[24]

If these "preceding political arrangements" were upheld by all concerned parties, and the local belligerents especially, the UN force had a good chance of succeeding. Moreover, it could succeed with a modus operandi based not on its strength in force of arms, but on moral authority drawn from its neutral status, its guarantee of working with the consent and cooperation from local factions, and its committal to using force only in self-defense. This modus operandi and the simple military objectives that followed from it could be accomplished by an ad hoc and loosely managed military force in a supportive environment. However, if that environment broke down, as it did in southern Lebanon, traditional UN military objectives were inadequate.

In environments even more challenging than that posed by Lebanon, the UN's post–Cold War operations experienced an incoherence between means and ends. Ambitious political mandates for missions to the former Yugoslavia and Somalia were passed by a United Security Council that then did not follow through in giving the UN the forces, command structure, and military capabilities it would need to realize the Security Council goals. The UN had to try and make old systems and procedures work in contested environments that did not support traditional operations. Moreover, attempts by the Blue Helmets to create supportive environments through force of arms were unsuccessful.

Large, complex, and dangerous military operations centered on ambitious military objectives required a political or military framework with more legitimacy and authority than the United Nations could muster. Attempts were made in both Somalia and the former Yugoslavia to work around this dilemma through the use of subcontractors for limited enforcement measures. However, these operations marginalized the United Nations and reinforced the role of individual states. Adam Roberts noted that "U.S. and allied actions [in Bosnia] confirmed the truism that the more force is used on behalf of the UN, the more central the role of individual states becomes."[25] More important, many observers noted that such missions discredited the impartiality of the organization itself—the very core of its unique (albeit limited) legitimacy and authority in the diplomatic realm. Former Assistant Secretary-General Giandomenico Picco wrote that "the more the UN tries to resemble a state, the more it will fade away and, most seriously perhaps, the UN will become no more than the sum of its members."[26]

In a similar vein, Paul Kennedy and Bruce Russett wrote that "these operations, hopes, and expectations far exceed the capabilities of the system as it is now constituted, and they threaten to overwhelm the United Nations and discredit it, perhaps forever, even in the eyes of its warmest supporters."[27] David Hendickson and Ernest Lefever have even written that an aggressive reach by the United Nations for a central role in international military affairs was unethical in a world of sovereign states.[28] That argument, over the rights and wrongs of collective security per se, is well beyond the scope of this book. However, what is clearly evident is that, as a practical matter of policy, the United Nations simply could not be the political entity that had the institutional legitimacy and functional competence to manage comprehensive military operations in contested environments. Two years after calling for the United Nations to assume a greater role, scholar Thomas Weiss admitted,

> *The means to plan, support, and command peacekeeping, let alone enforcement, is scarcely greater now than during the Cold War. Modest progress in establishing a situation room in New York and some consolidation in the UN administrative services are hardly sufficient to make the militaries of the major or middle powers feel at ease about placing the UN in charge of combat missions.*[29]

Attempts in the post–Cold War era to reinforce the United Nations with additional means made little difference, as they could not compensate for the inherent nature of the institution and the structure of the international arena.

The UN and Multinational Military Operations

In a 1995 study on structural issues in UN military operations, two Cambridge scholars noted,

> *To be both legitimate and effective, the plausible threat or actual use of military measures as an instrument of policy necessitates functional political-military institutions such as those developed by states whose coincident or overlapping interests cause them to unite either in formal alliances or in ad hoc coalitions. In each case, appropriate political-military institutions are established to carry out three indispensable functions: the input of military advice into the political decision-making process; the translation of political objectives into military missions; and the maintenance and exercise of political control over military activity. But, without exception, all such institutions, whether national or regional, have a common limitation when employed to manage collectively sanctioned military*

> *operations: they derive their legitimacy from, and are account-*
> *able to, the nation-state.*[30]

Thus the challenge for the United Nations, in attempting to play a global role in collective security, has always been how it could best coordinate its security role with those of nation-states, whose sovereignty it recognizes as the organizing principle of international relations. In doing so, the United Nations had to recognize its political and military constraints vis-à-vis member states. In the absence of collective security arrangements as envisaged in Chapter VII of the UN Charter, the principles of peacekeeping evolved commensurate with the limitations of the United Nations. These limitations are constant, and not just a product of the Cold War impasse on the Security Council. Former UN official Saadia Touval writes that "those limitations are ingrained. They are embedded in the very nature of intergovernmental organizations, and no amount of upgrading, expansion or revamping of UN powers can correct those flaws."[31]

Traditional UN military operations in accord with the principles of peacekeeping were appropriate to the UN's multilateral character, but not to many crises of the post–Cold War era. In many ways, missions the UN could manage suited the nature of the institution more than the nature of the tasks at hand. As a 1995 report of the United States Institute of Peace noted, the "operational forms and procedures developed to handle intervention situations by the UN and other multilateral organizations may respond to the abilities, limitations, and preferences of those organizations and impede adaptation to local circumstances."[32] UN military operations in the past were most successful when the constraints of the organization were congruent with the nature of the crisis. The United Nations could manage small and simple military operations whose operational imperatives were based on political and diplomatic success, rather than success through force of arms. Multinational combat operations, with their enormous military requirements, needed to be managed by a political entity with far greater political legitimacy and military authority. As Berdal noted in December 1994, "the inherent political and operational constraints on UN action also suggest that ad hoc 'coalitions of the willing' might often be a better alternative to UN-led action, especially in cases where enforcement is being considered."[33] The decision to deploy NATO's 60,000 troops to supervise the Bosnian peace accords in December 1995 showed that credible military alliances or coalitions of the willing led by a major military power were better solutions to these sorts of interventions than a UN–managed force.

In the post–Cold War era, the United Nations did indeed advance its role in international security, principally through a more comprehensive approach to peacekeeping, such as seen in the smaller recent missions to Namibia, El Salvador, Mozambique, and elsewhere. However, this more comprehensive role was in the diplomatic and political sphere, not in the realm of military operations. In this area, member states hold too dear the powers and responsibilities conferred by sovereignty to allow the United Nations to manage significant military operations in its own name and under its own authority. As Adam Roberts noted, "the UN, including its leading members, needs to recognize openly that the Charter was right to provide for a balance between self-defense and collective military action under UN auspices; but wrong to imply that the UN could have a central role in more than a very small number of crises."[34] The structure of the international arena, legitimized by the UN Charter, reserves for nation-states and smaller political entities the legitimacy and authority needed to competently manage all but the most simple military operations. As long as the fundamental structure of the international arena remains based on the sovereign state, the United Nations' attempts to under-take complex and dangerous military operations will be antithetical to its political nature and ultimately futile—and will hurt both the United Nations and the mission.

This conclusion might suggest that there is a definitive formula for which political entities should undertake certain types of multinational military opera-tions. Such a formula would hold that simple military missions such as observa-tion and traditional peacekeeping are the core competence of the UN, while more dynamic military operations should only be undertaken by rehearsed military alliances or coalitions led by a major military power. As in most issues of inter-national relations, this comparison must be tempered by several factors that show set prescriptions can be instructive, but most often are far from categorical. Conclusions drawn from a simple and narrow comparison of the strategic man-agement capabilities of the UN and multinational groups led by a major military power must be informed by other factors when applied to future circumstances.

For instance, if political legitimacy and military authority are the sole keys to the successful management of multinational military campaigns, then what accounts for the failure of the American-British-French multinational peace-keeping force (MNF) in Beirut in 1982–1984? At the strategic level, these three major military powers could bring an unsurpassed legitimacy and authority to the MNF, which was charged with the relatively uncomplicated mission of peace-keeping. In the end, the complexity of the conflict, the disagreements among the participants in the MNF over methods and objectives, and the subsequent lack of enthusiasm for pursuing an unclear mandate in the face of continuous threats defeated the mission. Similarly, the experiences of Somalia between 1992–1995 and Bosnia between 1992–1997 ultimately might provide more insights about the challenges inherent to those situations, rather than the management capabili-ties or strategic character of the institutions involved there. One can appreciate the differences in military effectiveness between UNITAF and UNOSOM II in Somalia or UNPROFOR and NATO in Bosnia while at the same time recognizing that the long-term challenges to the international community in Somalia and Bosnia might be well beyond the political will and military capabilities of both organizations. As noted in the introduction, the indicators of success in multinational military operations are much more complex than a simple comparison based on bureaucratic or organizational theory.

Nonetheless, the experiences of the UN, alliances, coalitions, states, and other political bodies managing multinational military operations suggest that certain institutions are more suited for some military operations than others. A better understanding of these parameters could help avoid situations such as those in Bosnia and Somalia, where great powers who were reluctant to squarely address complex situations then turned the task over to an under-equipped and overwhelmed United Nations. This does not imply that such problems might demand an either/or solution insomuch as the UN and other multinational entities or states are concerned. Rather, new patterns of collective security could develop based upon the recognition of how political legitimacy and military authority underpin the management of multinational military forces. For instance, as happened in Somalia, Bosnia, and Haiti, the international community might want to try small traditional UN military operations based on consent, impartiality, and the passive use of force before, if necessary, replacing it with a more muscular multinational force organized and controlled by an regional alliance or coalition.

Ironically, this emerging pattern (along with the possibility of other sanctions) closely resembles the series of possible responses to breaches of international peace and security that were put forth in Chapter VII of the UN Charter (especially Articles 40–42). However, the spirit of these Articles does not require the UN to provide the organizational core of every political and military effort associated with a collective response. There are many different ways in which to approach these challenges that satisfy the basic purpose of the UN idea and the Charter. The United Nations itself should not be asked to do too much, especially in the emotive and complicated business of mounting and controlling dynamic military campaigns. A cooperative approach that respects the immutable and profound military impact of sovereignty, and at the same time seeks to take advantage of the institutional strengths of the many entities that make up international society, is likely to be more successful in the difficult missions.

Epilogue: 1998–2000

After Bosnia, Somalia, Cambodia, Angola, and other episodes outlined in the latter half of this book, one would expect the UN to curb its military ambitions for some time. Surprisingly, as the new century dawns, the world sits on the cusp of another periodic upswing in the size, character, and ambitions of UN peacekeeping operations. Since the fall of 1999, the UN has mandated three large and complex peacekeeping operations—in East Timor, Sierra Leone, and the Democratic Republic of the Congo—in which the UN itself will direct significant military forces operating in difficult environments. In addition, there is the new UN mission to Kosovo, but in that mission NATO is handling the military tasks while the UN restricts itself to policing, administrative, and other basic governmental functions.

As this book shows, this latest movement can be characterized as periodic upswing because a survey of the fifty-two-year history of UN peacekeeping is one of recurrent phases—patterns that have been repeated several times in the past half century. In the first phase, small peacekeeping successes lead an emboldened international community to give the UN larger, more complex, and ambitious military operations in more belligerent environments. In the second phase, these sorts of operations quickly overwhelm the capabilities of the UN itself, which tries unsuccessfully to improvise in operations for which it has no institutional structure, authoritative management systems, or military competency. In the third phase, burned and discredited, the UN pulls back to a more traditional peacekeeping role that suits the institution. Finally, with time healing some of these wounds and challenges to the international community continuing to mount, short memories compel the international community to thrust the UN back onto the international security stage in a more ambitious and central role than before.

The lessons of each of these cycles are clear and enumerated in great detail herein. In essence, the UN itself has never had, nor was it ever intended to have, the authority, institutions, and procedures needed to successfully manage complex military operations in dangerous environments. Conversely, the UN—the world's most accepted honest broker—has exactly the characteristics needed to manage some peacekeeping operations undertaken in supportive political environments. Even then, the UN has struggled to competently direct small and innocuous operations. But the real problems for all involved have come when the international community puts the UN in a military role for which it is neither politically suited nor strategically structured. This book goes into great detail on exactly why the UN has shown—in almost fifty missions—that there are strict limits to its military role. Quite simply, the UN should not be in the business of running serious military operations. It has neither the legitimacy, authority, nor systems of accountability needed to build the means necessary to direct significant military forces.

Authoritative, specifically structured, and well-rehearsed military alliances or coalitions of the willing led by a major military power better manage multinational military operations of the sort recently seen in the former Yugoslavia, Somalia, and Africa. These sorts of organizations are specifically structured—legally, politically, and organizationally—to direct complex and coercive military operations in uncertain environments. The model the international community used in Kosovo and East Timor recently may work best. An alliance such as NATO, or a multinational coalition such as that Australia led in East Timor, can do the heavy lifting before turning it over to the UN.

How then did the UN manage to unlearn these lessons in time to undertake Sierra Leone and the Congo in 1999–2000? After all, by 1995, UN peacekeeping had been thoroughly discredited. The Blue Helmets' failure to halt political violence in Somalia, Rwanda, Haiti, and the former Yugoslavia was reinforced by images of peacekeepers held hostage in Bosnia, gunned down in Mogadishu, or butchered along with thousands in Kigali. The UN quickly retreated from its ambitions of the post–Cold War period, turning a nascent peacekeeping mission in Haiti over to a U.S.-led coalition, passing Bosnia off to NATO, and leaving Somalia to slip back into chaos. By 1997, UN peacekeeping was down to a more manageable level of some 15,000 Blue Helmets operating in more mundane environments and on a budget of around $1.2 billion. All stayed relatively quiet on the UN front until late 1999, when Kosovo, East Timor, Sierra Leone, and the Congo sprang onto the scene. If those missions go forward as planned, they will add at least 25,000 Blue Helmets and some $700 million to $1 billion in costs to the UN's plate. More important, several of those new missions, especially Sierra Leone and the Congo, look certain to take place in very uncertain and belligerent environments—the sort in which the UN rarely if ever succeeds.

To understand this phenomenon, one must understand the United States' role. This book can speak of "the UN did this" or "the UN did that," but one must be realistic about whose hand is really on the throttle. And, as the saying goes, "the UN is US." Thus, it is necessary to outline the U.S. role in this latest cycle—the

rise and fall of UN peacekeeping in the six years after the end of the Cold War—
to understand UN peacekeeping's possible future. This message is critical for
the U.S. policy community because, while many Americans think the UN acts
of its own accord, U.S. actions drive these peacekeeping episodes as much as
anything else. More coherence in U.S. policy would have done more to prevent
many of the recent disasters in places such as Somalia and Bosnia than changes
at the UN or in the field.

Moreover, while a broad range of observers drew the same basic conclusion
from peacekeeping's recent past—that the UN should not be in the business of
managing complex, dangerous, and ambitious military operations—most are
split on how it happened and whom to blame. Conservatives in the United States
charge the UN itself and especially a fiendishly ambitious Boutros Boutros-
Ghali, who openly tried to accrue more and more military legitimacy and power
for the UN itself. Liberal internationalists blame a parochial U.S. Congress that
pulled the United States out of Somalia at the first sign of trouble and is now
holding the United States' UN dues hostage to its provincial agenda.

Both views are off base. Ironically, those who put UN peacekeeping through
the wringer and hung the organization and its last secretary-general out to dry
were those U.S. internationalists most likely to promote a larger collective security role for the United Nations. Over the past seven years, U.S. officials sought
for the UN a much greater role in international security affairs. But even though
UN officials were philosophically amenable to that goal, they chose to propel the
UN into uncharted waters more out of political expediency rather than as a carefully crafted manifestation of their predisposition towards collective security. In
many cases a new role for the UN was not so much a matter of policy, but a way
of avoiding hard policy decisions such as those concerning the former Yugoslavia
and Somalia. In essence, the U.S. used the UN as an excuse, not a strategy.

Either way, U.S. officials, especially in the first Clinton administration,
pushed a reluctant UN into much greater military roles than it could hope to
handle. Once its failures were manifest, the same officials joined in the conventional wisdom that the UN itself "tried to do too much." Because of this, any
post–Cold War "advances" in collective security were negated by those very
internationalists who were so keen to champion the UN. As Paul Kennedy and
Bruce Russett warned, UN operations such as those to Bosnia and Somalia "far
exceed the capabilities of the system as it is now constituted, and they threaten
to overwhelm the United Nations and discredit it, perhaps forever, even in the
eyes of its warmest supporters."[1] What they did not consider was that some of
the UN's "warmest supporters" were those who were most responsible for
putting it in desperate straits in the first place.

Chapter six charts how advocates of collective security were almost giddy in
the months immediately following the Gulf War. Even Ronald Reagan gave a
speech at Oxford in 1992 calling for a UN army. In Boutros-Ghali's *An Agenda*

for Peace, the Secretary-General outlined a series of proposals that could take the UN well beyond its traditional military role of classic peacekeeping. Although these were largely theoretical and untested ideas, by the time they were published in July 1992, the Security Council had already implemented a similar agenda. A few months prior to *An Agenda for Peace,* large and ambitious UN missions to the former Yugoslavia and Cambodia were already approved and under way. The case can be made that the UN itself was merely trying to catch up to the ambitions its members had for it.

This initial episode reflected a pattern that would develop over the next several years. The UN, many times reluctantly so, would be thrust into an ambitious and dangerous series of missions and operations by a Security Council that was enthusiastic about new and enlarged mandates for UN peacekeepers—but not so keen on providing the support necessary to make them a success. In 1992, while the secretary-general was preparing (at the request of the world's most powerful leaders) a draft report on possible new departures in peacekeeping, a series of international crises plunged the organization into what UN official Shashi Tharoor called "a dizzying series of peacekeeping operations that bore little or no resemblance in size, complexity, and function to those that had borne the peacekeeping label in the past."[2]

In the former Yugoslavia, it soon became painfully obvious that despite the deployment of almost 40,000 combat troops, the UN was in over its head. Among U.S. leaders, it was fashionable in both political parties to bemoan the ineffectiveness of the UN peacekeepers, even though the United States was as responsible for what the UN was attempting to do in the former Yugoslavia as any other state or the organization itself. Between September 1991 and January 1996, the Security Council passed eighty-nine resolutions relating to the situation in the former Yugoslavia, of which the United States sponsored one-third. While Russia vetoed one resolution and joined China in abstaining on many others, the United States voted for all eighty-nine, to include those twenty resolutions that expanded the mandate or size of the UN peacekeeping mission in the Balkans.[3]

Far from the notion that the UN was pulling the international community into Bosnia, the U.S.-led Security Council was pushing a reluctant UN even further into a series of missions and mandates it could not hope to accomplish. Boutros-Ghali warned the members of the Security Council that "the steady accretion of mandates from the Security Council has transformed the nature of UNPROFOR's mission to Bosnia-Herzegovina and highlighted certain implicit contradictions. . . . The proliferation of resolutions and mandates has complicated the role of the Force."[4] His under secretary-general for peacekeeping, Kofi Annan, was more direct. Attempts to further expand the challenging series of missions being given to the UN were "building on sand."[5]

This did not seem to deter the U.S.-led Security Council, however, which was happy to expand the mission further while volunteering few additional resources to the force in Bosnia. A June 1993 episode noted earlier in the book demonstrates this pattern. Then, the UN field commander estimated he would need some 34,000 more peacekeepers to protect both humanitarian aid convoys and safe areas in Bosnia. The Security Council, having given him these missions in previous resolutions, instead approved a "light option" of 7,600 troops, of whom only 5,000 had deployed to Bosnia some nine months later. Quitting his post in disgust, the Belgian general in command remarked, "I don't read the Security Council resolutions anymore because they don't help me."

The Clinton administration, which had shown unbounded enthusiasm for UN peacekeeping in the first months of the administration, began to sour slightly on its utility by September 1993. By then Ambassador Madeleine Albright's doctrine of "assertive multilateralism" had given way to President Clinton beseeching the UN General Assembly to know "when to say no."[6] But it was the United States and its allies on the Security Council who kept saying yes for the United Nations. Even after that speech, Mrs. Albright voted for all five subsequent resolutions (and sponsored two) that again expanded the size or mandate of the UN peacekeeping mission to the former Yugoslavia. All the while, until the fall of 1995, the United States steadfastly resisted participating in the UN mission or intervening itself with military forces through some other forum.

As chapter seven showed, there was an even more direct pattern in Somalia. There the United States pushed an unwilling UN into a hugely ambitious nation-building mission. In its waning days, the Bush administration had put together a U.S.-led coalition that intervened to ameliorate the man-made famine in Somalia. From the very beginning of the mission, it had been the intention of the U.S. to turn the operation over to a UN peacekeeping force. Conversely, Boutros Boutros-Ghali, an Egyptian well acquainted with the challenge of nation-building in Somalia, wanted no part of the mission for the UN. Ambassador Robert Oakley, the U.S. envoy to Somalia, noted that in a meeting with the secretary-general and his assistants on 1 December 1992, "the top UN officials rejected the idea that the U.S. initiative should eventually become a UN peacekeeping operation."[7]

The U.S. kept up the pressure on the secretary-general, who was powerless to resist the idea if it gained momentum in the Security Council. The debate resembled what Chester Crocker called "bargaining in a bazaar" and "raged out of public view"[8] while the United States and the UN negotiated over the follow-on mission. For his part, Boutros-Ghali wanted the U.S.-led coalition to accomplish a series of ambitious tasks before the UN would take over. These included the establishment of a reliable cease-fire, the control of all heavy weapons, the disarming of lawless factions, and the establishment of a new Somali police force. For its part, the United States just wanted to leave Somalia as soon as possible. It was now time to put assertive multilateralism to the test. Madeleine Albright shrugged off the challenge to the world body and wrote that the difficulties that the UN was bound to encounter in Somalia were "symptomatic of the complexity of mounting international nation-building operations that included a military component."[9]

The debate, with Boutros-Ghali resisting up to the last, effectively ended on 26 March 1993 with the passage of Security Council resolution 814 establishing a new UN operation in Somalia. The resolution authorized, for the first time, Chapter VII enforcement authority for a UN-managed force. More importantly, the resolution greatly expanded the mandate of the UN to well beyond what the American force had accomplished. Former Ambassador T. Frank Crigler called the UN mandate a "bolder and broader operation intended to tackle underlying social, political, and economic problems and to put Somalia back on its feet as a nation."[10] In the meantime, the United States withdrew its heavily armed 25,000 troop force and turned the baton over to a lightly armed and still arriving UN force. The transition, set for early May 1993, was so rushed that on the day the UN took command its staff was at only 30 percent of its intended strength.[11] The undermanned and underequipped UN force was left holding a bag not even of its own making.

The travails of the UN mission in Somalia are fully explained in this book. Suffice it to say here that the United States, although no longer a direct player in Somalia, continued to lead the Security Council in piling new mandates on the UN mission there. The most consequential of these was the mandate to apprehend those Somalis responsible for the June 1993 killing of twenty-four Pakistani peacekeepers. The United States further complicated this explosive new mission with an aggressive campaign of disarmament capped by the deployment of a special operations task force that was to lead the manhunt for Mohammed Farah Aideed. This task force was not under UN command in any way and when it became engaged in the tragic Mogadishu street battle of 3 October 1993, the UN commanders knew nothing of it until the shooting started. Even Maj. Gen. Thomas Montgomery, the American commander and deputy UN commander, was told of the operation only forty minutes before its launch. A U.S. military report afterward noted that the principal command problems of the UN mission in Somalia were "imposed on the U.S. by itself."[12]

This fact—that the UN was not involved in the deaths of eighteen American soldiers in Mogadishu—was buried by the Clinton administration. Even more cynically, several top-level administration officials charged in 1995 with selling the Dayton Peace Accords to a skeptical U.S. public constantly noted that U.S. soldiers in the NATO mission to Bosnia would not be in danger because the UN would not be in command, as it was in Somalia. Few single events have been as damaging to the UN's reputation with the Congress and American public as the continued perception that it was the United Nations that was responsible for the disaster in Somalia. Not only has this myth been left to fester, it was indirectly used, along with the UN's many other U.S.-initiated problems, to call for Boutros Boutros-Ghali's head during the 1996 presidential campaign. Then, for the first time in years, the United States used its veto to stand alone against the Security Council and bring down the secretary-general who had resisted the U.S.-led events that so discredited him and his organization. Ironically for a liberal internationalist, Mrs. Albright rode this stand against the rest of the Security Council into the secretary of state's office.

After those particular episodes, UN peacekeeping was in 1997 happy to be, as a UN official told me, in "a bear market." Congress and the administration were happy as well with a low profile for UN military operations—especially as administration officials try to get Congress to pay America's share of the unprecedented peacekeeping debt. Fittingly, Madeleine Albright, as secretary of state, is now chiefly responsible for convincing Congress to pay the bill that she is tacitly accountable for because of her votes during that busy time on the Security Council.

Albright also played a central role as the official, more than any other in the Bush and Clinton administrations, who epitomized the keen hopes of liberal internationalists advocating a greater security role for the UN. In early 1993, her speeches were laced with talk of "a renaissance for the United Nations" and ensuring that "the UN is equipped with a robust capacity to plan, organize, lead, and service peacekeeping activities."[13] After Somalia, however, it became obvious that the inherent limitations of a large multinational organization would not allow it effectively to manage complex military operations, and Albright stated that "the UN has not yet demonstrated the ability to respond effectively when the risk of combat is high and the level of local cooperation is low."[14] Left unsaid was that the United States, more than any other member state, was responsible for giving the UN much to do in Somalia and Bosnia and little to do it with. It appeared, as Harvey Sicherman has written, that "the assertive multilateralists of 1992–93 placed more weight upon the UN than it could bear, while ignoring NATO and other regional coalitions."[15]

Regional coalitions or more narrowly focused military alliances were ignored both for reasons of philosophy and political expediency. Philosophically, legitimacy could be gained for collective security in general and the UN in particular by having it directly manage the more dynamic military operations of the post–Cold War era. Thomas Weiss typified this school of thought and wrote, "the UN is the logical convenor of future international military operations. Rhetoric about regional organizations risks slowing down or even making impossible more timely and vigorous action by the UN, the one organization most likely to fulfill adequately the role of regional conflict manager."[16] This appealed in particular to the officials of the Clinton administration who had developed and published many similar thoughts while in academia or the think-tank world.

But for the most part the U.S. promoted unprecedented UN missions to conflicts such as Bosnia and Somalia because they did not want the U.S. or its alliances to be principally responsible for difficult and protracted military operations in areas of limited interest. As Shashi Tharoor wrote, "it is sometimes argued that the peacekeeping deployment to Bosnia-Herzegovina reflected not so much a policy as the absence of policy; that [UN] peacekeeping responds to the need to 'do something' when policy makers are not prepared to expend the political, military, and financial resources required to achieve the outcome that the press and opinion leaders are clamoring for."[17]

The final irony is that the UN's adventurous new role in 1993–1995 and peacekeeping's subsequent demise came about not necessarily by the well intentioned but unsupported design of collective security's most ardent proponents. Instead, it came about by default as these same supporters thrust upon the UN difficult missions they would rather not have addressed more directly. Now, only a short while later, it looks as if the cycle could repeat itself again. Given the recent and renewed enthusiasm for more missions of the sort that will greatly challenge the UN, the international community would do well to keep the recent past in mind. But exactly who will take away what lessons from Sierra Leone in the summer of 2000 remains to be seen.

Notes

Preface to the Second Edition

1. Peter Maass, "It's Risky to Talk Tough on Kosovo," *The New York Times*, March 10, 1998, p. A23

Preface

1. The term was first used by John Mackinlay and Jarat Chopra in "Second-generation Multinational Operations," *The Washington Quarterly*, vol. 15, no. 3, Summer 1992, pp. 113–31. The term is widely accepted and also has been used by the United Nations in documents from the United Nations Department of Public Information (UNDPI), *United Nations Peacekeeping* (New York, 1993), pp. 8–10. The many other terms in vogue for these operations are discussed in Chapter Six.
2. A universal military definition taken from the United States Armed Forces Staff College, *Joint Staff Officer's Guide* (Norfolk, Va., 1993), pp. 5–24.
3. The examination of military objectives will be at the strategic and operational level. This study does not seek explicitly to examine tactical tasks, such as what the actual small units did. It focuses on the strategic and operational levels of the military mission. However, because many missions are quite small, tactical objectives can sometimes be strategic objectives as well.
4. British Army Field Manual, *Wider Peacekeeping*, 4th draft (London, 1994), pp. 1–9, 1–10.
5. James H. Allan, *Peacekeeping: Outspoken Observations by a Field Officer* (Westport, Conn., 1996), pp. 12–13.

6. Brian Urquhart notes the complexity of judging success in the many long UN military missions in "The Role of the UN in Maintaining and Improving International Security," *Survival*, vol. 28, no. 5, September–October 1986, pp. 388–93.

7. U.S. Army Field Manual 100-23, *Peace Operations* (Washington, D.C., 1994), p. vi.

8. Paul F. Diehl, *International Peacekeeping* (Baltimore, Md., 1993), p. 36.

9. UN Department of Public Information, *The Blue Helmets: A Review of United Nations Peacekeeping*, 2d ed. (New York, 1990), p. 64.

10. Adam Roberts and Benedict Kingsbury, "The UN's Roles in International Society," in *United Nations, Divided World* (Oxford, 1993), p. 15.

11. Ibid., p. 16.

12. The focus here is solidly on UN military operations, however, and although some non-UN missions are discussed briefly, this study does not comprehensively treat missions totally separate from the United Nations, such as the Multinational Force of Observers in the Sinai or the Commonwealth Forces in Zimbabwe.

13. See, for instance, Daniel Katz and Robert Kahn, *The Social Psychology of Organizations*, 2d ed. (New York, 1978), or Richard Cyert and James March, *A Behavioral Theory of the Firm* (Prentice-Hall, N.J., 1963).

14. Mats Berdal, *Whither UN Peacekeeping?* Adelphi Paper 281 (London, 1993), p. 9.

15. Boutros Boutros-Ghali, Supplement to *An Agenda for Peace: Position Paper of the Secretary-General on the Occasion of the Fiftieth Anniversary of the United Nations* (New York, 3 January 1995), para 4.

16. John Mackinlay, *The Peacekeepers: An Assessment of Peacekeeping Operations at the Arab–Israeli Interface* (London, 1989), p. 12.

17. Berdal, *Whither UN Peacekeeping?*, p. 75.

18. See Giandomenico Picco, "The UN and the Use of Force: Leave the Secretary-General out of It," *Foreign Affairs*, vol. 73, no. 5, September–October 1994, pp. 14–18.

19. These are the levels of military operations as defined by common military doctrine. Among many articles detailing this analytical division, see David Jablonsky, "Strategy and the Operational Level of War," *Parameters*, vol. 17, no. 1, Spring 1987, pp. 58–69.

20. Kenneth Allard, *Somalia Operations: Lessons Learned* (Washington, D.C., 1995), p. 6.

21. Francis Fukuyama, book review of Linda Melvern's *The Ultimate Book Crime*, in *Foreign Affairs*, vol. 75, no. 3, May–June 1996, p. 133.

Introduction

1. John J. Mearsheimer, "The False Promise of International Institutions," *International Security*, vol. 19, no. 3, Winter 1994–1995, p. 33.

2. Adam Roberts and Benedict Kingsbury, "The UN's Role in International Security," in *United World, Divided World*, 2d ed. (Oxford, 1993), p. 4.
3. "Final Declaration of the First Security Council Summit." New York: UN Department of Public Information, Press Release, 31 January 1992.
4. Boutros Boutros-Ghali, *An Agenda for Peace: Preventive Diplomacy, Peacemaking, and Peace-keeping* (New York, 1992), p. 26.
5. Alan James, "The History of Peacekeeping: An Analytical Perspective," *Canadian Defence Quarterly*, vol. 23, no. 1 (special no. 2), September 1993, p. 17. See also Brian Urquhart, "Security after the Cold War," in A. Roberts and B. Kingsbury, eds., *United Nations, Divided World*, 2d ed. (Oxford, 1993), pp. 86, 81–103.
6. For instance, Adam Roberts, "The United Nations and International Security," *Survival*, vol. 35, no. 2, Summer 1993, pp. 3–30, especially p. 15, and Mats Berdal, *Whither UN Peacekeeping?* Adelphi Paper 281 (London, 1993).
7. For example, see Gareth Evans, *Cooperating for Peace* (Sydney, 1993); Jeffrey Laurenti, *Partners for Peace: Strengthening Collective Security for the 21st Century* (New York, 1992); Michael Renner, *Critical Juncture: The Future of Peacekeeping*, WorldWatch Paper 114 (Washington, D.C., 1993); Indar J. Rikhye, *Strengthening UN Peacekeeping—New Challenges and Proposals* (Washington, D.C., 1992); Brian Urquhart and Erskine Childers, *Towards a More Effective United Nations* (Uppsala, Sweden, 1992); T. Lee, J. Pagenhardt, and J. Stanley, *To Unite Our Strength: Enhancing the United Nations Peace and Security System* (New York, 1992); and numerous conference reports listed in the bibliography.
8. A good example of the many scholarly articles in this vein of thinking is in Thomas G. Weiss, "New Challenges for UN Military Operations: Implementing an Agenda for Peace," *The Washington Quarterly*, vol. 16, no. 1, Winter 1993, pp. 51–66. Another good example is from Professor Keith Krause, "Canadian Defence and Security Policy in a Changing Global Context," *Canadian Defence Quarterly*, vol. 23, no. 4, Summer 1994, p. 7.
9. The United States Institute of Peace, *The Professionalization of Peacekeeping: A United States Institute of Peace Study Group Report* (Washington, D.C., August 1993), p. 2.
10. Boutros Boutros-Ghali, "Empowering the United Nations," *Foreign Affairs*, vol. 72, no. 1, Winter 1992–1993, p. 89.
11. UN Department of Public Information, *United Nations Peacekeeping* (New York, 1993), pp. 8–10.
12. Boutros Boutros-Ghali, Address to Chief Editors and High-Level Officials at the Seminar on "Germany and International Security" held by the Federal College for Security Policy Studies, Bad Godesberg, Germany, 19 January 1995.

13. Boutros Boutros-Ghali, UN Security Council, S/1995/1, Supplement to *An Agenda for Peace* (New York, 3 January 1995), para. 77.

Chapter One

1. Adam Roberts, "From San Francisco to Sarajevo: The UN and the Use of Force," *Survival*, vol. 37, no. 4, Winter 1995–1996, p. 8.
2. The Charter of the United Nations, signed on 26 June 1945, entered into force on 24 October 1945. Chapter I, Article 1, Paragraph 1.
3. Many scholars have written of the inherent tension in a system of collective security working through an organization that also is premised on the sovereign right of states to use military force. Along with the work of Innis Claude, see Hedley Bull, *Intervention in World Politics* (Oxford, 1984), and *The Anarchical Society* (New York, 1977).
4. See U.S. Department of State, *Foreign Relations of the United States, 1945, Malta and Yalta Documents* (Washington, D.C., 1963), pp. 665–712.
5. Brian Urquhart, *A Life in Peace and War* (London, 1987), p. 93. Others have echoed Urquhart's criticism about the supposed naïveté of the framers of the Charter. See Clark M. Eichelberger, *UN: The First Twenty Years* (New York, 1965), p. 159. In addition, much of the rhetoric of the time, especially from American leaders trying to rally domestic support, was unduly optimistic about the collective security prospects of the organization. See Arthur H. Vandenberg, Jr., *The Private Papers of Senator Vandenberg* (Boston, 1952), p. 119, and Samuel Rosenman, *The Public Papers and Addresses of Franklin D. Roosevelt*, vol. 13 (New York, 1969), p. 235.
6. Vandenberg, *Private Papers*, p. 198.
7. John B. Martin, *Adlai Stevenson of Illinois: The Life of Adlai E. Stevenson* (Garden City, 1976), p. 238. Lord Gladwyn was similarly skeptical. See *The Memoirs of Lord Gladwyn* (London, 1972), pp. 163–69. Other "realists" involved in the decisions included the leaders of the major powers. See Rosenman, *Public Papers and Addresses of Roosevelt*; the memoirs of Winston Churchill, *The Second World War: Triumph and Tragedy*, vol. 6, (London, 1954); Harry Truman, *Year of Decisions: 1945* (London, 1955); and Charles de Gaulle, *War Memoirs: Salvation, 1944–1946*, trans. by Murchie and Erskine (London, 1960).
8. Dean Acheson, *Present at the Creation: My Years in the State Department* (New York, 1969), p. 111.
9. J. Maney Patrick, *The Roosevelt Presence: A Biography of Franklin Delano Roosevelt* (New York, 1992). See also Rosenman, *The Public Papers and Addresses of Roosevelt*, p. 180.

10. Rosalyn Higgins, "The New United Nations and Former Yugoslavia," *International Affairs*, vol. 69, no. 3, 1993, p. 471. Higgins also writes, "It was not the intention of the Charter that collective security should only be available to an attacked state if others felt that they had a direct interest in assisting; if it could be guaranteed that assistance would entail no harm to their soldiers; and if the political and military outcome was clear from the outset. Becoming a member of the UN necessarily entails, at that moment, the decision that the national interests will lie in ensuring an efficacious collective security system."

11. This section is not intended to be a legal examination of the political or military capabilities of the United Nations, the UN Charter, or other UN organs. Such studies are numerous. The best remain: D. W. Bowett, *United Nations Forces: A Legal Study of United Nations Practice* (London, 1964); Rosalyn Higgins, *United Nations Peacekeeping: Documents and Commentary*, vols. 1–4 (Oxford, 1969, 1970, 1980, 1981); Finn Seyersted, *United Nations Forces in the Law of Peace and War* (Leiden, Netherlands, 1966); Frederic Kirgis, *International Organizations in Their Legal Setting*, 2d ed. (St. Paul, Minn., 1993); and Bruno Simma, Hermann Mosler, Helmut Brokelman, and Christian Rohde, eds., *The Charter of the United Nations: A Commentary* (Oxford, 1994).

12. Seyersted, *United Nations Force*, p. 402.

13. Gareth Evans, *Cooperating for Peace: The Global Agenda for the 1990's and Beyond* (St. Leonards, Australia, 1993), p. 23.

14. Philippe Kirsch, "The Legal Basis of Peacekeeping," *Canadian Defence Quarterly*, vol. 23, no. 1, September 1993, pp. 18–19.

15. UN Department of Public Information, *The Blue Helmets: A Review of United Nations Peace-keeping*, 2d ed. (New York, 1990), p. 5.

16. Conversation with the author, UN Headquarters, New York, 19 September 1995.

17. Adam Roberts and Benedict Kingsbury, "The UN's Roles in International Society," in *United Nations, Divided World*, 2d ed. (Oxford, 1993), p. 31.

18. For more on economic sanctions, see Robin Renwick, *Economic Sanctions* (Cambridge, Mass., 1981), and Gary Hufbauer et al., *Economic Sanctions Reconsidered* (Washington, D.C., 1990).

19. Not exactly nonmilitary, though, as military forces often are required to enforce such sanctions. However, Article 42 addresses more clearly military sanctions enforcement such as a blockade. An example of this is the naval and air blockade imposed on Iraq in 1990–1991 in support of Security Council Resolution 865. See Chapter eight.

20. Higgins, "The New UN and Former Yugoslavia," p. 466.

21. Ibid, p. 468. Higgins also notes that the question of whether Article 42 actions could occur in the absence of prior wider agreements under

Article 43 has been left open in international law, despite precedents in the Persian Gulf War, Somalia, and the former Yugoslavia (ibid, p. 467).

22. Brian Urquhart, like many observers, traces the incipient nature of the United Nations' collective security capability to the lack of Article 43-type agreements and forces. "Security after the Cold War," in Adam Roberts and Benedict Kingsbury, eds., *United Nations, Divided World*, 2d ed. (Oxford, 1993), p. 102.

23. The policy and legal implications of renegotiating and concluding such agreements in the 1990s are referred to in Boutros Boutros-Ghali, *An Agenda for Peace* (New York, 1992), and more comprehensively in Eugene Rostow, *Should Article 43 of the UN Charter Be Raised from the Dead?*, McNair Paper 19 (Washington, D.C., 1993).

24. The fascinating story of these negotiations is worth volumes and has in fact been extensively covered elsewhere. For a succinct examination, see Eric Grove, "UN Armed Forces and the Military Staff Committee," *International Security*, vol. 17, no. 4, Spring 1993, pp. 172–82. See also Lincoln Bloomfield, *International Military Forces* (Boston, 1964); D. W. Bowett, *United Nations Forces* (London, 1964); and William Frye, *A United Nations Peace Force* (London, 1957).

25. Roberts, "From San Francisco to Sarajevo: The UN and the Use of Force," p. 9.

26. Abba Eban, "The UN Idea Revisited," *Foreign Affairs*, vol. 74, no. 5, September–October 1995, p. 44.

27. Roberts, "From San Francisco to Sarajevo," p. 8.

28. Urquhart, "Security after the Cold War," p. 83.

29. Chapter VII, Article 47, Paragraph 1.

30. For discussion of this period, see the memoirs of the world statesmen and UN framers listed in editorial note 7 and *The Diaries of Edward Stettinius*, U.S. Secretary of State, 1943–1946, The Stettinius Papers Collection, The University of Virginia, Charlottesville.

31. For instance, UN Report MS/265, "General Principles Governing the Organization of the Armed Forces Made Available to the Security Council by Member Nations of the United Nations," UN Military Staff Committee, 30 April 1947; also labeled as Security Council report S/336.

32. Grove, "UN Armed Forces and the Military Staff Committee," pp. 175–81.

33. Michael Howard, "A History of the UN's Security Role," in Roberts and Kingsbury, eds., *United Nations, Divided World*, p. 66.

34. Roberts, "From San Francisco to Sarajevo," p. 9.

35. Evans, *Cooperating for Peace*, p. 20.

36. UNEF I was established by General Assembly Resolution 998(ES-1) of 4 November 1956, and UNSF was established by General Assembly Resolution 1752 (XVII) of 21 September 1962.

37. USIP, *The Professionalization of Peacekeeping* p. 24.

38. Roberts, "From San Francisco to Sarajevo, p. 8.

39. U.S. Government Accounting Office, *UN Peacekeeping: Lessons Learned in Managing Recent Missions*, GAO Report 94-9 (Washington, D.C., December 1993), p. 5.

40. This "explosion in peacekeeping" is fully charted in Chapter Six. However, it should be noted that in 1990, the United Nations was managing some 10,000 military personnel in eight observation and traditional peacekeeping missions. By 1993, it had control over some 80,000 troops (90,000 authorized) in eighteen different missions, including operations with complex multifunctional and enforcement mandates. From the UN Department of Public Information, "Peacekeeping Information Notes Update" (no. 2), November 1993, and UNDPI, *The Blue Helmets*, App. 2.

41. There are several good analyses of the organizational changes in the Secretariat in regards to UN military operations. In particular, see Mats Berdal, *Whither UN Peacekeeping?*, sect. 3; Berdal, "Reforming the UN's Organizational Capacity for Peacekeeping," in Ramesh Thakur and Carlyle Thayer, *A Crisis of Expectations: UN Peacekeeping in the 1990s* (Boulder, Colo., 1995), pp. 181–192; and William Durch, "Structural Issues and the Future of UN Peace Operations," in Don Daniel and Bradd Hayes, eds., *Beyond Traditional Peacekeeping* (New York, 1995), pp. 151–163.

42. Mission of the United States to the United Nations, "Peacekeeping Management Enhancements," Memorandum, 20 May 1995.

43. Boutros Boutros-Ghali, UN Security Council, S/1995/1, Supplement to *An Agenda for Peace* (New York, 3 January 1995), p. 9.

44. Jim Whitman and Ian Bartholomew, "UN Peace Support Operations: Political-Military Considerations," in Donald C. F. Daniel and Bradd C. Hayes, eds., *Beyond Traditional Peacekeeping* (New York, 1995), p. 173. For examples of many other prescriptions for reinforcing the UN Secretariat, see USIP, *The Professionalization of Peacekeeping*, or Steven Rader, *Strengthening the Management of UN Peacekeeping Operations* (Oslo, Norway, 1994).

45. Berdal, "Reforming the UN's Organizational Capacity for Peacekeeping," p. 182.

46. James H. Allan, *Peacekeeping: Outspoken Observations by a Field Officer* (Westport, Conn., 1996), p. xvi.

47. Paul F. Diehl, *International Peacekeeping* (London, 1993), p. 26.

48. This number does not include the peacekeepers killed in action in the UN Operation in the Congo (1960–1964), which used active force against belligerents at the cost of 245 UN soldiers killed in action. Because of this anomaly in an era of traditional peacekeeping missions, this study treats the Congo operation as a second-generation mission, along with

Somalia, former Yugoslavia, and others. Figures are from the UN Department of Public Information, *The Blue Helmets*, and *UN Peacekeeping* (August 1996).

49. Marrack Goulding, "The Evolution of United Nations Peacekeeping," *International Affairs*, June 1993, p. 455. The principles first appeared together in this form in S/11052/Rev. 27 October 1973 in reference to UNEF II.

50. John Mackinlay, *The Peacekeepers: An Assessment of Peacekeeping Operations at the Arab–Israeli Interface* (London, 1989), p. 199.

51. Ramesh Thakur, "UN Peacekeeping in the New World Disorder," in *A Crisis of Expectations*, p. 8.

52. Shashi Tharoor, special assistant to the under secretary-general for Peacekeeping Operations, "Should UN Peacekeeping Go Back to Basics?," *Survival*, vol. 37, no. 4, Winter 1995–1996, p. 53.

53. Boutros-Ghali, *An Agenda for Peace*, p. 11.

54. Boutros-Ghali, "Empowering the U.N.," p. 94.

55. *The Economist*, 26 December 1992, p. 57.

56. "UN Peacekeeping Information Notes Update (no. 2)," November 1993, and UNDPI, *The Blue Helmets*, App. 2.

57. Mats Berdal has noted that missions such as these, "although they involved new tasks, could be accommodated within existing administrative and management structures" (*Whither UN Peacekeeping*, p. 9). It is for this very reason that this book does not explicitly address these particular missions, but instead concentrates its analysis of second-generation peacekeeping operations on those large and complex military enterprises that were so different from the military efforts of traditional peacekeeping and gave the United Nations so much strategic angst in the early 1990s.

58. The rate of UN fatalities in these missions rose considerably faster than ever before. In 1993–1995, peacekeepers killed in action averaged well over 100 per year. The great majority of these were in second-generation peacekeeping missions. In the previous forty-four years of observation and traditional peacekeeping missions, fewer than 500 peacekeepers lost their lives (Congo mission excepted). GA/PK/125, 11 April 1994, and Boutros Boutros-Ghali, *Report on the Work of the Organization from the 47th–48th Session of the General Assembly* (New York, 1993), p. 178; 1994 Report, p. 160.

59. Berdal, *Whither UN Peacekeeping?*, p. 76.

60. For an impressive explanation of this important point, see Charles Dobbie, *A Concept for Post–Cold War Peacekeeping* (Oslo, 1994), and my Chapter Six.

61. British Army Field Manual, *Wider Peacekeeping*, pp. 1–9, 1–10.

62. The military doctrine of most nations notes the great differences between consent-based and nonconsensual operations. For instance, U.S. Army doctrine states that "U.S. policy distinguishes between peacekeeping and peace enforcement. Both are classified as peace operations. However, they are not part of a continuum allowing a unit to move freely from one to the other. A broad demarcation separates these operations." Field Manual 100-23, *Peace Operations* (Washington, D.C., 1994), p. 12.

Chapter Two

1. UN Department of Public Information, *The Blue Helmets: A Review of United Nations Peace-keeping*, 2d ed. (New York, 1990), p. 9.
2. Ibid., p. 432.
3. For a complete explanation of classic operational doctrine for UN forces, see the International Peace Academy's *Peacekeeper's Handbook*, 2d ed. (New York, 1984).
4. William J. Durch, ed., *The Evolution of UN Peacekeeping: Case Studies and Comparative Analysis* (New York, 1993), pp. 16–26.
5. Accordingly, the Security Council Resolutions authorizing UNTSO were dated May–July 1948 (res. 50 and 54), June 1956 (res. 114), June–July 1967 (res. 236 and S/8047), October 1973 (res. 339), and September 1982 (res. 521).
6. Security Council Document S/10611, Letter from the Representative of Lebanon to the President of the Security Council, annex, 29 March 1972.
7. S/628, Letter to the Security Council, 2 January 1948.
8. S/4022, Security Council Resolution, 11 June 1958.
9. UNDPI, *The Blue Helmets*, p. 389.
10. UNGOMAP observers arrived in Afghanistan on 25 April 1988, the same day the president of the Security Council provisionally approved the Geneva accords plan. Resolution 622, authorizing the mission, was not passed until 31 October 1988 (ibid., p. 318).
11. This same peace treaty was linked to the birth of UNTAG in Namibia (a second-generation peacekeeping mission).
12. D. W. Bowett, *United Nations Forces: A Legal Study of United Nations Practice* (London, 1964), p. 87.
13. Ibid., p. 70.
14. Taken from individual mission information in UN Department of Public Information, *United Nations Peace-keeping* (New York, 1996), and *The Blue Helmets*.
15. In 1948, UNTSO requested three hundred enlisted men to work as "auxiliary technical personnel." See A/648, Progress Report of UN Mediator to the General Assembly, GAOR, 3d session, suppl. II, pp. 32–33. With the entry into force of the General Armistice Agreements several months

later, UNTSO reverted to an observer strength averaging 120 officers and few other ranks.

16. S/4052, UNOGIL Interim Report to the Secretary-General, 17 July 1958.

17. Although lightly armed for self-defense only, this Yugoslav unit represented the first arms used by UN observers. UNDPI, *The Blue Helmets* p. 192.

18. S/5412, Report of the Secretary-General to the SC on UNYOM, 4 September 1963, pp. 154–157.

19. UNDPI, "Peacekeeping Information Notes," March 1993, pp. 17–18.

20. Unit numbers from Rosalyn Higgins, *United Nations Peacekeeping, 1946–1967, Documents and Commentary,* vol. I (London, 1970), p. 557, and UNDPI, *The Blue Helmets*, p. 181.

21. UNDPI, *The Blue Helmets*, p. 31.

22. The UNIPOM officers were from Brazil, Burma, Canada, Ceylon, Ethiopia, Ireland, Nepal, Holland, Nigeria, and Venezuela.

23. S/22692, Report of the secretary-general on UNIKOM, 12 June 1991, p. 1.

24. In UNAVEM II, the UN even contracted armed security guards to accompany unarmed UN military observers. UNDPI, "Peacekeeping Information Notes," 1993, p. 19. The great variety of force structure experiences makes a consistent pattern difficult to distinguish.

25. P. Chilton, O. Nasseur, D. Plesch, and J. Patten, *NATO, Peacekeeping, and the United Nations* (London, 1994), p. 33.

26. UNDPI, *The Blue Helmets*, p. 394.

27. Higgins, *UN Peacekeeping*, vol. II, p. 352.

28. UNDPI, *The Blue Helmets*, pp. 317–18.

29. Conversation with Sir Brian Urquhart, former Under Secretary-General for Special Political Affairs, 23 August 1994.

30. Interview by William Durch in Durch, *The Evolution of UN Peacekeeping*, p. 448.

31. Carl Van Horn, *Soldiering for Peace* (New York, 1967), p. 67.

32. In October of 1953, the UNTSO commander, General Bennike, was personally questioned by the Security Council about standard operational issues. Official Records of the Security Council, 8th Year, 635th Meeting, pp. 19–20.

33. UNDPI, *The Blue Helmets*, p. 17.

34. Van Horn, *Soldiering for Peace*, pp. 372–73.

35. Interview quoted in Durch, *The Evolution of UN Peacekeeping*, p. 98.

36. S/6782, a letter from the Secretary-General to the Representative of Pakistan, 13 October 1965.

37. S/4100, Report of the UNOGIL Commander to the Secretary-General, 29 September 1958.

38. Term used by D. W. Bowett, *United Nations Forces*, p. 78.

39. Security Council Official Records, 8th Year, 635th Meeting, pp. 19–20.
40. S/6651, Report of the Secretary-General on the Situation in Kashmir, 3 September 1965.
41. Van Horn, *Soldiering for Peace*, pp. 316–22.
42. UNDPI, "UN Peacekeeping Information Notes," 1993, p. 15.
43. Ibid., pp. 15–18.
44. UNDPI, *The Blue Helmets*, p. 398.
45. Or armed with side arms only.
46. UNDPI Document 1306/Rev.2, "UN Peacekeeping Operations Information Notes," New York, November 1993, pp. 19–26.
47. Durch, *Evolution of UN Peacekeeping*, p. 305.
48. Alan James, *Peacekeeping in International Politics* (London, 1990), pp. 255–56.
49. UNDPI, *The Blue Helmets*, p. 26.
50. S/3942, Report to the Security Council on the situation in the Middle East, 22 January 1958. This authority was not taken too seriously by the belligerents; in fact, the Israeli army occupied Government House during the six-day war of 1967 and escorted the UNTSO headquarters elsewhere.
51. Alan James, *Peacekeeping in International Politics*, pp. 166–67.
52. Ibid., pp. 305–6.
53. Ibid., p. 174.
54. UNDPI, *The Blue Helmets*, p. 4.

Chapter Three

1. Brian Smith, "The United Nations Iran–Iraq Military Observer Group," in William J. Durch, ed., *The Evolution of UN Peacekeeping: Case Studies and Comparative Analysis* (New York, 1993), p. 239. See also Brian Urquhart and Gary Sick, eds., *The United Nations and the Iran–Iraq War* (New York, 1987), p. 8.
2. UN Department of Public Information, *The Blue Helmets: A Review of United Nations Peace-Keeping*, 2d ed. (New York, 1990), p. 323.
3. For a survey of these factors, see Dilip Hiro, *The Longest War: The Iran–Iraq Military Conflict* (London, 1989).
4. UNDPI, *The Blue Helmets*, p. 442.
5. Elements remained in Iraq until 15 December 1988. S/20442. Report of the Secretary-General on UNIIMOG, 2 February 1989.
6. S/20242, Interim Report of the Secretary-General on UNIIMOG, 25 October 1988, p. 2.
7. Ibid., p. 3.
8. Ibid., p. 5.

9. S/20093, Report of the Secretary-General on the Implementation of Operative Paragraph 2 of Security Council Resolution 598 (1987), 7 August 1988, p. 3.

10. S/20442, p. 7.

11. S/21200, Report of the Secretary-General on UNIIMOG, 22 March 1990, p. 7.

12. Author's conversation with General Vadset, Stockholm, Sweden, 10 April 1995 and S/20093, p. 3.

13. UNDPI, *The Blue Helmets*, p. 327.

14. Alan James, *Peacekeeping in International Politics* (London, 1990), p. 173.

15. Hugh Smith, ed., *Peacekeeping: Challenges for the Future* (Canberra, Australia, 1993), p. 205.

16. S/20093, p. 2.

17. S/21960, Report of the Secretary-General on UNIIMOG, 23 November 1990, p. 8.

18. S/20093, p. 2.

19. S/20442, p. 6.

20. UNDPI, *The Blue Helmets*, p. 331.

21. S/21803, Report of the Secretary-General on UNIIMOG, 21 September 1990, p. 8.

22. U.S. Army, *Field Manual 100-5, Operations* (Washington, D.C., 1993), pp. 2–5.

23. Author's conversation with Sir Brian Urquhart, former under secretary-general for special political affairs, New York, September 1993.

24. Among many reports detailing the problems of the FOD–OSPA split is J. D. Murray, "Military Aspects of Peacekeeping: Problems and Recommendations," unpublished paper, International Peace Academy, New York 1976.

25. S/20093, pp. 1–2.

26. Smith, "The United Nations Iran–Iraq Military Observer Group," p. 246.

27. S/20242, p. 3.

28. U.S. Army, Field Manual 17-98, *Scout Platoon* (Washington, D.C., 1987), pp. 4–18.

29. S/20093, p. 4.

30. S/20862, Report of the Secretary-General on UNIIMOG, 22 September 1989, p. 5.

31. S/21200, p. 7.

32. Ibid., p. 8.

33. S/20242, p. 3.

34. S/21200, p. 5.

35. S/21803, p. 6.

36. Ibid., p. 4.

37. S/20442, p. 6.
38. S/20862, p. 5.
39. Smith, "United Nations Iran–Iraq Military Observer Group," p. 254.
40. See Lawrence Freedman and Efraim Karsh, *The Gulf Conflict, 1990–1991* (London, 1993), pp. 107–9, for a political account of this episode.
41. Ibid., p. 108.
42. S/21803, p. 6.
43. Ibid., p. 11.
44. S/22263, Report of the Secretary-General on UNIIMOG, 26 February 1991, p. 3.
45. Ibid., p. 4.
46. S/22148, Report of the Secretary-General on UNIIMOG, 28 January 1991, p. 4.
47. Smith, "United Nations Iran–Iraq Military Observer Group," p. 254.
48. James, *Peacekeeping in International Politics*, p. 174.
49. S/21960, p. 11.

Chapter Four

1. Paul F. Diehl, *International Peacekeeping* (London, 1993), p. 5.
2. British Army Field Manual, *Wider Peacekeeping*, 4th draft, (London, 1994), pp. C-3 to C-4.
3. Diehl, *International Peacekeeping*, p. 13.
4. William J. Durch, ed., *The Evolution of UN Peacekeeping: Case Studies and Comparative Analysis* (New York, 1993). p. xii.
5. This framework for analysis is taken from Durch, *The Evolution of UN Peacekeeping*, chap. 2, pp. 16–37.
6. A. B. Fetherston, *Towards a Theory of UN Peacekeeping* (London, 1994), p. 13.
7. General Assembly Resolution 998(ES-1), 4 November 1956.
8. A/3289, 4 November 1956, and A/3302, 6 November 1956.
9. Security Council Resolution 340, 25 October 1973.
10. A joint British, Greek Cypriot, and Turkish Cypriot force was established in December 1963 to patrol a neutral zone between Greek and Turkish communities in Nicosia. S/5508, 9 January 1964, and UN Department of Public Information, *The Blue Helmets*: *A Review of United Nations Peace-keeping,* 2d ed. (New York, 1990), p. 284.
11. Security Council Resolution 186, 4 March 1964.
12. General Assembly Resolution 1752 (XVII), 21 September 1962.
13. Security Council Resolution 350, 31 May 1974.

14. Roger Hilsman, *To Move a Nation* (New York, 1967), pp. 245–55. For a complete account of the politics behind ONUC's mandate, see Ernest W. Lefever, *Uncertain Mandate* (Baltimore, Md., 1967).

15. Durch, *The Evolution of UN Peacekeeping*, pp. 22–23.

16. General Assembly Resolution 997(ES-I), 2 November 1956, and 1000(ES-I), 5 November 1956, respectively.

17. Mona Ghali, "The United Nations Emergency Force I," in Durch, *The Evolution of UN Peacekeeping*, p. 113.

18. Diehl, *International Peacekeeping*, p. 75.

19. John Mackinlay, *The Peacekeepers: An Assessment of Peacekeeping Operations at the Arab–Israel Interface* (London, 1989), p. 230.

20. A phrase used by John Mackinlay in reference to UNDOF, ibid., p. 152.

21. A/3302, Report of the Secretary-General on the Plan for an Emergency United Nations Force, 6 November 1956.

22. A/3289, 4 November 1956, and A/3302, 6 November 1956.

23. Diehl, *International Peacekeeping*, p. 7.

24. James M. Boyd, *United Nations Peace-Keeping: A Military and Political Appraisal* (London, 1971), p. 122.

25. UNDPI, *The Blue Helmets*, p. 266. UNSF is considered a small security force merely reinforcing a mission centered on observation duties, not interpositional peacekeeping tasks. Viewed in this light, UNSF could be seen as similar to UNIKOM, an observation mission that also had an armed security contingent.

26. A/3943, Secretary-General's Summary Study of UNEF I, 9 October 1958.

27. UNDPI, *The Blue Helmets*, p. 83.

28. Mona Ghali, "UNDOF," in Durch, *The Evolution of UN Peacekeeping*, p. 158.

29. A/5172, Secretary-General's Progress Report on UNEF I, 22 August 1962.

30. Mona Ghali, "UNEF II," in Durch, *The Evolution of UN Peacekeeping*, p. 147. Mackinlay, *The Peacekeepers*, p. 164.

31. S/11137, Report of the Secretary-General on UNFICYP, 1 December 1973, para. 3.

32. UNDPI, *The Blue Helmets*, p. 438.

33. Ghali, "UNDOF," in Durch, *The Evolution of UN Peacekeeping*, p. 156.

34. James, *Peacekeeping in International Politics*, p. 328.

35. A/3493, Secretary-General's Summary Study of UNEF I, 9 October 1958.

36. UNDPI, *The Blue Helmets*, p. 421.

37. Ibid., pp. 423, 439; Mona Ghali, "UNIFIL, 1978–Present," in Durch, *The Evolution of UN Peacekeeping*, p. 190.

38. UNDPI, "UN Peacekeeping Notes Update 1994," May 1994, p. 10.

39. UNDPI, *The Blue Helmets*, p. 57.

40. See Susan R. Mills, *The Financing of United Nations Peacekeeping*, Occasional Paper 3 (New York, 1989).

41. S/11052/Rev. 1, Report of the Secretary-General on UNEF II, 27 October 1973.

42. UNDPI, *The Blue Helmets*, p. 55.

43. Karl Birgisson, "UNFICYP," in Durch, *The Evolution of UN Peacekeeping*, p. 232.

44. UNDPI, *The Blue Helmets*, p. 83.

45. Ibid., pp. 52–53.

46. Birgisson, "UNFICYP," in Durch, *The Evolution of UN Peacekeeping*, p. 227; James, *Peacekeeping in International Politics*, p. 226.

47. Rosalyn Higgins, *UN Peacekeeping, 1946–1967, Documents and Commentary*, vol. 4 (London, 1970), p. 162.

48. UNDPI, *The Blue Helmets*, p. 287.

49. Ibid., p. 88.

50. James, *Peacekeeping in International Politics*, pp. 321–22.

51. John Mackinlay noted that this forced 74 percent of UNDOF's logistics forces to be deployed on the Syrian side of the buffer zone while the main storage areas were in Israel. *The Peacekeepers*, p. 142.

52. Higgins, *UN Peacekeeping*, vol. 1, p. 302.

53. UNDPI, *The Blue Helmets*, p. 426.

54. J. D. Murray, "Military Aspects of Peacekeeping: Problems and Recommendations," pp. 21–22.

55. Boyd, *United Nations Peace-keeping*, p. 117.

56. UNDPI, *The Blue Helmets*, p. 58.

57. David Alberts and Richard Hayes, *Command Arrangements for Peace Operations* (Washington, D.C., 1995), p. 9.

58. U.S. Army Headquarters, *Field Manual 100-23: Peace Operations* (Washington, D.C., 1994), p. glossary-4.

59. Alberts and Hayes, *Command Arrangements for Peace Operations*, p. 10.

60. U.S. Army Headquarters, *Field Manual 100-23; Peace Operations*, p. glossary-12.

61. There are further subsets of command below operational control, including "tactical control," which is even more circumscribed in terms of time, functions, and location. Some have (overly) simplified tactical control to mean "short-term rental." Alberts and Hayes, *Command Arrangements for Peace Operations*, pp. 10–11.

62. UNDPI, *The Blue Helmets*, p. 55.

63 Ibid., pp. 421–24, 439–40.

64. Ibid., p. 77.

65. UNDPI, "United Nations Peacekeeping Notes," May 1994 update, p. 10.

66. UNDPI, *The Blue Helmets*, p. 49.

67. A/3943, Secretary-General's Summary Study of UNEF I, 9 October 1958.
68. There also was room for ambiguity about roles and responsibilities in UNSF, whose commander was on equal footing with the head of the UNTEA observation mission. UNDPI, *The Blue Helmets*, p. 268.
69. Indar J. Rikhye, *The Theory and Practice of International Peacekeeping* (New York, 1984), p. 206.
70. For instance, this phenomenon is highlighted throughout Murray, "Military Aspects of Peacekeeping," pp. 27–41. See also Mackinlay, *The Peacekeepers*, and Boyd, *United Nations Peace-keeping*.
71. Mackinlay, *The Peacekeepers*, p. 146–47.
72. UNDPI, *The Blue Helmets*, p. 414.
73. Murray, "Military Aspects of Peacekeeping," p. 18.
74. Mackinlay, *The Peacekeepers*, p. 145.
75. International Peace Academy, *The Peacekeeper's Handbook*, 2d ed. (New York, 1984). See especially the experiences of several missions highlighted by Murray, "Military Aspects of Peacekeeping," pp. 22–23.
76. Ibid., pp. 22–23.
77. Mackinlay, *The Peacekeepers*, p. 218.
78. Brigadier F. R. Henn, "Guidelines on Peacekeeping: Another View," *British Army Review*, no. 67, April 1981, p. 36.
79. Paul Lewis and Basil Zarov, "Soldiers for Peace," in *MHQ: The Quarterly Journal of Military History*, Autumn 1992, pp. 43, 67.
80. International Peace Academy, *The Peacekeeper's Handbook*, pp. 3–8.
81. UNDPI, *The Blue Helmets*, p. 70.
82. U.S. Army Headquarters, *Field Manual 100-23; Peace Operations*, p. glossary-2.
83. Ghali, "UNEF II," in Durch, *The Evolution of UN Peacekeeping*, p. 148.
84. Ramesh Thakur, "UN Peacekeeping in the New World Disorder," in Thakur and Carlyle Thayer, eds., *A Crisis of Expectations: UN Peacekeeping in the 1990s* (Boulder, Colo., 1995), p. 6.
85. E. L. M. Burns, *Between Arab and Israeli* (Toronto, 1962), p. 188.
86. A/4486, 13 September 1960, and A/4857, 30 August 1961, Progress Reports of the Secretary-General on UNEF I.
87. UNDPI, "UN Peacekeeping Notes Update," May 1994, p. 9, and *The Blue Helmets*, p. 308.
88. U.S. Army Headquarters, *Field Manual 7-8, Infantry Rifle Platoon Operations* (Ft. Benning, Ga., August 1984), pp. 4–20.
89. Mackinlay, *The Peacekeepers*, p. 14.
90. UNDPI, *The Blue Helmets*, p. 71.
91. S/12212, Report of the Secretary-General on UNEF II, 18 October 1976, and UNDPI, *The Blue Helmets*, pp. 96, 423.

92. UNSF was the only traditional peacekeeping mission where operations were not predicated on a linear buffer zone. In the first ten years of the Cyprus operation, the UN peacekeepers were not deployed in a buffer zone, but spread out around Cyprus much like the force deployment in UNSF. However, since the Turkish invasion of the island in 1974, the UN peacekeeping forces have occupied a linear buffer zone that stretches the width of the island.

93. UNDPI, *The Blue Helmets*, p. 71.

94. Ibid., p. 71.

95. Ibid., p. 88.

96. Ibid., p. 296.

97. British Army, *British Army Field Manual: Wider Peacekeeping* (London, 1994), pp. 2–7.

98. James, *Peacekeeping in International Politics*, p. 5.

99. UNDPI, "UN Peacekeeping Notes Update," May 1994, p. 9.

100. James, *Peacekeeping in International Politics*, p. 219.

101. Ghali, "UNEF II," in Durch, *The Evolution of UN Peacekeeping*, p. 148.

102. Diehl, *International Peace-keeping*, pp. 77–78. In the summary of his work on traditional peacekeeping, Paul Diehl lists securing support (great power and local), emphasizing interstate conflicts, deploying to a geographically "friendly" area, and the neutrality of the force as the keys to peacekeeping success (pp. 167–75).

Chapter Five

1. Sir Brian Urquhart, *A Life in Peace and War* (London, 1987), p. 288.

2. Security Council Resolution 425, 19 March 1978.

3. J. D. Murray, "UN Peacekeeping Force Deployment: UNIFIL 1978," International Peace Academy Paper, New York, 1978, p. 1.

4. Bjorn Skogmo, *UNIFIL, International Peacekeeping in Lebanon, 1978–1988* (London, 1989), p. 12.

5. The mission planning process can be found in a myriad of operational manuals of almost any professional armed force. These steps are based on U.S. doctrine in the U.S. Armed Forces Staff College's *Joint Staff Officer's Guide* (Norfolk, Va., 1993) and *Campaign Planning* (Carlisle Barracks, Penn., 1988). British Army doctrine for "wider peacekeeping" reaffirms the deliberate planning process in British Army, *British Army Field Manual: Wider Peacekeeping* (London, 1994), p. 6-2. The military establishments of most large states have thousands of personnel assigned to full-time deliberate planning in various headquarters. In the United States of America, much of this planning is done through sophisticated and automated systems such as the Joint Operational Planning and Execution System (JOPES).

6. S/12611, Report of the Secretary-General on the Implementation of Security Council Resolution 425, 19 March 1978, para. 4.

7. Skogmo, *UNIFIL, International Peacekeeping in Lebanon, 1978–1988,* p. 14.

8. S/12611, para 3.

9. See, for instance, Ramesh Thakur, *International Peacekeeping in Lebanon* (Boulder, Colo., 1987).

10. UN Department of Public Information, *The Blue Helmets,* 2d ed. (New York, 1990), p. 113.

11. Urquhart, *A Life in Peace and War,* p. 289.

12. Doran Kochavi, *The United Nations Peacekeeping Operations in the Arab–Israeli Conflict: 1973–1979* (Claremont, Calif., 1980), p. 106.

13. Durch, *Evolution of UN Peacekeeping,* p. 31.

14. S/12611, para. 4(d).

15. Murray, "UN Peacekeeping Force Deployment," p. 8.

16. Mona Ghali, "UNIFIL, 1978–present," in William J. Durch, ed., *Evolution of UN Peacekeeping*: *Case Studies and Comparative Analysis* (New York, 1993), p. 192.

17. S/13691, Report of the Secretary-General on UNIFIL for the Period 9 June–10 December 1979, para. 32.

18. "The composite mechanized company, referred to in my report of 13 October 1986, has now been set up as the force mobile reserve. It comprises elements of the Fijian, Finnish, Ghanaian, Irish, and Nepalese battalions. They will be assembled to begin operations as a unit with effect from mid-January 1987." S/18581, para. 9. See also Emmanual A. Erskine, *Mission with UNIFIL* (London, 1989), pp. 31–32, 71–87.

19. S/15557, Report of the Secretary-General on UNIFIL, 13 January 1983, para. 8.

20. S/12620 Addition 5, 13 June 1978, para. 8(m).

21. S/12620, Progress Report of the Secretary-General on the UNIFIL, 23 March 1978, para. 4.

22. S/13691, para. 12; S/15194, para. 12; and S/15863, Report of the Secretary-General on UNIFIL for the Period 19 January–12 July 1983, para. 7.

23. S/12611, paragraph 9(c).

24. S/12675, Letter from the Secretary-General to the President of the Security Council, 1 May 1978.

25. Security Council Resolution 501, 25 February 1982.

26. The estimate from *The London Times,* 12 April 1978, p. 6, was 11,000 PLO guerillas. The UN forecast of PLO "armed elements" in the UNIFIL area has always been consistently lower.

27. The very conservative estimate used by the United Nations for DFF numbers was 1,500 in June 1978 (UNDPI, *The Blue Helmets,* p. 128).

28. Ibid., p. 121.
29. Kochavi, *The United Nations Peacekeeping Operations in the Arab–Israeli Conflict: 1973–1979*, p. 118.
30. Durch, *Evolution of UN Peacekeeping*, p. 28.
31. In fact, the government of Lebanon suggested the mandate be revised. S/12834, Letter from the Representative of Lebanon to the Secretary-General, 5 September 1978, para. 7.
32. S/12626, Letter from the Secretary-General to the President of the Security Council, 21 March 1978.
33. Had the fundamentalist Iran of Khomeini proposed participation in UNIFIL, it would have surely been denied. From the 1980s, Iran's interest and influence in Lebanon was considerable and carried out through Hezbollah and other Shiite organizations it supported.
34. Kochavi, *The United Nations Peacekeeping Operations in the Arab–Israeli Conflict: 1973–1979*, p. 114.
35. S/20416 Report of the Secretary-General on UNIFIL for the Period 26 July 1988–24 January 1989, para. 5.
36. Emmanuel A. Erskine, *Mission with UNIFIL* (London, 1989), p. 86.
37. S/18581, Report of the Secretary-General on UNIFIL for the Period 11 July 1986–11 January 1987, para. 8.
38. S/17557, Report of the Secretary-General on UNIFIL for the Period 12 April–10 October 1985, para. 12.
39. UNDPI, *The Blue Helmets*, pp. 427–28.
40. Ghali, "UNIFIL 1978–Present," pp. 191–92.
41. Ibid.
42. John Mackinlay, *The Peacekeepers: An Assessment of Peacemaking Operations at the Arab–Israeli Conflict* (London, 1989), p. 59.
43. Erskine, *Mission with UNIFIL*, p. 204.
44. The Force Commander's HQ in Jerusalem, the Main HQ established by the French temporarily at Zahrani, and Forward HQ at Naqoura. Murray, "UN Peacekeeping Force Deployment," p. 13.
45. Erskine, *Mission with UNIFIL*, p. 41, and Urquhart, *A Life in Peace and War*, p. 293.
46. See the reports in S/13691, para. 45; S/12929, para. 9; S/13258, para. 18; S/13254; and Erskine, *Mission with UNIFIL*, p. 82.
47. Mackinlay, *The Peacekeepers*, p. 58.
48. S/12620, addition 5, para. 21.
49. Murray, "UN Peacekeeping Force Deployment," p. 14.
50. Marianne Heiberg, "Peacekeepers and Local Populations: Some Comments on UNIFIL," in Indar Rikhye and K. Skjelsbaek, eds., *The UN and Peacekeeping: Results, Limitations, and Prospects* (New York, 1991), p. 156.
51. Murray, "UN Peacekeeping Force Deployment," p. 39.

52. Mackinlay, *The Peacekeepers*, p. 44.
53. Erskine, *Mission with UNIFIL*, p. 21.
54. Bjorn Skogmo, *The UN Security Council and the Crisis in Lebanon* (Oslo, 1986), p. 171.
55. John Mackinlay, "Improving Multifunctional Forces," *Survival*, vol. 36, no. 3, Autumn 1994, p. 166.
56. U.S. Army Headquarters, *FM 100-5: Operations* (Washington, D.C., 1993), pp. 2–8, 2–9.
57. Mackinlay, *The Peacekeepers*, p. 46.
58. Ibid., pp. 58–59.
59. Marianne Heiberg, "Observations of UN Peacekeeping in Lebanon," NUPI note 305, Norwegian Institute of International Affairs, Oslo, September 1984, p. 34.
60. Naomi J. Weinberger, "Peacekeeping Operations in Lebanon," *Middle East Journal*, vol. 37, no. 3, summer 1983, p. 347.
61. Ghali, "UNIFIL 1978–Present," p. 190.
62. The Israelis even documented evidence of these differing approaches. See Ze'ef Schiff and Ehud Ya'arip, *Israel's Lebanon War* (New York, 1984), p. 94, and Nathan Pelcovits, *Peacekeeping on Arab–Israeli Fronts* (Baltimore, Md., 1984), p. 19.
63. Kochavi, *United Nations Peacekeeping Operations in the Arab–Israeli Conflict, 1973–1979*, pp. 123–24.
64. Alan James, *Peacekeeping in International Politics* (London, Macmillan, 1990), p. 348.
65. Heiberg, "Peacekeepers and Local Populations: Some Comments on UNIFIL," p. 168 (ff. 11), and Mackinlay, *The Peacekeepers*, p. 60.
66. Mackinlay, *The Peacekeepers*, p. 60.
67. Ibid., p. 54.
68. Security Council Resolution 425, para. 3.
69. S/12611, para. 8.
70. Mackinlay, *The Peacekeepers*, p. 45.
71. UNDPI, *The Blue Helmets*, p. 121.
72. Ibid., p. 129.
73. Skogmo, *UNIFIL, International Peacekeeping in Lebanon*, p. 22.
74. S/14295, Report of the Secretary-General on UNIFIL for the Period June–December 1980.
75. UNDPI, *The Blue Helmets*, p. 126.
76. Ibid., pp. 126, 123, 127.
77. S/15194, para. 12.
78. S/12620, Add. 4, para. 24.
79. The most thorough discussion of this interesting and perplexing issue, on which opinions still vary widely, is in F. T Liu, *United Nations Peacekeeping and the Non-use of Force* (Boulder, Colo., 1992).

80. James, *Peacekeeping in International Politics*, p. 344.

81. S/1994/62, para. 10.

82. Ibid., para. 12.

83. Ibid., para. 26.

84. S/20416, para. 32.

85. Erskine, *Mission with UNIFIL*, p. 24.

86. S/12611, para. 2(d) and 6.

87. Tasks are specified in S/12845, para. 27.

88. Erskine, *Mission with UNIFIL*, p. 33.

89. S/12620, Add. 4, para. 17.

90. UNDPI, *The Blue Helmets*, p. 131.

91. Erskine, *Mission with UNIFIL*, p. 114.

92. S/13384, Report of the Secretary-General on UNIFIL for the Period from 13 January–8 June 1979, para. 9.

93. S/15194, para. 9.

94. Heiberg, "Peacekeepers and Local Populations: Some Comments on UNIFIL," in Rikhye and Skjeslbaek, *The UN and Peacekeeping*, p. 165.

95. Indar Rikhye, *The Theory and Practice of International Peacekeeping* (New York, 1984), p. 105.

96. S/1994/62, Report of the Secretary-General on UNIFIL for the Period 21 July 1993–20 January 1994, para. 7, and Peacekeeping Notes Update, November 1996.

97. James, *Peacekeeping in International Politics*, p. 345.

98. S/12845, para. 49–50.

99. S/15455, Report of the Secretary-General on UNIFIL, 14 October 1982, para. 14.

100. Heiberg, "Peacekeepers and Local Populations," p. 150–51.

101. S/13026, para. 34.

102. S/15455, para. 25, and S/16036, Report of the Secretary-General on UNIFIL for the Period 13 July–12 October 1983, para. 22.

103. UN Secretary-General Kurt Waldheim, quoted in Erskine, *Mission with UNIFIL*, p. 37.

104. Erskine, *Mission with UNIFIL*, p. 38.

Chapter Six

1. Boutros Boutros-Ghali, *An Agenda for Peace: Preventive Diplomacy, Peacemaking and Peace-keeping* (New York, 1992), p. 11.

2. Boutros Boutros-Ghali, "An Agenda for Peace: One Year Later," *Orbis*, vol. 37, no. 3, Summer 1993, p. 328.

3. Mats R. Berdal, "Peacekeeping in Europe," in *European Security after The Cold War*, Papers from the September 1993 IISS Annual Conference, Adelphi Paper 284 (London, 1994), p. 71.

4. Richard Haass, *Intervention: The Use of American Military Force in the Post–Cold War World* (Washington, D.C., 1994), p. 82.

5. Respectively, 4,493 and 6,250 troops. In UN Department of Public Information, *The Blue Helmets: A Review of UN Peace-Keeping*, 2d ed. (New York, 1990), pp. 359–60, and UN Peacekeeping Notes Update, November 1993, p. 77.

6. Mats R. Berdal, *Whither UN Peacekeeping?*, Adelphi Paper 281, International Institute of Strategic Studies (London, 1993), p. 27.

7. SC Resolutions 770, 13 August 1992; 816, 31 March 1993; and 836, 4 June 1993.

8. Once against air targets and seven times against ground targets. United States Air Force Europe South, *Operation Deny Flight Update*, 22 March 1995, p. 1.

9. Quoted in the *International Herald Tribune*, 30 September 1993, p. 2.

10. "Lessons from UNPROFOR," a presentation to a conference on "The Application of the Law of War Rules and Principles in Armed Conflict," Garmisch-Partenkirchen, Germany, 5–7 December 1994.

11. A. B. Fetherston, *Towards a Theory of UN Peacekeeping* (London, 1994), p. 26.

12. Less so in UNOSOM II, which was chosen for the case study because it provides the closest evidence of some *attempt* at peace enforcement, although some supporters would still subjectively classify it as principally peacekeeping in nature. Fetherston, for instance, classifies UNOSOM II as peace enforcement and writes that in UNOSOM II, "theory and practice met." *Towards a Theory of UN Peacekeeping*, p. 25. Admiral Jonathan Howe, the special representative of the secretary-general to Somalia, disagrees with Fetherston. He told the author that UNOSOM II was definitely not structured for enforcement tasks and did not seek to undertake them as the principal acts in UNOSOM II's strategy (interview with Admiral Jonathan Howe, Stockholm, Sweden, 11 April 1995, handwritten notes).

13. John Gerard Ruggie, "Peacekeeping and U.S. Interests," *The Washington Quarterly*, vol. 17, no. 4, Autumn 1994, p. 181.

14. Among others, a thoughtful study that takes this approach is Gareth Evans's *Cooperating for Peace: The Global Agenda for the 1990s and Beyond* (St. Leonards, Australia, 1993).

15. Boutros-Ghali, *An Agenda for Peace*, p. 26.

16. See Don Daniel, "Securing the Observance of UN Mandates through the Employment of Military Forces," paper presented to the Use of Force in Peace Operations Conference, Stockholm, 10–11 April 1995. Daniel notes that some missions granted Chapter VII authority are much closer in their conduct of operations to traditional peacekeeping than enforcement.

17. ONUC is not reexamined in detail because of the many good studies done of that mission. See in particular Georges Abi-Saab, *The United Nations Operation in the Congo: 1960–1962* (Oxford, 1978); Conor Cruise O'Brien, *To Katanga and Back* (London, 1962); and Ernest W. Lefever, *Uncertain Mandate* (Baltimore, Md., 1967).

18. Boutros-Ghali, *An Agenda for Peace*, p. 7, and Evans, *Cooperating for Peace*, pp. 20–22.

19. Thirteen missions were authorized between 1948 and 1988. Twenty missions were authorized between 1988 and 1993. UNDPI, *Information Notes*, May 1994.

20. UNDPI, *The Blue Helmets*, App. 2, and UN Peacekeeping, "Information Notes Update" (no. 2), November 1993.

21. See William J. Durch, ed., *Evolution of UN Peacekeeping: Case Studies and Comparative Analysis* (New York, 1993), pp. 26–29, and Evans, *Cooperating for Peace*, p. 109. Conversely, Paul F. Diehl maintains that historically, a clear mandate in itself may have "little impact on the ultimate success of the operation" if other more critical conditions for success are not met *International Peace-keeping*, (London, 1993), p. 173.

22. Durch, *Evolution of UN Peacekeeping*, pp. 26–27. See also Diehl, *International Peace-keeping*, p. 75.

23. UN Department of Public Information, *The United Nations and the Situation in the Former Yugoslavia* (New York, 15 March 1994), pp. 72–157.

24. Boutros Boutros-Ghali, *Report on the Work of the Organization from the 47th–48th Session of the General Assembly* (New York, September 1993), p. 101.

25. Fetherston, *Towards a Theory of United Nations Peacekeeping*, p. xvi.

26. In just one example, a U.S. government report noted in 1993 that the UN's "small staff could not prepare detailed operational plans for all UNTAC's activities prior to deployment and this hindered operations" (U.S. General Accounting Office, *UN Peacekeeping: Lessons Learned in Managing Recent Missions*, GAO/NSIAD-94-9 [Washington, D.C., December 1993], p. 5).

27. Berdal, "Peacekeeping in Europe," p. 66.

28. Berdal, *Whither UN Peacekeeping?*, p. 9. See chapter 3 of this Adelphi Paper for a complete explanation of this issue.

29. Fetherston, *Towards a Theory of UN Peacekeeping*, p. 42.

30. Lewis Mackenzie, "Military Realities of UN Peacekeeping Operations," *RUSI Journal*, February 1993, p. 22.

31. At a conference on the Use of Force in Peace Operations (Stockholm, 10–11 April 1995), ex-UN commanders, political representatives, and analysts were split over whether a heavy UN force provoked belligerents and damaged the UN's impartial standing or provided the UN force a

deterrent capability because mobility and protection allow it to perform its impartial operations even more effectively. There is no clear pattern of evidence to support either side, but UN peacekeepers in second-generation missions are unanimous in their support for the protection afforded by heavy mechanized and armored force structures.

32. Report of the Secretary-General on the Situation in the Former Yugoslavia, (S/25264), 10 February 1993, p. 6.

33. John Pomfret, "Bosnian Serbs Report 9 Dead after Pounding by UN Tanks," *The International Herald Tribune*, 2 May 1994, p. 4, and a presentation by General Percurt Green, Chief of Joint Operations Staff, Sweden, to the Conference on the Use of Force in Peace Operations, Stockholm, 10–11 April 1995.

34. S/1995/1, "Supplement to an Agenda for Peace," p. 4.

35. Major General J. A. MacInnis, presentation to the Conference on the Applicability of the Laws of War in Humanitarian Conflict, Garmisch-Partenkirchen, Germany, 5–7 December 1994.

36. Trevor Findlay, *Cambodia: Lessons and Legacy of UNTAC* (Oxford, 1995), p. 117.

37. UNPROFOR and UNOSOM II represented the heaviest of the second-generation peacekeeping operations, but other missions in this category had a sophisticated and complex force composition as well. The sheer scale and complexity of the military tasks facing most second-generation peacekeeping missions necessitated a combined arms force structure with air and naval elements. UNTAC had 10 fixed-wing aircraft as well as 26 helicopters to facilitate transportation and logistics. It also had a naval element of 30 boats (sea patrol, river patrol, landing, and other) and almost 400 sailors of all ranks. S/23613, Report of the Secretary-General on Cambodia, 19 February 1992, p. 19.

38. UNDPI, "Peacekeeping Notes Update" no. 2, November 1993.

39. S/1994/300, Report of the Secretary-General Pursuant to Resolution 871, 16 March 1994, pp. 18–20.

40. UNDPI, "United Nations Peacekeeping Update," December 1994, p. 108.

41. UN Department of Public Information, *The United Nations and the Situation in the Former Yugoslavia* (New York, 1994), p. 15.

42. Ibid., p. 16.

43. S/1994/300, p. 12.

44. S/1995/1, p. 4.

45. Findlay, *Cambodia: Lessons and Legacy of UNTAC*, p. 27.

46. S/1994/300, pp. 18–20.

47. Ibid.

48. U.S. GAO, *UN Peacekeeping: Lessons Learned in Managing Recent Missions*, p. 41, and Findlay, *Cambodia: Lessons and Legacy of UNTAC*, p. 34.

49. Comment to the author, 1995.

50. S/1994/300, p. 12.

51. U.S. GAO, *UN Peacekeeping: Lessons Learned in Managing Recent Missions*, p. 44.

52. Mark Heinrich, "Russian UN Commander in Croatia Dismissed," *The Times* (London), 12 April 1995, p. 6, and Berdal, "Peacekeeping in Europe," p. 71.

53. Findlay, *Cambodia: Lessons and Legacy of UNTAC*, p. 139.

54. U.S. GAO, *UN Peacekeeping: Lessons Learned in Managing Recent Missions*, p. 44.

55. This is the number of member states contributing troops to UNPROFOR. UNTAC had 32, ONUC 31, ONUMOZ 24, and UNTAG 19. UNDPI, *The Blue Helmets*, App. 2, and UNDPI, Information Notes Update, December 1994.

56. U.S. GAO, *UN Peacekeeping: Lessons Learned in Managing Recent Missions*, p. 51.

57. Findlay, *Cambodia: Lessons and Legacy of UNTAC*, p. 141.

58. Ibid., p. 143. In particular, Findlay highlights the different attitudes of the UNTAC contingents and the deleterious effect this had on mission cohesion.

59. General Ole Kandborg (Denmark), presentation to the Use of Force in Peace Operations conference, Stockholm, 10–11 April 1995.

60. Major General J. A MacInnis, conference paper, Garmisch-Partenkirchen, December 1994.

61. Berdal, *Whither UN Peacekeeping?*, p. 26.

62. Findlay, *Cambodia: Legacy and Lessons of UNTAC*, p. 124.

63. Mats Berdal, presentation to the Use of Force in Peace Operations conference, Stockholm, 10–11 April 1995.

64. Berdal, "Peacekeeping in Europe," p. 67.

65. Adam Roberts, *The Crisis in Peacekeeping* (Oslo, 1994), p. 25.

66. Trevor Findlay, *Cambodia: The Legacy and Lessons of UNTAC*, pp. 33–34.

67. Ibid., pp. 23, 26, 115.

68. UNDPI, *The United Nations and the Situation in the Former Yugoslavia*, p. 21.

69. U.S. Government Accounting Office, *Humanitarian Intervention: The Effectiveness of UN Operations in Bosnia*, GAO/NSIAD-94-156BR (Washington, D.C., April 1994), pp. 32–33.

70. S/1994/300, p. 15, and U.S. GAO, *Humanitarian Intervention: The Effectiveness of UN Operations in Bosnia*, p. 15.

71. Suzanne Schafer, "Officials Vow Further Airstrikes If U.S. Goes into Bosnia," *European Stars and Stripes*, 21 March 1994.

72. Christopher Bellamy, "Military Agree on How to Make Peace," *The Independent*, 7 July 1994, p. 4. Other reports throughout 1994 include Roger Cohen, "Who's in Charge in Bosnia? UN and NATO Fight It Out," *International Herald Tribune*, 30 October 1994, p. 7, and Michael Evans, "UN-NATO Link Brought Near to Breaking Point," *The Times* (London), 25 April 1994, p. 3.

73. Berdal, presentation to the Use of Force in Peace Operations conference, Stockholm, 10–11 April 1995.

74. Ibid.

75. U.S. GAO, *Humanitarian Intervention: The Effectiveness of UN Operations in Bosnia*, pp. 39–40.

76. Berdal, "Peacekeeping in Europe," p. 70. Berdal also highlighted the same phenomenon in UNTAC, *Whither UN Peacekeeping?*, pp. 42–43.

77. U.S. GAO, *Humanitarian Intervention: The Effectiveness of UN Operations in Bosnia*, p. 40.

78. U.S. GAO, *UN Peacekeeping: Lessons Learned in Managing Recent Missions*, p. 51.

79. Address to the Royal United Services Institute, London, 12 October 1993.

80. Berdal, *Whither UN Peacekeeping?*, p. 42.

81. Findlay, *Cambodia: Legacy and Lessons of UNTAC*, p. 135.

82. Mats Berdal, "Peacekeeping in Europe," p. 62.

83. Most lucidly argued by Charles Dobbie in *A Concept for Post–Cold War Peacekeeping* (Oslo, 1994), and the British Army's *British Army Field Manual: Wider Peacekeeping* (London, 1994).

84. Articulated in particular in numerous articles and monographs by J. Chopra, J. Mackinlay, G. Ruggie, J. J. Holst, T. Weiss, D. Daniel, and B. Hayes.

85. Shashi Tharoor, "Should UN Peacekeeping Go back to Basics?" *Survival*, vol. 37, no. 4, Winter 1994–1995, p. 60.

86. MacInnis, conference paper, Garmisch-Partenkirchen, Germany, December 1994.

87. Don Daniel and Bradd Hayes, *Securing Observance of UN Mandates through the Employment of Military Forces* (Newport, R.I., 1995), p. 6.

88. Berdal, "Peacekeeping in Europe," p. 71.

89. Adam Roberts, *The Crisis in Peacekeeping* (Oslo, 1994), p. 37.

90. Adam Roberts, "From San Francisco to Sarejevo: The UN and the Use of Force," *Survival* 37, Winter 1995–1996, p. 25.

91. Berdal, "Peacekeeping in Europe," p. 67.

92. S/25264, Further Report of the Secretary-General Pursuant to SC Resolution 743 (establishing UNPROFOR), 10 February 1993.

93. Some analysts, such as Mats Berdal, claim it is closer to fifteen times up to 1994. Berdal, "Peacekeeping in Europe," p. 67.

94. SC Resolutions 743, 21 February 1992, and 749, 7 April 1992; SC Resolution 758, 8 June 1992; SC Resolutions 761, 29 June 1992, and 764, 13 July 1992; SC Resolution 762, 30 June 1992; SC Resolution 769, 7 August 1992; SC Resolutions 770, 13 August 1992, and 776, 14 September 1992; SC Resolution 779, 6 October 1992; SC Resolutions 781, 9 October 1992, and 786, 10 November 1992; SC Resolution 795, 11 December 1992; SC Resolution 816, 31 March 1993; SC Resolutions 819, 16 April 1993, 824 6 May 1993, and 908, 31 March 1994, and SC Resolution 836, 4 June 1993, respectively.

95. Berdal, *Whither UN Peacekeeping?*, p. 31.

96. Quoted in A. B. Fetherston, *Towards a Theory of UN Peacekeeping* (London, 1994), p. 86, from "Belgian Commander Wants to Quit" Reuters News Service, 4 January 1994.

97. Interview with LTC Jack Clarke, coauthor of U.S. Army Field Manual 100-23, *Peace Operations* (Washington, D.C., 1994), December 1994, Garmisch-Partenkirchen, Germany.

98. S/1994/300, p. 11.

99. S/1994/300, p. 15.

100. S/23613, Report of the Secretary-General on Cambodia, 19 February 1992, p. 14. Findlay, *Cambodia: Legacy and Lessons of UNTAC*, p. 36.

101. Findlay, *Cambodia: Legacy and Lessons of UNTAC*, p. 37.

102. It is not necessary to go into a military explanation of why a peacekeeping force of twelve battalions, hastily thrown together, could not wage a campaign of offensive coercion against the Khmer Rouge or other parties. This quite obvious point has been reinforced by John Mackinlay in the *International Spectator*, November 1993, Gerald Segal and Mats Berdal in *Jane's Intelligence Review*, March 1993, and the author's conversations with the UNTAC commander and some of his staff, Stockholm, April 1995.

103. Alan James, *Peacekeeping in International Politics* (London, 1990), p. 296.

104. S/24578, Second Progress Report of the Secretary-General on the UNTAC, 21 September 1992, p. 5.

105. Findlay, *Cambodia: Legacy and Lessons of UNTAC*, p. 39.

106. Ibid., p. 112. He also noted that the UNTAC commander would be the first to admit that there were large elements of hope and luck involved in UNTAC's mission (pp. 134–35).

107. U.S. GAO, *Humanitarian Intervention: Effectiveness of UN Operations in Bosnia*, p. 25.

108. SC Resolution 770, 13 August 1992.

109. SC Resolution 776, 14 September 1992.

110. S/24848, Further Report of the Secretary-General Pursuant to SC Resolution 743, 24 November 1992, p. 16, and Fetherston, *Towards a Theory of UN Peacekeeping*, p. 82.

111. Lecture by General Sir David Ramsbotham, George C. Marshall European Center for Security Studies, Garmisch-Partenkirchen, Germany, 2 December 1994.

112. Noted in UNTAC by General Sanderson, the force commander. Comment at the Use of Force in Peace Operations conference, Stockholm, 10–11 April 1995.

113. U.S. GAO, *Humanitarian Intervention: Effectiveness of UN Operations in Bosnia*, p. 35.

114. Berdal, "Peacekeeping in Europe," p. 65.

115. See Edward Luttwak, "Meddling by Outside Powers Has Prolonged the Balkan War," *International Herald Tribune*, 11 August 1995, p. 7; John Hillen, *Killing with Kindness: The UN Intervention in Bosnia*, Foreign Policy Briefing 34, The CATO Institute, (Washington, D.C., June 1995); and Shapiro and Thompson, "No, the Only Solution Is a Compromise with the Bosnian Serbs," *International Herald Tribune*, 16 May 1995.

116. Berdal, "Peacekeeping in Europe," p. 64.

117. S/25264, p. 2.

118. Ibid., Corr. 1.

119. Roger Cohen, "UN Peace Force Loses Credibility," *International Herald Tribune*, 10 May 1995, p. 2; Barbara Crossette, "UN Chief Wants to Rethink Role in Bosnia," *International Herald Tribune*, 18 May 1995, p. 1; and Anthony Lloyd, "Safe Areas Hold Troops to Ransom," *The Times* (London) 22 May 1995, p. 1.

120. James Schear, "The Conflicts of Bosnia: Assessing the Role of the UN," in Stephen Blank, ed., *Yugoslavia's Wars: The Problem from Hell* (Carlisle Barracks, Penn., 1995), p. 40. A Report of the Secretary-General in March 1994 also noted that the operations to protect the safe areas were all predicated against one party and threatened UNPROFOR's impartiality (S/1994/300, p. 12).

121. S/1994/300, p. 11.

122. Andrew Bair, "What Happened in Yugoslavia? Lessons for Future Peacekeepers," in *European Security*, vol. 3, no. 2, Summer 1994, p. 345.

123. SC Resolution 836, 4 June 1993.

124. Major General Ole L. Kandborg (Denmark), presentation to the Use of Force in Peace Operations conference, Stockholm, 10–11 April 1995.

125. Noted in a paper presented by Wolfgang Biermann to the Use of Force in Peace Operations conference, Stockholm, 10–11 April 1995.

126. Quoted in ibid. NATO Secretary-General Willy Claes, statement to the North Atlantic Assembly, Washington, D.C., 18 November 94.

127. Major General J. A. MacInnis, presentation to the Application of Law of War Rules conference, Garmisch-Partenkirchen, Germany, 5–7 December 1994.

128. See Roger Cohen, "Raids Countereffective," *International Herald Tribune*, 27 May 1995, p. 1.

129. John Pomfret, "British–French Force in Bosnia Tells UN: You Don't Control Us," *The Washington Post*, 16 August 1995, p. A16.

130. Rick Atkinson, "Near-Catastrophe Forced West to Prop Up UN in Bosnia," *The Washington Post*, 30 July 1995, p. A21.

131. Shashi Tharoor, "UN Peacekeeping in Europe," *Survival*, vol. 37, no. 2, Summer 1995, p. 125.

132. S/25264, Corr. 1, p. 3.

133. S/1994/300, p. 8.

134. Ibid.

135. Berdal, "Peacekeeping in Europe," p. 61.

136. See Craig Whitney, "NATO's New Ultimatum to Serbs," *International Herald Tribune*, 23 April 1994, p. 1.

137. See Boutros-Ghali, *Supplement to An Agenda for Peace*.

138. The assessment given in Trevor Findlay's study of UNTAC, *Cambodia: The Lessons and Legacy of UNTAC*, p. 103. However, as Cambodia has slipped back into instability, others have disagreed. See William Shawcross, *Cambodia's New Deal* (Washington, D.C., 1993), and Nate Thayer, "Medellin on the Mekong," *Far Eastern Economic Review*, 23 November 1995, pp. 24–31.

139. Durch, *The Evolution of UN Peacekeeping*, p. 8.

140. Mackinlay, "Improving Multifunctional Forces," *Survival*, vol. 36, no. 3, Autumn 1994, p. 152.

141. S/1994/300, p. 15.

142. John Gerard Ruggie, "Wandering the Void: Charting the UN's New Strategic Role," *Foreign Affairs*, vol. 72, no. 5 (November–December 1993), p. 28.

143. Berdal, *Whither UN Peacekeeping?*, p. 11.

144. Schear, "The Conflicts of Bosnia," p. 43.

Chapter Seven

1. S/24480, Report of the Secretary-General on the Situation in Somalia, 24 August 1992, pp. 5–6.

2. A phrase used in John L. Hirsch and Robert B. Oakley, *Somalia and Operation Restore Hope: Reflections on Peacemaking and Peacekeeping* (Washington, D.C., 1995), p. xii.

3. UN Department of Public Information, *The United Nations and the Situation in Somalia*, reference paper (New York, 1 May 1994) p. 1. For a

trenchant criticism of the failure of the international community to intervene earlier, see Jeffrey Clark, "Debacle in Somalia," *Foreign Affairs*, vol. 72, no. 1, January–February 1993, pp. 109–23.

4. SC Resolution 751, 24 April 1992.

5. SC Resolution 775, 28 August 1992, and S/24480, p. 8.

6. UNDPI, *The United Nations and the Situation in Somalia*, p. 5.

7. S/24868, Letter of the Secretary-General to the Security Council, 29 November 1992.

8. For an insider's account of the American policy machinations leading up to this decision, see Hirsch and Oakley, *Somalia and Operation Restore Hope*, pp. 40–44, and Dan Oberdorfer, "Anatomy of a Decision: How Bush Made Up His Mind to Send Troops to Somalia," *The International Herald Tribune*, 7 December 1992, p. 1.

9. SC Resolution 794, 3 December 1992.

10. Quoted in Robert Oakley, "An Envoy's Perspective," *Joint Force Quarterly*, no. 2, Autumn 1993, p. 46. See also Hirsch and Oakley, *Somalia and Operation Restore Hope*, p. 152.

11. Joseph P. Hoar, "A Commander-in-Chief's Perspective," *Joint Force Quarterly*, no. 2, Autumn 1993, p. 62.

12. Hirsch and Oakley, *Somalia and Operation Restore Hope*, p. xviii.

13. Ibid., p. 45.

14. Quoted in ibid., p. 104. See also remarks of the White House Press Secretary in IHT staff dispatches, "Bush Wants Troops out of Somalia by Jan. 20," *The International Herald Tribune*, 4 December 1992, p. 1.

15. IHT staff dispatches, "Bush Sends Troops to Somalia, With First Marines Due to Land Monday," *The International Herald Tribune*, 5–6 December 1992, p. 1.

16. S/24992, Report of the Secretary-General on the Implementation of Resolution 794, 19 December 1992, p. 12.

17. S/24992, pp. 7–9.

18. Chester Crocker in Hirsch and Oakley, *Somalia and Operation Restore Hope*, pp. xi, 111.

19. Oakley, "An Envoy's Perspective," p. 55.

20. T. Frank Crigler, "The Peace-Enforcement Dilemma," *Joint Force Quarterly*, no. 2, Autumn 1993, p. 66.

21. Jonathan Stevenson, "Hope Restored in Somalia," *Foreign Policy*, Summer 1993, p. 138.

22. Hirsch and Oakley, *Somalia and Operation Restore Hope*, p. 153.

23. S/24992, p. 10.

24. S/25354, Further Report of the Secretary-General Submitted in Pursuance of Paragraphs 18 and 19 of Resolution 794, 3 March 1993, p. 15.

25. Ibid., pp. 16–17.

26. Colonel Gary Anderson, "UNOSOM II: Not Failure, Not Success," in *Beyond Traditional Peacekeeping*, p. 273, and Harold E. Bullock, *Peace by Committee: Command and Control Issues in Multinational Peace Enforcement Operations* (Maxwell Air Force Base, Ala., 1995), p. 41.

27. UNOSOM II had some Russian helicopters but would not use them because of prohibitive insurance costs (ibid., p. 274). The Pakistani contingent was later given some older U.S. helicopters by the United States, along with tanks and armored personnel carriers. U.S. GAO Report NSIAD-94-175, *Withdrawal of U.S. Troops from Somalia* (Washington, D.C., 1994), p. 7.

28. Admiral Jonathan Howe interview with the author, Stockholm, Sweden, 11 April 1995, handwritten notes.

29. S. L. Arnold, "Somalia: An Operation Other than War," *Military Review*, vol. 73, no. 12, December 1993, p. 35.

30. S/26738, Further Report of the Secretary-General in Pursuance of Paragraph 19 of Resolution 814 and Paragraph 5 of Resolution 865, 12 November 1993, p. 13.

31. W. D. Freeman, R. B. Lambert, and J. D. Mims, "Operation Restore Hope: A U.S. CENTCOM Perspective," *Military Review*, September 1993, p. 62, and Hoar, "A CINC's Perspective," pp. 56–57.

32. Ibid. and the Brown Report (unclassified), unpublished Department of Defense lessons-learned report (Washington, D.C., 1993).

33. S/24480, p. 8.

34. Hirsch and Oakley, *Somalia and Operation Restore Hope*, p. 41.

35. United States Central Command, Public Affairs Office, "Somalia Statistics," Tampa, Fla., 25 March 1994.

36. Statistics from the Office of the President, "Report to Congress on U.S. Military Operations in Somalia," U.S. Department of State Dispatch, 25 October 1993, Annex III, p. 25.

37. S/24992, pp. 12–13.

38. S/25354, pp. 15–16.

39. S/26738, pp. 11–13.

40. S/26317, Further Report of the Secretary-General Submitted in Pursuance of Paragraph 18 of Resolution 814, 17 August 1993, pp. 2–3.

41. U.S. Central Command Public Affairs Office, "Somalia Statistics," Tampa, Fla., 25 March 1994.

42. S/26317, p. 18.

43. S/1994/12, Further Report of the Secretary-General submitted in Pursuance of the Security Council Resolution 886 (1993), 6 January 1994, pp. 13–14.

44. UNDPI, *The United Nations and Situation in Somalia*, p. 3.

45. According to U.S. Marine Commander Major General Anthony Zinni, in Bullock, *Peace by Committee*, p. 23.

46. The Special Representative of the Secretary-General characterized these units as "two of the most capable and well-equipped contingents" (Jonathan Howe, "The United States and the United Nations in Somalia: The Limits of Involvement," *The Washington Quarterly*, vol. 18, no. 3, Summer 1995, p. 53).

47. Author's conversation with Canadian military attaché, Washington, D.C., August 1995.

48. Bullock, *Peace by Committee*, p. 37. Among the many examples cited was the propensity of some contingents to display poor fire discipline when harassed and threatened by the ubiquitous Somali snipers and rock-throwing mobs. Much of this can be attributed to vast differences in training, equipment, and doctrinal capabilities. For instance, to protect vulnerable U.S. forces on the ground so that they could exercise restraint against snipers and mobs, these ground forces often were supported by elite sniper teams or combat air support. Not all contingents had these resources or were trained in their use. Subsequently, they tended to lash out at crowds around them when confronted by an unseen enemy. Bullock also noted that even nations such as Pakistan deployed their elite combat units for service with UNITAF and replaced them with under-equipped conscript units for UNOSOM II.

49. Germany, Greece, Italy, Norway, Turkey, the United States, Korea, Kuwait, Morocco, Saudi Arabia, Tunisia, and the United Arab Emirates all withdrew. (Further Report of the Secretary-General on the UN Operation in Somalia Submitted in Pursuance of Paragraph 14 of SC Resolution 897 (1994), 24 May 1994 (S/1994/614), pp. 5–6.

50. S/26738, p. 22.

51. Hirsch and Oakley, *Somalia and Operation Restore Hope*, p. 115.

52. Bullock, *Peace by Committee*, p. 62, and Stevenson, "Hope Restored in Somalia?," p. 140.

53. As noted in Chapter Six, the disparity in capabilities is especially apparent in support forces. When suitable replacement forces could not be found, U.S. logistics forces were replaced (at much greater expense) by civilian contractors (S/26738, p. 25).

54. Ibid., p. 11.

55. Admiral Jonathan Howe noted that the problem of force turbulence plagued UNOSOM II as it has done other missions (see UNIFIL case study). Deployment, rotation, and withdrawal decisions were made by member states in varying degrees of coordination with the United Nations. Interview with the author, Stockholm, Sweden, 11 April 1995, handwritten notes.

56. Howe, "The U.S. and the UN in Somalia," p. 54.

57. Bullock, *Peace by Committee*, p. 60.

58. Kenneth Allard, *Somalia Operations: Lessons Learned* (Washington, D.C., 1995), p. 32.

59. S/26317, p. 4.

60. Hirsch and Oakley, *Somalia and Operation Restore Hope*, p. 141.

61. Admiral Jonathan Howe, interview with the author, Stockholm, Sweden, 11 April 1995, handwritten notes.

62. Howe, "The U.S. and the UN in Somalia," p. 53.

63. Gary Anderson, "UNOSOM II: Not Failure, Not Success," in Daniel and Hayes, *Beyond Traditional Peacekeeping*, p. 269.

64. Chester Crocker, "The Lessons of Somalia: Not Everything Went Wrong," *Foreign Affairs*, vol. 74, no. 3, May–June 1995, p. 5.

65. Hoar, "A CINC's Perspective," p. 62.

66. Bullock, *Peace by Committee*, p. 15.

67. Ibid., pp. 14, 40.

68. Frances Kennedy, "Italian Views on Somalia Deserve a Better Hearing," *The International Herald Tribune*, 23 July 1993, p. 8, and Kenneth C. Allard, *Somalia Operations: Lessons Learned* (Washington, D.C., 1995), p. 57.

69. Bullock, *Peace by Committee*, p. 13.

70. S/26317, p. 19.

71. United States Institute of Peace, *Restoring Hope: The Real Lessons of Somalia for the Future of Intervention* (Washington, D.C., July 1995), p. 11.

72. Hirsch and Oakley, *Somalia and Operation Restore Hope*, p. xiv.

73. Allard, *Somalia Operations: Lessons Learned*, p. 31.

74. Tactical control is even more limited than operational control, allowing the tactical commander to give forces temporary and local directives in accordance with missions already assigned (Ibid., p. 29).

75. Ibid., p. 59.

76. Any connection relied on coordination between the ranger task force commander, an Army general, and Montgomery in his role as U.S. forces commander with tactical control of the QRF, which supported the ranger task force operations. Allard, *Somalia Operations: Lessons Learned*, pp. 57–58.

77. Admiral Jonathan Howe, vignette related to the SIPRI conference on the Use of Force in Peace Operations, Stockholm, Sweden, 10 April 1995, handwritten notes.

78. Rick Atkinson, "U.S. Expedition in Somalia: The Making of a Disaster," *The International Herald Tribune*, 31 January 1994, p. 1.

79. Allard, *Somalia Operations: Lessons Learned*, p. 60.

80. Ibid., p. 34.

81. Admiral Jonathan Howe, interview with the author, Stockholm, Sweden, 11 April 1995, handwritten notes.

82. Ibid.

83. Bullock, *Peace by Committee*, p. 35.

84. Allard, *Somalia Operations: Lessons Learned*, p. 5.

85. Office of the President, "Report to Congress on U.S. Military Operations in Somalia," p. 14.

86. A very thorough operational analysis of the transition is presented in Jonathan T. Dworken, *Operation Restore Hope: Preparing and Planning the Transition to UN Operations*, Center for Naval Analysis Report CRM 93-14B (Alexandria, Va., 1994). See also Allard, *Somalia Operations: Lessons Learned*, p. 26.

87. Freeman, Lambert, and Mims, "Operation Restore Hope: A U.S. CENT-COM Perspective," p. 71.

88. Quoted in Bullock, *Peace by Committee*, p. 11.

89. S/24992, p. 13.

90. Chester Crocker, "The Lessons of Somalia," p. 5.

91. Chester Crocker in Hirsch and Oakley, *Somalia and Operation Restore Hope*, p. ix.

92. Hoar, "A CINC's Perspective," p. 63.

93. Ibid., pp. 55–56, and Robert Oakley, "An Envoy's Perspective," p. 47.

94. U.S. Envoy Robert Oakley noted that, surprisingly, there was little realization among outsiders that UNOSOM II was attempting to do much more with much less (Hirsch and Oakley, *Somalia and Operation Restore Hope*, p. 123).

95. Admiral Jonathan Howe, interview with the author, Stockholm, Sweden, 11 April 1995, handwritten notes.

96. Crigler, "The Peace-Enforcement Dilemma," p. 67.

97. Howe, "The U.S. and UN in Somalia," p. 52. Admiral Howe reemphasized the gap between UNOSOM II's resources and aspirations in an interview with the author, Stockholm, Sweden, 11 April 1995, handwritten notes.

98. Admiral Jonathan Howe, interview with the author, Stockholm, Sweden, 11 April 1995, handwritten notes.

99. USIP, "Restoring Hope," p. 12.

100. S/25354, pp. 12–13.

101. Crocker, "The Lessons of Somalia," p. 6.

102. Oakley, "An Envoy's Perspective," p. 52.

103. UN CENTCOM OPPLAN JTF Somalia, quoted in Freeman, Lambert, and Mims, "Operation Restore Hope: A U.S. CENTCOM Perspective," p. 64.

104. U.S. Central Command Operations Plan for Joint Task Force Somalia, December 1992. Taken from Jonathan T. Dworken, *Operation Restore Hope: Preparing and Planning the Transition to UN Operations*, pp. 7–9.

105. Ibid., p. 9.

106. IHT staff dispatches, "Bush Wants Troops out of Somalia by Jan. 20," p. 1.

107. Walter S. Clarke, "Testing the World's Resolve in Somalia," *Parameters*, vol. 23, no. 4, Winter 1993–1994, p. 55.

108. S/25354, p. 13.

109. Oberdorfer, "Anatomy of a Decision," p. 1.

110. Hoar, "A CINC's Perspective," p. 62.

111. These include the deputy U.S. special envoy Walter Clarke and Army Colonel Bruce Clarke (Bullock, *Peace by Committee*, pp. 11, 23, 42).

112. Admiral Jonathan Howe, interview with the author, Stockholm, Sweden, 11 April 1995, handwritten notes.

113. Freeman, Lambert, and Mims, "Operation Restore Hope: A U.S. CENT-COM Perspective," p. 64.

114. Howe, "The U.S. and UN in Somalia," p. 51.

115. S/24992, p. 10.

116. Allard, *Somalia Operations: Lessons Learned*, p. 64.

117. Arnold, "Somalia: An Operation Other than War," p. 31.

118. Oakley, "An Envoy's Perspective," pp. 48, 51.

119. Crocker, "The Lessons of Somalia," p. 6.

120. Hoar, "A Commander in Chief's Perspective," p. 58.

121. F. M. Lorenz, "Law and Anarchy in Somalia," *Parameters*, vol. 23, no. 4, Winter 1993–1994, pp. 31, 36, and Clarke, "Testing the World's Resolve in Somalia," p. 45.

122. USIP, "Restoring Hope," p. 10.

123. Dworken, *Preparing and Planning the Transition to UN Operations*, p. 23.

124. Clarke, "Testing the World's Resolve in Somalia," p. 51.

125. S/26317, p. 4.

126. S/25354, p. 19.

127. Res. 814, 26 March 1993.

128. S/26317, p. 17.

129. Hirsch and Oakley, *Somalia and Operation Restore Hope*, p. x.

130. Bullock, *Peace by Committee*, p. 41.

131. SC Resolution 897, 4 February 1994.

132. S/1994/614, Report of Secretary-General on situation in Somalia, May 1994, p. 7.

133. Office of the President, "Report to Congress on U.S. Military Operations in Somalia," p. 1.

134. Crocker, "The Lessons of Somalia," p. 6.

135. Oakley, "An Envoy's Perspective," p. 55.
136. Adam Roberts, "From San Francisco to Sarajevo: The UN and the Use of Force," *Survival* vol. 37, no. 4, Winter 1995–1996, pp. 7–28.
137. S/26317, p. 18.

Chapter Eight

1. Adam Roberts, "Laws of War in the 1990–91 Gulf Conflict," *International Security*, vol. 18, no. 3, January–February 1994, p. 146.
2. Security Council Resolutions S/1501, 25 June 1950, and S/1511, 27 June 1950.
3. Blair House meeting minutes and report of J. F. Dulles to the Secretary of State, in *Foreign Relations of the United States,* vol. 7: 1950 (Washington, D.C., 1976), pp. 160, 237.
4. S/1588, 7 July 1950, and Rosalyn Higgins, *United Nations Peacekeeping, 1946–1967: Documents and Commentary,* vol. 2 (London, 1970), p. 195.
5. D. W. Bowett, *United Nations Forces: A Legal Study of United Nations Practice*, pp. 33ff.
6. SC Resolution 660, 2 August 1990.
7. Security Council Resolutions 665, 678, 686.
8. Lawrence Freedman and Efraim Karsh, *The Gulf Conflict, 1990–1991* (London, 1993), p. 146.
9. Quoted in the *UN Chronicle*, vol. 28, no. 1, January 1991, p. 49.
10. United Nations Information Service, *Yearbook of the United Nations* (New York, 1950), pp. 224–29.
11. William R. Frye, *A UN Peace Force* (London, 1957), pp. 181–90.
12. U.S. Department of State, *United States Participation in the United Nations: 1951*, Publication 4583 (Washington, D.C., 1952), pp. 273–88.
13. Michael Carver, *War Since 1945* (New York, 1981), pp. 16–19, 112.
14. H. Norman Schwarzkopf, *It Doesn't Take a Hero* (London, 1992), pp. 401–3.
15. U.S. Department of Defense, *The Conduct of the Persian Gulf War* (Washington, D.C., 1992), pp. 109–14.
16. Ibid., p. 218.
17. General Julian Thompson quoted in James Gow, ed., *Iraq, the Gulf Conflict and the World Community* (London, 1993), p. 150.
18. Trygve Lie, *In the Cause of Peace* (New York, 1954), p. 334.
19. C. Kenneth Allard, *Command, Control, and the Common Defense* (New Haven, Conn., 1990), p. 29.
20. Evan Luard, *A History of the United Nations,* vol. 1 (London, 1982), p. 244.

21. "Military Situation in the Far East," Hearings before the Committee on Armed Services and the Committee on Foreign Relations of the U.S. Senate, 82d Congress, 1st Session (1951), pp. 1937, 10.

22. UN General Assembly Official Record, 6th Session, Supplement No. 13, *Report of the Collective Measures Committee, 1951*, p. 46.

23. Robert O'Neill, "Problems of Command in Limited Warfare: Thoughts from Korea and Vietnam," in Lawrence Freedman, Richard Hayes, and Robert O'Neill, eds., *War, Strategy, and International Politics* (Oxford, 1992), p. 270.

24. Foreign Broadcast Information Service, Near East–South Asia edition, Washington, D.C., U.S. State Department, 14 January 1991, pp. 35–36.

25. Jeffrey McCausland, *The Gulf Conflict: A Military Analysis*, Adelphi Paper 282, (London, 1993), p. 56, and Schwarzkopf, *It Doesn't Take a Hero*, p. 373.

26. Dean Acheson speech to the American Newspaper Guild, 29 June 1950, quoted in Evan Luard, *A History of the United Nations* (London, 1982), p. 245.

27. Douglas A. MacArthur, *Reminiscences* (New York, 1964), pp. 346–51.

28. NSC 81/1, in *The Foreign Relations of the United States* vol. 7, pp. 712–16.

29. General Assembly Resolution 376(V), 7 October 1950.

30. For a complete account of the frenetic U.S. campaign to gain support for offensive action, see Freedman and Karsh, *The Gulf Conflict*, pp. 228–34.

31. Quoted in James Gow, ed., *Iraq, the Gulf Conflict and the World Community* (London, 1993), p. 6.

32. O'Neill, "Problems of Command in Limited Warfare," p. 266.

Conclusions

1. Innis Claude, *Swords into Plowshares: The Problems and Process of International Organization*, 4th ed. (New York, 1971), p. 14.

2. Ronald Steel, *Temptations of a Superpower* (Cambridge, Mass., 1995), p. 86.

3. Paul Kennedy and Bruce Russett, "Reforming the United Nations," *Foreign Affairs*, vol. 74, no. 5, September–October 1995, pp. 57, 59.

4. Andrei Raevsky, "Peacekeeping Operations: Problems of Command and Control," in Ramesh Thakur and Carlyle Thayer, eds., *A Crisis of Expectations: UN Peacekeeping in the 1990s* (Boulder, Colo., 1995), p. 200.

5. Adam Roberts, "The United Nations and International Security," *Survival*, vol. 35, no. 2, Summer 1993, p. 15.

6. Abba Eban, "The UN Idea Revisited," *Foreign Affairs* vol. 74, no. 5, September–October 1995, p. 48.

7. William J. Durch, ed., *The Evolution of UN Peacekeeping: Case Studies and Comparative Analysis* (New York, 1993), p. 28.

8. David Hendrickson, "The Ethics of Collective Security," *Ethics and International Affairs*, vol. 3, 1993, pp. 2–3.

9. Thomas G. Weiss, "New Challenges for UN Military Operations: Implementing an Agenda for Peace," *The Washington Quarterly*, vol. 16, no. 1, Winter 1993, pp. 51, 63, discussing Boutros Boutros-Ghali, *An Agenda for Peace: Preventive Diplomacy, Peacemaking and Peace-keeping* (New York, 1992).

10. Thomas G. Weiss, "The United Nations at Fifty: Recent Lessons," *Current History*, May 1995, p. 225.

11. Quoted in Shashi Tharoor, "Should UN Peacekeeping Go back to Basics?," *Survival*, vol. 37, no. 4, Winter 1995–1996, p. 57; Secretary-General's speech given to Twenty-Fifth Vienna Seminar, 2 March 1995 (UN Information Service Press Release 1310), p. 4.

12. Weiss, "The United Nations at Fifty," p. 224.

13. Harvey Sicherman, "The Revenge of Geopolitics," *Orbis: A Journal of World Affairs*, vol. 41, no. 1, Winter 1997, p. 11.

14. British Broadcasting Corporation Television Special, *A Soldier's Peace*, 1994.

15. Tharoor, "Should UN Peacekeeping Go back to Basics?," p. 59.

16. Steel, *Temptations of a Superpower*, p. 135.

17. John Mearsheimer, "The False Promise of International Institutions," *International Security*, 19, no. 3 (Winter 1994–1995), p. 32.

18. Weiss, "New Challenges for UN Military Operations," p. 51.

19. Raevsky, "Peacekeeping Operations," p. 194.

20. Peacekeeper J. D. Murray wrote that the "UN's non-military considerations can transform a peacekeeping force into one incapable of effecting its commander's strategy" ("Military Aspects of Peacekeeping: Problems and Recommendations," International Peace Academy, 1976).

21. Charles Lipson, "Is the Future of Collective Security Like the Past?," in George Downs, ed., *Collective Security beyond the Cold War* (Ann Arbor, Mich., 1994), p. 114.

22. Thakur, "Peacekeeping in the New World Disorder," in Thakur and Thayer, *A Crisis of Expectations*, p. 12.

23. Emmanuel Erskine, *Mission with UNIFIL* (London, 1989), p. 205.

24. John Mackinlay, *The Peacekeepers: An Assessment of Peacekeeping Operations at the Arab–Israel Interface* (London, 1989), p. 203.

25. Adam Roberts, "From San Francisco to Sarajevo: The UN and the Use of Force," *Survival* vol. 37, no. 4, Winter 1995–1996, p. 24.

26. Giandomenico Picco, "The UN and the Use of Force," October 1994, pp. 15–18.
27. Kennedy and Russett, "Reforming the United Nations," p. 57.
28. David C. Hendrickson, "The Ethics of Collective Security," *Ethics and International Affairs 7*, 1993, pp. 1–15, and Ernest W. Lefever, "Reining in the UN," *Foreign Affairs*, vol. 72, no. 3, Summer 1993, pp. 17–20.
29. Weiss, "The United Nations at Fifty," p. 226.
30. Jim Whitman and Ian Bartholomew in Donald Daniel and C. F. Hayes, *Beyond Traditional Peacekeeping* (New York, 1995), p. 170.
31. Saadia Touval, "Why the UN Fails," *Foreign Affairs*, vol. 73, no. 5, September–October 1994, p. 45.
32. United States Institute of Peace, "Restoring Hope: The Real Lessons of Somalia for the Future of Intervention," USIP Press, 1995, p. 19.
33. Mats Berdal, "The UN at Fifty: Its Role in Global Security," Ditchley Conference Report No. D94/15, Ditchley Park, England, 1994.
34. Roberts, "From San Francisco to Sarajevo," p. 26.

Epilogue

1. Kennedy and Russett, *Foreign Affairs*, ibid, p. 57.
2. Shashi Tharoor, "Should UN Peacekeeping Go Back to Basics?" *Survival*, vol. 37, no. 5, Winter 1995–96, p. 53.
3. UN Department of Public Information, "The United Nations and the Situation in the Former Yugoslavia," Updates 1992–97.
4. S/1994/300, Report of the Secretary-General to the Security Council, 16 March 1994.
5. BBC special, "Soldiers for Peace" broadcast January 1995.
6. Bill Clinton address to the UN General Assembly, September 1993.
7. Hirsch and Oakley, *Somalia and Operation Restore Hope*, op. cit. p. 45.
8. Chester Crocker in ibid, p. xi and p. 111.
9. Madeleine K. Albright, "Yes, There Is a Reason to be in Somalia, *The New York Times*, August 10, 1993, p. A19.
10. T. Frank Crigler, *Joint Force Quarterly*, op. cit. p. 66.
11. Freeman, Lambert, and Mims, *Military Review*, op. cit. p. 71.
12. Kenneth Allard, *Somalia Operations,* op. cit. p. 60.
13. See especially "What You Need to Know About the United Nations," a speech by Albright in *Vital Speeches of the Day*, 1 June 1993.
14. Testimony of Ambassador Madeleine K. Albright before the U.S. Senate Committee on Foreign Relations, 20 October 1993.
15. Harvey Sicherman, *Orbis*, op. cit. p. 11.
16. Thomas G. Weiss, *The Washington Quarterly*, op. cit. pp. 51 and 63.
17. Tharoor, *Survival*, op. cit. p. 59.

Bibliography

Books and Monographs

General

Abi-Saab, Georges. *The United Nations Operations in the Congo, 1960–1964.* Oxford: Oxford University Press, 1978.

Acheson, Dean. *Present at the Creation: My Years in the State Department.* New York: Norton, 1969.

Alberts, David S., and Richard Hayes. *Command Arrangements for Peace Operations.* Washington, D.C.: National Defense University Press, 1995.

Allard, C. Kenneth. *Command, Control, and the Common Defense.* New Haven, Conn.: Yale University Press, 1990.

———. *Somalia Operations: Lessons Learned.* Washington, D.C.: National Defense University Press, 1995.

Baehr, Peter, and Leon Gordenker. *The United Nations in the 1990's.* New York: St. Martin's Press, 1992.

Bailey, Sydney. *How Wars End: The United Nations and the Termination of Armed Conflicts, 1946–1964.* Oxford: Clarendon Press, 1982.

———. *The United Nations.* London: Pall Mall Press, 1963.

Berdal, Mats R. *Whither UN Peacekeeping?* Adelphi Paper 281. International Institute of Strategic Studies. London: Brassey's, 1993.

Bloomfield, Lincoln P., ed. *International Military Forces: The Question of Peacekeeping in an Armed and Disarming World.* Boston: Little, Brown, 1964.

Bowett, D. W. *United Nations Forces: A Legal Study of United Nation Practice.* London: Stevens and Sons, 1964.

Boyd, James M. *United Nations Peace-Keeping: A Military and Political Appraisal.* London: Praeger, 1971.

Bull, Hedley. *Intervention in World Politics*. Oxford: Clarendon Press, 1984.

Bullock, Harold E. *Peace by Committee: Command and Control Issues in Multinational Peace Enforcement Operations*. Maxwell Air Force Base, Ala.: Air University Press, 1995.

Burns, A. L., and N. Heathcote. *Peace-Keeping by UN Forces*. London: Praeger, 1963.

Caesse, Antonio, ed. *United Nations Peacekeeping: Legal Essays*. Alphen aan den Rijn, Netherlands: Sijthoff and Noordhoff, 1978.

Claude, Inis. *Swords into Plowshares: The Problems and Progress of International Organization*, 4th ed. New York: Random House, 1971.

Clements, Kevin, and Robin Ward, eds. *Building International Community: Cooperating for Peace Case Studies*. St. Leonards, Australia: Allen and Unwin, 1994.

Connaughton, R. M. *Peacekeeping and Military Intervention*. Camberley, UK: The Strategic and Combat Studies Institute, 1992.

———. *Swords and Ploughshares: Coalition Operations, the Nature of Future Conflict and the United Nations*. Camberley, UK: The Strategic and Combat Studies Institute, 1993.

Daniel, Donald C. F., and Bradd C. Hayes, eds. *Beyond Traditional Peacekeeping*. New York: St. Martin's Press, 1995.

Daniel, Donald C. F., and Bradd C. Hayes. *Securing Observance of UN Mandates through the Employment of Military Forces*. Newport, R.I.: U.S. Naval War College, 1995.

Diehl, Paul F. *International Peacekeeping*. London: The Johns Hopkins University Press, 1993.

Dobbie, Charles. *A Concept for Post–Cold War Peacekeeping*. Oslo: Norwegian Institute for Defense Studies, 1994.

Doll, William, and Steven Metz. *The US Army and Multinational Peace Operations: Problems and Solutions*. Carlisle, Penn.: Strategic Studies Institute U.S. Army War College, 1993.

Durch, William J., ed. *The Evolution of UN Peacekeeping: Case Studies and Comparative Analysis*. New York: St. Martin's Press, 1993.

Dworken, Jonathan T. *Operation Restore Hope: Preparing and Planning the Transition to UN Operations*. Center for Naval Analyses Report CRM 93-14B. Alexandria, Va.: Center for Naval Analyses, 1994.

Eichelberger, Clark M. *UN: The First Twenty Years*. New York: Harper and Row, 1965.

Erskine, Emmanuel A. *Mission with UNIFIL*. London: Hurst and Company, 1989.

Evans, Gareth. *Cooperating for Peace: The Global Agenda for the 1990's and Beyond*. St. Leonards, Australia: Allen and Unwin, 1993.

Fabian, Larry L. *Soldiers without Enemies: Preparing the United Nations for Peacekeeping.* Washington, D.C.: The Brookings Institution, 1971.

Fetherston, A. B. *Towards a Theory of United Nations Peacekeeping.* London: St. Martin's Press, 1994.

Findlay, Trevor. *Cambodia: The Legacy and Lessons of UNTAC.* Oxford: Oxford University Press, 1995.

Finkelstein, L., ed. *Politics and the United Nations System.* Durham, N.C.: Duke University Press, 1988.

Freedman, Lawrence, Richard Hayes, and Robert O'Neill, eds. *War, Strategy, and International Politics.* Oxford: Clarendon Press, 1992.

Frye, William R. *A United Nations Peace Force.* London: Stevens and Sons, 1957.

Gladwyn, Baron Hubert Miles Gladwyn Jebb. *The Memoirs of Lord Gladwyn.* London: Weidenfeld and Nicolson, 1972.

Goodrich, Leland M., and Anne P. Simons. *The United Nations and the Maintenance of International Peace and Security.* Washington, D.C.: The Brookings Institution, 1955.

Gordenker, Leon. *The UN Secretary-General and the Maintenance of Peace.* New York: Columbia University Press, 1967.

———. *The United Nations in the 1990's.* New York: St. Martin's Press, 1992.

Gordenker, Leon, and Thomas Weiss, eds. *Soldiers, Peacekeepers, and Disasters.* New York: St. Martin's Press, 1991.

Haass, Richard N. *Intervention: The Use of American Military Force in the Post–Cold War World.* Washington, D.C.: Carnegie Endowment, 1994.

Harbottle, Michael. *The Blue Berets.* London: Leo Cooper, 1971.

Higgins, Rosalyn. *United Nations Peacekeeping, 1946–1967, Documents and Commentary,* vols. 1–4. London: Oxford University Press, 1970.

Higgins, Rosalyn, and Michael Harbottle. *United Nations Peacekeeping: Past Lessons and Future Prospects.* London: The David Davies Memorial Institute of International Studies, 1971.

Hirsch, John L., and Robert B. Oakley. *Somalia and Operation Restore Hope: Reflections on Peacemaking and Peacekeeping.* Washington, D.C.: United States Institute of Peace Press, 1995.

International Committee of the Red Cross. *Report on a Symposium on Humanitarian Action and Peacekeeping Operations.* Geneva: ICRC, 1994.

International Peace Academy. *Peacekeepers Handbook.* Elmsford, N.Y.: Pergamon, 1984.

James, Alan. *Peacekeeping in International Politics.* London: Macmillan, 1990.

———. *The Politics of Peacekeeping.* New York: Praeger, 1969.

Jockel, Joseph T. *Canada and International Peacekeeping*. Washington, D.C.: Center for Strategic and International Studies, 1994.

Kissinger, Henry. *Diplomacy*. New York: Simon & Schuster, 1994.

Kochavi, Doron. *The United Nations Peacekeeping Operations in the Arab–Israeli Conflict, 1973–1979*. Doctoral Dissertation, Claremont Graduate School, Calif., 1980.

Laurenti, Jeffrey. *The Common Defense: Peace and Security in a Changing World*. New York: United Nations Association of the USA, 1992.

Laurenti, Jeffrey, et al., *Partners for Peace: Strengthening Collective Security for the 21st Century*. New York: United Nations Association of the USA, 1992.

Lewis, W. H., ed. *Military Implications of United Nations Peacekeeping Operations*. Washington, D.C.: National Defense University Press, 1993.

———. *Peacekeeping: The Way Ahead?* Washington, D.C.: National Defense University Press, 1993.

Lie, Trygve. *In the Cause of Peace*. New York: Macmillan, 1954.

Liu, F. T. *United Nations Peacekeeping: Management and Operations*. Occasional Paper 4. New York: International Peace Academy, 1990.

Liu, F. T. *United Nations Peacekeeping and the Non-use of force*. New York: International Peace Academy, 1992.

Luard, Evans. *The United Nations: How It Works and What It Does*. London: Macmillan, 1975.

Luard, Evans. *A History of the United Nations*, vol. 1. London: Macmillan, 1982.

Mackinlay, John. *The Peacekeepers: An Assessment of Peacekeeping Operations at the Arab–Israel Interface*. London: Unwin Hyman, 1989.

Mackinlay, John, and Jarat Chopra. *A Draft Concept of Second Generation Multinational Operations, 1993*. Thomas J. Watson Jr. Institute for International Studies. Providence, R.I.: Brown University, 1993.

Maney, Patrick J. *The Roosevelt Presence: A Biography of Franklin Delano Roosevelt*. New York: Twayne Publishers, 1992.

Martin, John Bartlow. *Adlai Stevenson of Illinois: The Life of Adlai E. Stevenson*. Garden City, N.Y.: Doubleday, 1976.

Metz, Steven. *The Future of the United Nations: Implications for Peace Operations*. Carlisle, Penn.: Strategic Studies Institute, U.S. Army War College, 1993.

Mokhtari, Fariborz L., ed. *Peacemaking, Peacekeeping and Coalition Warfare: The Future Role of the United Nations*. Washington, D.C.: National Defense University Press, 1994.

Moskos, Charles. *Peace Soldiers: The Sociology of a United Nations Military Force*. Chicago: University of Chicago Press, 1976.

Murphy, John F. *The United Nations and the Control of International Violence*. Manchester: Manchester University Press, 1983.

Naidu, M. V. *Collective Security and the United Nations*. London: Macmillan, 1974.

Norton, Augustus, and Thomas G. Weiss. *UN Peacekeepers: Soldiers with a Difference*. Paper #292. New York: Foreign Policy Association, 1990.

Parsons, Anthony. *From Cold War to Hot Peace: UN Interventions, 1947–1994*. London: Michael Joseph, 1995.

Pelcovits, Nathan. *Peacekeeping on the Arab–Israeli Fronts: Lessons from the Sinai and Lebanon*. Boulder, Colo.: Westview, 1984.

Quinn, Dennis J., ed. *Peace Support Operations and the U.S. Military*. Washington, D.C.: National Defense University Press, 1994.

Reid, Escott. *On Duty: A Canadian at the Making of the United Nations, 1945–1946*. Kent, Ohio: Kent State University Press, 1983.

Renner, Michael. *Critical Juncture: The Future of Peacekeeping*. Worldwatch Paper 114. Washington, D.C.: Worldwatch Institute, 1993.

Rikhye, Indar J. *The Theory and Practice of International Peacekeeping*. London: Hurst and Company, 1984.

———. *Military Advisor to the Secretary-General: UN Peacekeeping and the Congo Crisis*. New York: St. Martin's Press, 1992.

———. *Strengthening UN Peacekeeping—New Challenges and Proposals, United States Institute of Peace*. Washington, D.C.: 1992.

Rikhye, Indar J., Michael Harbottle, and Bjorn Egge. *The Thin Blue Line: International Peacekeeping and Its Future*. New Haven, Conn.: Yale University Press, 1974.

Rikhye, Indar J., and Kjell Skjeslbaek, eds. *The United Nations and Peacekeeping: Results, Limitations, and Prospects—The Lessons of 40 Years of Experience*. New York: St. Martin's Press, 1991.

Roberts, Adam. *The Crisis in Peacekeeping*. Oslo: Norwegian Institute for Defence Studies, 1994.

Roberts, Adam, and Benedict Kingsbury, eds. *United Nations, Divided World*. 2nd ed. Oxford: Clarendon Press, 1993.

Rosen, Samuel I. *The Public Papers and Addresses of Franklin D. Roosevelt. Vol 13: Victory and the Threshold of Peace, 1944–1945*. New York: Russell & Russell, 1969.

Rostow, Eugene V. *Should Article 43 of the United Nations Charter Be Raised from the Dead?* Washington, D.C.: National Defense University Press, 1993.

Seyersted, Finn. *United Nations Forces: In the Law of Peace and War*. Leiden, Netherlands: AW Sijthoff, 1966.

Skogmo, Bjorn. *UNIFIL, International Peacekeeping in Lebanon, 1978–1988*. London: Lynne Rienner, 1989.

Smith, Hugh, ed. *Peacekeeping: Challenges for the Future.* Canberra: Australian Defence Studies Centre, 1993.

———. *International Peacekeeping: Building on the Cambodian Experience.* Canberra: Australian Defense Studies Centre, 1994.

Smith, Richard. *The Requirement for the United Nations to Develop an Internationally Recognized Doctrine for the Use of Force in Intra-State Conflict.* Camberley: The Strategic and Combat Studies Institute, 1994.

Snow, Donald M. *Peacekeeping, Peacemaking, and Peace-enforcement: The US Role in the New International Order.* Carlisle Barracks, Penn.: Strategic Studies Institute, U.S. Army War College 1993.

Thakur, Ramesh. *International Peacekeeping in Lebanon: United Nations Authority and Multinational Force.* Boulder, Colo.: Westview, 1987.

Thakur, Ramesh, and Carlyle Thayer, eds. *A Crisis of Expectations: UN Peacekeeping in the 1990's.* Boulder, Colo.: Westview, 1995.

Urquhart, Brian. *A Life in Peace and War.* London: Weidenfeld and Nicolson, 1987.

Vandenberg, Arthur H., Jr. *The Private Papers of Senator Vandenberg.* Boston: Houghton Mifflin, 1952.

Wainhouse, David. *International Peacekeeping at the Crossroads: National Support Experience and Prospects.* Baltimore, Md.: Johns Hopkins University Press, 1973.

Weiss, Thomas G., ed. *Collective Security in a Changing World.* Boulder, Colo.: Lynne Rienner, 1993.

Wiseman, Henry, ed. *Peacekeeping: Appraisals and Proposals.* New York: Pergamon, 1983.

The Korean Conflict

Farrar-Hockley, Anthony. *The British Part in the Korean War: A Distant Obligation,* vol. 1; *An Honourable Discharge,* vol. 2. London: Her Majesty's Stationery Office, 1990, 1994.

Goodrich, Leland M. *Korea: A Study of US Policy in the United Nations.* New York: The Council on Foreign Relations, 1956.

Gordenker, Leon. *The United Nations and the Peaceful Unification of Korea: The Politics of Field Operations, 1947–1950.* The Hague: Martinus Nijhoff, 1959.

Leckie, Robert. *The Korean War.* London: Barrie and Rockliff with Pall Mall Press, 1962.

MacArthur, Douglas A. *Reminiscences.* New York: McGraw-Hill, 1964.

Matray, James I. *Historical Dictionary of the Korean War.* London: Greenwood, 1991.

Ministry of National Defense, Republic of Korea. *The History of the United Nations Forces in the Korean War,* 6 vols. Seoul: War History Compilation Commission, 1975.

O'Neill, Robert. "Problems of Command in Limited Warfare: Thoughts from Korea and Vietnam," in Lawrence Freedman, Richard Hayes, and Robert O'Neill, eds. *War, Strategy, and International Politics*. Oxford: Clarendon Press, 1992.

Yoo, Tae-Ho. *The Korean War and the United Nations*. Louvain, Belgium: Librairie Desbarax, 1965.

The Gulf Conflict

Dannreuther, Roland. *The Gulf Conflict: A Political and Strategic Analysis*. Adelphi Paper 264. International Institute for Strategic Studies. London: Brassey's, 1992.

Gow, James, ed. *Iraq, the Gulf Conflict and the World Community*. London: Brassey's, 1993.

Freedman, Lawrence, and Efraim Karsh. *The Gulf Conflict, 1990–1991*. London: Faber and Faber, 1993.

Hiro, Dilip. *Desert Shield to Desert Storm: The Second Gulf War*. London: Harper Collins, 1992.

Matthews, Ken. *The Gulf Conflict and International Relations*. London: Routledge Press, 1993.

Mazarr, M. J., Snider, D. M., and J. A. Blackwell. *Desert Storm: The Gulf War and What We Learned*. Oxford: Westview, 1993.

McCausland, Jeffrey. *The Gulf Conflict: A Military Analysis*. Adelphi Paper 282. International Institute for Strategic Studies. London: Brassey's, 1993.

Maurer, Martha. *Coalition Command and Control*. Washington, D.C.: National Defense University Press, 1994.

Pimlott, J., and S. Badsey, eds. *The Gulf War Assessed*. London: Arms and Armour Press, 1992.

Schwarzkopf, Norman H. *The Autobiography: It Doesn't Take a Hero*. London: Bantam Press, 1992.

Sessions, Sterling D., and Carl R. Jones. *Interoperability: A Desert Storm Case Study*. Washington, D.C.: National Defense University Press, 1993.

U.S. News and World Report. *Triumph without Victory: The Unreported History of the Persian Gulf War*. New York: Random House, 1992.

Watson, Bruce W., ed. *Military Lessons of the Gulf War*. London: Greenhill Books, 1991.

UN Documents

Boutros-Ghali, Boutros. *An Agenda for Peace: Preventive Diplomacy, Peacemaking and Peace-keeping*. New York: United Nations, 1992.

———. *Report on the Work of the Organization from the 47th–48th Session of the General Assembly*. New York: United Nations, 1993.

———. *Supplement to "An Agenda for Peace": Position Paper of the Secretary-General on the Occasion of the Fiftieth Anniversary of the United Nations.* New York: United Nations, 3 January 1995.

United Nations Department of Public Information. *The Blue Helmets: A Review of United Nations Peace-keeping,* 2nd ed. New York: United Nations, 1990.

———. *The Blue Helmets: A Review of United Nations Peace-keeping.* 3d ed. New York: United Nations, 1996.

———. *Charter of the United Nations and Statute of the International Court of Justice.* New York: United Nations, 1991.

———. *United Nations Peace-keeping* (Update). New York: United Nations, 1993.

———. *United Nations Peace-keeping* (Update). New York: United Nations, May 1994.

———. *United Nations Peace-keeping* (Update). New York: United Nations, May 1996.

———. *The United Nations and the Situation in the Former Yugoslavia.* New York: United Nations, 15 March 1994.

———. *The United Nations and the Situation in Somalia.* New York: United Nations, 1 May 1994.

Mission Documents from the United Nations Security Council The United Nations Iran–Iraq Military Observer Group (UNIIMOG), 1988–1991; The United Nations Interim Force in Lebanon (UNIFIL), 1978–1995; The United Nations Operation in Somalia (UNOSOM I & II), 1992–1995; and various other documents.

National Government Documents

British Army. *British Army Field Manual. vol. 5: Operations Other than War, part 2, Wider Peacekeeping.* London, Her Majesty's Stationery Office, 1994.

Office of the President of the United States. *The Clinton Administration's Policy on Reforming Multilateral Peace Operations* (PDD-25). Washington, D.C.: Office of the President, May 1994.

United States Armed Forces Staff College. *The Joint Staff Officer's Guide.* Norfolk, Va., 1993.

United States Army-Air Force Center for Low Intensity Conflict. *Peacekeeping Tactics, Techniques, and Procedures.* Langley Air Force Base, Va., 1989.

United States Army Center for Lessons Learned. *U.S. Army Operations in Support of UNOSOM II.* Ft. Leavenworth, Kansas, 1994.

United States Army Command and General Staff College. *Military Operations in Low Intensity Conflict.* Army Correspondence Course Program IS 7005. Ft. Leavenworth, Kansas, 1991.

United States Army Headquarters. *Field Manual 100-5: Operations.* Washington, D.C., June 1993.

———. *Field Manual 100-23: Peace Operations.* Washington, D.C., December 1994.

United States Army War College. *Campaign Planning.* Strategic Studies Institute. Carlisle Barracks, Penn., 1988.

United States Congressional Research Service. *The Cambodian Peacekeeping Operation: Background, Prospects, and U.S. Policy Concerns.* Washington, D.C.: The Library of Congress, 3 March 1993.

———. *Peacekeeping in Future U.S. Foreign Policy.* Washington, D.C.: The Library of Congress, 10 May 1994.

———. *Peacekeeping: Issues of U.S. Military Involvement.* Washington, D.C.: The Library of Congress, 25 July 1994.

———. *Peacekeeping and U.S. Foreign Policy: Implementing* (PDD-25). Washington, D.C.: The Library of Congress, 5 August 1994.

———. *United Nations Peacekeeping: Historical Overview and Current Issues.* Washington, D.C.: The Library of Congress, 31 January 1990.

———. *United Nations Peacekeeping: Issues for Congress.* Washington, D.C.: The Library of Congress, 3 August 1994.

———. *United Nations Peacekeeping Operations, 1988–1993: Background Information.* Washington, D.C.: The Library of Congress, 28 February 1994.

———. *Yugoslavia: The United Nations Protection Force (UNPROFOR) and Other Multilateral Missions.* Washington, D.C.: The Library of Congress, 19 April 1993.

United States General Accounting Office. *Humanitarian Intervention: Effectiveness of UN Operations in Bosnia.* Washington, D.C.: U.S. Government Printing Office, April 1994.

———. *Peace Operations: Information on U.S. and UN Activities.* Washington, D.C.: U.S. Government Printing Office, February 1995.

———. *United Nations: How Assessed Contributions for Peacekeeping Operations Are Calculated.* Washington, D.C.: U.S. Government Printing Office, August 1994.

———. *UN Peacekeeping: Lessons Learned in Managing Recent Missions.* Washington, D.C.: U.S. Government Printing Office, December 1993.

———. *UN Peacekeeping: Observations on Mandates and Operational Capability.* Washington, D.C.: U.S. Government Printing Office, June 1993.

———. *U.S. Participation in Peacekeeping Operations.* Washington, D.C.: U.S. Government Printing Office, September 1992.

Articles

Abizaid, John P. "Lessons for Peacekeepers." *Military Review* 58 (March 1993): 11–19.

Allen, William W., Antoinette D. Johnson, and John T. Nelson. "Peacekeeping and Peace Enforcement Operations." *Military Review* 58 (October 1993): 53–61.

Arnold, S. L. "Somalia: An Operation Other than War." *Military Review* (December 1993): 26–35.

Arnold, S. L. "Somalia and Operations Other than War." *Parameters* (Winter 1993–1994): 4–58.

Bailey, Sydney D. "The United Nations and the Termination of Armed Conflict, 1946–64." *International Affairs* (Summer 1982): 465–75.

Bair, Andrew. "What Happened in Yugoslavia? Lessons for Future Peacekeepers." *European Security* 3 (Summer 1994): 340–49.

Baker, James H. "Policy Challenges of UN Peace Operations." *Parameters* (Spring 1994): 13–26.

Berdal, Mats. "Fateful Encounter: US and Peacekeeping." *Survival* 36 (Spring 1994): 30–50.

———. "Peacekeeping in Europe." In *European Security after the Cold War.* Adelphi Paper 284. London: International Institute of Strategic Studies, January 1994.

Betts, Richard K. "The Delusion of Impartial Intervention." *Foreign Affairs* 73 (November–December 1994): 20–33.

Boutros-Ghali, Boutros. "An Agenda for Peace: One Year Later." *Orbis* (Summer 1993): 323–32.

———. "Empowering the United Nations." *Foreign Affairs* 72 (Winter–Spring 1992–1993): 89–102.

Brady, Christopher, and Sam Daws. "UN Operations: The Political–Military Interface." *International Peacekeeping* 1 (Spring 1994): 59–79.

Childers, Erskine. "Assuming Our Responsibilities: The United Nations in a World of Conflict." *Oxford International Review* (Spring 1995): 9–17.

Cohen, Eliot A. "The Mystique of U.S. Air Power." *Foreign Affairs* 73 (January–February 1994): 15–27.

Crigler, T. Frank. "A Peace Enforcement Dilemma." *Joint Forces Quarterly* (Autumn 1993): 64–70.

Crocker, Chester A. "The Lessons of Somalia." *Foreign Affairs* 74 (May–June 1995): 2–8.

Diehl, Paul F. "Institutional Alternatives to Traditional U.N. Peacekeeping: An Assessment of Regional and Multinational Options." *Armed Forces and Society* 19, no. 2 (Winter 1993): 209–30.

Dixon, Anne M. "The Whats and Whys of Coalitions." *Joint Forces Quarterly* (Winter 1993–1994): 26–28.

Dobbie, Charles. "A Concept for Post–Cold War Peacekeeping." *Survival* 36 (Autumn 1994): 121–48.

Durch, William J. "Building on Sand, UN Peacekeeping in the Western Sahara." *International Security* 14, no. 4 (Spring 1993): 151–71.

Eban, Abba. "The UN Idea Revisited." *Foreign Affairs* 74 (September–October 1995): 44–55.

The Economist Staff. "United Nations Peacekeeping: Trotting to the Rescue." *The Economist* (25 June 1994): 19–22.

Freedman, Lawrence. "Humanitarian War, The New United Nations and Peacekeeping." *International Affairs* 68, no. 2 (June 1993): 425–27.

Freeman, W. D., R. B. Lambert, and J. D. Mims. "Operation Restore Hope: A U.S. CENTCOM Perspective." *Military Review* (September 1993): 61–72.

Gerlach, Jeffrey R. "A UN Army for the New World Order?" *Orbis* (Summer 1993): 223–36.

Goulding, Marrack. "The Evolution of United Nations Peacekeeping." *International Affairs* 69, no. 3 (June 1993): 451–64.

Greenberg, Keith Elliot. "The Essential Art of Empathy." *MHQ, The Quarterly Journal of Military History* (Autumn 1992): 64–69.

Grove, Eric. "UN Armed Forces and the Military Staff Committee: A Look Back." *International Security* 14, no. 4 (Spring 1993): 172–92.

Hagglund, Gustav. "Peace-keeping in a modern war zone." *Survival* 32 (May–June 1990): 233–40.

Hall, Brian. "Blue Helmets, Empty Guns." *The New York Times Magazine* (2 January 1994): 19–43.

Hendrickson, David C. "The Ethics of Collective Security." *Ethics and International Affairs* 7 (1993): 1–15.

Higgins, Rosalyn. "The New United Nations and Former Yugoslavia." *International Affairs* 69, no. 3 (June 1993): 465–83.

Hoar, Joseph P. "Somalia: A CINC's Perspective." *Joint Forces Quarterly* (Autumn 1993): 56–63.

Hoffman, Carl W. "The UN Secretary-General's Peacekeeping Proposals." In *Essays on Strategy*, vol. XI. Washington, D.C.: National Defense University Press, 1994.

Holst, Johan Jorgen. "Enhancing peace-keeping operations." *Survival* 32 (May–June 1990): 264–75.

Huntington, Samuel P. "New Contingencies, Old Roles." *Joint Forces Quarterly* (Autumn 1993): 38–43.

James, Alan. "Peacekeeping in the post–Cold War Era." *International Journal* (Spring 1995): 241–65.

Kennedy, Paul, and Bruce Russett. "Reforming the United Nations." *Foreign Affairs* 74 (September–October 1995): 56–67.

Krepon, Michael, and Jeffrey P. Tracey. "Open Skies and UN peace-keeping." *Survival* 32 (May–June 1990): 251–63.

Lefever, Ernest W. "Reining In the U.N." *Foreign Affairs* 72, no. 3 (Summer 1993): 17–20.

Lewis, Paul. "A Short History of United Nations Peacekeeping." *MHQ, The Quarterly Journal of Military History* (Autumn 1992): 33–47.

Luck, Edward C., and Toby Trister Gati. "Whose Collective Security?" *The Washington Quarterly* (Spring 1992): 43–56.

Mackenzie, Lewis. "Military Realities of UN Peacekeeping Operations." *RUSI Journal* (February 1993): 21–24.

Mackinlay, John. "Defining a Role beyond Peacekeeping." In W. H. Lewis, ed., *Military Implications of United Nations Peacekeeping Operations.* Washington, D.C.: National Defense University Press, 1993, pp. 32–38.

———. "Improving Multifunctional Forces." *Survival* 36 (Autumn 1994): 149–73.

———. "Powerful Peace-keepers." *Survival* 32 (May–June 1990): 241–50.

Mackinlay, John, and Jarat Chopra. "Second Generation Multinational Operations." *The Washington Quarterly* (Summer 1992): 113–31.

Martin, Laurence. "Peacekeeping as a Growth Industry." *The National Interest* (Summer 1993): 3–11.

Mearsheimer, John. "The False Promise of International Institutions." *International Security* 19, no. 3 (Winter 1994–1995): 5–49.

Morillon, Philippe. "UN Operations in Bosnia: Lessons and Realities." *RUSI Journal* (December 1993): 31–35.

Morrison, David C. "Make Peace—or Else!" *The National Journal* no. 40 (3 October 1992): 2250–54.

Morrow, Lance. "An Interview: The Man in the Middle." *MHQ, The Quarterly Journal of Military History* (Autumn 1992): 48–51.

Norton, Augustus, and Thomas G. Weiss. "Superpowers and peace-keepers." *Survival* 32 (May–June 1990): 212–20.

Oakley, Robert. "An Envoy's Perspective." *Joint Forces Quarterly* (Autumn 1993): 44–55.

Oakley, Robert, and McGeorge Bundy. "A UN Volunteer Force—The Prospects." *The New York Review of Books* (15 July 1993): 52–56.

Paschall, Rod. "The Impartial Buffer." *MHQ, The Quarterly Journal of Military History* (Autumn 1992): 52–53.

Picco, Giandomenico. "The UN and the Use of Force." *Foreign Affairs* (September–October 1994): 15–18.

Puchala, Donald J. "Outsiders, Insiders, and UN Reform." *The Washington Quarterly* 17, no. 4 (Autumn 1994): 161–73.

Ramsbotham, David. "UN Operations: The Art of the Possible." *RUSI Journal* (December 1993): 25–30.

Roberts, Adam. "The Crisis in UN Peacekeeping." *Survival* 36 (Autumn 1994): 93–120.

———. "From San Francisco to Sarajevo: The UN and the Use of Force." *Survival* 37 (Winter 1995–1996): 7–28.

———. "Humanitarian War: Military Intervention and Human Rights." *International Affairs* 69, no. 3 (June 1993): 429–49.

———. "Presiding over Anarchy." *Oxford Today* (Michaelmas Term 1993): 6–8.

———. "The United Nations and International Security." *Survival* 35 (Summer 1993): 3–30.

Roberts, Adam, and Benedict Kingsbury. "Roles of the United Nations after the Cold War." *Oxford International Review* (Spring 1995): 4–8.

Rostow, Eugene. "Is UN Peacekeeping a Growth Industry?" *Joint Forces Quarterly* (Spring 1994): 100–105.

Ruggie, John G. "Peacekeeping and U.S. Interests." *The Washington Quarterly* 17, no. 4 (Autumn 1994): 175–84.

Sewall, John. "Standing Up Coalitions: Implications for UN Peacekeeping." *Joint Forces Quarterly* (Winter 1993–1994): 29–33.

Smith, Hugh. "Intelligence and UN Peacekeeping." *Survival* 36 (Autumn 1994): 174–92.

Stevenson, Jonathan. "Hope Restored in Somalia?" *Foreign Policy* no. 91 (Summer 1993): 138–54.

Tharoor, Shashi. "Peace-Keeping: Principles, Problems, Prospects." *U.S. Naval War College Review* (Spring 1994): 9–22.

———. "Should UN Peacekeeping Go Back to Basics?" *Survival* 37 (Winter 1995–1996): 52–64.

Touval, Saadia. "Why the UN Fails." *Foreign Affairs* 73 (September–October 1994): 44–57.

Urquhart, Brian. "Beyond the Sheriff's Posse." *Survival* 32 (May–June 1990): 196–205.

———. "For a UN Volunteer Military Force." *The New York Review of Books* (10 June 1993): 3–4.

Weiss, Thomas G. "Intervention: Whither the United Nations?" *The Washington Quarterly* (Winter 1994): 109–28.

———. "New Challenges for UN Military Operations: Implementing an Agenda for Peace." *The Washington Quarterly* (Winter 1993): 51–66.

———. "The United Nations and Civil Wars." *The Washington Quarterly* 17, no. 4 (Autumn 1994): 139–59.

Speeches, Presentations, and Conference Papers

Albright, Madeleine K. Untitled. Remarks to the National Defense University, Washington, D.C., September 23, 1993.

Berdal, Mats. "The Future of UN Peacekeeping: Problems of Management and Institutional Reform." Remarks to the Symposium on Collective Responses to Common Threats, Royal Ministry of Foreign Affairs, Oslo, June 22–23, 1993.

———. "The United Nations at Fifty: Its Role in Global Security." An essay presented at a Ditchley Foundation conference, Ditchley Park, Oxfordshire, England, December 2–4, 1994.

Boutros-Ghali, Boutros. "Building a New Strategy: Collective Security through the United Nations." Speech to the Security Council's first Summit meeting, New York, January 1992.

———. "The Role of the United Nations in Maintaining Peace and Security: What to Expect from Germany." Address to chief editors and high-level officials at the seminar on "Germany and International Security" held by the Federal College for Security Policy Studies, Bad Godesberg, Germany, January 19, 1995.

Dallen, Russell M. "A UN Revitalized." A compilation of UNA–USA recommendations on strengthening the role of the United Nations in peacemaking, peacekeeping, and conflict prevention, United Nations Association of the USA, New York, 1992.

Dennehy, Edward J., William J. Droll, Gregory P. Harper, Stephen M. Speakes, and Fred A. Treyz. "A Blue Helmet Combat Force." A National Security Program Policy Analysis Paper, John F. Kennedy School of Government, Cambridge, Harvard University, 1993.

Doyle, Sarah, Kimberly Smith, and Kemper Vest. "The Changing Shape of Peacekeeping." A Center for National Security Negotiations Conference Report, SAIC Corporation, June 14–15, 1994.

Eyre, Dana P. "Nontraditional Missions—Peacekeeping and Peace Enforcement: A Preliminary Assessment of Future U.S. Army Roles and Force Training Issues." A paper prepared for the 1993 biennial meeting of the Inter-University Seminar on Armed Forces and Society, Baltimore, Md., October 20–22, 1993.

Gati, Toby, and Peter Romero. "Peacekeeping: What Works? America's Future Peacekeeping Policy." A conference report from a roundtable of American policymakers and academics sponsored by the U.S. Department of State, Meridian International Center, Washington, D.C., February 7, 1994.

Henrikson, Alan K. "Toward a Practical Vision of Collective Action for International Peace and Security." A discussion paper prepared for the Roundtable on Defining a New World Order, Boston: Tufts University, May 2–3, 1991.

Lake, Anthony. "From Containment to Enlargement." Remarks to the Johns Hopkins University School of Advanced International Studies, Washington, D.C., September 21, 1993.

Last, D. M. "Peacekeeping Doctrine and Conflict Resolution Techniques." A paper prepared for the 1993 biennial meeting of the Inter-University Seminar on Armed Forces and Society, Baltimore, Md., October 20–22, 1993.

Laurenti, Jeffrey. "Directions and Dilemmas in Collective Security." A paper drawn from the Roundtable on Defining a New World Order, Boston: Tufts University, May 2–3, 1991.

MacInnis, J. A. "Lessons from UNPROFOR: Peacekeeping from a Force Commander"s Perspective." A Presentation to the Application of Law of War Rules and Principles in Armed Conflict Conference, Garmish, Germany, December 5–7, 1994.

Mackinlay, John, and Jarat Chopra. "A Draft Concept of Second Generation Multinational Operations 1993." A Report of the Thomas J. Watson Jr. Institute for International Studies at Brown University, Providence, R.I., 1993.

Murray, J. D. "Military Aspects of Peacekeeping: Problems and Recommendations." International Peace Academy, 1976.

———. "Peacekeeping Force Deployment: UNIFIL—1978." International Peace Academy, 1979.

Ramsbotham, David. "UN Peacekeeping: The Art of the Possible." International Security Information Service Briefing no. 44, London, Royal United Services Institute, October 1994.

Rifkind, Malcom. "Peacekeeping or Peacemaking." Speech to the Royal United Services Institute, London, February 20, 1993.

Salacuse, Jeswald W., et al. "The Conference Report." The Roundtable on Defining a New World Order, Boston: Tufts University, May 2–3, 1991.

Segal, David R. "The Phases of UN Peacekeeping and Patterns of American Participation." A paper prepared for the 1993 biennial meeting of the Inter-University Seminar on Armed Forces and Society, Baltimore, Md., October 20–22, 1993.

Sutterlin, James S. "Enhancing the Capacity of the United Nations in Maintaining Peace and International Security." A UNSA–USA occasional paper, United Nations Association of the USA, New York, 1992.

U.S. Department of State. "Peacekeeping: What Works? America's Future Peacekeeping Policy." A Conference Report sponsored by the Office of Research and the Office of Politico-Military Analysis, Washington, D.C., February 7, 1994.

Formal Interviews by Author

Baril, Major General Maurice. Senior military advisor to the secretary-general. United Nations Headquarters, New York, 27 July 1994.

Breed, Henry. Special assistant to the under-secretary-general for Peacekeeping. United Nations Headquarters, New York, 27 July 1994.

Clark, Lieutenant General Wesley. Senior U.S. military representative to the United Nations Military Staffs Committee. The Pentagon, Arlington, Va., 16 September 1994.

Clarke, Lieutenant Colonel John L. Co-author of *U.S. Army Doctrine on Peace Operations* (Field Manual 100-23). Garmisch, Germany, 15 December 1994.

Coleman, Christopher. First officer (policy and analysis), Department of Peacekeeping Operations. United Nations Headquarters, New York, 27 July 1994.

Helis, Colonel James. Executive officer to the military advisor to the UN secretary-general. UN Headquarters, New York, 20 September 1995.

Howe, Admiral (Ret.) Jonathon. Former special representative of the secretary-general to Somalia (UNOSOM II). Stockholm, Sweden, 11 April 1995.

Johnstone, Ian. Senior associate, The International Peace Academy. New York, 26 July 1994.

Leclerq, Lieutenant Colonel Jean-Marie. Deputy chief, Situation Center, Department of Peacekeeping Operations. United Nations Headquarters, New York, 27 July 1994.

MacDonald, Colonel Bill, Colonel James McCallum, Professor Mark Walsh. U.S. Army Peacekeeping Institute. Carlisle Barracks, Penn., 2 September 1994.

Mackinlay, Professor John. Author, *The Peacekeepers* (1989) and director, Project on Peace Support Operations, Thomas J. Watson, Jr., Institute for International Studies, Brown University. Garmisch, Germany, 7 and 16 December 1994. Stockholm, Sweden, 11–12 April 1995. Baltimore, Md., 20–21 October 1995.

Roan, Colonel Richard. Deputy military advisor, United States Mission to the United Nations. New York, 19 September 1995.

Tharoor, Shashi. Special assistant to the under secretary-general for Peacekeeping. U.N. Headquarters, New York, 19 September 1995.

Urquhart, Sir Brian. Formerly under secretary-general of the United Nations for Special Political Affairs, now Scholar in Residence, The Ford Foundation. New York, 17 September 1993.

Williams, Michael. Former press spokesman for UNTAC and UNPROFOR, International Institute of Strategic Studies. London, 2 June 2.

Informal Communications

Berdal, Mats. Author, *Whither UN Peacekeeping?* (1993). Research fellow, International Institute of Strategic Studies. London, October 1994 to April 1995.

Dobbie, Lieutenant Colonel (Ret.) Charles. Author, *Wider Peacekeeping* (1994), and *A Concept for Post Cold War Peacekeeping* (1994). London, Oxford, October 1994 to June 1995.

Evans, Senator Gareth. Australian foreign minister and author, *Cooperating for Peace* (1993). Stockholm, Sweden, April 1995.

Furuhovde, Lieutenant General Trond. Former commander of UNIFIL. Stockholm, Sweden, April 1995.

Hautamaki, Lieutenant General Jussi. Former chief of staff, UNIFIL. Stockholm, Sweden, April 1995.

Hayes, Captain Bradd. Co-editor, *Beyond Traditional Peacekeeping* (1995). Stockholm, Sweden, April 1995.

Healy, Lieutenant Colonel Damien. Assistant to LTG John Sanderson, military commander of UNTAC. Stockholm, Sweden, April 1995.

Lichtenstein, Ambassador Charles. Former deputy U.S. ambassador to the United Nations. Washington, D.C., October 1995 to December 1996.

MacInnis, Lieutenant General J. A. Former deputy commander, UNPRO-FOR. Garmisch, Germany, December 1994.

Ramsbotham, General Sir David. Consultant on peacekeeping to the secretary general. Oxford, UK; Garmisch, Germany, November, December 1994.

Rinaldo, Richard. Co-author, *U.S. Army Doctrine on Peace Operations* (Field Manual 100-23). September 1993 to September 1995.

Vadset, Lieutenant General (Ret.) Martin. Former commander, UNTSO. Stockholm, Sweden, April 1995.

Index

About the Author

A former U.S. Army combat officer and public policy scholar with a doctorate from Oxford University, John Hillen is currently a senior executive at a leading new-economy firm on Wall Street. While on active duty with the U.S. Army, Hillen served as a paratrooper and reconnaissance officer in Asia, Europe, and the Middle East. He was decorated for his actions in combat against the Iraqi Republican Guard during the Persian Gulf War. After leaving the Army, he worked as an international security scholar and analyst at several different think tanks in Washington, D.C. In addition to *Blue Helmets*, he is the editor/co-author of *Future Visions for U.S. Defense Policy* and numerous articles in journals and newspapers such as *Foreign Affairs*, the *Wall Street Journal*, *Slate*, the *Washington Post*, *National Review*, and many others. He is a regular guest commentator about military affairs on CNN, NPR, MSNBC, PBS, and every major network. Hillen is a Henry Crown Fellow at the Aspen Institute, where he moderates leadership and management seminars for top business executives and senior public leaders. He is a member of the Council on Foreign Relations, the International Institute for Strategic Studies, a senior fellow at the Foreign Policy Research Institute, and a life member of the Veterans of Foreign Wars. He lives with his wife, Maria, and young son, Jack, in the New York City area.